New Dreams for Old

New Dreams for Old

MIKE RESNICK

Introduction by NANCY KRESS

an imprint of **Prometheus Books**
Amherst, NY

Published 2006 by Pyr®, an imprint of Prometheus Books

Inquiries should be addressed to
Pyr
59 John Glenn Drive
Amherst, New York 14228–2197
VOICE: 716–691–0133, ext. 207
FAX: 716–564–2711
WWW.PYRSF.COM

10 09 08 07 06   5 4 3 2 1

Library of Congress Cataloging-in-Publication Data

Resnick, Michael D.
    New dreams for old / Mike Resnick.
        p. cm.
    ISBN 1–59102–441–2 (pbk. : alk. paper)
    ISBN 978–1–59102–441–5
    I. Title.

PS3568.E698N49 2006
813'.54—dc22

2006008903

Printed in the United States on acid-free paper

To Carol, as always,

And to Janis Ian—
Singer, musician, songwriter,
poet, science fiction writer,
and spiritual kid sister

Contents

Introduction

BY NANCY KRESS

Once there was an orbital built to revive a dead African culture.

Once there was a robot faithful to its mistress beyond all human devotion.

Once there were elephants carrying a very old, very deep grudge.

If you see in these thumbnail synopses a wedding of the mundane and the marvelous, you are right. Many third world people might like to revive a pre-Colonial culture—but on an *orbital*? Elephants are commonly attributed with long memory, but not usually in the form of grudges. And robots, that staple of SF, are more often portrayed as menaces (see any Hollywood movie) than as the biblical ideal of "good and faithful servant."

Still, the juxtaposition of these ideas is not that startling within the context of science fiction's long and diverse history. What is startling is the treatment that Mike Resnick brings to them: complex, vital, compassionate, and sad. The sadness needs some explanation, for two reasons.

First, "sad" can mean "depressing"—but not in Mike's stories. These stories are *funny*. Some of them are laugh-out-loud funny, with lines like "This is the fifth time Mr. Spinoza has died this year. All this dying has to be hard on his system." The stories are never sad in a gloomy, hopeless, get-out-the-Prozac kind of way. Instead, they are sad the way the best fiction is always sad: It encompasses all of humanity's yearnings. That inevitably includes some things we cannot obtain, some things we should not obtain, and some things we obtain only to lose again, too soon. Mike Resnick understands this. And so even as his stories make us laugh, they also are infused with a complex sadness for beings that desire so much and struggle for it so hard.

The second reason the sadness is startling is that Mike himself is not a sad person. Exuberant, large, he is given to quips and wit and amiable teasing. The first time I read "For I Have Touched the Sky," I had trouble matching it to the Mike Resnick with whom I'd shared panels, lunches, and an ongoing feud about mud-rasslin' (don't ask). This is a complicated man. To echo Whitman, he contains multitudes.

And so do his stories. The book you hold in your hand teems with memorable characters doing their absolute, flat-out best to move Heaven and Earth. If this is the first time you meet Kamari, Bernard Goldmeiere, or Hermes the Antarean, I envy you. They are completely, achingly, humanly true, even the ones that aren't human. To quote the elephants on Neptune, "Our nature is that we always tell the truth. Our tragedy is that we always remember it." The same could be said for their creator. There is truth in these stories, and tragedy, and remembrance of how hard it can be to want something, anything, with passion and struggle.

Once—there was a wonderful writer.

Robots Don't Cry

One day I was in Barnes & Noble or Borders (I spend a lot of time in both), thumbing through a new coffee-table book on Kilimanjaro, when I came to a photograph of Dr. Richard Leakey holding up a mildly human skull, and in my haste I thought at first that the caption said he was displaying a newly discovered specimen of *Australopithecus robotus*.

I did a double take and went back and read it more carefully, and of course what he had in his hand was the skull of an *Australopithecus robotus*. Made a lot more sense.

But all the way home I kept wondering what an *Australopithecus robotus* might be like, and before I went to bed that night I had written "Robots Don't Cry." It was a Hugo nominee in 2004, was made into an amateur film (titled *Metal Tears*) as a film school graduation project by a young director named Jake Bradbury (damned good name for a science fiction director, don't you agree?), and is currently under option to Grand Illusions.

11

They call us graverobbers, but we're not.

What we do is plunder the past and offer it to the present. We hit old worlds, deserted worlds, worlds that nobody wants any longer, and we pick up anything we think we can sell to the vast collectibles market. You want a seven-hundred-year-old timepiece? A thousand-year-old bed? An actual printed book? Just put in your order, and sooner or later we'll fill it.

Every now and then we strike it rich. Usually we make a profit. Once in a while we just break even. There's only been one world where we actually lost money; I still remember it—Greenwillow. Except that it wasn't green, and there wasn't a willow on the whole damned planet.

There was a robot, though. We found him, me and the Baroni, in a barn, half-hidden under a pile of ancient computer parts and self-feeders for mutated cattle. We were picking through the stuff, wondering if there was any market for it, tossing most of it aside, when the sun peeked in through the doorway and glinted off a prismatic eye.

"Hey, take a look at what we've got here," I said. "Give me a hand digging it out."

The junk had been stored a few feet above where he'd been standing and the rack broke, practically burying him. One of his legs was bent at an impossible angle, and his expressionless face was covered with cobwebs. The Baroni lumbered over—when you've got three legs you don't glide gracefully—and studied the robot.

"Interesting," he said. He never used whole sentences when he could annoy me with a single word that could mean almost anything.

"He should pay our expenses, once we fix him up and get him running," I said.

"A human configuration," noted the Baroni.

"Yeah, we still made 'em in our own image until a couple of hundred years ago."

"Impractical."

"Spare me your practicalities," I said. "Let's dig him out."

"Why bother?"

Trust a Baroni to miss the obvious. "Because he's got a memory cube," I answered. "Who the hell knows what he's seen? Maybe we'll find out what happened here."

"Greenwillow has been abandoned since long before you were born and I was hatched," replied the Baroni, finally stringing some words together. "Who cares what happened?"

"I know it makes your head hurt, but try to use your brain," I said, grunting as I pulled at the robot's arm. It came off in my hands. "Maybe whoever he worked for hid some valuables." I dropped the arm onto the floor. "Maybe he knows where. We don't just have to sell junk, you know; there's a market for the good stuff, too."

The Baroni shrugged and began helping me uncover the robot. "I hear a lot of ifs and maybes," he muttered.

"Fine," I said. "Just sit on what passes for your ass, and I'll do it myself."

"And let you keep what we find without sharing it?" he demanded, suddenly throwing himself into the task of moving the awkward feeders. After a moment he stopped and studied one. "Big cows," he noted.

"Maybe ten or twelve feet at the shoulder, judging from the size of the stalls and the height of the feeders," I agreed. "But there weren't enough to fill the barn. Some of those stalls were never used."

Finally we got the robot uncovered, and I checked the code on the back of his neck.

"How about that?" I said. "The son of a bitch must be five hundred years old. That makes him an antique by anyone's definition. I wonder what we can get for him?"

The Baroni peered at the code. "What does AB stand for?"

"Aldebaran. Alabama. Abrams' Planet. Or maybe just the model number. Who the hell knows? We'll get him running and maybe he can tell us." I tried to set him on his feet. No luck. "Give me a hand."

"To the ship?" asked the Baroni, using sentence fragments again as he helped me stand the robot upright.

"No," I said. "We don't need a sterile environment to work on a robot. Let's just get him out in the sunlight, away from all this junk, and then we'll have a couple of mechs check him over."

We half-carried and half-dragged him to the crumbling concrete pad beyond the barn, then laid him down while I tightened the muscles in my neck, activating the embedded micro-chip, and directed the signal by pointing to the ship, which was about half a mile away.

"This is me," I said as the chip carried my voice back to the ship's computer. "Wake up Mechs 3 and 7, feed them everything you've got on robots going back a millennium, give them repair kits and anything else they'll need to fix a broken robot of indeterminate age, and then home in on my signal and send them to me."

"Why those two?" asked the Baroni.

Sometimes I wondered why I partnered with anyone that dumb. Then I remembered the way he could sniff out anything with a computer chip or cube, no matter how well it was hidden, so I decided to give him a civil answer. He didn't get that many from me; I hoped he appreciated it.

"Three's got those extendable eyestalks, and it can do micro-surgery, so I figure it can deal with any faulty microcircuits. As for Seven, it's strong as an ox. It can position the robot, hold him aloft, move him any way that Three directs it to. They're both going to show up filled to the brim with everything the ship's data bank has on robots, so if he's salvageable, they'll find a way to salvage him."

I waited to see if he had any more stupid questions. Sure enough, he had.

"Why would anyone come here?" he asked, looking across the bleak landscape.

"I came for what passes for treasure these days," I answered him. "I have no idea why you came."

"I meant originally," he said, and his face started to glow that shade of pea-soup green that meant I was getting to him. "Nothing can grow, and the ultraviolet rays would eventually kill most animals. So why?"

"Because not all humans are as smart as me."

"It's an impoverished world," continued the Baroni. "What valuables could there be?"

"The usual," I replied. "Family heirlooms. Holographs. Old kitchen implements. Maybe even a few old Republic coins."

"Republic currency can't be spent."

"True—but a few years ago I saw a five-credit coin sell for three hundred Maria Teresa dollars. They tell me it's worth twice that today."

"I didn't know that," admitted the Baroni.

"I'll bet they could fill a book with all the things you don't know."

"Why are Men so sardonic and ill-mannered?"

"Probably because we have to spend so much time with races like the Baroni," I answered.

Mechs Three and Seven rolled up before he could reply.

"Reporting for duty, sir," said Mech Three in his high-pitched mechanical voice.

"This is a very old robot," I said, indicating what we'd found. "It's been out of commission for a few centuries, maybe even longer. See if you can get it working again."

"We live to serve," thundered Mech Seven.

"I can't tell you how comforting I find that." I turned to the Baroni. "Let's grab some lunch."

"Why do you always speak to them that way?" asked the Baroni as we walked away from the mechs. "They don't understand sarcasm."

"It's my nature," I said. "Besides, if they don't know it's sarcasm, it must sound like a compliment. Probably pleases the hell out of them."

"They are machines," he responded. "You can no more please them than offend them."

"Then what difference does it make?"

"The more time I spend with Men, the less I understand them," said the Baroni, making the burbling sound that passed for a deep sigh. "I look forward to getting the robot working. Being a logical and unemotional entity, it will make more sense."

"Spare me your smug superiority," I shot back. "You're not here because Papa Baroni looked at Mama Baroni with logic in his heart."

The Baroni burbled again. "You are hopeless," he said at last.

We had one of the mechs bring us our lunch, then sat with our backs propped against opposite sides of a gnarled old tree while we ate. I didn't want to watch his snakelike lunch writhe and wriggle, protesting every inch of the way, as he sucked it down like the long, living piece of spaghetti it was, and he had his usual moral qualms, which I never understood, about watching me bite into a sandwich. We had just about finished when Mech Three approached us.

"All problems have been fixed," it announced brightly.

"That was fast," I said.

"There was nothing broken." It then launched into a three-minute explanation of whatever it had done to the robot's circuitry.

"That's enough," I said when it got down to a dissertation on the effect of mu-mesons on negative magnetic fields in regard to prismatic eyes. "I'm wildly impressed. Now let's go take a look at this beauty."

I got to my feet, as did the Baroni, and we walked back to the concrete pad. The robot's limbs were straight now, and his arm was restored, but he still lay motionless on the crumbling surface.

"I thought you said you fixed him."

"I did," replied Mech Three. "But my programming compelled me not to activate it until you were present."

"Fine," I said. "Wake him up."

The little mech made one final quick adjustment and backed away as the robot hummed gently to life and sat up.

"Welcome back," I said.

"Back?" replied the robot. "I have not been away."

"You've been asleep for five centuries, maybe six."

"Robots cannot sleep." He looked around. "Yet everything has changed. How is this possible?"

"You were deactivated," said the Baroni. "Probably your power supply ran down."

"Deactivated," the robot repeated. He swiveled his head from left to right, surveying the scene. "Yes. Things cannot change this much from one instant to the next."

"Have you got a name?" I asked him.

"Samson 4133. But Miss Emily calls me Sammy."

"Which name do you prefer?"

"I am a robot. I have no preferences."

I shrugged. "Whatever you say, Samson."

"Sammy," he corrected me.

"I thought you had no preferences."

"I don't," said the robot. "But *she* does."

"Has she got a name?"

"Miss Emily."

"Just Miss Emily?" I asked. "No other names to go along with it?"

"Miss Emily is what I was instructed to call her."

"I assume she is a child," said the Baroni, with his usual flair for discovering the obvious.

"She was once," said Sammy. "I will show her to you."

Then somehow, I never did understand the technology involved, he projected a full-sized holograph of a small girl, perhaps five years old, wearing a frilly purple-and-white outfit. She had rosy cheeks and bright shining blue eyes, and a smile that men would die for someday if given half the chance.

It was only after she took a step forward, a very awkward step, that I realized she had a prosthetic left leg.

"Too bad," I said. "A pretty little girl like that."

"Was she born that way, I wonder?" said the Baroni.

"I love you, Sammy," said the holograph.

I hadn't expected sound, and it startled me. She had such a happy voice. Maybe she didn't know that most little girls came equipped with two legs. After all, this was an underpopulated colony world; for all I knew, she'd never seen anyone but her parents.

"It is time for your nap, Miss Emily," said Sammy's voice. "I will carry you to your room." Another surprise. The voice didn't seem to come from the robot, but from somewhere . . . well, offstage. He was recreating the scene exactly as it had happened, but we saw it through his eyes. Since he couldn't see himself, neither could we.

"I'll walk," said the child. "Mother told me I have to practice walking, so that someday I can play with the other girls."

"Yes, Miss Emily."

"But you can catch me if I start to fall, like you always do."

"Yes, Miss Emily."

"What would I do without you, Sammy?"

"You would fall, Miss Emily," he answered. Robots are always so damned literal.

And as suddenly as it had appeared, the scene vanished.

"So that was Miss Emily?" I asked.

"Yes," said Sammy.

"And you were owned by her parents?"

"Yes."

"Do you have any understanding of the passage of time, Sammy?"

"I can calibrate time to within three nanoseconds of . . ."

"That's not what I asked," I said. "For example, if I told you that scene we just saw happened more than five hundred years ago, what would you say to that?"

"I would ask if you were measuring by Earth years, Galactic Standard years, New Calendar Democracy years . . ."

"Never mind," I said.

Sammy fell silent and motionless. If someone had stumbled upon him at just that moment, they'd have been hard-pressed to prove that he was still operational.

"What's the matter with him?" asked the Baroni. "His battery can't be drained yet."

"Of course not. They were designed to work for years without recharging."

And then I knew. He wasn't a farm robot, so he had no urge to get up and start working the fields. He wasn't a mech, so he had no interest in fixing the feeders in the barn. For a moment I thought he might be a butler or a majordomo, but if he was, he'd have been trying to learn my desires to serve me, and he obviously wasn't doing that. That left just one thing.

He was a nursemaid.

I shared my conclusion with the Baroni, and he concurred.

"We're looking at a *lot* of money here," I said excitedly. "Think of it—a fully functioning antique robot nursemaid! He can watch the kids while his new owners go rummaging for more old artifacts."

"There's something wrong," said the Baroni, who was never what you could call an optimist.

"The only thing wrong is we don't have enough bags to haul all the money we're going to sell him for."

"Look around you," said the Baroni. "This place was abandoned, and it was never prosperous. If he's that valuable, why did they leave him behind?"

"He's a nursemaid. Probably she outgrew him."

"Better find out." He was back to sentence fragments again.

I shrugged and approached the robot. "Sammy, what did you do at night after Miss Emily went to sleep?"

He came to life again. "I stood by her bed."

"All night, every night?"

"Yes, sir. Unless she woke and requested pain medication, which I would retrieve and bring to her."

"Did she require pain medication very often?" I asked.

"I do not know, sir."

I frowned. "I thought you just said you brought it to her when she needed it."

"No, sir," Sammy corrected me. "I said I brought it to her when she *requested* it."

"She didn't request it very often?"

"Only when the pain became unbearable." Sammy paused. "I do not fully understand the word 'unbearable,' but I know it had a deleterious effect upon her. My Miss Emily was often in pain."

"I'm surprised you understand the word 'pain,'" I said.

"To feel pain is to be nonoperational or disfunctional to some degree."

"Yes, but it's more than that. Didn't Miss Emily ever try to describe it?"

"No," answered Sammy. "She never spoke of her pain."

"Did it bother her less as she grew older and adjusted to her handicap?" I asked.

"No, sir, it did not." He paused. "There are many kinds of disfunction."

"Are you saying she had other problems, too?" I continued.

Instantly we were looking at another scene from Sammy's past. It was the same girl, now maybe thirteen years old, staring at her face in a mirror. She didn't like what she saw, and neither did I.

"What *is* that?" I asked, forcing myself not to look away.

"It is a fungus disease," answered Sammy as the girl tried unsuccessfully with cream and powder to cover the ugly blemishes that had spread across her face.

"Is it native to this world?"

"Yes," said Sammy.

"You must have had some pretty ugly people walking around," I said.

"It did not affect most of the colonists. But Miss Emily's immune system was weakened by her other diseases."

"What other diseases?"

Sammy rattled off three or four that I'd never heard of.

"And no one else in her family suffered from them?"

"No, sir."

"It happens in my race, too," offered the Baroni. "Every now and then a genetically inferior specimen is born and grows to maturity."

"She was not genetically inferior," said Sammy.

"Oh?" I said, surprised. It's rare for a robot to contradict a living being, even an alien. "What was she?"

Sammy considered his answer for a moment.

"Perfect," he said at last.

"I'll bet the other kids didn't think so," I said.

"What do they know?" replied Sammy.

And instantly he projected another scene. Now the girl was fully grown, probably about twenty. She kept most of her skin covered, but we could see the ravaging effect her various diseases had had upon her hands and face.

Tears were running down from these beautiful blue eyes over bony, parchmentlike cheeks. Her emaciated body was wracked by sobs.

A holograph of a robot's hand popped into existence and touched her gently on the shoulder.

"Oh, Sammy!" she cried. "I really thought he liked me! He was always so nice to me." She paused for breath as the tears continued unabated. "But I saw his face when I reached out to take his hand, and I felt him shudder when I touched it. All he really felt for me was pity. That's all any of them ever feel!"

"What do they know?" said Sammy's voice, the same words and the same inflections he had just used a moment ago.

"It's not just him," she said. "Even the farm animals run away when I approach them. I don't know how anyone can stand being in the same room with me." She stared at where the robot was standing. "You're all I've got, Sammy. You're my only friend in the whole world. Please don't ever leave me."

"I will never leave you, Miss Emily," said Sammy's voice.

"Promise me."

"I promise," said Sammy.

And then the holograph vanished and Sammy stood mute and motionless again.

"He really cared for her," said the Baroni.

"The boy?" I said. "If he did, he had a funny way of showing it."

"No, of course not the boy. The robot."

"Come off it," I said. "Robots don't have any feelings."

"You heard him," said the Baroni.

"Those were programmed responses," I said. "He probably has three million to choose from."

"Those are emotions," insisted the Baroni.

"Don't you go getting all soft on me," I said. "Any minute now you'll be telling me he's too human to sell."

"*You* are the human," said the Baroni. "*He* is the one with compassion."

"I've got more compassion than her parents did, letting her grow up like that," I said irritably. I confronted the robot again. "Sammy, why didn't the doctors do anything for her?"

"This was a farming colony," answered Sammy. "There were only 387 families on the entire world. The Democracy sent a doctor once a year at the beginning, and then, when there were less than 100 families left, he stopped coming. The last time Miss Emily saw a doctor was when she was fourteen."

"What about an offworld hospital?" asked the Baroni.

"They had no ship and no money. They moved here in the second year of a seven-year drought. Then various catastrophes wiped out their next six crops. They spent what savings they had on mutated cattle, but the cattle died before they could produce young or milk. One by one all the families began leaving the planet as impoverished wards of the Democracy."

"Including Miss Emily's family?" I asked.

"No. Mother died when Miss Emily was nineteen, and Father died two years later."

Then it was time for me to ask the Baroni's question.

"So when did Miss Emily leave the planet, and why did she leave you behind?"

"She did not leave."

I frowned. "She couldn't have run the farm—not in her condition."

"There was no farm left to run," answered Sammy. "All the crops had died, and without Father there was no one to keep the machines working."

"But she stayed. Why?"

Sammy stared at me for a long moment. It's just as well his face was incapable of expression, because I got the distinct feeling that he thought the question was too simplistic or too stupid to merit an answer. Finally he projected another scene. This time the girl, now a woman approaching thirty, hideous open pustules on her face and neck, was sitting in a crudely crafted hoverchair, obviously too weak to stand any more.

"No!" she rasped bitterly.

"They are your relatives," said Sammy's voice. "And they have a room for you."

"All the more reason to be considerate of them. No one should be forced to associate with me—especially not people who are decent enough to make the offer. We will stay here, by ourselves, on this world, until the end."

"Yes, Miss Emily."

She turned and stared at where Sammy stood. "You want to tell me to leave, don't you? That if we go to Jefferson IV I will receive medical attention and they will make me well—but you are compelled by your programming not to disobey me. Am I correct?"

"Yes, Miss Emily."

The hint of a smile crossed her ravaged face. "Now you know what pain is."

"It is . . . uncomfortable, Miss Emily."

"You'll learn to live with it," she said. She reached out and patted the robot's leg fondly. "If it's any comfort, I don't know if the medical specialists could have helped me even when I was young. They certainly can't help me now."

"You are still young, Miss Emily."

"Age is relative," she said. "I am so close to the grave I can almost taste the dirt." A metal hand appeared, and she held it in ten incredibly fragile fingers. "Don't feel sorry for me, Sammy. It hasn't been a life I'd wish on anyone else. I won't be sorry to see it end."

"I am a robot," replied Sammy. "I cannot feel sorrow."

"You've no idea how fortunate you are."

I shot the Baroni a triumphant smile that said: *See? Even Sammy admits he can't feel any emotions.*

And he sent back a look that said: *I didn't know until now that robots could lie*, and I knew we still had a problem.

The scene vanished.

"How soon after that did she die?" I asked Sammy.

"Seven months, eighteen days, three hours, and four minutes, sir," was his answer.

"She was very bitter," noted the Baroni.

"She was bitter because she was born, sir," said Sammy. "Not because she was dying."

"Did she lapse into a coma, or was she cogent up to the end?" I asked out of morbid curiosity.

"She was in control of her senses until the moment she died," answered Sammy. "But she could not see for the last eighty-three days of her life. I functioned as her eyes."

"What did she need eyes for?" asked the Baroni. "She had a hover-chair, and it is a single-level house."

"When you are a recluse, you spend your life with books, sir," said Sammy, and I thought: *The mechanical bastard is actually lecturing us!*

With no further warning, he projected a final scene for us.

The woman, her eyes no longer blue, but clouded with cataracts and something else—disease, fungus, who knew?—lay on her bed, her breathing labored.

From Sammy's point of view, we could see not only her, but, much closer, a book of poetry, and then we heard his voice: "Let me read something else, Miss Emily."

"But that is the poem I wish to hear," she whispered. "It is by Edna St. Vincent Millay, and she is my favorite."

"But it is about death," protested Sammy.

"All life is about death," she replied so softly I could barely hear her. "Surely you know that I am dying, Sammy?"

"I know, Miss Emily," said Sammy.

"I find it comforting that my ugliness did not diminish the beauty around me, that it will remain after I am gone," she said. "Please read."

Sammy read:

"There will be rose and rhododendron
When you are dead and under ground;
Still will be heard from white syringas . . ."

Suddenly the robot's voice fell silent. For a moment I thought there was a flaw in the projection. Then I saw that Miss Emily had died.

He stared at her for a long minute, which means that we did, too, and then the scene evaporated.

"I buried her beneath her favorite tree," said Sammy. "But it is no longer there."

"Nothing lasts forever, even trees," said the Baroni. "And it's been five hundred years."

"It does not matter. I know where she is."

He walked us over to a barren spot about thirty yards from the ruin of the farmhouse. On the ground was a stone, and neatly carved into it was the following:

> Miss Emily
> 2298–2331 G.E.
> There will be rose
> and rhododendron

"That's lovely, Sammy," said the Baroni.

"It is what she requested."

"What did you do after you buried her?" I asked.

"I went to the barn."

"For how long?"

"With Miss Emily dead, I had no need to stay in the house. I remained in the barn for many years, until my battery power ran out."

"Many years?" I repeated. "What the hell did you do there?"

"Nothing."

"You just stood there?"

"I just stood there."

"Doing nothing?"

"That is correct." He stared at me for a long moment, and I could have sworn he was studying me. Finally he spoke again. "I know that you intend to sell me."

"We'll find you a family with another Miss Emily," I said. *If they're the highest bidder.*

"I do not wish to serve another family. I wish to remain here."

"There's nothing here," I said. "The whole planet's deserted."

"I promised my Miss Emily that I would never leave her."

"But she's dead now," I pointed out.

"She put no conditions on her request. I put no conditions on my promise."

I looked from Sammy to the Baroni, and decided that this was going to take a couple of mechs—one to carry Sammy to the ship and one to stop the Baroni from setting him free.

"But if you will honor a single request, I will break my promise to her and come away with you."

Suddenly I felt like I was waiting for the other shoe to drop, and I hadn't heard the first one yet.

"What do you want, Sammy?"

"I told you I did nothing in the barn. That was true. I was incapable of doing what I wanted to do."

"And what was that?"

"I wanted to cry."

I don't know what I was expecting, but that wasn't it.

"Robots don't cry," I said.

"Robots *can't* cry," replied Sammy. "There is a difference."

"And that's what you want?"

"It is what I have wanted ever since my Miss Emily died."

"We rig you to cry, and you agree to come away with us?"

"That is correct," said Sammy.

"Sammy," I said, "you've got yourself a deal."

I contacted the ship, told it to feed Mech Three everything the medical library had on tears and tear ducts, and then send it over. It arrived about ten minutes later, deactivated the robot, and started fussing and fiddling. After about two hours it announced that its work was done, that Sammy now had tear ducts and had been supplied with a solution that could produce six hundred authentic saltwater tears from each eye.

I had Mech Three show me how to activate Sammy and then sent it back to the ship.

"Have you ever heard of a robot wanting to cry?" I asked the Baroni.

"No."

"Neither have I," I said, vaguely disturbed.

"He loved her."

I didn't even argue this time. I was wondering which was worse, spending thirty years trying to be a normal human being and failing, or spending thirty years trying to cry and failing. None of the other stuff had gotten to me; Sammy was just doing what robots do. It was the thought of his trying so hard to do what robots couldn't do that suddenly made me feel sorry for him. That in turn made me very irritable; ordinarily I don't even feel sorry for Men, let alone machines.

And what he wanted was such a simple thing compared to the grandiose ambitions of my own race. Once Men had wanted to cross the ocean; we crossed it. We'd wanted to fly; we flew. We wanted to reach the stars; we reached them. All Sammy wanted to do was cry over the loss of his Miss Emily. He'd waited half a millennium and had agreed to sell himself into bondage again, just for a few tears.

It was a lousy trade.

I reached out and activated him.

"Is it done?" asked Sammy.

"Right," I said. "Go ahead and cry your eyes out."

Sammy stared straight ahead. "I can't," he said at last.

"Think of Miss Emily," I suggested. "Think of how much you miss her."

"I feel pain," said Sammy. "But I cannot cry."

"You're sure?"

"I am sure," said Sammy. "I was guilty of having thoughts and longings above my station. Miss Emily used to say that tears come from the heart and the soul. I am a robot. I have no heart and no soul, so I cannot cry, even with the tear ducts you have given me. I am sorry to have wasted your time. A more complex model would have understood its limitations at the outset." He paused, and then turned to me. "I will go with you now."

"Shut up," I said.

He immediately fell silent.

"What is going on?" asked the Baroni.

"You shut up, too!" I snapped.

I summoned Mechs Seven and Eight and had them dig Sammy a grave right next to his beloved Miss Emily. It suddenly occurred to me that I didn't even know her full name, that no one who chanced upon her headstone would ever know it. Then I decided that it didn't really matter.

Finally they were done, and it was time to deactivate him.

"I would have kept my word," said Sammy.

"I know," I said.

"I am glad you did not force me to."

I walked him to the side of the grave. "This won't be like your battery running down," I said. "This time it's forever."

"She was not afraid to die," said Sammy. "Why should I be?"

I pulled the plug and had Mechs Seven and Eight lower him into the ground. They started filling in the dirt while I went back to the ship to do one last thing. When they were finished, I had Mech Seven carry my handiwork back to Sammy's grave.

"A tombstone for a robot?" asked the Baroni.

"Why not?" I replied. "There are worse traits than honesty and loyalty." I should know: I've stockpiled enough of them.

"He truly moved you."

Seeing the man you could have been will do that to you, even if he's all metal and silicone and prismatic eyes.

"What does it say?" asked the Baroni as we finished planting the tombstone.

I stood aside so he could read it:

> "Sammy"
> Australopithecus Robotus

"That is very moving."

"It's no big deal," I said uncomfortably. "It's just a tombstone."

"It is also inaccurate," observed the Baroni.

"He was a better man than I am."

"He was not a man at all."

"Fuck you."

The Baroni doesn't know what it means, but he knows it's an insult, so he came right back at me like he always does. "You realize, of course, that you have buried our profit?"

I wasn't in the mood for his notion of wit. "Find out what he was worth, and I'll pay you for your half," I replied. "Complain about it again, and I'll knock your alien teeth down your alien throat."

He stared at me. "I will never understand Men," he said.

All that happened twenty years ago. Of course the Baroni never asked for his half of the money, and I never offered it to him again. We're still partners. Inertia, I suppose.

I still think about Sammy from time to time. Not as much as I used to, but every now and then.

I know there are preachers and ministers who would say he was just a machine, and to think of him otherwise is blasphemous, or at least wrongheaded, and maybe they're right. Hell, I don't even know if there's a God at all—but if there is, I like to think He's the God of *all* us Australopithecines.

Including Sammy.

The Elephants on Neptune

I have absolutely no idea where the notion for this story came from. Once it did come, it seemed so totally unlike any story I'd previously written or even thought about writing that I was sure it wouldn't work. I wrote a little, looked at it, decided to write a little more, considered what I'd done again, and kept it up all the way to the end, pretty much unconvinced that it was even marketable—until I finished it, and then I read it through and fell in love with it.

Despite that fact that I don't write hard science (hell, I don't even write soft science; I write *limp* science), I've sold upward of twenty-five stories to *Asimov's*. This is the only one that editor Gardner Dozois ever returned for fixing.

It didn't bother him that there were elephants on Neptune. It didn't bother him that they could forage for food. It didn't bother him that they could breathe the air. It didn't bother him that they could speak English. It didn't bother him that they could remember events that transpired three thousand years ago. But he knows that Neptune is a gas giant, and it bothered the hell out of him that the elephants were walking on its surface, so he insisted that I insert a line or two explaining how they managed it. (When it won the Asimov's

Readers Poll, in my acceptance speech I thanked
Gardner for turning me into a hard science writer
at long last.)

"The Elephants on Neptune" was a Hugo
and Nebula nominee in 2001.

The elephants on Neptune led an idyllic life.

None ever went hungry or were sick. They had no predators. They
never fought a war. There was no prejudice. Their birth rate exactly
equalled their death rate. Their skins and bowels were free of parasites.

The herd traveled at a speed that accomodated the youngest and
weakest members. No sick or infirm elephant was ever left behind.

They were a remarkable race, the elephants on Neptune. They
lived out their lives in peace and tranquility, they never argued among
themselves, the old were always gentle with the young. When one was
born, the entire herd gathered to celebrate. When one died, the entire
herd mourned its passing. There were no animosities, no petty jeal-
ousies, no unresolved quarrels.

Only one thing stopped it from being Utopia, and that was the fact
that an elephant never forgets.

Not ever.

No matter how hard he tries.

When men finally landed on Neptune in 2473 A.D., the elephants
were very apprehensive. Still, they approached the spaceship in a spirit
of fellowship and goodwill.

The men were a little apprehensive themselves. Every survey of
Neptune told them it was a gas giant, and yet they had landed on solid
ground. And if their surveys were wrong, who knew what else might
be wrong as well?

A tall man stepped out onto the frozen surface. Then another. Then a third. By the time they had all emerged, there were almost as many men as elephants.

"Well, I'll be damned!" said the leader of the men. "You're elephants!"

"And you're men," said the elephants nervously.

"That's right," said the men. "We claim this planet in the name of the United Federation of Earth."

"You're united now?" asked the elephants, feeling much relieved.

"Well, the survivors are," said the men.

"Those are ominous-looking weapons you're carrying," said the elephants, shifting their feet uncomfortably.

"They go with the uniforms," said the men. "Not to worry. Why would we want to harm you? There's always been a deep bond between men and elephants."

That wasn't exactly the way the elephants remembered it.

326 B.C.

Alexander the Great met Porus, King of the Punjab of India, in the Battle of the Jhelum River. Porus had the first military elephants Alexander had ever seen. He studied the situation, then sent his men out at night to fire thousands of arrows into extremely sensitive trunks and underbellies. The elephants went mad with pain and began killing the nearest men they could find, which happened to be their keepers and handlers. After his great victory, Alexander slaughtered the surviving elephants so that he would never have to face them in battle.

217 B.C.

The first clash between the two species of elephants. Ptolemy IV took his African elephants against Antiochus the Great's Indian elephants.

The elephants on Neptune weren't sure who won the war, but they knew who lost. Not a single elephant on either side survived.

Later that same 217 B.C.

While Ptolemy was battling in Syria, Hannibal took thirty-seven ele-phants over the Alps to fight the Romans. Fourteen of them froze to death, but the rest lived just long enough to absorb the enemy's spear thrusts while Han-nibal was winning the Battle of Cannae.

"We have important things to talk about," said the men. "For example, Neptune's atmosphere is singularly lacking in oxygen. How do you breathe?"

"Through our noses," said the elephants.

"That was a serious question," said the men, fingering their weapons ominously.

"We are incapable of being anything *but* serious," explained the elephants. "Humor requires that someone be the butt of the joke, and we find that too cruel to contemplate."

"All right," said the men, who were vaguely dissatisfied with the answer, perhaps because they didn't understand it. "Let's try another question. What is the mechanism by which we are communicating? You don't wear radio transmitters, and because of our helmets we can't hear any sounds that aren't on our radio bands."

"We communicate through a psychic bond," explained the ele-phants.

"That's not very scientific," said the men disapprovingly. "Are you sure you don't mean a telepathic bond?"

"No, though it comes to the same thing in the end," answered the elephants. "We know that we sound like we're speaking English to you, except for the man on the left who thinks we're speaking Hebrew."

"And what do we sound like to you?" demanded the men.

"You sound exactly as if you're making gentle rumbling sounds in your stomachs and your bowels."

"That's fascinating," said the men, who privately thought it was a lot more disgusting than fascinating.

"Do you know what's *really* fascinating?" responded the elephants. "The fact that you've got a Jew with you." They saw that the men didn't comprehend, so they continued: "We always felt we were in a race with the Jews to see which of us would be exterminated first. We used to call ourselves the Jews of the animal kingdom." They turned and faced the Jewish spaceman. "Did the Jews think of themselves as the elephants of the human kingdom?"

"Not until you just mentioned it," said the Jewish spaceman, who suddenly found himself agreeing with them.

42 B.C.

The Romans gathered their Jewish prisoners in the arena at Alexandria, then turned fear-crazed elephants loose on them. The spectators began jumping up and down and screaming for blood—and, being contrarians, the elephants attacked the spectators instead of the Jews, proving once and for all that you can't trust a pachyderm.

(When the dust had cleared, the Jews felt the events of the day had reaffirmed their claim to be God's chosen people. They weren't the Romans' chosen people, though. After the soldiers killed the elephants, they put all the Jews to the sword, too.)

"It's not his fault he's a Jew any more than it's your fault that you're elephants," said the rest of the men. "We don't hold it against either of you."

"We find that difficult to believe," said the elephants.

"You do?" said the men. "Then consider this: the Indians—that's the good Indians, the ones from India, not the bad Indians from America—worshipped Ganesh, an elephant-headed god."

"We didn't know that," admitted the elephants, who were more impressed than they let on. "Do the Indians still worship Ganesh?"

"Well, we're sure they would if we hadn't killed them all while we were defending the Raj," said the men. "Elephants were no longer in the military by then," they added. "That's something to be grateful for."

Their very last battle came when Tamerlane the Great went to war against Sultan Mahmoud. Tamerlane won by tying branches to buffalos' horns, setting fire to them, and then stampeding the buffalo herd into Mahmoud's elephants, which effectively ended the elephant as a war machine, buffalo being much less expensive to acquire and feed.

All the remaining domesticated elephants were then trained for elephant fighting, which was exactly like cockfighting, only on a larger scale. Much larger. It became a wildly popular sport for thirty or forty years until they ran out of participants.

"Not only did we worship you," continued the men, "but we actually named a country after you—the Ivory Coast. *That* should prove our good intentions."

"You didn't name it after *us*," said the elephants. "You named it after the parts of our bodies that you kept killing us for."

"You're being too critical," said the men. "We could have named it after some local politician with no vowels in his name."

"Speaking of the Ivory Coast," said the elephants, "did you know that the first alien visitors to Earth landed there in 1883?"

"What did they look like?"

"They had ivory exoskeletons," answered the elephants. "They took one look at the carnage and left."

"Are you sure you're not making this all up?" asked the men.

"Why would we lie to you at this late date?"

"Maybe it's your nature," suggested the men.

"Oh, no," said the elephants. "Our nature is that we always tell the truth. Our tragedy is that we always remember it."

The men decided that it was time to break for dinner, answer calls of nature, and check in with Mission Control to report what they'd found. They all walked back to the ship, except for one man, who lingered behind.

All of the elephants left too, except for one lone bull. "I intuit that you have a question to ask," he said.

"Yes," replied the man. "You have such an acute sense of smell, how did anyone ever sneak up on you during the hunt?"

"The greatest elephant hunters were the Wanderobo of Kenya and Uganda. They would rub our dung all over their bodies to hide their own scent, and would then silently approach us."

"Ah," said the man, nodding his head. "It makes sense."

"Perhaps," conceded the elephant. Then he added, with all the dignity he could muster, "But if the tables were turned, I would sooner die than cover myself with *your* shit."

He turned away and set off to rejoin his comrades.

Neptune is unique among all the worlds in the galaxy. It alone recognizes the truism that change is inevitable, and acts upon it in ways that seem very little removed from magic.

For reasons the elephants couldn't fathom or explain, Neptune encourages metamorphosis. Not merely adaption, although no one could deny that they adapted to the atmosphere and the climate and the fluctuating surface of the planet and the lack of acacia trees—but *metamorphosis*. The elephants understood at a gut level that Neptune had somehow imparted to them the ability to evolve at will, though they had been careful never to abuse this gift.

And since they were elephants, and hence incapable of carrying a grudge, they thought it was a pity that the men couldn't evolve to the point where they could leave their bulky spacesuits and awkward helmets behind, and walk free and unencumbered across this most perfect of planets.

The elephants were waiting when the men emerged from their ship and strode across Neptune's surface to meet them.

"This is very curious," said the leader.

"What is?" asked the elephants.

The leader stared at them, frowning. "You seem smaller."

"We were just going to say that you seemed larger," replied the elephants.

"This is almost as silly as the conversation I just had with Mission Control," said the leader. "They say there aren't any elephants on Neptune."

"What do they think we are?" asked the elephants.

"Hallucinations or space monsters," answered the leader. "If you're hallucinations, we're supposed to ignore you."

He seemed to be waiting for the elephants to ask what the men were supposed to do if they were space monsters, but elephants can be as stubborn as men when they want to be, and that was a question they had no intention of asking.

The men stared at the elephants in silence for almost five minutes. The elephants stared back.

Finally the leader spoke again.

"Would you excuse me for a moment?" he said. "I suddenly have an urge to eat some greens."

He turned and marched back to the ship without another word.

The rest of the men shuffled their feet uncomfortably for another few seconds.

"Is something wrong?" asked the elephants.

"Are we getting bigger or are you getting smaller?" replied the men.

"Yes," answered the elephants.

"I feel much better now," said the leader, rejoining his men and facing the elephants.

"You look better," agreed the elephants. "More handsome, somehow."

"Do you really think so?" asked the leader, obviously flattered.

"You are the finest specimen of your race we've ever seen," said the elephants truthfully. "We especially like your ears."

"You do?" he asked, flapping them slightly. "No one's ever mentioned them before."

"Doubtless an oversight," said the elephants.

"Speaking of ears," said the leader, "are you African elephants or Indian? I thought this morning you were African—they're the ones with the bigger ears, right?—but now I'm not sure."

"We're Neptunian elephants," they answered.

"Oh."

They exchanged pleasantries for another hour, and then the men looked up at the sky.

"Where did the sun go?" they asked.

"It's night," explained the elephants. "Our day is only fourteen hours long. We get seven hours of sunlight and seven of darkness."

"The sun wasn't all that bright anyway," said one of the men with a shrug that set his ears flapping wildly.

"We have very poor eyesight, so we hardly notice," said the elephants. "We depend on our senses of smell and hearing."

The men seemed very uneasy. Finally they turned to their leader.

"May we be excused for a few moments, sir?" they asked.

"Why?"

"Suddenly we're starving," said the men.

"And I gotta use the john," said one of them.

"So do I," said a second one.

"Me too," echoed another.

"Do you men feel all right?" asked the leader, his enormous nose wrinkled in concern.

"I feel great!" said the nearest man. "I could eat a horse!"

The other men all made faces.

"Well, a small forest, anyway," he amended.

"Permission granted," said the leader. The men began walking rapidly back to the ship. "And bring me a couple of heads of lettuce, and maybe an apple or two," he called after them.

"You can join them if you wish," said the elephants, who were coming to the conclusion that eating a horse wasn't half as disgusting a notion as they had thought it would be.

"No, my job is to make contact with aliens," explained the leader. "Although when you get right down to it, you're not as alien as we'd expected."

"You're every bit as human as *we* expected," replied the elephants.

"I'll take that as a great compliment," said the leader. "But then, I would expect nothing less from traditional friends such as yourselves."

"Traditional friends?" repeated the elephants, who had thought nothing a man said could still surprise them.

"Certainly. Even after you stopped being our partners in war, we've always had a special relationship with you."

"You have?"

"Sure. Look how P. T. Barnum made an international superstar out of the original Jumbo. That animal lived like a king—or at least he did until he was accidentally run over by a locomotive."

"We don't want to appear cynical," said the elephants, "but how do you *accidentally* run over a seven-ton animal?"

"You do it," said the leader, his face glowing with pride, "by inventing the locomotive in the first place. Whatever else we may be, you must admit we're a race that can boast of magnificent accomplishments: the internal combustion engine, splitting the atom, reaching the planets, curing cancer." He paused. "I don't mean to denigrate you, but truly, what have you got to equal that?"

"We live our lives free of sin," responded the elephants simply. "We respect each other's beliefs, we don't harm our environment, and we have never made war on other elephants."

"And you'd put that up against the the heart transplant, the silicon chip, and the three-dimensional television screen?" asked the leader with just a touch of condescension.

"Our aspirations are different from yours," said the elephants. "But we are as proud of our heroes as you are of yours."

"You have heroes?" said the leader, unable to hide his surprise.

"Certainly." The elephants rattled off their roll of honor: "The Kilimanjaro Elephant. Selemundi. Mohammed of Marsabit. And the Magnificent Seven of Krueger Park: Mafunyane, Shingwedzi, Kambaki, Joao, Dzombo, Ndlulamithi, and Phelwane."

"Are they here on Neptune?" asked the leader as his men began returning from the ship.

"No," said the elephants. "You killed them all."

"We must have had a reason," insisted the men.

"They were there," said the elephants. "And they carried magnificent ivory."

"See?" said the men. "We *knew* we had a reason."

The elephants didn't like that answer much, but they were too polite to say so, and the two species exchanged views and white lies all through the brief Neptunian night. When the sun rose again, the men voiced their surprise.

"Look at you!" they said. "What's happening?"

"We got tired of walking on all fours," said the elephants. "We decided it's more comfortable to stand upright."

"And where are your trunks?" demanded the men.

"They got in the way."

"Well, if that isn't the damnedest thing!" said the men. Then they looked at each other. "On second thought, *this* is the damnedest thing! We're bursting out of our helmets!"

"And our ears are flapping," said the leader.

"And our noses are getting longer," said another man.

"This is most disconcerting," said the leader. He paused. "On the other hand, I don't feel nearly as much animosity toward you as I did yesterday. I wonder why?"

"Beats us," said the elephants, who were becoming annoyed with the whining quality of his voice.

"It's true, though," continued the leader. "Today I feel like every elephant in the universe is my friend."

"Too bad you didn't feel that way when it would have made a difference," said the elephants irritably. "Did you know you killed sixteen million of us in the twentieth century alone?"

"But we made amends," noted the men. "We set up game parks to preserve you."

"True," acknowledged the elephants. "But in the process you took away most of our habitat. Then you decided to cull us so we wouldn't exhaust the park's food supply." They paused dramatically. "That was when Earth received its second alien visitation. The aliens examined the theory of preserving by culling, decided that Earth was an insane asylum, and made arrangements to drop all their incurables off in the future."

Tears rolled down the men's bulky cheeks. "We feel just terrible about that," they wept. A few of them dabbed at their eyes with short, stubby fingers that seemed to be growing together.

"Maybe we should go back to the ship and consider all this," said the men's leader, looking around futilely for something large enough in which to blow his nose. "Besides, I have to use the facilities."

"Sounds good to me," said one of the men. "I got dibs on the cabbage."

"Guys?" said another. "I know it sounds silly, but it's much more comfortable to walk on all fours."

The elephants waited until the men were all on the ship, and then went about their business, which struck them as odd, because before the men came they didn't *have* any business.

"You know," said one of the elephants. "I've got a sudden taste for a hamburger."

"I want a beer," said a second. Then: "I wonder if there's a football game on the subspace radio?"

"It's really curious," remarked a third. "I have this urge to cheat on my wife—and I'm not even married."

Vaguely disturbed without knowing why, they soon fell into a restless, dreamless sleep.

Sherlock Holmes once said that after you eliminate the impossible, what remains, however improbable, must be the truth.

Joseph Conrad said that truth is a flower in whose neighborhood others must wither.

Walt Whitman suggested that whatever satisfied the soul was truth.

Neptune would have driven all three of them berserk.

"Truth is a dream, unless my dream is true," said George Santayana.

He was just crazy enough to have made it on Neptune.

"We've been wondering," said the men when the two groups met in the morning. "Whatever happened to Earth's last elephant?"

"His name was Jamal," answered the elephants. "Someone shot him."

"Is he on display somewhere?"

"His right ear, which resembles the outline of the continent of Africa, has a map painted on it and is in the Presidential Mansion in Kenya. They turned his left ear over—and you'd be surprised how many left ears were thrown away over the centuries before someone somewhere thought of turning them over—and another map was painted, which now hangs in a museum in Bombay. His feet were turned into a matched set of barstools, and currently grace the Aces High Show Lounge in Dallas, Texas. His scrotum serves as a tobacco pouch for an elderly Scottish politician. One tusk is on display at the British Museum. The other bears a scrimshaw and resides in a store window in Beijing. His tail has been turned into a fly swatter, and is the proud possession of one of the last *vaqueros* in Argentina."

"We had no idea," said the men, honestly appalled.

"Jamal's very last words before he died were 'I forgive you,'" continued the elephants. "He was promptly transported to a sphere higher than any man can ever aspire to."

The men looked up and scanned the sky. "Can we see it from here?" they asked.

"We doubt it."

The men looked back at the elephants—except that they had evolved yet again. In fact, they had eliminated every physical feature for which they had ever been hunted. Tusks, ears, feet, tails, even scrotums, all had undergone enormous change. The elephants looked exactly like human beings, right down to their spacesuits and helmets.

The men, on the other hand, had burst out of their spacesuits (which had fallen away in shreds and tatters), sprouted tusks, and found themselves conversing by making rumbling noises in their bellies.

"This is very annoying," said the men who were no longer men. "Now that we seem to have become elephants," they continued, "perhaps you can tell us what elephants *do*?"

"Well," said the elephants who were no longer elephants, "in our spare time, we create new ethical systems based on selflessness, forgiveness, and family values. And we try to synthesize the work of Kant, Descartes, Spinoza, Thomas Aquinas, and Bishop Barkley into something far more sophisticated and logical, while never forgetting to incorporate emotional and aesthetic values at each stage."

"Well, we suppose that's pretty interesting," said the new elephants without much enthusiasm. "Can we do anything else?"

"Oh, yes," the new spacemen assured them, pulling out their .550 Nitro Expresses and .475 Holland & Holland Magnums and taking aim. "You can die."

"This can't be happening! You yourselves were elephants yesterday!"

"True. But we're men now."

"But why kill us?" demanded the elephants.

"Force of habit," said the men as they pulled their triggers.

Then, with nothing left to kill, the men who used to be elephants boarded their ship and went out into space, boldly searching for new life-forms.

Neptune has seen many species come and go. Microbes have been spontaneously generated nine times over the eons. It has been visited by aliens thirty-seven different times. It has seen forty-three wars, five of them atomic, and the creation of 1,026 religions, none of which possessed any universal truths. More of the vast tapestry of galactic history has been played out on Neptune's foreboding surface than any other world in Sol's system.

Planets cannot offer opinions, of course, but if they could, Neptune would almost certainly say that the most interesting creatures it ever hosted were the elephants, whose gentle ways and unique perspectives remain fresh and clear in its memory. It mourns the fact that they became extinct by their own hand. Kind of.

A problem would arise when you asked whether Neptune was referring to the old-new elephants who began life as killers, or the new-old ones who ended life as killers.

Neptune just hates questions like that.

Travels with My Cats

Writing is a form of immortality. If you don't believe in an afterlife, it's comforting to think that long after you're dead, some vital part of you will be alive again for the length of time that someone picks up one of your books and reads it. I've heard other writers say it often enough; I've occasionally said it myself.

I thought it might be interesting to write a story about it, not from the writer's point of view, but rather from the viewpoint of someone who fondly remembers a cherished volume, one that changed his life, or at least made it a little more tolerable, and was written by an author he can never know, someone who died before he was born—as *I* wish I could have met a couple of authors who had profound influences on me when I was first starting to read.

Hence, "Travels with My Cats." It won me my fifth Hugo, my fifth Asimov's Readers Poll, my eleventh Nebula nomination, and my twenty-seventh Hugo nomination. I think it's one of my two or three best.

I found it in the back of a neighbor's garage. They were retiring and moving to Florida, and they'd put most of their stuff up for sale rather than pay to ship it south.

I was eleven years old, and I was looking for a Tarzan book, or maybe one of Clarence Mulford's Hopalong Cassidy epics, or perhaps (if my mother was looking the other way) a forbidden Mickey Spillane novel. I found them, too—and then the real world intruded. They were 50 cents each (and a whole dollar for *Kiss Me Deadly*), and all I had was a nickel.

So I rummaged some more, and finally found the only book that was in my price range. It was called *Travels with My Cats*, and the author was Miss Priscilla Wallace. Not Priscilla, but Miss Priscilla. For years I thought Miss was her first name.

I thumbed through it, hoping it at least had some photos of half-naked native girls hidden in its pages. There weren't any pictures at all, just words. I wasn't surprised; somehow I had known that an author called Miss wasn't going to plaster naked women all over her book.

I decided that the book itself felt too fancy and feminine for a boy who was trying out for the Little League later in the day—the letters on the cover were somehow raised above the rest of the surface, the endpapers were an elegant satin, the boards were covered with a russet, velvetlike cloth, and it even had a bookmark which was a satin ribbon attached to the binding. I was about to put it back when it fell open to a page that said that this was Number 121 of a Limited Printing of 200.

That put a whole new light on things. My very own limited edition for a nickel—how could I say No? I brought it to the front of the garage, dutifully paid my nickel, and waited for my mother to finish looking (she always looked, never shopped—shopping implies parting with money, and she and my father were Depression kids who never bought what they could rent cheaper or, better yet, borrow for free).

That night I was faced with a major decision. I didn't want to read a book called *Travels with My Cats* by a woman called Miss, but I'd spent my last nickel on it—well, the last until my allowance came due again next week—and I'd read all my other books so often you could almost see the eyetracks all over them.

So I picked it up without much enthusiasm, and read the first page, and then the next—and suddenly I was transported to Kenya Colony and Siam and the Amazon. Miss Priscilla Wallace had a way of describing things that made me wish I was there, and when I finished a section I felt like I'd *been* there.

There were cities I'd never heard of before, cities with exotic names like Maracaibo and Samarkand and Addis Ababa, some with names like Constantinople that I couldn't even find on the map.

Her father had been an explorer, back in the days when there still *were* explorers. She had taken her first few trips abroad with him, and he had undoubtedly give her a taste for distant lands. (My own father was a typesetter. How I envied her!)

I had half hoped the African section would be filled with rampaging elephants and man-eating lions, and maybe it was—but that wasn't the way she saw it. Africa may have been red of tooth and claw, but to her it reflected the gold of the morning sun, and the dark, shadowy places were filled with wonder, not terror.

She could find beauty anywhere. She would describe two hundred flower sellers lined up along the Seine on a Sunday morning in Paris, or a single frail blossom in the middle of the Gobi Desert, and somehow you knew that each was as wondrous as she said.

And suddenly I jumped as the alarm clock started buzzing. It was the first time I'd ever stayed up for the entire night. I put the book away, got dressed for school, and hurried home after school so that I could finish it.

I must have read it six or seven more times that year. I got to the point where I could almost recite parts of it word-for-word. I was in love with those exotic faraway places, and maybe a little bit in love with the author, too. I even wrote her a fan letter addressed to "Miss Priscilla Wallace, Somewhere," but of course it came back.

Then, in the fall, I discovered Robert A. Heinlein and Louis L'Amour, and a friend saw *Travels with My Cats* and teased me about its fancy cover and the fact that it was written by a woman, so I put it on a shelf and over the years I forgot about it.

I never saw all those wonderful, mysterious places she wrote about. I never did a lot of things. I never made a name for myself. I never got rich and famous. I never married.

By the time I was forty, I was finally ready to admit that nothing unusual or exciting was ever likely to happen to me. I'd written half of a novel that I was never going to finish or sell, and I'd spent twenty years looking fruitlessly for someone I could love. (That was Step One; Step Two—finding someone who could love me—would probably have been even more difficult, but I never got around to it.)

I was tired of the city, and of rubbing shoulders with people who had latched onto the happiness and success that had somehow eluded me. I was Midwestern born and bred, and eventually I moved to Wisconsin's North Woods, where the most exotic cities were small towns like Manitowoc and Minnaqua and Wausau—a far cry from Macau and Marrakech and the other glittering capitals of Priscilla Wallace's book.

I worked as a copy editor for one of the local weekly newspapers—the kind where getting the restaurant and real estate ads right was more important than spelling the names in the news stories correctly. It wasn't the most challenging job in the world, but it was pleasant enough, and I wasn't looking for any challenges. Youthful dreams of triumph had gone the way of youthful dreams of love and passion; at this late date, I'd settled for tranquility.

I rented a small house on a little nameless lake, some fifteen miles out of town. It wasn't without its share of charm: it had an old-fashioned veranda, with a porch swing that was almost as old as the house. A pier for the boat I didn't own jutted out into the lake, and there was even a water trough for the original owner's horses. There was no air-conditioning, but I didn't really need it—and in the winter I'd sit by the fire, reading the latest paperback thriller.

It was on a late summer's night, with just a bit of a Wisconsin chill in the air, as I sat next to the empty fireplace, reading about a rip-roaring gun-blazing car chase through Berlin or Prague or some other city I'll never see, that I found myself wondering if this was my future: a lonely old man, spending his evenings reading pop fiction by a fireplace, maybe with a blanket over his legs, his only companion a tabby cat . . .

And for some reason—probably the notion of the tabby—I remembered *Travels with My Cats*. I'd never owned a cat, but *she* had; there had been two of them, and they'd gone everywhere with her.

I hadn't thought of the book for years. I didn't even know if I still had it. But for some reason, I felt an urge to pick it up and look through it.

I went to the spare room, where I kept all the stuff I hadn't unpacked yet. There were maybe two dozen boxes of books. I opened the first of them, then the next. I rummaged through Bradburys and Asimovs and Chandlers and Hammetts, dug deep beneath Ludlums and Amblers and a pair of ancient Zane Grays—and suddenly there it was, as elegant as ever. My one and only Limited Numbered Edition.

So, for the first time in perhaps thirty years, I opened the book and began reading it. And found myself just as captivated as I had been the first time. It was every bit as wonderful as I remembered. And, as I had done three decades ago, I lost all track of the time and finished it just as the sun was rising.

I didn't get much work done that morning. All I could do was think about those exquisite descriptions and insights into worldsthat no longer existed—and then I began wondering if Priscilla Wallace herself still existed. She'd probably be a very old lady, but maybe I could update that old fan letter and finally send it.

I stopped by the local library at lunchtime, determined to pick up everything else she had written. There was nothing on the shelves or in their card file. (They were a friendly old-fashioned rural library; computerizing their stock was still decades away.)

I went back to the office and had my computer run a search on her. There were thirty-seven distinct and different Priscilla Wallaces. One was an actress in low-budget movies. One taught at Georgetown University.

One was a diplomat stationed in Bratislava. One was a wildly successful breeder of show poodles. One was the youthful mother of a set of sextuplets in South Carolina. One was an inker for a Sunday comic strip.

And then, just when I was sure the computer wouldn't be able to find her, the following came up on my screen:

"Wallace, Priscilla, b. 1892, d. 1926. Author of one book: *Travels with My Cats*."

1926. So much for fan letters, then or now; she'd died decades before I'd been born. Even so, I felt a sudden sense of loss, and of resentment—resentment that someone like that had died so young, and that all her unlived years had been taken by people who would never see the beauty that she found everywhere she went.

People like me.

There was also a photo. It looked like a reproduction of an old sepia-toned tintype, and it showed a slender, auburn-haired young woman with large dark eyes that seemed somehow sad to me. Or maybe the sadness was my own, because I knew she would die at thirty-four and all that passion for life would die with her. I printed up a hard copy, put it in my desk drawer, and took it home with me at the end of the day. I don't know why. There were only two sentences on it. Somehow a life—any life—deserved more than that. Especially one that could reach out from the grave and touch me and make me feel, at least while I was reading her book, that maybe the world wasn't quite as dull and ordinary as it seemed to me.

That night, after I heated up a frozen dinner, I sat down by the fireplace and picked up *Travels with My Cats* again, just thumbing through it to read my favorite passages here and there. There was the one about the stately procession of elephants against the backdrop of snow-capped Kilimanjaro, and another about the overpowering perfume of the flowers as she walked through the gardens of Versailles on a May morning. And then, toward the end, there was what had become my favorite of all:

"There is so much yet to see, so much still to do, that on days like this I wish I could live forever. I take comfort in the heartfelt belief that long after I am gone, I will be alive again for as long as someone picks up a copy of this book and reads it."

It *was* a comforting belief, certainly more immortality than I ever aspired to. I'd made no mark, left no sign by which anyone would know I'd ever been here. Twenty years after my death, maybe thirty at most, no one would ever know that I'd even existed, that a man named Ethan Owens—my name; you've never encountered it before, and you doubtless never will again—lived and worked and died here, that he tried to get through each day without doing anyone any harm, and that was the sum total of his accomplishments.

Not like her. Or maybe very much like her. She was no politician, no warrior queen. There were no monuments to her. She wrote a forgotten little travel book and died before she could write another. She'd been gone for more than three-quarters of a century. Who remembered Priscilla Wallace?

I poured myself a beer and began reading again. Somehow, the more she described each exotic city and primal jungle, the less exotic and primal they felt, the more they seemed like an extension of home. As often as I read it, I couldn't figure out how she managed to do that.

I was distracted by a clattering on the veranda. *Damned raccoons are getting bolder every night*, I thought—but then I heard a very distinct *meow*. My nearest neighbor was a mile away, and that seemed a long way for a cat to wander, but I figured the least I could do was go out and look, and if it had a collar and a tag I'd call its owner. And if not, I'd shoo it away before it got into the wrong end of a disagreement with the local raccoons.

I opened the door and stepped out onto the veranda. Sure enough, there was a cat there, a small white one with a couple of tan markings on its head and body. I reached down to pick it up, and it backed away a couple of steps.

"I'm not going to hurt you," I said gently.

"He knows that," said a feminine voice. "He's just shy."

I turned—and there she was, sitting on my porch swing. She made a gesture, and the cat walked across the veranda and jumped up onto her lap.

I'd seen that face earlier in the day, staring at me in sepia tones. I'd studied it for hours, until I knew it's every contour.

It was *her*.

"It's a beautiful night, isn't it?" she said as I kept gaping at her. "And quiet. Even the birds are asleep." She paused. "Only the cicadas are awake, serenading us with their symphonies."

I didn't know what to say, so I just watched her and waited for her to vanish.

"You look pale," she noted after a moment.

"You look real," I finally managed to croak.

"Of course I do," she replied with a smile. "I *am* real."

"You're Miss Priscilla Wallace, and I've spent so much time thinking about you that I've begun hallucinating."

"Do I look like an hallucination?"

"I don't know," I admitted. "I don't think I've ever had one before, so I don't know what they look like—except that obviously they look like you." I paused. "They could look a lot worse. You have a beautiful face."

She laughed at that. The cat jumped, startled, and she began stroking it gently. "I do believe you're trying to make me blush," she said.

"*Can* you blush?" I asked, and then of course wished I hadn't.

"Of course I can," she replied, "though I had my doubts after I got back from Tahiti. The things they *do* there!" Then, "You were reading *Travels with My Cats*, weren't you?"

"Yes, I was. It's been one of my most cherished possessions since I was a child."

"Was it a gift?" she asked.

"No, I bought it myself."

"That's very gratifying."

"It's very gratifying to finally meet the author who's given me so much pleasure," I said, feeling like an awkward kid all over again.

She looked puzzled, as if she was about to ask a question. Then she changed her mind and smiled again. It was a lovely smile, as I had known it would be.

"This is very pretty property," she said. "Is it yours all the way up to the lake?"

"Yes."

"Does anyone else live here?"

"Just me."

"You like your privacy," she said. It was a statement, not a question.

"Not especially," I answered. "That's just the way things worked out. People don't seem to like me very much."

Now why the hell did I tell you that? I thought. *I've never even admitted it to myself.*

"You seem like a very nice person," she said. "I find it difficult to believe that people don't like you."

"Maybe I overstated the case," I admitted. "Mostly they don't notice me." I shifted uncomfortably. "I didn't mean to unburden myself on you."

"You're all alone. You have to unburden yourself to *someone*," she replied. "I think you just need a little more self-confidence."

"Perhaps."

She stared at me for a long moment. "You keep looking like you're expecting something terrible to happen."

"I'm expecting you to disappear."

"Would that be so terrible?"

"Yes," I said promptly. "It would be."

"Then why don't you simply accept that I'm here? If you're wrong, you'll know it soon enough."

I nodded. "Yeah, you're Priscilla Wallace, all right. That's exactly the kind of answer she'd give."

"You know who *I* am. Perhaps you'll tell me who *you* are?"

"My name is Ethan Owens."

"Ethan," she repeated. "That's a nice name."

"You think so?"

"I wouldn't say so if I didn't." She paused. "Shall I call you Ethan, or Mr. Owens?"

"Ethan, by all means. I feel like I've known you all my life." I felt another embarrassing admission coming on. "I even wrote you a fan letter when I was a kid, but it came back."

"I would have liked that," she said. "I never once got a fan letter. Not from anyone."

"I'm sure hundreds of people wanted to write. Maybe they couldn't find your address either."

"Maybe," she said dubiously.

"In fact, just today I was thinking about sending it again."

"Whatever you wanted to say, you can tell me in person." The cat jumped back down onto the veranda. "You look very uncomfortable, perched on the railing like that, Ethan. Why don't you come and sit beside me?"

"I'd like that very much," I said, standing up. Then I thought it over. "No, I'd better not."

"I'm thirty-two years old," she said in amused tones. "I don't need a chaperone."

"Not with me, you don't," I assured her. "Besides, I don't think we have them anymore."

"Then what's the problem?"

"The truth?" I said. "If I sit next to you, at some point my hip will press against yours, or perhaps I'll inadvertently touch your hand. And . . ."

"And what?"

"And I don't want to find out that you're not really here."

"But I am."

"I hope so," I said. "But I can believe it a lot easier from where I am."

She shrugged. "As you wish."

"I've had my wish for the night," I said.

"Then why don't we just sit and enjoy the breeze and the scents of the Wisconsin night?"

"Whatever makes you happy," I said.

"Being here makes me happy. Knowing my book is still being read makes me happy." She was silent for a moment, staring off into the darkness. "What's the date, Ethan?"

"April 17."

"I mean the year."

"2004."

She looked surprised. "It's been that long?"

"Since . . . ?" I said hesitantly.

"Since I died," she said. "Oh, I know I must have died a long time ago. I have no tomorrows, and my yesterdays are all so very long ago. But the new millennium? It seems"—she searched for the right word—"excessive."

"You were born in 1892, more than a century ago," I said.

"How did you know that?"

"I had the computer run a search on you."

"I don't know what a computer is," she said. Then, suddenly: "Do you also know when and how I died?"

"I know when, not how."

"Please don't tell me," she said. "I'm thirty-two, and I've just written the last page of my book. I don't know what comes next, and it would be wrong for you to tell me."

"All right," I said. Then, borrowing her expression, "As you wish."

"Promise me."

"I promise."

Suddenly the little white cat tensed and looked off across the yard.

"He sees his brother," said Priscilla.

"It's probably just the raccoons," I said. "They can be a nuisance."

"No," she insisted. "I know his body language. That's his brother out there."

And sure enough, I heard a distinct *meow* a moment later. The white cat leaped off the veranda and headed toward it.

"I'd better go get them before they become completely lost," said Priscilla, getting to her feet. "It happened once in Brazil, and I didn't find them for almost two days."

"I'll get a flashlight and come with you," I said.

"No, you might frighten them, and it wouldn't do to have them run away in strange surroundings." She stood up and stared at me. "You seem like a very nice man, Ethan Owens. I'm glad we finally met." She smiled sadly. "I just wish you weren't so lonely."

She climbed down to the yard and walked off into the darkness before I could lie and tell her I led a rich full life and wasn't lonely at all. Suddenly I had a premonition that she wasn't coming back. "Will we meet again?" I called after her as she vanished from sight.

"That depends on you, doesn't it?" came her answer out of the darkness.

I sat on the porch swing, waiting for her to reappear with the cats. Finally, despite the cold night air, I fell asleep. I woke up when the sun hit the swing in the morning.

I was alone.

It took me almost half the day to convince myself that what had happened the night before was just a dream. It wasn't like any other dream I'd ever had, because I remembered every detail of it, every word she said, every gesture she made. Of course she hadn't really visited me, but just the same I couldn't get Priscilla Wallace out of my mind, so I finally stopped working and used my computer to try to learn more about her.

There was nothing more to be found under her name except for that single brief entry. I tried a search on *Travels with My Cats* and came up empty. I checked to see if her father had ever written a book about his explorations; he hadn't. I even contacted a few of the hotels she had stayed at, alone or with her father, but none of them kept records that far back.

I tried one line of pursuit after another, but none of them proved fruitful. History had swallowed her up almost as completely as it would someday swallow me. Other than the book, the only proof I had that she had ever lived was that one computer entry, consisting of ten words and two dates. Wanted criminals couldn't hide from the law any better than she'd hidden from posterity.

Finally I looked out the window and realized that night had fallen and everyone else had gone home. (There's no night shift on a weekly paper.) I stopped by a local diner, grabbed a ham sandwich and a cup of coffee, and headed back to the lake.

I watched the 10:00 news on TV, then sat down and picked up her book again, just to convince myself that she really *had* lived once upon a time. After a couple of minutes I got restless, put the book back on a table, and walked out for a breath of fresh air.

She was sitting on the porch swing, right where she had been the night before. There was a different cat next to her, a black one with white feet and white circles around its eyes.

She noticed me looking at the cat. "This is Goggle," she said. "I think he's exceptionally well-named, don't you?"

"I suppose," I said distractedly.

"The white one is Giggle, because he loves getting into all sorts of mischief." I didn't say anything. Finally she smiled. "Which of them has your tongue?"

"You're back," I said at last.

"Of course I am."

"I was reading your book again," I said. "I don't think I've ever encountered anyone who loved life so much."

"There's so much to love!"

"For some of us."

"It's all around you, Ethan," she said.

"I prefer seeing it through your eyes. It was like you were born again into a new world each morning," I said. "I suppose that's why I kept your book, and why I find myself rereading it—to share what you see and feel."

"You can feel things yourself."

I shook my head. "I prefer what *you* feel."

"Poor Ethan," she said sincerely. "You've never loved anything, have you?"

"I've tried."

"That isn't what I said." She stared at me curiously. "Have you ever married?"

"No."

"Why not?"

"I don't know." I decided I might as well give her an honest answer. "Probably because none of them ever measured up to you."

"I'm not that special," she said.

"To me you are. You always have been."

She frowned. "I wanted my book to enrich your life, Ethan, not ruin it."

"You didn't ruin it," I said. "You made it a little more bearable."

"I wonder . . ." she mused.

"About what?"

"My being here. It's puzzling."

"Puzzling is an understatement," I said. "Unbelievable is more the word for it."

She shook her head distractedly. "You don't understand. I remember last night."

"So do I—every second of it."

"That's not what I meant." She stroked the cat absently. "I was never brought back before last night. I wasn't sure then. I thought perhaps I forgot after each episode. But today I remember last night."

"I'm not sure I follow you."

"You can't be the only person to read my book since I died. Or even if you were, I've never been called back before, not even by you." She stared at me for a long moment. "Maybe I was wrong."

"About what?"

"Maybe what brought me here wasn't the fact that I needed to be read. Maybe it's because *you* so desperately need someone."

"I—" I began heatedly, and then stopped. For a moment it seemed like the whole world had stopped with me. Then the moon came out from behind a cloud, and an owl hooted off to the left.

"What is it?"

"I was about to tell you that I'm not that lonely," I said. "But it would have been a lie."

"It's nothing to be ashamed of, Ethan."

"It's nothing to brag about, either." There was something about her that made me say things I'd never said to anyone else, including myself. "I had such high hopes when I was a boy. I was going to love my work, and I was going to be good at it. I was going find a woman to love and spend the rest of my life with. I was going to see all the places you described. Over the years I saw each of those hopes die. Now I settle for paying my bills and getting regular checkups at the doctor's." I sighed deeply. "I think my life can be described as a fully realized diminished expectation."

"You have to take risks, Ethan," she said gently.

"I'm not like you," I said. "I wish I was, but I'm not. Besides, there aren't any wild places left."

She shook her head. "That's not what I meant. Love involves risk. You have to risk getting hurt."

"I've *been* hurt," I said. "It's nothing to write home about."

"Maybe that's why I'm here. You can't be hurt by a ghost."

The hell I can't, I thought. Aloud I said: "*Are* you a ghost?"

"I don't feel like one."

"You don't look like one."

"How *do* I look?" she asked.

"As lovely as I always knew you were."

"Fashions change."

"But beauty doesn't," I said.

"That's very kind of you to say, but I must look very old-fashioned. In fact, the world I knew must seem primitive to you." Her face brightened. "It's a new millennium. Tell me what's happened."

"We've walked on the moon—and we've landed ships on Mars and Venus."

She looked up into the night sky. "The moon!" she exclaimed. Then: "Why are you here when you could be there?"

"I'm not a risk-taker, remember?"

"What an exciting time to be alive!" she said enthusiastically. "I always wanted to see what lay beyond the next hill. But *you*—you get to see what's beyond the next star!"

"It's not that simple," I said.

"But it will be," she persisted.

"Someday," I agreed. "Not during my lifetime, but someday."

"Then you should die with the greatest reluctance," she said. "I'm sure I did." She looked up at the stars, as if envisioning herself flying to each of them. "Tell me more about the future."

"I don't know anything about the future," I said.

"*My* future. Your present."

I told her what I could. She seemed amazed that hundreds of millions of people now traveled by air, that I didn't know anyone who didn't own a car, and that train travel had almost disappeared in America. The thought of television fascinated her; I decided not to tell her what a vast wasteland it had been since its inception. Color movies, sound movies, computers—she wanted to know all about them. She was eager to learn if zoos had become more humane, if *people* had become more humane. She couldn't believe that heart transplants were actually routine.

I spoke for hours. Finally I just got so dry I told her I was going to have to take a break for a couple of minutes while I went into the kitchen and got us some drinks. She'd never heard of Fanta or Dr. Pepper, which is what I had, and she didn't like beer, so I made her an iced tea and popped open a Bud for me. When I brought them out to the porch, she and Goggle were gone.

I didn't even bother looking for her. I knew she had returned to the *somewhere* from which she had come.

She was back again the next three nights, sometimes with one cat, sometimes with both. She told me about her travels, about her over-whelming urge to see what there was to see in the little window of time alotted us humans, and I told her about the various wonders she would never see.

It was strange, conversing with a phantom every night. She kept assuring me she was real, and I believed it when she said it, but I was still afraid to touch her and discover that she was just a dream after all. Somehow, as if they knew my fears, the cats kept their distance too; not once in all those evenings did either of them ever so much as brush against me.

"I wish I'd seen all the sights *they've* seen," I said on the third night, nodding toward the cats.

"Some people thought it was cruel to take them all over the world with me," replied Priscilla, absently running her hand over Goggle's back as he purred contentedly. "I think it would have been more cruel to leave them behind."

"None of the cats—these or the ones that came before—ever caused any problems?"

"Certainly they did," she said. "But when you love something, you put up with the problems."

"Yeah, I suppose you do."

"How do you know?" she asked. "I thought you said you'd never loved anything."

"Maybe I was wrong."

"Oh?"

"I don't know," I said. "Maybe I love someone who vanishes every night when I turn my back." She stared at me, and suddenly I felt very awkward. I shrugged uncomfortably. "Maybe."

"I'm touched, Ethan," she said. "But I'm not of this world, not the way you are."

"I haven't complained," I said. "I'll settle for the moments I can get." I tried to smile; it was a disaster. "Besides, I don't even know if you're real."

"I keep telling you I am."

"I know."

"What would you do if you *knew* I was?" she asked.

"Really?"

"Really."

I stared at her. "Try not to get mad," I began.

"I won't get mad."

"I've wanted to hold you and kiss you since the first instant I saw you on my veranda," I said.

"Then why haven't you?"

"I have this . . . this *dread* that if I try to touch you and you're not here, if I prove conclusively to myself that you don't exist, then I'll never see you again."

"Remember what I told you about love and risk?"

"I remember."

"And?"

"Maybe I'll try tomorrow," I said. "I just don't want to lose you yet. I'm not feeling that brave tonight."

She smiled, a rather sad smile I thought. "Maybe you'll get tired of reading me."

"Never!"

"But it's the same book all the time. How often can you read it?"

I looked at her, young, vibrant, maybe two years from death, certainly less than three. I knew what lay ahead for her; all she could see was a lifetime of wonderful experiences stretching out into the distance.

"Then I'll read one of your other books."

"I wrote others?" she asked.

"Dozens of them," I lied.

She couldn't stop smiling. "Really?"

"Really."

"Thank you, Ethan," she said. "You've made me very happy."

"Then we're even."

There was a noisy squabble down by the lake. She quickly looked around for her cats, but they were on the porch, their attention also attracted by the noise.

"Raccoons," I said.

"Why are they fighting?"

"Probably a dead fish washed up on the shore," I answered. "They're not much for sharing."

She laughed. "They remind me of some people I know." She paused. "Some people I *knew*," she amended.

"Do you miss them—your friends, I mean?"

"No. I had hundreds of acquaintences, but very few close friends. I was never in one place long enough to make them. It's only when I'm with you that I realize they're gone." She paused. "I don't quite understand it. I know that I'm here with you, in the new millennium—but I feel like I just celebrated my thirty-second birthday. Tomorrow I'll put flowers on my father's grave, and next week I set sail for Madrid."

"Madrid?" I repeated. "Will you watch them fight the brave bulls in the arena?"

An odd expression crossed her face. "Isn't that curious?" she said.

"Isn't *what* curious?"

"I have no idea what I'll do in Spain . . . but you've read all my books, so *you* know."

"You don't want me to tell you," I said.

"No, that would spoil it."

"I'll miss you when you leave."

"You'll pick up one of my books and I'll be right back here," she said. "Besides, I went more than seventy-five years ago."

"It gets confusing," I said.

"Don't look so depressed. We'll be together again."

"It's only been a week, but I can't remember what I did with my evenings before I started talking to you."

The squabbling at the lake got louder, and Giggle and Goggle began huddling together.

"They're frightening my cats," said Priscilla.

"I'll go break it up," I said, climbing down from the veranda and heading off to where the raccoons were battling. "And when I get back," I added, feeling bolder the farther I got from her, "maybe I'll find out just how real you are after all."

By the time I reached the lake, the fight was all but over. One large raccoon, half a fish in its mouth, glared at me, totally unafraid. Two others, not quite as large, stood about ten feet away. All three were bleeding from numerous gashes, but it didn't look like any of them had suffered a disabling injury.

"Serves you right," I muttered.

I turned and started trudging back up to the house from the lake. The cats were still on the veranda, but Priscilla wasn't. I figured she'd stepped inside to get another iced tea, or perhaps use the bathroom— one more factor in favor of her not being a ghost—but when she didn't come out in a couple of minutes I searched the house for her.

She wasn't there. She wasn't anywhere in the yard, or in the old empty barn. Finally I went back and sat down on the porch swing to wait.

A couple of minutes latter Goggle jumped up on my lap. I'd been idly petting him for a couple of minutes before I realized that he was real.

I bought some cat food in the morning. I didn't want to set it out on the veranda, because I was sure the raccoons would get wind of it and drive Giggle and Goggle off, so I put it in a soup bowl and placed it on the counter next to the kitchen sink. I didn't have a litter box, so I left the kitchen window open enough for them to come and go as they pleased.

I resisted the urge to find out any more about Priscilla with the computer. All that was really left to learn was how she died, and I didn't want to know. How does a beautiful, healthy, world-traveling woman die at thirty-four? Torn apart by lions? Sacrificed by savages? Victim of a disfiguring tropical disease? Mugged, raped, and killed in New York? Whatever it was, it had robbed her of half a century. I didn't want to think of the books she could have written in that time, but rather of the joy she could have felt as she traveled from one new destination to another. No, I very definitely didn't want to know how she died.

I worked distractedly for a few hours, then knocked off in midafternoon and hurried home. To her.

I knew something was wrong the moment I got out of my car. The porch swing was empty. Giggle and Goggle jumped off the veranda, raced up to me, and began rubbing against my legs as if for comfort.

I yelled her name, but there was no response. Then I heard a rustling inside the house. I raced to the door, and saw a raccoon climbing out through the kitchen window just as I entered.

The place was a mess. Evidently he had been hunting for food, and since all I had were cans and frozen meals, he just started ripping the house apart, looking for anything he could eat.

And then I saw it: *Travels with My Cats* lay in tatters, as if the raccoon had had a temper tantrum at the lack of food and had taken it out on the book, which I'd left on the kitchen table. Pages were ripped to shreds, the cover was in pieces, and he had even urinated on what was left.

I worked feverishly on it for hours, tears streaming down my face for the first time since I was a kid, but there was no salvaging it—and that meant there would be no Priscilla tonight, or any night until I found another copy of the book.

In a blind fury I grabbed my rifle and a powerful flashlight and killed the first six raccoons I could find. It didn't make me feel any better—especially when I calmed down enough to consider what she would have thought of my bloodlust.

I felt like morning would never come. When it did, I raced to the office, activated my computer, and tried to find a copy of Priscilla's book at www.abebooks.com and www.bookfinder.com, the two biggest computerized clusters of used book dealers. There wasn't a single copy for sale.

I contacted some of the other book dealers I'd used in the past. None of them had ever heard of it.

I called the copyright division at the Library of Congress, figuring they might be able to help me. No luck: *Travels with My Cats* was never officially copyrighted; there was no copy on file. I began to wonder if I hadn't dreamed the whole thing, the book as well as the woman.

Finally I called Charlie Grimmis, who advertises himself as The Book Detective. He does most of his work for anthologists seeking rights and permissions to obscure, long-out-of-print books and stories, but he didn't care who he worked for, as long as he got his money.

It took him nine days and cost me $600, but finally I got a definitive answer:

Dear Ethan:

You led me on a merry chase. I'd have bet halfway through it that the book didn't exist, but you were right: evidently you did own a copy of a limited, numbered edition.

Travels with My Cats *was self-published by one Priscilla Wallace (d.*

1926), *in a limited, numbered edition of 200. The printer was the long-defunct Adelman Press of Bridgeport, Connecticut. The book was never copyrighted or registered with the Library of Congress.*

Now we get into the conjecture part. As near as I can tell, this Wallace woman gave about 150 copies away to friends and relatives, and the final 50 were probably trashed after her death. I've checked back, and there hasn't been a copy for sale anywhere in the past dozen years. It's hard to get trustworthy records farther back than that. Given that she was an unknown, that the book was a vanity press job, and that it went only to people who knew her, the likelihood is that no more than 15 or 20 copies still exist, if that many.

Best,

Charlie

When it's finally time to start taking risks, you don't think about it—you just do it. I quit my job that afternoon, and for the past year I've been criss-crossing the country, hunting for a copy of *Travels with My Cats*. I haven't found one yet, but I'll keep looking, no matter how long it takes. I get lonely, but I don't get discouraged.

Was it a dream? Was she a hallucination? A couple of acquaintances I confided in think so. Hell, I'd think so too—except that I'm not traveling alone. I've got two feline companions, and they're as real and substantial as cats get to be.

So the man with no goal except to get through another day finally has a mission in life, an important one. The woman I love died half a century too soon. I'm the only one who can give her back those years, if not all at once then an evening and a weekend at a time—but one way or another she's going to get them. I've spent all my yesterdays and haven't got a thing to show for them; now I'm going to start stockpiling her tomorrows.

Anyway, that's the story. My job is gone, and so is most of my money. I haven't slept in the same bed twice in close to four hundred days. I've lost a lot of weight, and I've been living in these clothes for longer than I care to think. It doesn't matter. All that matters is that I find a copy of that book, and someday I know I will.

Do I have any regrets?

Just one.

I never touched her. Not even once.

A Princess of Earth

I grew up reading Edgar Rice Burroughs, especially his Martian stories. To this day there is something very romantic, and even comforting, about the notion of essentially *wishing* yourself to Mars as John Carter did.

I am deeply in love with my wife, Carol, and have been for the forty-plus years we've been married. I always took it as a given that I'd die first. Then one day I got to wondering just what I would do if *she* died first.

I combined the two notions, and came up with "A Princess of Earth." It's probably a little more meaningful for me than for anyone else, but it did please enough voters to become a 2005 Hugo nominee.

When Lisa died I felt like my soul had been ripped out of my body, and what was left wasn't worth the powder to blow it to hell. To this day I don't even know what she died of; the doctors tried to tell me why she had collapsed and what had killed her, but I just tuned them out. She was dead and I would never talk to her or touch her again, never share a million unimportant things with her, and that was the only fact that mattered. I didn't even go to the funeral; I couldn't bear to look at her in her coffin.

I quit my job—we'd been counting the days to my retirement so we could finally spend all our time together—and I considered selling the house and moving to a smaller place, but in the end I couldn't do it. There was too much of her there, things I'd lose forever if I moved away.

I left her clothes in the closet, just the way they'd always been. Her hairbrush and her perfume and her lipstick remained on the vanity where she'd kept them neatly lined up. There was a painting of a New England landscape that I'd never liked much, but since she had loved it I left it hanging where it was. I had my favorite photos of her blown up and framed, and put them on every table and counter and shelf in the house.

I had no desire to be with other people, so I spent most of my days catching up on my reading. Well, let me amend that. I started a lot of books; I finished almost none of them. It was the same thing with movies: I'd rent a few, begin playing them, and usually turn them off within fifteen or twenty minutes. Friends would invite me out, I'd refuse, and after awhile they stopped calling. I barely noticed.

Winter came, a seemingly endless series of bleak days and frigid nights. It was the first time since I'd married Lisa that I didn't bring a Christmas tree home to decorate. There just didn't seem much sense to it. We'd never had any children, she wasn't there to share it, and I wasn't going to have any visitors.

As it turned out, I was wrong about the visitor: I spotted him maybe an hour before midnight, wandering naked across my backyard during the worst blizzard of the season.

At first I thought I was hallucinating. Five inches of snow had fallen, and the wind chill was something like ten below zero. I stared in disbelief for a full minute, and when he didn't disappear, I put on my coat, climbed into my boots, grabbed a blanket, and rushed outside. When I reached him he seemed half-frozen. I threw the blanket around him and led him back into the house.

I rubbed his arms and legs vigorously with a towel, then sat him down in the kitchen and poured him some hot coffee. It took him a few minutes to stop shivering, but finally he reached out for the cup. He warmed his hands on it, then lifted it and took a sip.

"Thank you," he whispered hoarsely.

Once I was sure that he wasn't going to die, I stood back and took a look at him. He was actually pretty good-looking now that his color was returning. He might have been thirty, maybe a couple of years older. Lean body, dark hair, gray eyes. A couple of scars, but I couldn't tell what they were from, or how fresh they were. They could have been from one of the wars in Iraq, or old sports injuries, or perhaps just the wind whipping frozen bushes against him a few minutes ago.

"Are you feeling better?" I asked.

He nodded. "Yes, I'll be all right soon."

"What the hell were you doing out there without any clothes on?"

"Trying to get home," he said with an ironic smile.

"I haven't seen you around," I said. "Do you live near here?"

"No."

"Is there someone who can pick you up and take you there?"

He seemed about to answer me, then changed his mind and just shook his head.

"What's your name?" I asked.

"John." He took another swallow from the cup and made a face.

"Yeah, I know," I said. "The coffee's pretty awful. Lisa made it better."

"Lisa?"

"My wife," I said. "She died last year."

We were both silent for a couple of minutes, and I noticed still more color returning to his face.

"Where did you leave you clothes?" I asked.

"They're very far away."

"Just how far did you walk in this blizzard?"

"I don't know."

"Okay," I said in exasperation. "Who do I call—the cops, the hospital, or the nearest asylum?"

"Don't call anyone," said John. "I'll be all right soon, and then I'll leave."

"Dressed like that? In this weather?"

He seemed surprised. "I'd forgotten. I guess I'll have to wait here until it's over. I'm sorry to impose, but . . ."

"What the hell," I said. "I've been alone a long time and I'm sure Lisa would say I could use a little company, even from a naked stranger. At any rate she wouldn't want me to throw you out in the cold on Christmas Eve." I stared at him. "I just hope you're not dangerous."

"Not to my friends."

"I figure pulling you out of the snow and giving you shelter qualifies as an act of friendship," I said. "Just what the hell were you doing out there and what happened to your clothes?"

"It's a long story."

"It's a long night, and I've got nothing to do."

"All right," said John with a shrug. "I am a very old man; how old I do not know. Possibly I am a hundred, possibly more; but I can't tell because I have never aged as other men, nor do I remember any childhood."

"Stop," I said.

"What is it?"

"I don't know what game you're playing, but I've heard that before—a long, long time ago. I don't know where, but I've heard it."

He shook his head. "No you haven't. But perhaps you've *read* it before."

I searched through my memory, mentally scanning the bookshelves of my youth—and there I found it, right between *The Wizard of Oz* and *King Solomon's Mines*. "God, it's been close to half a century! I loved that book when I was growing up."

"Thank you," said John.

"What am I thanking you for?"

"I wrote it."

"Sure you did," I said. "I read the damned thing fifty years ago, and it was an old book then. Look at yourself in a mirror."

"Nevertheless."

Wonderful, I thought. *Just what I needed on Christmas Eve. Other people get carolers; I get you.* Aloud I said: "It wasn't written by a John. It was written by an Edgar."

"He *published* it. *I* wrote it."

"Sure," I said. "And your last name is Carter, right?"

"Yes, it is."

"I should have called the loony bin to begin with."

"They couldn't get here until morning," said John. "Trust me: you're perfectly safe."

"The assurances of a guy who walks around naked in a snowstorm and thinks he's John Carter of Mars aren't exactly coin of the realm," I said. The second I said it I kind of tensed and told myself I should be humoring him, that I was a sixty-four-year-old man with high blood pressure and worse cholesterol and he looked like a cruiserweight boxer. Then I realized that I didn't really care whether he killed me or not, that I'd just been going through the motions of living since Lisa had died, and I decided not to humor him after all. If he picked up a kitchen knife and ran me through, Warlord of Mars style, at least it would put an end to the aching loneliness that had been my constant companion for almost a year.

"So why do you think you're John Carter?" I asked him.

"Because I am."

"Why not Buck Rogers or Flash Gordon—or the Scarlet Pimpernel for that matter?"

"Why aren't you Doc Savage or the Shadow?" he replied. "Or James Bond for that matter?"

"I never claimed to be a fictional character," I said.

"Neither did I. I am John Carter, formerly of Virginia, and I am trying to return to my princess."

"Stark naked in a blizzard?"

"My clothes do not survive the transition, and I am not responsible for the weather," he said.

"That's a reasonably rational explanation for a crazy man."

He stared at me. "The woman I love more than life itself is millions of miles from here. Is it so crazy to want to return to her?"

"No," I admitted. "It's not crazy to want to be with her. But it's crazy to think she's on Mars."

"Where do *you* think she is?" he asked.

"How the hell should *I* know?" I shot back. "But I know nothing's on Mars except a bunch of rocks. It's below zero in the summer, there's no oxygen, and if anything ever lived there, it died out fifty or sixty million years ago. What have you got to say to that?"

"I have spent close to a century on Barsoom. Perhaps it is some other world than the one you know as Mars. Perhaps when I traverse the void, I also traverse the eons. I'm not interested in explanations, only in results. As long as I can once again hold my incomparable princess in my arms, I'll leave the answers to the scientists and the philosophers."

"And the psychiatrists," I added.

He looked grimly amused. "So if you had your way, I would be locked away in an institution until they convinced me that the woman I love doesn't exist and that my entire life has been a meaningless fantasy. You strike me as a very unhappy man; would that make you happier?"

"I'm just a realistic man," I said. "When I was a kid, I wanted so badly to believe *A Princess of Mars* was true that I used to stand in my backyard every night and reach my hands out to Mars, just the way you did. I kept waiting to get whisked away from the mundane life I'd been living and transported to Barsoom." I paused. "It never happened. All I got from all that reaching was sore shoulders and a lot of teasing from friends who didn't read books."

"Perhaps you had no reason to go to Barsoom," he said. "You were a child, with your entire life ahead of you. I think that Barsoom can be very choosy about who it allows to visit."

"So now you're saying that a planet is sentient?"

"I have no idea if it is," replied John. "Do you know for an absolute fact that it isn't?"

I stared at him irritably. "You're better at this than I am," I said. "You sound so fucking reasonable. Of course, you've had a lot more practice."

"More practice at what?"

"Fooling people by sounding normal."

"More practice than you?"

"See?" I said. "That's what I mean. You've got an answer for everything, and if you don't, then you respond with a question that'll make *me* sound like a fool if I answer it. But *I* wasn't wandering around naked in a blizzard in the middle of the night, and I don't think I live on Mars."

"Do you feel better now?" he said.

"Not much," I admitted. "You want some more coffee?"

"Actually, what I'd like to do is walk around a little and get some life back in my limbs."

"Outside?"

He shook his head. "No, not outside."

"Fine," I said, getting up. "It's not as big or stately as a Martian palace, but I'll give you the chef's tour."

He got to his feet, adjusted the blanket around himself, and fell into step behind me. I led him into the living room, then stopped.

"Are you still cold?"

"A little."

"I think I'll light a fire," I said. "I haven't used the damned fireplace all winter. I might as well get my money's worth."

"It's not necessary," he said. "I'll be all right."

"It's no bother," I said, opening the screen and tossing a couple of logs onto the grate. "Look around while I'm doing it."

"You're not afraid I might rob you?"

"Have you got any pockets to put your loot in?" I asked.

He smiled at that. "I guess it's my good luck that I'm not a thief."

I spent the next couple of minutes positioning the kindling and starting the fire. I don't know which rooms he'd seen, but he was just returning when I straightened up.

"You must have loved her very much," he said. "You've turned the house into a shrine to her."

"Whether you're John Carter or merely think you're John Carter, you should be able to understand what I felt."

"How long has she been gone?"

"She died last February," I said, then added bitterly: "On Valentine's Day."

"She was a lovely woman."

"Most people just get older," I said. "She got more beautiful every day. To me, anyway."

"I know."

"How could you know? You never met her, never saw her."

"I know because my princess grows more beautiful with every passing moment. When you are truly in love, your princess always grows more beautiful."

"And if she's Barsoomian, she stays young for a thousand years, give or take," I said, remembering the book.

"Perhaps."

"Perhaps? Don't you know?"

"Does it really make a difference, as long as she remains young and beautiful in my eyes?"

"That's pretty philosophical for a guy who thinks he makes his living lopping off heads with a longsword," I said.

"I want nothing more than to live in peace," he replied, sitting in the armchair that was closest to the fire. "I resent every second that I am away from my Dejah Thoris."

"I envy you," I said.

"I thought I was supposed to be insane," he said wryly.

"You are. It makes no difference. Whether your Dejah Thoris is real or whether she's a figment of a deranged mind, you believe she exists and that you're going to join her. My Lisa is dead; I'll never see her again."

He made no reply, but simply stared at me.

"You may be crazy as a loon," I continued, seating myself on the sofa, "but you're convinced you're going to see your Princess of Mars. I'd give up every last vestige of sanity if I could believe, even for a minute, that I would see my Princess of Earth one more time."

"I admire your courage," said John.

"Courage?" I repeated, surprised.

"If my princess were to die, I would have no desire to live another day, even another moment, without her."

"It has nothing to do with a desire to live."

"Then what is it?"

I shrugged. "Instinct. Inertia. I don't know. I certainly haven't enjoyed being alive the past year."

"And yet you have not ended it."

"Maybe it's not courage at all," I said. "Maybe it's cowardice."

"Or maybe there is a reason."

"For living? I can't give you one."

"Then perhaps it was Fate that I should appear at your house."

"You didn't magically appear," I said. "You walked here from wherever it was you left your clothes."

"No," he said, shaking his head firmly. "One moment I was strolling through the gardens of my palace in Helium, hand in hand with my princess, and the next I was standing in your yard, without my harness or my weapons. I tried to return, but I couldn't see Barsoom through the swirling snow, and if I can't see it I can't reach out to it."

"You've got a smooth answer for everything," I said wearily. "I'll bet you ace all your Rorschach tests, too."

"You know all your neighbors," said John. "Have you ever seen me before? How far do you think a naked man could get in this blizzard? Have the police come by to warn you of an escaped madman?"

"It's a terrible night to be out, even for the police, and you seem like a harmless enough madman," I replied.

"Now who has the smooth answer?"

"Okay, fine—you're John Carter, and Dejah Thoris is up there somewhere waiting for you, and it was Fate that brought you here, and tomorrow morning a very worried man won't show up looking for his missing cousin or brother."

"You have my books," he said. "Some of them anyway. I saw them on a shelf in your study. Use them. Ask me anything you want."

"What would that prove? There's probably a thousand kids who can recite them word for word."

"Then I guess we'll spend the night in silence."

"No," I said. "I'll ask you some questions—but the answers won't be in the books."

"Fine."

"All right," I said. "How can you be so smitten with a woman who was hatched from an egg?"

"How can you love a woman of Irish or Polish or Brazilian descent?" he asked. "How can you love a black woman, or a red one, or a white one? How can you love a Christian or a Jew? I love my princess because of what she is, not what she might have been." He paused. "Why are you smiling?"

"I was thinking that we're growing a perceptive crop of madmen this year."

He gestured to one of Lisa's photos. "I take it she had nothing in common with you."

"She had everything in common with me," I said. "Except heritage and religion and upbringing. Odd, isn't it?"

"Why should it be?" he asked. "I never thought it was odd to love a Martian woman."

"I suppose if you can believe there are people on Mars, even people who have hatched from eggs, it's easy enough to believe you love one of them."

"Why do you feel it's so insane to believe in a better world, a world of grace and chivalry, of manners and nobility? And why should I not love the most perfect woman that world has to offer? Would it not be mad to feel otherwise? Once you met your princess, would it have been rational to cast her aside?"

"We're not talking about my princess," I said irritably.

"We are talking about love."

"Lots of people fall in love. No one else has had to go to Mars because of it."

"And now we are talking about the sacrifices one makes for love." He smiled ruefully. "For example, here I am, in the middle of the night, forty million miles from my princess, with a man who thinks I belong in an asylum."

"Why did you come back from Mars, then?" I asked.

"It was not an act of volition." He paused, as if remembering. "The first time it happened, I thought the Almighty must be testing me as He had tested Job. I spent ten long years here before I could return."

"And you never once questioned if it had really happened?"

"The ancient cities, the dead sea bottoms, the battles, the fierce green-skinned warriors, I could have imagined them. But I could never have imagined my love for my princess; it remained with me every minute of every day—the sound of her voice, the feel of her skin, the scent of her hair. No, I could not have invented that."

"It must have been a comfort during your exile," I said.

"A comfort and a torture," he replied. "To look up in the sky every day and know that she and the son I had never seen were so unthinkably far away."

"But you never doubted?"

"Never," he said. "I still remember the last words I wrote: 'I believe that they are waiting for me, and something tells me I shall soon know.'"

"True or not, at least you could believe it," I said. "You didn't watch your princess die in front of you."

He stared at me, as if trying to decide what to say next. Finally he spoke. "I have died many times, and if Providence wills it, I shall die again tomorrow."

"What are you talking about?"

"Only my consciousness can traverse the void between worlds," he said. "My body remains behind, a lifeless hulk."

"And it doesn't decay or rot, it just waits for you to return?" I said sarcastically.

"I can't explain it," he said. "I can only take advantage of it."

"And this is supposed to comfort me—that a madman who thinks he's John Carter is hinting that my Lisa might somehow be alive on Mars?"

"It would comfort *me*," he said.

"Yeah, but you're crazy."

"Is it crazy to think she might have done what I did?"

"Absolutely," I said.

"If you had a terminal disease, would it be crazy to seek out every quack in the world who thought he could cure it rather than to sit around passively waiting to die?"

"So now you're a quack instead of a madman?"

"No," he said. "I'm just a man who is less afraid of death than of losing his princess."

"Bully for you," I said. "I've already lost mine."

"For ten months. I lost mine for ten years."

"There's a difference," I pointed out. "Mine's dead; yours wasn't."

"There's another difference," he replied. "I had the courage to find mine."

"Mine isn't lost. I know exactly where she is."

He shook his head. "You know where the unimportant part of her is."

I sighed deeply. "I'd settle for your madness if I had your faith."

"You don't need faith. You only need the courage to believe, not that something is true, but that it is possible."

"Courage is for Warlords," I replied, "not for sixty-four-year-old widowers."

"Every man has untapped wells of courage," he said. "Maybe your princess is not on Barsoom. Maybe there is no Barsoom, and I am every bit as crazy as you think I am. Are you really content to accept things as they are, or have you the courage to hope that I'm right?"

"Of course I hope you're right," I said irritably. "So what?"

"Hope leads to belief, and belief leads to action."

"It leads to the funny farm."

He looked at me, a sad expression on his face. "Was your princess perfect?"

"In every way," I said promptly.

"And did she love you?"

I saw his next question coming, but I couldn't help answering him. "Yes."

"Could a perfect princess have loved a coward or a madman?" he said.

"Enough!" I snapped. "It's been hard enough staying sane these last ten months. Then you come along and make the alternative sound too attractive. I can't spend the rest of my life thinking that I'll somehow find a way to see her again!"

"Why not?"

At first I thought he was kidding. Then I saw that he wasn't.

"Aside from the fact that it's crazy, if I bought into it I wouldn't accomplish a damned thing."

"What are you accomplishing now?" he asked.

"Nothing," I admitted, suddenly deflated. "I get up each morning and all I do is wait for the day to drag to a close so I can go to sleep and not see her face in front of me until I wake up again."

"And you consider this the rational behavior of a sane man?"

"Of a realistic man," I replied. "She's gone and she's not coming back."

"Reality is greatly overrated," he responded. "A realist sees silicon; a madman sees a machine that can think. A realist sees bread mold; a madman sees a drug that miraculously cures infection. A realist looks at the stars and asks, why bother? A madman looks at those same stars and asks, why not bother?" He paused and stared intently at me. "A realist would say, My princess is dead. A madman would say, John Carter found a way to overcome death, so why couldn't she?"

"I wish I could say that."

"But?" he said.

"I'm not a madman."

"I feel very sorry for you."

"I don't feel sorry for *you*," I replied.

"Oh? What do you feel?"

"Envy," I said. "They'll come by tonight or tomorrow or the next day to pick you up and take you back to wherever you wandered off from, and you will believe just as devoutly then as you do now. You'll know beyond any doubt that your princess is waiting for you. You'll spend your every waking moment trying to escape, trying to get back to Barsoom. You'll have belief and hope and purpose, which is a pretty impressive triumvirate. I wish I had any one of them."

"They're not unattainable."

"Maybe not to Warlords, but they are to aging widowers with bad knees and worse blood pressure," I said, getting to my feet. He looked at me curiously. "I've had enough craziness for one night," I told him. "I'm going to bed. You can sleep on the sofa if you want, but if I were you I'd leave before they came looking for me. If you go to the basement you'll find some clothes and an old pair of boots you can have, and you can take my coat from the hall closet."

"Thank you for your hospitality," he said as I walked to the staircase. "I'm sorry to have brought back painful memories of your princess."

"I cherish my memories," I replied. "Only the present is painful."

I climbed the stairs and lay down on the bed, still dressed, and fell asleep to visions of Lisa alive and smiling, as I did every night.

When I awoke in the morning and went downstairs he was gone. At first I thought he'd taken my advice and gotten a head start on his keepers—but then I looked out the window and saw him, right where I'd spotted him the night before.

He was face-down in the snow, his arms stretched out in front of him, naked as the day he was born. I knew before I checked for a pulse that he was dead. I wish I could say that he had a happy smile on his face, but he didn't; he looked as cold and uncomfortable as when I'd first found him.

I called the police, who showed up within the hour and took him away. They told me they had no reports of any nut cases escaping from the local asylum.

I checked in with them a few times in the next week. They simply couldn't identify him. His fingerprints and DNA weren't on file anywhere, and he didn't match any missing persons descriptions. I'm not sure when they closed the file on him, but nobody showed up to claim the body and they finally planted him, with no name on his headstone, in the same cemetery where Lisa was buried.

I visited Lisa every day, as usual, and I started visiting John's grave as well. I don't know why. He'd gotten me thinking crazy, uncomfortable thoughts that I couldn't shake, blurring the line between wishes and possibilities, and I resented it. More to the point, I resented him: he died with the absolute knowledge that he would soon see his princess, while I lived with the absolute knowledge that I would never again see mine.

I couldn't help wondering which of us was truly the sane one—the one who made reality conform by the sheer force of his belief, or the one who settled for old memories because he lacked the courage to try to create new ones.

As the days passed I found myself dwelling more and more on what John had said, turning it over in my mind again and again—and then, on February 13, I read an item in the newspaper that tomorrow Mars would be closer to Earth than at any time in the next sixteen years.

I turned my computer on for the first time in months and verified the item on a couple of Internet news services. I thought about it for a while, and about John, and about Lisa. Then I phoned the Salvation Army and left a message on their answering device, giving them my address and telling them that I would leave the house unlocked and they were welcome to everything in it—clothes, food, furniture, anything they wanted.

I've spent the past three hours writing these words, so that whoever reads them will know that what I am about to do I am doing willingly, even joyfully, and that far from giving in to depression I am, at long last, yielding to hope.

It's almost three in the morning. The snow stopped falling at midnight, the sky is clear, and Mars should come into view any moment now. A few minutes ago I gathered my favorite photos of Lisa; they're lined up on the desk right beside me, and she seems more beautiful than ever.

Very soon I'll take off my clothes, fold them neatly on my desk chair, and walk out into the yard. Then it's just a matter of spotting what I'm looking for. Is it Mars? Barsoom? Something else? It makes no difference. Only a realist sees things as they are, and it was John who showed me the limitations of reality—and how could someone as perfect as my princess not transcend those limitations?

I believe she is waiting for me, and something tells me I shall soon know.

Down Memory Lane

What if you and the one person you were meant to spend your life with—in my case, Carol—were born a century apart? My answer was "Travels with My Cats."

What if the person you love dies first? My answer was "A Princess of Earth."

And what if the person you love doesn't die first, but instead comes down with an all-too-common condition whereby she is no longer the person you've known? How would you communicate with her? At what level could you once again connect? My answer for the third of what I think of as my Carol Trilogy of short stories was "Down Memory Lane."

Last minute note: As this book was going to press, I was informed that "Down Memory Lane" has just been honored with my twenty-eighth Hugo nomination.

Gwendolyn sticks a finger into her cake, pulls it out, and licks it with a happy smile on her face.

"I *like* birthdays!" she says, giggling with delight.

I lean over and wipe some frosting off her chin. "Try to be a little neater," I say. "You wouldn't want to have to take a bath before you open your present."

"Present?" she repeats excitedly, her gaze falling on the box with the colorful wrapping paper and the big satin bow. "Is it time for my present now? Is it?"

"Yes, it is," I answer. I pick up the box and hand it to her. "Happy birthday, Gwendolyn."

She tears off the paper, shoves the card aside, and opens the box. An instant later she emits a happy squeal and pulls out the rag doll. "This is my very favorite day of my whole life!" she announces.

I sigh and try to hold back my tears.

Gwendolyn is eighty-two years old. She has been my wife for the last sixty of them.

I don't know where I was when Kennedy was shot. I don't know what I was doing when the World Trade Center collapsed under the onslaught of two jetliners. But I remember every single detail, every minute, every second, of the day we got the bad news.

"It may not be Alzheimer's," said Dr. Castleman. "Alzheimer's is becoming a catchword for a variety of senile dementias. Eventually we'll find out exactly which dementia it is, but there's no question that Gwendolyn is suffering from one of them."

It wasn't a surprise—after all, we knew something was wrong; that's why she was being examined—but it was still a shock.

"Is there any chance of curing it?" I asked, trying to keep my composure.

He shook his head sadly. "Right now we're barely able to slow it down."

"How long have I got?" said Gwendolyn, her face grim, her jaw set.

"Physically you're in fine shape," said Castleman. "You could live another ten to twenty years."

"How long before I don't know who anyone is?" she persisted.

He shrugged helplessly. "It proceeds at different rates with different people. At first you won't notice any diminuition, but before long it will become noticeable, perhaps not to you, but to those around you. And it doesn't progress in a straight line. One day you'll find you've lost the ability to read, and then, perhaps two months later, you'll see a newspaper headline, or perhaps a menu in a restaurant, and you'll read it as easily as you do today. Paul here will be elated and think you're regaining your capacity, and he'll call me and tell me about it, but it won't last. In another day, another hour, another week, the ability will be gone again."

"Will I know what's happening to me?"

"That's almost the only good part of it," replied Castleman. "You know now what lies ahead of you, but as it progresses you will be less and less aware of any loss of your cognitive abilities. You'll be understandably bitter at the start, and we'll put you on antidepressants, but the day will come when you no longer need them because you no longer remember that you ever had a greater mental capacity than you possess at that moment."

She turned to me. "I'm sorry, Paul."

"It's not your fault," I said.

"I'm sorry that you'll have to watch this happen to me."

"There must be something we can do, some way we can fight it . . ." I muttered.

"I'm afraid there isn't," said Castleman. "They say there are stages you go through when you know you're going to die: disbelief, then anger, then self-pity, and finally acceptance. No one's ever come up with a similar list for the dementias, but in the end what you're going to have to do is accept it and learn to live with it."

"How long before I have to go to . . . to wherever I have to go when Paul can't care for me alone?"

Castleman took a deep breath, let it out, and pursed his lips. "It varies. It could be five or six months, it could be two years, it could be longer. A lot depends on you."

"On me?" said Gwendolyn.

"As you become more childlike, you will become more curious

about things that you no longer know or recognize. Paul tells me you've always had a probing mind. Will you be content to sit in front of the television while he's sleeping or otherwise occupied, or will you feel a need to walk outside and then forget how to get back home? Will you be curious about all the buttons and switches on the kitchen appliances? Two-year-olds can't open doors or reach kitchen counters, but *you* will be able to. So, as I say, it depends on you, and that is something no one can predict." He paused. "And there may be rages."

"Rages?" I repeated.

"In more than half the cases," he replied. "She won't know why she's so enraged. You will, of course—but you won't be able to do anything about it. If it happens, we have medications that will help."

I was so depressed I was thinking of suicide pacts, but Gwendolyn turned to me and said, "Well, Paul, it looks like we have a lot of living to cram into the next few months. I've always wanted to take a Caribbean cruise. We'll stop at the travel agency on the way home."

That was her reaction to the most horrific news a human being can receive.

I thanked God that I'd had sixty years with her, and I cursed Him for taking away everything that made her the woman I loved before we'd said and done all the things we had wanted to say and do.

She'd been beautiful once. She still was. Physical beauty fades, but inner beauty never does. For sixty years we had lived together, loved together, worked together, played together. We got to where we could finish each other's sentences, where we knew each other's tastes better than we knew our own. We had fights—who doesn't?—but we never once went to bed mad at each other.

We raised three children, two sons and a daughter. One son was killed in Vietnam; the other son and the daughter kept in touch as best they could, but they had their own lives to lead, and they lived many states away.

Gradually our outside social contacts became fewer and fewer; we were all each other needed. And now I was going to watch the only thing I'd ever truly loved become a little less each day, until there was nothing left but an empty shell.

The cruise went well. We even took the train all the way to the rum factory at the center of Jamaica, and we spent a few days in Miami before flying home. She seemed so normal, so absolutely herself, that I began thinking that maybe Dr. Castleman's diagnosis had been mistaken.

But then it began. There was no single incident that couldn't have occurred fifty years ago, nothing that you couldn't find a reasonable excuse for—but things kept happening. One afternoon she put a roast in the oven, and at dinnertime we found that she'd forgotten to turn the oven on. Two days later we were watching *The Maltese Falcon* for the umpteenth time, and suddenly she couldn't remember who killed Humphrey Bogart's partner. She "discovered" Raymond Chandler, an author she'd loved for years. There were no rages, but there was everything else Dr. Castleman had predicted.

I began counting her pills. She was on five different medications, three of them twice a day. She never skipped them all, but somehow the numbers never came out quite right.

I'd mention a person, a place, an incident, something we'd shared together, and one time out of three she couldn't recall it—and she'd get annoyed when I'd explain that she had forgotten it. In a month it became two out of three times. Then she lost interest in reading. She blamed it on her glasses, but when I took her to get a new prescription, the optometrist tested her and told us that her vision hadn't changed since her last visit two years earlier.

She kept fighting it, trying to stimulate her brain with crossword puzzles, math problems, anything that would cause her to think. But each month the puzzles and problems got a little simpler, and each month she solved a few less than she had the month before. She still loved music, and she still loved leaving seeds out for the birds and watching them come by to feed—but she could no longer hum along with the melodies or identify the birds.

She had never allowed me to keep a gun in the house. It was better, she said, to let thieves steal everything then to get killed in a shootout—they were just possessions; we were all that counted—and I honored her wishes for sixty years. But now I went out and bought a small handgun and a box of bullets, and kept them locked in my desk against the day that she was so far gone she no longer knew who I was. I told myself that when that day occurred, I would put a bullet into her head and another into my own . . . but I knew that I couldn't. Myself, yes; the woman who'd been my life, never.

I met her in college. She was an honor student. I was a not-very-successful jock—third-string defensive end in football, backup power forward in basketball, big, strong, and dumb—but she saw something in me. I'd noticed her around the campus—she was too good-looking not to notice—but she hung out with the brains, and our paths almost never crossed. The only reason I asked her out the first time was because one of my frat brothers bet me ten dollars she wouldn't give me the time of day. But for some reason I'll never know she said yes, and for the next sixty years I was never willingly out of her presence. When we had money we spent it, and when we didn't have money we were every bit as happy; we just didn't live as well or travel as much. We raised our kids, sent them out into the world, watched one die and two move away to begin their own lives, and wound up the way we'd started—just the two of us.

And now one of us was vanishing, day by day, minute by minute.

One morning she locked the bathroom door and couldn't remember how to unlock it. She was so panicky that she couldn't hear me giving her instructions from the other side. I was on the the phone, calling the fire department, when she appeared at my side to ask why I was talking to them and what was burning.

"She had no memory of locking herself in," I explained to Dr. Castleman the next day. "One moment she couldn't cope with a lock any three-year-old could manipulate, and the next moment she opened the door and didn't remember having any problem with it."

"That's the way these things progress," he said.

"How long before she doesn't know me any more?"

Castleman sighed. "I really don't know, Paul. You've been the most important thing in her life, the most constant thing, so it stands to reason that you'll be the last thing she forgets." He sighed again. "It could be a few months, or a few years—or it could be tomorrow."

"It's not fair," I muttered.

"Nobody ever said it was," he replied. "I had her checked over while she was here, and for what it's worth she's in excellent physical health for a woman of her age. Heart and lungs are fine, blood pressure's normal."

Of course her blood pressure was normal, I thought bitterly. She didn't spend most of her waking hours wondering what it would be like when the person she had spent her life with no longer recognized her.

Then I realized that she didn't spend most of her waking hours thinking of *anything*, and I felt guilty for pitying myself when she was the one whose mind and memories were racing away at an ever-faster rate.

Two weeks later we went shopping for groceries. She wandered off to get something—ice cream, I think—and when I'd picked up what I needed and went over to the frozen food section she wasn't there. I looked around, checked out the next few aisles. No luck.

I asked one of the stock girls to check the women's rest room. It was empty.

I started getting a panicky feeling in the pit of my stomach. I was just about to go out into the parking lot to look for her when a cop brought her into the store, leading her very gently by the arm.

"She was wandering around looking for her car," he explained. "A 1961 Nash Rambler."

"We haven't owned that car in forty years or more," I said. I turned to Gwendolyn. "Are you all right?"

Her face was streaked by tears. "I'm sorry," she said. "I couldn't remember where we parked the car."

"It's all right," I said.

She kept crying and telling me how sorry she was. Pretty soon everyone was staring, and the store manager asked if I'd like to take her to his office and let her sit down. I thanked him, and the cop, but decided she'd be better off at home, so I led her out to the Ford we'd owned for the past five years and drove her home.

As we pulled into the garage and got out of the car, she stood back and looked at it.

"What a pretty car," she said. "Whose is it?"

"They're not sure of anything," said Dr. Castleman. "But they think it's got something to do with the amyloid beta protein. An abundance of it can usually be found in people suffering from Alzheimer's or Down syndrome."

"Can't you take it out, or do something to neutralize it?" I asked.

Gwendolyn sat in a chair, staring at the wall. We could have been ten thousand miles away as far as she was concerned.

"If it was that simple, they'd have done it."

"So it's a protein," I said. "Does it come in some kind of food? Is there something she shouldn't be eating?"

He shook his head. "There are all kinds of proteins. This is one you're born with."

"Is it in the brain?"

"Initially it's in the spinal fluid."

"Well, can't you drain it out?" I persisted.

He sighed. "By the time we know it's a problem in a particular individual, it's too late. It forms plaques on the brain, and once that happens, the disease is irreversible." He paused wearily. "At least it's irreversible today. Someday they'll cure it. They should be able to slow it down before too long. I wouldn't be surprised to see it eradicated within a quarter of a century. There may even come a day when they can test embryos for an amyloid beta imbalance and correct it in utero. They're making progress."

"But not in time to help Gwendolyn."

"No, not in time to help Gwendolyn."

Gradually, over the next few months, she became totally unaware that she even had Alzheimer's. She no longer read, but she watched the television incessantly. She especially liked children's shows and cartoons. I would come into the room and hear the eighty-two-year-old woman I loved singing along with the Mickey Mouse Club. I had a feeling that if they still ran test patterns she could watch one for hours on end.

And then came the morning I had known would come: I was fixing her breakfast—some cereal she'd seen advertised on television—and she looked up at me, and I could tell that she no longer knew who I was. Oh, she wasn't afraid of me, or even curious, but there was absolutely no spark of recognition.

The next day I moved her into a home that specialized in the senile dementias.

"I'm sorry, Paul," said Dr. Castleman. "But it really is for the best. She needs professional care. You've lost weight, you're not getting any sleep, and to be blunt, it no longer makes any difference to her who feeds and cleans and medicates her."

"Well, it makes a difference to *me*," I said angrily. "They treat her like an infant!"

"That's what she's become."

"She's been there two weeks, and I haven't seen them try—really *try*—to communicate with her."

"She has nothing to say, Paul."

"It's there," I said. "It's somewhere inside her brain."

"Her brain isn't what it once was," said Castleman. "You have to face up to that."

"I took her there too soon," I said. "There *must* be a way to connect with her."

"You're an adult, and despite her appearance, she's a four-year-old child," said Castleman gently. "You no longer have anything in common."

"We have a lifetime in common!" I snapped.

I couldn't listen to any more, so I got up and stalked out of his office.

I decided that depending on Dr. Castleman was a dead end, and I began visiting other specialists. They all told me pretty much the same thing. One of them even showed me his lab, where they were doing all kinds of chemical experiments on the amyloid beta protein and a number of other things. It was encouraging, but nothing was going to happen fast enough to cure Gwendolyn.

Two or three times each day I picked up that pistol I'd bought and toyed with ending it, but I kept thinking: what if there's a miracle— medical, religious, whatever kind? What if she becomes Gwendolyn again? She'll be all alone with a bunch of senile old men and women, and I'll have deserted her.

So I couldn't kill myself, and I couldn't help her, and I couldn't just stand by and watch her. Somehow, somewhere, there had to be a way to connect with her, to communicate on the same level again. We'd faced some pretty terrible problems together—losing a son, suffering a miscarriage, watching each of our parents die in turn—and as long as we were together we were able to overcome them. This was just one more problem—and every problem is capable of solution.

I found the solution, too. It wasn't where I expected, and it certainly wasn't *what* I expected, but she was eighty-two years old and sinking fast, and I didn't hesitate.

That's where things stand this evening. Earlier today I bought this notebook, and this marks the end of my first entry.

Friday, June 22. I'd heard about the clinic while I was learning everything I could about the disease. The government outlawed it and shut it down, so they moved it lock, stock, and barrel to Guatamala. It wasn't much to look at, but then, I wasn't expecting much. Just a miracle of a different sort.

They make no bones about what they anticipate if the experiment goes as planned. That's why they only accept terminal patients—and because they have so few and are so desperate for volunteers, that's also why they didn't challenge me when I told them I had a slow-acting cancer. I signed a release that probably wouldn't hold up in any court of law outside Guatamala; they now have my permission to do just about anything they want to me.

Saturday, June 23. So it begins. I thought they'd inject it into my spine, but instead they went through the carotid artery in my neck. Makes sense; it's the conduit between the spine and the brain. If anything's going to get the protein where it can do its work, that's the ticket. I thought it would hurt like hell, but it's just a little sore. Except for that, I don't feel any different.

Wednesday, June 27. Fourth day in a row of tedious lectures explaining how some of us will die but a few may be saved and all humanity will benefit, or something like that. Now I have an inkling of how lab rats and guinea pigs feel. They're not aware that they're dying; and I guess before too long, we won't be either.

Wednesday, July 3. After a week of having me play with the most idiotic puzzles, they tell me that I've lost six percent of my cognitive functions and that the condition is accelerating. It seems to please them to no end. I'm not convinced; I think if they'd give me a little more time I'd do better on these damned tests. I mean, it's been a long time since I was in school. I'm out of practice.

Sunday, July 7. You know, I think it's working. I was reading down in the lounge, and for the longest time I couldn't remember where my room was. Good. The faster it works, the better. I've got a lot of catching up to do.

Tuesday, July 16. Today we got another talking-to. They say the shots are stronger and the symptons are appearing even faster than they'd hoped, and it's almost time to try the anecdote. Anecdote. Is that the right word?

Friday, July 26. Boy am I lucky. At the last minute I remembered why I went there in the furst place. I wated until it was dark and snuck out. When I got to the airport I didnt have any money, but they asked to see my wallet and took out this plastic card and did something with it and said it was OK and gave me a ticket.

Saturday, july 27. I wrote down my address so I wouldnt forget, and boy am i lucky I did, because when I got a cab at the airporte I coudlnt' remember what to tell him. We drove and we drove and finally I remembered I had wrote it down, but when we got home i didnt' have a key. i started pounding on the door, but no one was there to let me in, and finally they came with a loud siren and took me somewere else. i cant stay long. I have to find gwendolyn before it is too late, but i cant remember what it wood be too late for.

Mundy, august. He says his name is Doctr Kasleman and that i know him, and he kept saying o paul why did you do this to yourself, and i told him i didn't remember but i know I had a reason and it had something to do with gwendolyn. do you remember her he said. of course i do i said, she is my love and my life. I askt when can i see her & he said soon.

wensday. they gave me my own room, but i dont want my own room i want to be with gwendolyn. finaly they let me see her and she was as beutiful as ever and i wanted to hug her and kiss her but wen i walked up to her she started krying and the nurse took her away

it has been 8 daz since i rote here. or maybe 9. i keep forgeting to. today i saw a prety littl girl in the hall, with prety white hair. she reminds me of someone but i dont know who. tomorrow if i remember i will bring her a prezent

i saw the pretti gurl again today. i took a flower from a pot and gave it to her and she smiled and said thank you and we talkt alot and she said i am so glad we met & i am finaly happy. i said so am i. i think we are going to be great friends becauz we like each other and have so mucch in commmon. i askt her name and she couldnt remember, so i will call her gwendolyn. i think i nu someone called gwendolyn once a long time ago and it is a very pretti name for a very pretti new frend.

The Chinese Sandman

A JOHN JUSTIN MALLORY STORY

The only fantasy novel I've written to date (as opposed to over four dozen science fiction novels) is *Stalking the Unicorn*, which stars John Justin Mallory, a down-on-his-luck private eye who finds himself transported to a different Manhattan, the one you can just barely see out of the corner of your eye but isn't there when you turn to look at it head-on, a Manhattan that *seems* familiar, but is filled with elves, leprechauns, gorgons, and the like—and the most powerful demon of all, the Grundy.

I had a lot of fun writing it, but when it was done I figured Mallory was permanently retired. Various editors figured differently, and I've had to bring him out of retirement for Lawrence Watt-Evans, Kristine Kathryn Rusch, Martin H. Greenberg, Bill Fawcett, and in this instance Dave Truesdale when he was editing *Black Gate* magazine.

When I write, I always play music on the stereo, and since I happen to think that all good pop music ended the first time some jerk plugged his guitar into a socket, I find myself playing a lot of swing from the 1940s. Among my very favorite performers are the Andrews

Sisters—and as you'll see, one of their songs was the inspiration for this story.

Mallory put the final thumbtack into his Playmate centerspread, then stood back to admire it as it hung above his desk in all its pneumatic glory.

"Just what the Mallory & Carruthers Detective Agency needed to make me feel at home," he said at last.

"I wish you wouldn't do that, John Justin," said his partner, turning her head away in distaste.

"And I wish you wouldn't keep drawing underwear on them with your magic marker every month," replied Mallory. "We each have to learn to live with disappointment."

"It's indecent," snorted Winnifred Carruthers.

Mallory stared at the centerspread. "You know," he remarked, "I don't think it's silicon at all."

"Certainly it is," said Winnifred.

He shook his head. "Nope. I think it's helium."

He waited for her to smile at his joke. When no smile was forthcoming, he sat down at the desk and picked up a *Racing Form*.

"I see Flyaway is running again today," he noted.

"How many has he lost now?" asked Winnifred. "Something like forty in a row?"

"Forty-two," said Mallory.

"Forty-three," purred a feminine voice. "You're forgetting the one at Saratoga where he refused to leave the gate."

"That doesn't count," said Mallory. "They refunded all the bets."

"Forty-three," persisted the voice.

"Why don't you go kill a fish or something?" muttered Mallory.

A feminine figure jumped down from her perch atop a magic mirror that continually played the fourth inning of a 1932 American Association game between the Stranger City Mauve Devils and the Raddish

River Geldings. She was young and slender, and looked human at first glance—but her limbs were covered with a fine orange down faintly striped with black, while her face, neck, and chest were cream-colored. Her orange irises were those of a cat, her canines were quite pronounced, and she had whiskers—feline, not human—growing out of her upper lip. Her ears were a little too rounded, her face a touch too oval, her nails long and lethal-looking. She wore a single garment, a short tan dress that looked like it had been rescued from a trash can.

"Because," she said.

"Because why?"

"That's what humans are for," said Felina. "The God of the cat people put you here to feed us and keep us warm and dry and to scratch between our shoulder blades."

"Well, I'm glad we got that straight," said Mallory sardonically. "I've often wondered what I was put here for."

She lay, stomach down, on his desk. "Now you know."

He reached forward and scratched between her shoulder blades for a moment. When her purring became too loud and annoying he stopped.

Felina sat up, her legs dangling over the edge, and stared out the window into the fog.

"What do you see?" asked Mallory, also looking out.

"Nothing," she said, staring intently.

"OK, what don't you see?"

"Quiet!" said Felina. "I'm listening!"

"For what?"

"Hush!" snapped Felina, extending the claws on her right hand and taking a halfhearted swipe at Mallory's face.

Mallory's hand shot out, and he grabbed her by the nape of the neck. "You do that once more and I'll throw all ninety pounds of you out on your ass. This is a place of business and you're the office cat, who is here on sufferance. Try not to forget it."

She hissed at him, then turned her attention back to the window. Finally she relaxed.

"He's not here yet," she said to Winnifred.

"Who's not here?" demanded Mallory. "What are you talking about?"

"It's nothing, John Justin," said his partner. "Just forget it."

"How can I forget what I don't know?" said Mallory. "Are you expecting someone?"

Winnifred sighed. "No, not really."

Mallory shrugged. He was used to not understanding Felina, but Winnifred was always an open book, and her demeanor disturbed him. He decided to cheer her up.

"Why did the politician cross the street?" he asked.

Winnifred merely stared at him.

"What's a politician?" asked Felina. "Is it something to eat?"

"To get back to the middle of the road," said Mallory, laughing at his own joke.

Winnifred sighed and made no comment.

"Okay, maybe I won't become a nightclub comic after all," said Mallory.

A tear rolled down Winnifred's cheek.

"It was *that* bad?" asked Mallory.

"Do be quiet, John Justin," she said.

"You want to tell me what's wrong?"

"Nothing's wrong."

"This is your partner you're talking to," said Mallory. "I know better. You're sixty-eight years old, so it can't be PMS."

"That was an uncalled-for remark!" said Winnifred heatedly.

"Okay, I apologize. Now will you tell me what's wrong?"

"No."

"Aha!" said Mallory. "A minute ago nothing was wrong. Now you simply don't want to tell me."

"There's nothing you can do about it, John Justin."

"How do you know, if you don't tell me?"

"I don't want to talk about it."

He turned to Felina. "Has this got something to do with whoever you were listening for?"

Felina smiled at him. "Yes. No. Maybe. Certainly. Perhaps."

"I see you're about as helpful as ever."

"Get me a parakeet and I'll tell you."

"You will not!" yelled Winnifred.

Felina stared at her for a moment, then turned back to Mallory. "Three parakeets. And a macaw." She lowered her head in thought, then looked up. "And a goldfish."

"Why not ask for the Robert Redford of the cat people while you're at it?"

"I never thought of it," admitted Felina, her face suddenly animated with interest.

"Don't think of it now."

"Whatever you say."

"I say our friend has a problem, and you're not helping either of us solve it."

"I am too!" Felina shot back. "I told her he probably won't be coming today. Now she doesn't have to stay here and wait for him."

"He's *never* coming," said Winnifred, and suddenly Mallory had the odd experience of watching his partner cry, her burly body wracked by sobs.

Mallory walked over to where she sat and knelt down next to her, taking a gentle hold of her plump pink hand.

"What *is* it?" he asked gently. "You are the bravest woman—the bravest *anything*—I've ever known. You spent thirty years as a white hunter, facing gorgons and dragons and things that would have had hunters on *my* world running for cover. When the Grundy declared war on me, you were the only person in the whole of this Manhattan who didn't desert me."

"*I* didn't either," said Felina. "Exactly," she added thoughtfully.

"Shut up," said Mallory. He turned back to Winnifred. "You're not just my partner. You're my only friend in this world. If something's wrong, you've got to let me help you."

"No one can help me," said Winnifred miserably.

"Come on," urged Mallory. "My business is helping people."

She wiped her eyes and finally faced him. "Can you seize the wind? Can you catch a moment of time and put it in a box?"

"Not without a lot of special equipment," said Mallory wryly. "You're not about to tell me someone has stolen the wind?"

She shook her head. "No. Just that what's been stolen is as hard to retrieve."

"It'd help if you told me what it is."

"Do you remember a conversation we had when we first met?"

"We had a lot of conversations," said Mallory.

"This one was about my lover."

Mallory frowned. "I didn't know you had a lover."

"I didn't," said Winnifred.

"Uh . . . I'm a little confused."

She closed her eyes. "I remember it as if it were yesterday," she said. "I remember silver moonlight over a tropical lagoon, and the smell of jasmine. I remember the feel of a strong hand on mine, and the whisper of words over the rippling of the water." Suddenly she opened her eyes. "Except that I'm just mouthing the words. I don't remember it at all."

"That's because you made it up," said Mallory. "It never happened."

"Maybe it did, maybe it didn't," said Winnifred. "It's harder than you think to know what's a dream and what isn't."

"I don't want to be obtuse, but I still don't understand the problem."

"Look at me, John Justin," she said. "I'm a fat, ugly old woman."

"Not to me."

"Thank you for that, but I know what I am. Well, fifty years ago I was a fat, ugly young woman. I went into the jungle to make my fortune, because I knew I could never compete with other women for a man's love. And when I came out of the jungle thirty years later, I knew I'd made the right decision." She paused. "One thing kept me sane all those years, the same thing that kept me sane until the day I met you two years ago and you gave me a new purpose in life—and that thing was my memory of that one romantic night. Did it really happen? It's been so long that I don't know, I can't be sure—but whether or not the night was real, the *memory* was real. It was my most cherished possession." Tears welled up in her eyes again. "And now it's gone."

"But you just described it to me," said Mallory, puzzled.

"I can describe it, but I can't *feel* it any longer!" wept Winnifred.

"It was the old man with the horse," said Felina.

Mallory turned to her. "What old man? What are you talking about?"

"He's like the old clothes man, only different," said Felina helpfully.

"I was a fool!" whispered Winnifred.

"Tell me about this man," said Mallory.

"He's the Chinese Sandman," replied Winnifred dully.

"The Chinese Sandman?" repeated Mallory.

"Did you ever hear the Andrews Sisters sing about the Japanese Sandman?"

"I don't think so. Why?"

"It's about an old secondhand man, the kind who drives his horse-drawn wagon through your alley, collecting things you don't want. In the case of the Japanese Sandman, he trades new days for old."

"It's an interesting notion, trading new days for old," remarked Mallory. "But what does he have to do with the Chinese Sandman?"

"They're cousins," said Winnifred.

"So does the Chinese Sandman trade new days for old, too?"

She shook her head. "No, John Justin. He trades new *dreams* for old."

"And you're saying that—?" began Mallory.

"That I traded him my most precious possession," said Winnifred bitterly.

"But why?"

"I didn't believe in him," she replied. "I didn't think he could do it."

"You know the kind of magic that goes on in this Manhattan. You've seen what creatures like the Grundy can do. You should have known better."

"You're right, you're right," said Winnifred miserably. "To tell you the truth, I thought that dream was getting shopworn. It comforted me like nothing else in the world, but it's been inside my head for almost half a century. I thought I might find something newer and more exciting." She dabbed at her eyes with a handkerchief. "God, what a fool I was!"

"You wouldn't believe how many regretful husbands and wives I've heard that from," said Mallory sympathetically. "They're always sorry, and they never realize what they had until it's gone."

"What makes us behave so self-destructively, John Justin?" she asked.

He sighed deeply. "You're asking a guy whose wife ran off with his partner, and whose sole possessions after forty-three years of life are two beat-up suits and the office cat."

"I'm sorry," said Winnifred. "I don't want to burden you with my problem."

"It's *our* problem now," said Mallory, as Felina raced to the window and pushed her face up against it. "What I don't understand is this guy's racket. I mean, who the hell would want to buy *your* old dream?"

"That's easy," said a low voice with a strange accent, and Mallory turned to see a thin, almost emaciated Oriental man, his hair in a braid down his back, decked out in a patchwork outfit of old, unmatched silks and satins, standing in his doorway.

"It's *him!*" exclaimed Winnifred.

"That's figures," said Mallory. "Nothing else has gone right this month." He stood up and faced the old man. "You were about to say something?"

"You wanted to know who would buy an old dream," said the Chinese Sandman with a smile. "The person who traded it, of course."

"Every customer wants it back?" asked Mallory.

"Of course," said the Sandman. "But they never know it until they've lost it."

"Then trade it back to her."

The Chinese Sandman chuckled. "I made a fair trade for it. I gave her a wonderful dream, full of excitement and romance, of distant and exotic terrains, of handsome men and beautiful women, and she was the most beautiful of all."

"I don't want it!" said Winnifred.

"Of course you don't want it," agreed the Sandman. "It's not *yours*."

"So take it back, give her her own dream, and we'll call it square," said Mallory.

"How would I stay in business if I did that?" replied the Chinese Sandman. "She traded a valueless dream to me. But now it *has* a value, doesn't it? Quite a high one."

"All right," said Mallory. "Name your price, and try to remember that we're not made of money."

"I'm not some nondescript huckster," said the Sandman, making a face. "I don't *sell*—I *trade*."

"Look around the place," said Mallory. "We'll trade anything you want for it."

"Even the cat woman?"

Felina hissed at him and displayed her claws.

"No!" said Winnifred firmly.

Felina jumped lightly onto the back of Winnifred's chair, purring loudly.

"Anything but the cat," said Mallory.

The Sandman looked around the room. "No, I don't think so,"

he said. "There's nothing here that I want—not even the cat woman."

"Don't be foolish," said Mallory. "No one else in the world wants Winnifred's dream. If you want to unload it, you've got to deal with us."

"Oh, I didn't say we couldn't do business," said the Sandman. "I merely remarked that there's nothing in your office that I want."

"You were here before, when you traded dreams, so you knew there was nothing in the place that you wanted," said Mallory. "So cut the crap and tell us what you *do* want."

"How very astute of you, Mr. Mallory," said the Chinese Sandman. "You give me hope that we may be able to reach an equitable agreement."

"You name it, and I'll tell you if we have a deal."

"Very well," said the Sandman. "I want *you*, Mr. Mallory."

"*Me?*" said Mallory, surprised.

"Well, not you personally. But I want your skill. In fact, I shall be perfectly forthright: I want an item, a trinket, a tribute if you will, that I think only you can secure for me. If you bring me what I desire, I will return Colonel Carruthers's dream to her. If not, well . . ." He shrugged his shoulders regretfully and let the sentence hang in midair, unfinished.

"Don't do it, John Justin," said Winnifred. "It was *my* blunder. I'll live with the consequences."

"It can't hurt to hear him out," said Mallory.

"*I* heard him out," Winnifred pointed out.

"He doesn't have anything I want," said Mallory.

"You'd be surprised," said the old Chinese man with a smile.

"Spare me your surprises and just tell me what you want."

"There is an amber egg," said the Sandman, outlining its size with his gnarled fingers. "Inside it is a tiny pegasus, a blood-bay colt with three white feet and golden wings. I want it."

"What's the catch?" said Mallory. "Why don't you just buy it instead of having me rob whatever store is selling it?"

"It's not in a store, John Justin Mallory," said the Sandman.

"Shit!" muttered Mallory. "I don't even want to think about what you're going to say next."

"It resides on the nightstand next to the Grundy's bed."

"I knew it!"

"When you bring it to me, I will give your partner what she wants."

"Why don't you ask for something easy, like the key to Fort Knox?"

"Each dream has its own price," answered the Sandman. "For the partner of John Justin Mallory, the price is higher than most."

"Why?" demanded Mallory.

"Because no one else can retrieve it for me. You, at least, have a chance of success, however small and unlikely."

"Your optimism is heartwarming."

"Just get it, John Justin Mallory," said the Sandman, turning to leave.

"Wait a minute!" said Mallory. "Assuming that God drops everything else and I get the thing, how do we contact you?"

"I will know when you have succeeded," answered the Sandman. "I will contact *you* to effect the trade."

He closed the door behind him. Mallory looked out the window, but fog obscured his vision. All he could hear was the *clop-clop-clop* of a horse's hooves as it trudged down the street, pulling its wagonload of dreams at the behest of its Oriental master.

The Grundy's castle seemed to rise right out of the middle of Central Park. It was a huge Gothic structure, replete with spires and turrets, hundreds of feet long on each side. A single drawbridge lay across a moat that seemed alive with the kind of things that haunted children's nightmares. The stone walls glistened in the light rain.

"Well, I guess this is it," said Mallory, hoping desperately that he was mistaken.

His companion stared at the moat. "I'm hungry."

A hideous sea creature surfaced, glared at them, bared its enormous teeth, and then vanished beneath the water.

"So is *he*," said Mallory.

"What good is water if you can't catch some fish in it?" asked Felina.

"This particular water has probably got some inhabitants who are wondering what good is land if you can't catch some cat people on it."

"If we're not going fishing, why are you just standing here?" asked Felina.

"I'm casing the joint."

"I thought you were trying to work up the courage to go in," said Felina.

"That, too," admitted Mallory.

"It won't be so bad, John Justin," said Felina. "There's probably nothing but goblins and gorgons and minotaurs and medusas and maybe some yetis." She paused thoughtfully. "At least, until we get to the dangerous parts."

"Thanks," said Mallory sardonically. "I feel all better now."

"I knew you would," replied Felina. "I have that effect on people. Scratch my back."

"Be quiet."

"Scratching cat people's backs is one of the very best things human people do," continued Felina. "You'll feel much better if you just reach over and scratch between my shoulder blades."

Mallory ignored her and continued looking at the castle. Not much had changed since he had started looking five minutes earlier: it still appeared impregnable.

"Well," he said finally, "let's get started."

"We're going fishing now?"

Mallory took a couple of tentative steps across the drawbridge. "We're going into the castle now. If you smell or sense anything approaching us, let me know."

"Anything?"

"Anything dangerous."

"Oh," said Felina. Suddenly she smiled. "There are four moat monsters swimming toward us right now."

"They're in the water. We're up here."

Felina nodded her head agreeably. "Probably only two of them can reach us."

Mallory increased his pace. Ominous swirls in the water below implied that the creatures had adjusted their routes and were tracking him. He reached the end of the drawbridge and uttered a sigh of relief. He looked around for Felina, who was nowhere to be seen.

"Who goes there?" demanded a deep, gruff voice.

"John Justin Mallory," replied the detective. "And a friend. We're here to see the Grundy."

This was met by a peal of laughter. "Mallory? To see the Grundy?" Another laugh. "Don't you know you're his greatest enemy, Mallory?"

"Just tell him I'm here and that I've got a proposition for him."

"Oh, I'd dearly love to tell him you're here," the voice assured him. "But I'm under orders to kill anyone who crosses the moat."

The owner of the voice stepped forward, and Mallory saw that it was a broad, muscular, green-skinned troll, no more than four feet tall, holding a wicked-looking battle axe.

"Just give him my message," said Mallory. "He'll want to see me."

"I can't imagine why," said the troll. "You're the ugliest human I've ever laid eyes on." He raised the axe over his head. "Prepare to die!"

"My friend won't like that."

"Hah!" said the troll. "I don't see any friend!"

At that moment Felina, who had been walking along the chain that supported the drawbridge from overhead, dropped lightly to the ground.

"Felina," said Mallory, "take that thing away from him before I lose my temper."

"Wait a minute!" said the troll, backing up a step. "She's the friend you were referring to?"

"That's right."

"But that's unfair! Trolls are afraid of cat people! Everyone knows that!"

"Too bad," said Mallory, as Felina, the moonlight glinting off her claws, slowly approached the troll.

"This is against the rules of engagement!" whined the troll. "There's nothing in my contract that says I have to fight cat people! I'm issuing a formal complaint to the union steward first thing in the morning!"

"If you live that long," said Mallory.

"What are you talking about?" shrieked the troll. "Of course I'll live that long! You wouldn't make me face her now that you know how terrified I am!"

"Why not?"

"What kind of a fiend are you, Mallory? Surely you can't be enjoying this situation! Where's your heart?"

"Between my lungs and my spleen, last time I looked," said Mallory. "Now, are you going to let us pass?"

"The Grundy says no one can enter."

"The Grundy doesn't have to fight my friend. You do."

"You're giving me a terrible headache!" whined the troll.

"Looks like you're between a rock and a hard place," said Mallory without sympathy.

"What rock?" shrieked the troll. "I'm between the Grundy and a cat person!"

"Six of one, half a dozen of the other."

"Oh my God!" said the troll, looking fearfully into the shadows. "You've got five more cat people with you?"

"One's enough," said Mallory as Felina took another step toward the troll, a hungry grin on her catlike face.

"Help!" screamed the troll. "Somebody! Anybody! I'm being theatened by a small puppy!"

"A small puppy?" repeated Mallory, puzzled.

"Well, they might not come if I said I was being threatened by something formidable," explained the troll.

"If they're all like you, I don't think they're going to be much help."

"Keep a civil tongue in your head, Mallory!" said the troll. "I'm not afraid of detectives. I'll be busy disemboweling you with my axe while my comrades are turning your pet into a tennis racket."

"I don't think they string rackets with catgut any more," said Mallory.

"They do at the Grundy's castle," was the reply.

And then, suddenly, two leprechauns and an emaciated elf appeared beside the troll.

"It took you long enough to get here!" complained the troll.

"They were rerunning an old Ann Rutherford movie," replied the elf. "We had to wait for the commercial." He surveyed the situation. "Now, what do you want us to do?"

"Kill the cat person while I take care of Mallory."

Felina turned to them and hissed.

"Uh . . . I've got nothing against cat people," said the taller leprechaun. "How about you, Merv?"

"Not a thing," said the smaller leprechaun, staring hypnotically at Felina's glistening claws. "Some of my best friends are cat people."

"Are they really?" asked the elf.

"Well, they would be if I ever took the trouble to get to know them," said Merv. He turned to the troll. "I have a better plan. You kill the cat woman and the detective. We'll set fire to their funeral pyre."

"I can't. Trolls have an instinctive fear of cat people."

"Yeah?" replied Merv. "Well, leprechauns have an instinctive fear of dying. So there."

They all turned to the elf. "How about you?"

"I'm not afraid of either of them," said the elf.

"Good," said Merv. "*You* kill them."

"I'd love to," said the elf. "But I'm just an accountant. You want my roommate. He specializes in maiming and pillaging."

"So get him down here!" demanded the troll.

"I wish I could, but he ran off to California and joined a cult that worships rutabagas." The elf grimaced. "I think they eat them, too. Raw."

"I'd like to spend all night listening to you explain why none of you are going to stop us from entering," said Mallory. "But since none of you *are* going to stop us from entering . . ."

He took a step forward. The troll, the leprechauns, and the elf practically fell over each other while retreating.

"Come on, Felina."

"Don't I get to kill even one of them?" she asked unhappily.

"Maybe later."

The troll looked down at his wrist. "Hey, my shift's almost over!" He turned to Felina. "You can kill the next troll on duty. I give you my blessing."

"How do you know it's over?" asked Merv. "You're not even wearing a watch."

"I lost it in a strip poker game three years ago," answered the troll, "but if I *had* one, I'm sure it would say that my shift's over." And with that he turned and headed to the interior of the castle at breakneck speed.

"Some security team," snorted Mallory contemptuously.

"So we're not the Pretorian guard," replied the elf. "You're not Sherlock Holmes, either."

He raced off into the darkness, accompanied by the two leprechauns, before Mallory could reply.

Mallory looked into the interior of the castle. It seemed empty and foreboding.

"Felina, can you smell anyone?" he asked.

There was no response.

He turned, and saw Feline lying on her belly, reaching a clawed hand into the water, trying to snare a fish.

"Get up!" he yelled, rushing over to her and lifting her to her feet.

"You're mean to me," sniffed Felina.

"Not as mean as *he* would have been," said the detective, pointing to a moat monster that surfaced exactly where her hand had been.

She stared at the monster, then at Mallory, then back at the monster, which was just disappearing beneath the surface.

"I forgive you," she said. "This one time."

"I can't tell you how grateful I am," said Mallory. "Now, can you sense anyone else?"

"Just the Grundy."

"He's here now?" asked Mallory.

"Kind of."

"Does he know we're here?"

She nodded her head. "He's the Grundy," she said, as if that explained everything. "He wants to see you."

"How do you know that?"

She smiled. "Cat people know things that human people can never know."

"Do they know enough not to get eaten by moat monsters while I go speak to the Grundy?" asked Mallory.

"Probably."

"I haven't got time to argue," said Mallory. "I can always handcuff you to the castle gate."

She leaped to the chain that held the drawbridge. "You'd have to catch me first."

"I don't want to catch you. Just see to it that no one else does, either."

He turned and entered the castle. He looked around, trying to figure out what to do next, when a liveried goblin approached him.

"Please follow me, Mr. Mallory," said the goblin with a thick Cockney accent.

"You know me?"

"You was expected."

Mallory followed him up a flight of stone stairs and down a long corridor that displayed various torture devices.

"Interesting decor," he remarked.

"The master likes it well enough."

"I assume they're just for show."

"When they ain't in use," answered the goblin.

They came to a large pentagonal room, and the goblin came to a stop.

"I'll leave you here, Mr. Mallory, sir," he said. "Just walk right in and make yourself to home." He paused. "Oh—and don't go feedin' the pets."

He turned and began walking back the way they had come, and Mallory entered the room. There was a huge bed against the back wall, covered with sheets of red satin. On a nightstand embossed with gargoyles was the amber egg he sought. There were four windows, all barred. A golden bookcase held various grimoires and books of spells, all leatherbound and embossed.

There were six spherical cages suspended from the high ceiling by golden chains. Inside one was a gremlin, in another was a small sphinx. A third held a small nude gold-skinned woman, no more than three feet tall but in perfect proportion, who was weeping copiously. A winged warrior in medieval armor was in a fourth. The final two held creatures Mallory had never seen, except perhaps during those nightmares that visited him when he'd mixed too many drinks in his youth.

"What do you think of my pets, John Justin Mallory?" said a deep voice.

Mallory looked around but couldn't see anything. Then, suddenly, the Grundy materialized in the middle of the room. He was tall, a few inches over six feet, with two prominent horns protruding from his hairless head. His eyes were a burning yellow, his nose sharp and aquiline, his teeth white and gleaming, his skin a bright red. His shirt and pants were crushed velvet, his cloak satin, his collar and cuffs made of the fur of some white polar animal. He wore gleaming black gloves and boots, and he had two mystic rubies suspended from his neck on a golden chain. When he exhaled, small clouds of vapor emanated from his mouth and nostrils.

"They're impressive," admitted Mallory.

"Perhaps you would like to join them," suggested the Grundy ominously.

"I'll take a rain check."

"You still don't fear me," noted the demon, frowning in puzzlement. "Why not? You know what damage I can do."

"I know you're a rational creature," responded Mallory. "Perhaps the only one in this Manhattan besides me. You know I wouldn't come here without a reason, and I know you won't kill me without a reason."

"Ah, but I have a reason," said the Grundy. "It is my nature to kill, to bring chaos out of order, to destroy that which is beautiful."

"No one ever called me beautiful before."

"I was generalizing."

"I know. But you're not going to kill me before you hear me out."

"No, I'm not, though I'm not quite sure why." The Grundy stared at him. "You are the first man ever to willingly enter my domicile."

"It wasn't all that difficult," replied Mallory. "On a 10 scale, I give your security team a minus 3."

"They're here only to make a commotion."

"I beg your pardon?"

"You don't really think that *I* need protection?"

"No, I suppose not."

"They're here to make noise. I heard them all the way over in Queens."

"I thought you just controlled Manhattan."

"I control all the five boroughs." The Grundy pointed to a wicked-looking shears hanging on the wall over his bed. "It used to be Kings before I became annoyed with my last surrogate."

"Remind me never to become your surrogate."

"It seems unlikely. We *are* mortal enemies, after all."

"I'm not here as your enemy," said Mallory. "At least, not this time."

"Of course you are," said the Grundy. "You're here on an errand for the Chinese Sandman."

"You're pretty good, I'll give you that," said Mallory. "I wasn't sure you'd know about him."

"I know everything that goes on in my domain."

"Then you know I'm not here to steal anything on his behalf."

"Only because you know you can't," said the Grundy. He held his hand out, and the amber egg seemed to leap to it from the nightstand. "This is why you're here, is it not?"

"Indirectly."

"Explain."

"Actually, I'm here as a supplicant," said Mallory.

The Grundy laughed a harsh, grating laugh as blue vapor almost obscured his features. "Do you expect me to believe that?"

"Why not?" said Mallory. "You run New York City as surely as Tammany Hall ran it in *my* Manhattan a century ago. I live in New York City. I'm here to file a complaint about the Chinese Sandman."

"You, who have opposed and hindered me in the past, dare to ask for my intervention!" bellowed the Grundy, and the volume of his voice made all his caged beings tremble with fear.

"He's poaching on your territory."

"I do not steal dreams."

"So you're telling me that it's okay for anyone to steal from your subjects, as long as they steal things you don't want?"

The Grundy stared at him for a long moment. "There may be something to what you say."

"He's made my partner miserable," continued Mallory. "I thought making people miserable was *your* function."

"It's possible," mused the Grundy. "Not likely, but possible."

"It's more than possible," said Mallory. "He's out there right now, stealing dreams."

The Grundy shook his head irritably. "You do not understand."

"Enlighten me."

"It's possible that he's in the employ of my Opponent."

"I thought your Opponent worked for Good, just as you work for Evil."

"That is because you never listen to me. Good and Evil are relative terms; what is Good one century may be Evil in another." He paused. "My opponent represents Order; I represent Chaos."

"How does stealing a sweet old lady's only romantic dream lead to order?" asked Mallory.

"Dreams are irrational. I realize that it gave her comfort, but it was not an orderly comfort."

"That seems like an awfully convoluted chain of reasoning."

"Nothing is as simple as it seems," answered the Grundy. "When you are a mere mortal, you cannot begin to realize the complexity of the universe."

"Okay, maybe he works for your Opponent," said Mallory. "That makes it even more imperative that we get rid of him."

"I can reach out and choke the life from him this instant," agreed the Grundy, flexing his long, lean fingers.

"*No!*" shouted Mallory.

The Grundy stared at him silently.

"He's still got Winnifred's dream! I've got to get it back before you do anything to him."

"What do I care about an old woman's dream?"

"You said it yourself: her mind, her whole world, is more orderly without it. We've got to make the Sandman return it."

"I could torture it out of him," said the Grundy. "He could provide me with an entire evening's amusement before he finally succumbs."

Mallory stared at the demon for a long moment. "I don't think you want to get anywhere near him."

"Why not?"

"What if he stole your dream of empire?" suggested Mallory. "What if you no longer dreamed of defeating your Opponent?"

"I am supreme in my domain," answered the Grundy. "He can do nothing to me here."

"Maybe so, maybe not, but are you willing to bet everything you have on it?" asked Mallory. "Why expose yourself, when you don't know *how* he steals dreams?"

"Why do you think I don't know?"

"Because if you did, you'd have been stealing them for years."

"True," admitted the Grundy. "I have more effective ways of destroying dreams."

"I've seen you kill dozens of men in an instant. I've seen you destroy whole city blocks. I've seen you make the stock market crash. But I've never seen you steal a dream, or have to protect yourself from a dream thief. I think we'd better do this my way."

"What *is* your way, John Justin Mallory?"

Mallory held his hand out. "May I see that amber egg, please?"

The Grundy handed it to him, and Mallory held it up to the dim light.

"That pegasus looks very real," he noted.

"It *is* real."

"I didn't know they came that small."

"They don't—unless someone puts a curse on them and *makes* them that small."

"Why did you do it?"

"He was beautiful. He was innocent. He was filled with love. What better reasons could I want?"

"And he belonged to the Sandman?"

"Once upon a time. Before he escaped. I found him in a stable at the north end of Central Park."

"I believe I know the place," said Mallory.*

*See *Stalking the Unicorn*.

"And once you trade this to the Sandman for your partner's dream, what then?"

"I'll think of something."

"See that you do," said the Grundy, handing him the amber egg and somehow becoming less substantial. "You are all that stands between him and a death so hideous that I hope you cannot even imagine it."

The Grundy continued fading from sight, until nothing was left but his face.

"Once again we find ourselves on the same side, John Justin Mallory," he said.* "I am beginning to wonder if you are my successor rather than my antagonist."

And then he was gone.

"Mr. Mallory, sir?" said a Cockney voice, and Mallory turned to find himself facing the liveried goblin. "Come this way, please, and I'll see you to the front door."

"I can find it myself," said Mallory.

"No doubt you can, sir," replied the goblin, "but if you're with me, the gorgon and the banshees will leave you alone." A roar and a trio of high-pitched shrieks punctuated his statement, and Mallory dutifully followed him. When they reached the front door, Mallory took a single step outside and heard the portal slam into place behind him.

"Felina?"

"Up here," said a familiar voice.

Mallory looked up, and found the cat woman perched on a window ledge, chewing on the last bite of something with feathers.

"Come on," he said, trying not to show his disgust for her dietary practices. "We're leaving."

She dropped lightly to the ground beside him.

"I don't know why fish like worms so much," she said as they began walking across the drawbridge.

---

*See "Posttime in Pink"

"You ate a worm?"

"Just one."

"Tasted pretty bad, did it?"

"Oh, it tasted fine," said Felina. "But it whined and pleaded all the way down." She looked at him, an annoyed expression on her face. "I just hate it when they do that."

Mallory sighed. Every time he thought he was getting used to his new Manhattan, something like that came from out of left field and made the Grundy seem normal by comparison.

"You're back!" exclaimed Winnifred as Mallory entered the office.

"You didn't expect me to survive?"

"With the Grundy?" She shuddered. "You never know." She paused. "Still, the Grundy does seem to spend more time talking to you than to anyone else."

"Maybe that's because I'm the only one who ever tells him the truth."

"Did you . . . ?" began Winnifred hesitantly. "I mean . . ."

Mallory reached into his pocket, withdrew the amber egg, and held it up for her to see. "I got it."

She walked over and peered into it. "It really does have a pegasus in it, doesn't it? A blood-bay colt with golden wings."

"Same color as Citation, except for the wings," replied Mallory. "And Citation didn't need them."

"What did you have to give him for it?"

"A favor."

"What *kind* of favor?" Winnifred asked suspiciously. "If you have to break any laws . . ."

"Relax," said Mallory. "It's the same favor I'm doing for you."

"I don't understand. Surely the Grundy isn't afraid of the Chinese Sandman!"

"I don't think he's afraid of anything," agreed Mallory. "But he *is* cautious. Why should he dirty his hands if I'll do it for him?"

"So what do we do now?"

"We wait. The Sandman has to show up sooner or later." Mallory walked to an easy chair in front of the magic mirror. "Let's have a movie."

"What will it be today?" asked the mirror, which was still showing the ancient baseball game.

"A nice adventure film, I think."

"How about *The Man Who Would Be King?*"

"I've seen it."

"Not *this* version."

"Connery and Caine, right?"

"No."

"You also showed me the Gable and Bogart version that John Huston tried to make in the 1940s, before he ran out of money," said the detective.

"This is the one he tried to make in the early 1960s, with Marlon Brando and Richard Burton."

"Okay, that sounds good," said Mallory. "Let me get a beer and we're in business."

"You don't have time for a beer," said the mirror.

"You're starting that soon?"

"You are about to have a visitor."

"If she comes in with a dead squirrel in her mouth, I'm throwing her right back out."

"Not Felina," said the mirror. "Well," it corrected itself, "Felina too."

"All right," said Mallory. "Take a break."

"Thank you," said the mirror, suddenly displaying Tuffy Bresheen scattering her opponents to the four winds in a 1949 roller derby.

"Come on," said Mallory to Winnifred.

"Where are we going?"

"If it's who I think it is, and he does what I think he's going to do, we don't want to be inside."

"But the backyard is so small," complained Winnifred.

"True," said Mallory. "But it has one definite advantage."

"What's that?"

"No roof."

They went outside and walked around to the yard.

"Hi, John Justin," said Felina, perched on a branch on the only tree. She wiped some feathers from her mouth and emitted a small, ladylike burp. "I've been waiting for you."

"Have you really?"

"No," she admitted. "But it sounded good."

"I've been waiting for *you*," said Mallory.

"Oh?" She leaped into space, did a double somersault, and landed lightly on her feet right next to the detective.

"Yeah," he said. "I'm going to need your help in a couple of minutes."

"Do you want me to scare another troll?"

"No."

"More leprechauns?"

"Shut up and listen!" snapped Mallory. He handed her a small object and spent the next thirty seconds giving her instructions. "Now do you think you can do it?"

"Not until you apologize for yelling at me."

"I didn't yell."

"Did too."

"All right—I apologize."

"And you'll never yell at me again, and you'll buy me my very own fish pond, and—"

"Don't push it."

At that moment the Chinese Sandman joined them, decked out in a new outfit that was even more patchwork than the last.

"You have it," he announced. "I could sense it all the way from Grammercy Park."

"I've got it," confirmed Mallory, withdrawing the egg from a pocket and holding it up for the Sandman to see. "Where's your horse and wagon?"

"I don't need them any longer. I will give your partner her dream and you will give me my horse."

"I don't think so," said Mallory.

"What are you talking about?"

"I think the egg's worth more than that."

"John Justin!" cried Winnifred.

"Not to worry," he assured her. "Our friend knows it's worth more than one dream."

"We had a deal!" growled the Sandman.

"We still do," said Mallory. "I have something you want. You have something I want. Only the conditions have changed."

"How many dreams do you want?" demanded the Sandman.

"All of them."

"*What?*"

"Give back every dream you've stolen or it's no deal." He smiled. "Why not admit that you want this pegasus every bit as much as the people you cheated want their dreams?"

"You go to hell, Mallory!" yelled the Sandman. "I'll trade you Colonel Carruthers's dream for the egg. That's the only deal I'll make! Take it or leave it!"

"Good-bye, Sandman," said Mallory calmly.

"I'll be back for it!" promised the Sandman ominously.

"It won't do you much good," said Mallory. "As soon as you leave the yard, I'm throwing it against the brick wall of the house as hard as I can."

"You can't! It has mystic powers that only I can tap!"

"Sure I can," said Mallory with a shrug. "Its powers are no use to me."

The Sandman looked like he was about to explode. Then, suddenly, his whole body relaxed, as if all the air had gone out of it. "All right, it's a deal."

"Fine. Give them back."

The Sandman muttered something in Chinese, made a strange gesture in the air, and bowed. "It is done."

"Winnifred?" said Mallory, turning to her.

A blissful smile crossed her face. "It's back!"

"Grundy!" yelled Mallory. "Is he telling the truth?"

A cloud suddenly took on the features of the Grundy's face. "He's telling the truth," it said in the Grundy's voice. "He has returned all the dreams."

"I don't suppose you'd like to tell me exactly what powers your pegasus has?" said Mallory.

"As you yourself said, they're of no use to you," replied the Sandman. "Only I can tap them, and I have no intention of sharing my knowledge with you, now or ever." He held out his hand. "My egg?"

Mallory handed it over to him.

The Sandman murmured another chant over it, then placed it on the ground. The amber egg seemed to glow with power, then began to shake. A moment later the amber shattered, leaving a tiny pegasus standing in the yard. Gradually it began to grow, and within ninety seconds it was full-sized. It stared curiously at the three humans and the cat girl, then lowered its head and begin nibbling on the grass.

"That's it?" said Mallory. "The deal's done?"

"The deal's done," asknowledged the Sandman.

"Then I've got something to say to you."

"Oh?"

"Yeah," said Mallory angrily, pushing the Sandman in the chest. "I don't like your business, I don't like your attitude, I don't like anything about you." He pushed him again, harder this time. "I don't ever want to see you in this neighborhood again, understand?"

Suddenly the Sandman reached out to Mallory's wrist, and an instant later the detective found himself flying through the air. He landed with a loud *thud!*

"How dare you lay your hands on my person!" raged the Sandman.

"I am the Chinese Sandman! Who are you to tell *me* where I can and can't go!"

He walked to the pegasus, grabbed its mane, and swung himself up to its back—and yelped in surprise.

"What's going on?" he demanded, trying without success to free his hands from the blood-bay colt's black mane.

"Wrong question," said Mallory, getting to his feet and approaching horse and rider. "It's 'What's going away?'"

"What have you done to me?" cried the Sandman. He lifted a leg preparatory to jumping off, and found that he was stuck to the colt's back as well.

"While you were busy demonstrating your martial arts on me, Felina covered your horse's mane and back with glue." Felina proudly held up the paint brush and the empty bucket of glue for the Sandman to see.

"Fool!" grated the Sandman. "It will wear off in five minutes, and when it does . . ."

"Oh, I think it will last a little longer than that," said Mallory with a smile. He looked up to the heavens. "What do *you* think?"

"With the spell I put on it, it will outlive the pegasus," said the Grundy's stern voice.

Mallory raised his hand and brought it down with a resounding *smack!* on the colt's rump. It whistled in surprise, then began flapping its golden wings. A moment later it was almost fifty feet above them.

"You can't get away with this, John Justin Mallory!" bellowed the Chinese Sandman. "I'll be back!"

"I don't think so," said Mallory. "In fact, I can almost visualize a strong wind blowing you all the way to Mongolia, and blowing you right back there every time you try to leave."

The largest cloud in the sky suddenly took on the Grundy's features and, pursing its lips, blew the pegasus so fast and so far that in a handful of seconds it was totally out of sight.

Mallory turned to Winnifred, a triumphant smile on his face, only to discover that his partner was crying.

"What happened?" he demanded. "Did that bastard manage to steal it again?"

"No, John Justin," she sobbed. "It's mine."

"Then why——?"

"It's so *beautiful!*" she explained.

"But you cried when he took it away from you. Why are you crying now?"

"You wouldn't understand."

Mallory sighed. "I guess not." He walked over to Felina. "Come on," he said. "I'll buy you a fish sandwich."

"Not now, John Justin," said Felina, leaping up to a branch of the tree.

"Why not?"

"I'm having a conversation."

"With whom?"

"With the snake I just ate, of course."

Mallory walked around to the front of the office. Just before he entered, he looked up at the cloud that had so recently possessed the Grundy's features.

"Don't go too far away," he muttered. "You just may be the only sensible person I can talk with."

He sighed deeply and entered the office.

"Okay," he said to the magic mirror. "Let's get on with the movie."

"I'm not in the mood any more."

"All right," said Mallory. "What *do* you want to show me?"

He spent the next two hours watching Tuffy Bresheen turn the 1949 roller derby into a preview of World War III.

Guardian Angel

When I found out that the Science Fiction Book Club was originating an occasional anthology rather than just reprinting mass-market books, I sought out editor Ellen Asher at the 2003 Worldcon and suggested that she let me edit an anthology consisting of six novellas, all hard-boiled science fictional mysteries, to be titled *Down These Dark Spaceways*.

There would be no Sherlocks or Wimseys or Poirots here; instead, there would be the descendants of those fallen angels who stalked the dark alleys, who understood going in that the odds were against them, who were not surprised when their enemies lied to them and their friends deserted them, who knew that the rewards would never measure up to the risks but took those risks anyway.

Ellen okayed the project, I hunted up five of the best writers around, and of course I assigned one to myself as well. In the archtypal Chandleresque hard-boiled story, there is of course a mystery to be solved, but it is never quite as important as the hero's quest to correct the moral inequities he encounters. I kept that in mind while I was writing "Guardian Angel," and enjoyed the experience so much that I have a feeling I'll be providing Jake Masters with another case one of these days.

Her skin had cost her a bundle. It was smoother than silk, and at least thirty years younger than her eyes, which had a hard glitter to them that she couldn't quite hide. She had a hell of a figure, but there was no way to know how much of it was hers and how much was courtesy of the same guys who gave her that skin. She wore a ring that was brilliant enough to have given her the tan she sported, and another one that could have eaten the first one for breakfast.

She told me her name was Beatrice Vanderwycke. I didn't know if I believed her. You get used to being lied to in my line of work, and eventually you assume everything you're told is a lie until you know for a fact that it isn't. Still, she looked enough like a Beatrice Vanderwycke that I was willing to accept it for the moment.

Besides, I needed the work.

"And that was the last time I saw him," she was saying as she toyed with a bracelet that was worth more than I earn in a decade. "I'm terribly worried that something has happened to him, Mr. Masters."

"Call me Jake," I replied.

"Do you think you can help me?" She shifted her position and the chair instantly adjusted to accommodate her, then gently wrapped itself around her. I envied the chair.

"I can try," I said. "But I'll be honest with you: the police have far more resources than a private detective does. Have you spoken to them?"

"They sent me to you. I'm sure he's not on Odysseus, and that means he's beyond their jurisdiction. A very nice officer named Selina Hernandez recommended you."

Well, that's one way for Selina to make sure I take her out for that dinner I owe her.

"All right," I said. "Let me start making a record of this so I don't make too many mistakes." I activated my computer.

She almost laughed at it. "That machine must be a leftover from the last century. Does it still work?"

"Most of the time."

"Why don't you get a new one?"

"I've got a fondness for old broken-down machines," I said. "Can I have his name again?"

"Andy."

"Age?"

"Nineteen."

"He's legally of age on every world in the whole Albion Cluster," I pointed out. "Even if I find him, I can't make him come back with me if he doesn't want to."

She pulled out a wad of money that could choke damned near any animal I've ever seen. "You're a resourceful man. You'll find a way."

I stopped myself from leaping for the money and reached for it with some slight measure of restraint. It was mostly Democracy credits, but there were some Far London pounds, Maria Theresa dollars, and New Stalin rubles.

"I'm a resourceful man," I echoed, sliding the cash into a desk drawer. "I'll find a way." I paused. "Have you got a picture of him— holo, portrait, whatever?"

She placed a small cube on my desk and activated it. The image of a nice-looking kid with blue eyes and wavy brown hair suddenly appeared, hovering in the air.

"Can I keep it?" I asked.

"Of course."

"Can you supply me with a list of his friends, and how to contact them?"

"He didn't have many," she said.

"How about a girlfriend?"

"Certainly not, Mr. Masters," she said firmly. "He's just a boy."

He's a boy who looks to be about two inches taller than I am, I thought, but decided to keep my mouth shut.

"Any alien friends?"

She gave me a haughty stare. "No."

"You've got to give me a little more to go on than just an image of him, Mrs. Vanderwycke," I said. "It's a big galaxy out there."

She produced another cube. "This contains the names and addresses of all of his friends that I know about, plus some of his teachers and a list of all the schools he's attended."

"Where is he presently going to school?"

"He quit last year."

"All right—where does he work?"

"He doesn't."

"What does he do with his time?"

"He's been ill," she said. "That's why I'm so worried about him."

"He looks pretty healthy in the holo," I said.

"It's very difficult for me to discuss," she said uncomfortably. "He has . . . *emotional* problems."

"The kind that would make him wander off and forget who he is and where he lives?" I asked.

She shook her head. "No, Mr. Masters. But he needs to continue his treatment, and he's already missed three sessions with his therapist."

"I'll want the name and address of the therapist."

"It's on the cube."

"And you say he disappeared three days ago?"

"That's right. I had an appointment. He was in his room when I left, and gone when I returned." She stared at me with cold clear eyes that looked more like a predator than a distraught mother. "I'll pay your daily fee and cover all your expenses while you're looking for him. When you return him to me, there will be a substantial bonus."

"You already gave me one."

"That was an inducement, not a bonus," she said. "Will you find my son?"

"I'll give it my best shot," I promised.

"Good." She got to her feet, tall and elegant and reeking of money, a real knockout—and with her money and her cosmetic surgeons, she'd look just as good at seventy, or even ninety. "I will expect frequent reports."

"You'll get them."

She stared at me. I used to stare at things I was about to dissect in biology class the same way. "Don't disappointment me, Mr. Masters."

I walked her to the door, it irised to let her pass through, and then I was alone with all that beautiful money and the promise of a lot more to come if I could just find one missing kid.

I fed the cube with the info to my computer. It spit it out. I put it in again, waiting to make sure the machine wasn't going to turn it into an appetizer, then sat back down at my desk and began sifting through the data she'd given me. There were four teenaged boys and a couple of teachers—names, addresses, holos. I decided to put them off until I'd spoken to the therapist to find out what was wrong with the kid, but he wouldn't break doctor-patient confidentiality without Andy's permission. I told him I could get Beatrice Vanderwycke's permission, and he explained that since Andy was legally of age that wouldn't change anythng.

So I began hunting up the names from school. One teacher had died, another was guiding tourists through the ruins of Archimedes II. Two of the boys were in offworld colleges, a third was in the Navy and posted half a galaxy away. That left Rashid Banerjee, a slightly built young man with a thick shock of black hair. I managed to get him on the holophone, which saved me a trip out to his place, and introduced myself.

"I'm looking for Andy Vanderwycke," I explained.

"I didn't know he was missing," said Banerjee.

"He's been gone for three days," I said. "Is he the kind of kid who would go off on a lark?"

"I hardly knew him," said Banerjee. "He never struck me as irresponsible, but I don't know . . ."

"Is there anyone who *would* know?"

"Try his girlfriend."

"His mother told me he didn't have any girlfriends."

"He's got one. Or at least he did. His mother did her best to break it up."

"Any reason why?" I asked.

"Who knows?" he said. "She was a strange one, that lady. I don't think she liked him, even though he was her son."

"Can you give me the girl's name and tell me how to get in touch with her?"

"Melanie Grimes," answered Banerjee. He gave me her contact information. I thanked him, and went to the hospital where Melanie Grimes worked. They told me I'd have to wait in the cafetaria for her until she was on her break. It was a big, bustling room, with enough anti-grav sensors that any patient who found any kind of exertion difficult could simply float to a table. I found an empty table, and the moment I sat down a menu appeared a few inches above the table. Then a disembodied voice listed the day's specials.

"Just coffee," I said.

"Please press your thumb against the illuminated circle on the table," said the voice.

I did so.

"Your coffee will be billed to your account at the Odysseus branch of the Bank of Deluros."

I still don't know how the coffee got to the table. I turned away for a moment to watch a very proud, very stubborn old man insist on walking with crutches rather than let the room waft him to a chair, and when I turned back the coffee was already there.

I lit a smokeless cigar, and amused myself guessing the professions of every patient and visitor who walked by. Since there was no one to correct me, I gave myself a score of 90 percent.

Then a young woman began walking across the cafeteria toward me. She was very slender, almost thin, with short-cropped red hair and big brown eyes. While I was trying to guess whether she was a fourth-level computer programmer or an apprentice pastry chef, she came to a halt.

"Jake Masters?" she said. "I'm Melanie Grimes."

I stood up. "I want to thank you for seeing me."

"I haven't got much time. We've already had eight deliveries today."

"So you're an obstetrics nurse?"

"No, I'm not."

"You're too young to be a doctor."

"I'm a lab technician," she explained. "Every time a baby is born, we take some umbilical stem cells so we can clone its various organs should they ever need replacement. It's not very exciting," she continued, then added defensively: "But it *is* important."

"I don't doubt it," I said, handing her a business card. She studied my name and seemed fascinated by the little animated figure stalking the bad guys. Finally she looked up at me.

"This is about Andy, isn't it?"

"Yeah. According to his mother he went missing three nights ago."

"He's not missing," she said. "He ran away."

"From you?"

She shook her head. "From her."

"Are you talking about his mother?"

"Yes. He was frightened."

"Of her?"

"Yes."

I drained the last of my coffee. "Can you think of any reason why he should be frightened of her?"

"You've met her. Wouldn't you be afraid of her?"

Not much scares me besides the prospect of poverty these days, but I saw her point.

"If you wanted to find him, where would you look?"

"I don't know." Then: "He had this friend . . ."

"His mother gave me a list of his friends. I've spoken to Rashid Banerjee, and none of the others are on the planet."

"His mother didn't think this one could possibly be a friend, so of course she wouldn't give you his name—but he was the closest friend Andy had. Maybe his only real friend."

"Can you give me his name?"

"Crozchziim."

"Either you're choking or he's an alien," I said.

"He's a Gromite."

"What's a Gromite?"

"A native of Barsoti IV."

"Humanoid?"

"Yes."

"How long has he known Andy?"

"A long time," replied Melanie. "Andy's mother was too busy to bother with him, so he pretty much raised Andy. Over the years he was a nursemaid, a tutor, and a paid companion."

"Could Andy be staying with him?"

She shook her head. "He lived in an outbuilding on the Vanderwycke estate. A little shack, really, hidden from sight in a grove of trees. She'd have looked there before she contacted a detective."

I showed her the list of friends I'd been given. "Can you add any names to this?"

She studied the list. "Not really. I don't think Andy would have considered any of them friends. They were just classmates he knew."

"What about Andy's father?" I asked. "Dead?"

She smiled, the first smile I'd seen from her. "Didn't she tell you? But of course she wouldn't. It might ruin her social standing."

"You want to let me in on the joke?" I said.

"Andy's father is Ben Jeffries."

"Hatchet Ben Jeffries?" I said. "The kingpin of the Corvus system?"

"That's him."

"There's an outstanding murder warrant for him right here on Odysseus," I noted. "They've been trying to extradite him for years."

"That's why he never comes to the Iliad system," said Melanie.

"I assume he and Beatrice are divorced?"

"Andy says they were never married."

"Andy knows him?"

"Of course. He's been paying all Andy's expenses since he was born. He just can't visit him on Odysseus. He's flown Andy out to Corvus II a few times."

"Do they get along well?"

"I guess so."

"Could Andy be on Corvus now?" I asked.

She shrugged. "I don't know. Maybe."

I thanked her for her time, then went back to the office to check on Crozchziim's whereabouts. I had the computer access the Alien Registry. He'd reported once a week to the Department of Alien Affairs for close to fifteen years . . . but he'd skipped his last check-in, and the Department had no idea where he was.

Which meant my next step was to talk to Hatchet Ben Jeffries. I'd much rather have spoken to him via computer or subspace radio, but he was my only remaining lead, and I figured I'd better have a face-to-face with him, so I contacted the spaceport and booked an economy ticket to Corvus II.

Corvus was seventeen light-years from Iliad. I don't know who or what Corvus was, or why they named a star for it, but I thought the guy who named the planets was pretty unimaginative. They were Corvus I through Corvus XIV. It made Iliad's planets—Achilles, Odysseus, Ajax, Hektor, and the rest—look pretty classy by comparison.

We took off bright and early the next morning. I watched a holo of a murderball game for a couple of hours, then took a nap until the robot host woke me and asked if I wanted something to eat. I always

get nauseous when I eat at light speeds or traveling through worm-
holes in hyperspace, so I took a pass and went back to sleep until just
before we touched down.

I'd sent a message that I wanted to see Jeffries about his son, but
I'd left before there was any reply, and I hoped I hadn't wasted a trip.
It's been my experience that criminal kingpins are often reluctant to
speak to any kind of detective, even private ones. I cleared Customs,
then rented an aircar, punched in the address of Jeffries's estate, and
settled back to watch the countryside whiz past as we skimmed along
a few inches above the ground.

When we got to our destination there was a stone wall around the
entire place, all ten or twelve acres of it, and there were half a dozen
robots patrolling the exterior. The aircar stopped at the gate, its sensors flashing, and a few seconds later a mechanical voice came through
its speaker system:

"State your name and business. We will not be responsible for you or
your vehicle if you attempt to enter the grounds without permission."

"I'm Jake Masters, and I'm expected. Tell your boss I need to talk
to him."

"Please wait."

I waited a full two minutes. Then the gate vanished, and I realized
I'd been looking at one hell of a hologram. I suspected that the entire
wall was nothing but a carefully constructed image. For all I knew, so
were the robots. The aircar began moving forward, and once we were
inside the estate I ordered it to stop. Then, just to see if my guess about
how the place was really protected was right, I picked up a titanium
drinking mug that came with the vehicle and tossed it at the wall. It
was instantly atomized, which is exactly what would happen to anyone
who tried to enter without first being cleared.

We glided up to the front door of a mansion that would have been
impressive on any world and especially out here on the edge of the
Inner Frontier, and I found three men—*real* men, not images or robots

—waiting for me. Nobody was displaying any weapons, but they each had a few telltale bulges under their tunics.

"Well?" said the smallest of them.

"He is carrying a laser pistol," replied the aircar.

"Anything else?"

"A wallet, a passport, thirty-seven credits in change, two Maria Theresa dollars . . ."

"That's enough. Please hand me your burner, butt first, and step out of the vehicle, Mr. Masters."

I did as he said, and the two larger men frisked me about as thoroughly as I'd ever been frisked.

"What was that for?" I asked when they had finished.

"Mr. Jeffries has a lot of enemies," the small man explained. "And of course there are always bounty hunters."

"Yeah, but you've already scanned me and got my burner."

"You can't be too careful, Mr. Masters," he replied. "Last week a man tried to enter the house with a ceramic gun that got past every sensor. Step over here, please."

I walked over to a scanner that read my retina, my bone structure, and my fingerprints and checked them against my passport. Then they checked my passport against the registry office back on Odysseus. Finally they were satisfied that I was who I claimed to be, and that if I tried to kill their boss it wouldn't be with any weapons that had gotten past them.

"Please follow me," said the small man, turning and entering the mansion. We passed through a huge foyer with a floor made of marble with the distinctive blue tint that identified it as coming from far Antares, then down a corridor lined with alien artifacts on quartz shelves, and finally entered a luxurious study lined with books—not disks or cubes, but real books made of paper. The carpet was very thick, and seemed to shape itself around my feet with each step I took.

A tall man was standing beside a desk made of half a dozen different alien hardwoods. He was a steel gray man—hair, clothing, even his expression—and I knew he had to be Ben Jeffries. I half-expected to see the hatchet that made his reputation and gave him his sobriquet displayed on a wall or in a glass case, but there was no sign of it.

"Mr. Masters?" he said, extending his hand.

I took it. The grip was as firm and steel gray as the rest of him.

"Call me Jake."

"Have a seat, Jake," he said, snapping his fingers, and a chair quickly floated over to me, as responsive as a well-trained dog. "Can I get you something to drink?"

"Whatever you're having," I said.

"Cygnian cognac, I think," he said, and before he could ask for it a robot had entered with two half-filled glasses. I took one, so did he, and as the robot exited, he nodded to the man who had brought me to the study, and he left too. Now it was just the two of us.

"I've checked you out thoroughly, Jake," he said. "A man in my position has to be very careful. After all, you're a detective and there are close to eighty warrants for my arrest all across the Cluster. You've been scanned, so I know you're not carrying any recording devices, but just the same we're going to need some ground rules. You said you wanted to talk to me about my son. Fine—but that's the only subject that's open for discussion. Is that okay with you?"

I had a feeling that if it wasn't agreeable, I probably wouldn't live to make it back to the spaceport.

"That's fine," I said.

"I assume Andy's mother hired you?"

I nodded. "Mrs. Vanderwycke, right." I took a sip of the cognac. I'd heard of Cygnian cognac for years, but I could never afford it. I guess I'm used to cheap booze; I didn't like this stuff all. But since it was Hatchet Ben's cognac, I figured I'd better keep that observation to myself.

"Mrs. Vanderwycke," he repeated with an amused chuckle. "When

I knew her she was just plain Betty Wickes. Well, maybe not so plain."
He took a sip of his cognac. "All right, what do you need to know?"

"Your son has gone missing," I said, "and I've been hired to find him."

"Yeah, I gathered as much," said Jeffries.

"Has he been in contact with you? Asked for money or help?"

"No. He'd never show that much initiative."

"I take it you don't think too much of him?"

"He's a decent enough kid," said Jeffries. "But he's a weakling."

"He looked pretty sturdy in the holos I've seen."

"There are all kinds of weaklings," said Jeffries. "He's the kind I
have no use for. If you push him, he won't push back. He never stands
up to Betty, which is an open invitation to get walked all over. The
kid's got no guts. He lets every little thing get to him. Hell, he was
actually catatonic for a while back when he was five or six. You
wouldn't believe how much I had to pay a team of shrinks to snap him
out of it."

"Sounds like an unhappy kid," I said.

"I was an unhappy kid too," said Jeffries. "You learn to overcome
it—if you're tough enough. Andy isn't." He paused. "Maybe he'd have
turned out better if I'd raised him. It's hard to develop toughness
growing up around Betty."

"Tell me about her," I said.

"Watch your back around her," he said. "You know what I do for a
living, I'm not going to lie about it. I deal with the scum of the galaxy
every day—killers and worse." He stared at me. "Believe me when I
tell you she's more dangerous than any of them."

"If that's so, why did you hook up with her?"

"She was young and gorgeous, and I was young and foolish. It
didn't last long. I was gone before Andy was born."

"When's the last time you saw her?"

"Maybe fifteen or sixteen years ago," he said. "No, wait a minute.
I saw her a couple of years ago when Milos Arum was inaugurated as

Governor of Beta Capanis III. I didn't talk to her, but I saw her across the room."

"Beta Capanis," I said. "That's way to hell and gone, out on the Rim. I take it Arum's a close friend?"

"That's not part of our ground rules, Jake," he said with a hint of steel beneath the friendly smile. "Stick to Andy."

"Sorry," I said. "What can you tell me about a Gromite called Crozchziim?"

"I never met him, but Andy talked about him a lot."

"Any idea where he might be?"

"He? You mean the alien? Isn't he back on Odysseus?"

"Not as far as I can tell," I said.

"So you think he's with Andy?"

"It makes sense," I said. "They're friends, and they're both missing."

"Interesting," said Jeffries. "All I know about him is that he used to be an entertainer, a juggler or tumbler or something. He broke an arm or a leg, I don't remember which, when he was on Odysseus, and they let him go. Betty hired him to amuse the kid."

"He performed on stage?" If he worked for a theatre company that played human worlds, he had to belong to a union, and that would make him a little easier to trace.

"In a circus or a carnival, something like that." I must have looked my disappointment, because he added: "I'll have one of my men find out exactly where it was and get the information to you."

"Thanks," I said. "I guess that covers everything."

"Almost. Now I've got one for you."

"Fair is fair. Go ahead and ask."

"Twelve years ago you put three of my men away for a long time on Odysseus. You were a good cop. Why did you quit?"

"I wasn't corrupt enough," I said.

He chuckled. "Yeah, I heard about your problems when you arrested the wrong guys."

"Right guys, wrong administration," I replied. I wanted to ask if they were his, but I knew he wouldn't answer, so I got to my feet and he did the same.

"Have you got any idea where he might be?" he asked.

"Not yet," I said. "But I'll find him sooner or later—unless Mrs. Vanderwycke gets tired of paying my expenses and per diems."

"I'll tell you what," said Jeffries, walking me to the door of the study. "If she stops paying you, I'll pick up the tab and you'll report to me."

I looked at him for a moment without saying anything.

"What are you staring at?" he said.

"I'm trying to picture you as a concerned father."

Suddenly he was all steel again. "Just find him."

Then I was being escorted back to the car by another of his men, and an hour later I was on a spaceliner bound for Odysseus. When the trip was a little less than half over, the robot host handed me the printout of a subspace message that had just arrived from the Corvus system:

"The show Crozchziim worked for is long defunct. There are presently 137 circuses and carnivals touring the Albion Cluster. For what it's worth, only one of them, the Benzagari Carnival and Sideshow, is owned by a Gromite, Crozchziim's former partner in a juggling act."

It was as good a place as any to start, so before we landed I ran a check and learned that the carny had been playing on Brutus II for eight days and was slated to be there for four more. I didn't even leave the Odysseus spaceport; half an hour after we touched down I was en route to the Alpha Pirias system, where I'd transfer to a local ship that hit all the inhabited worlds within a three-system radius, including Brutus II.

When I got to Brutus I found that the carny had been kicked off the planet for running crooked games, which at least showed that the management had some respect for tradition, and was now on New Rhodesia. It took me another day to make connections. We touched down on nightside, and I got off with perhaps ten other passengers while the ship continued on toward its ultimate destination in the Roosevelt system.

I got in line to pass through Customs. When it was my turn I stepped up and handed over my passport disk to the robot Customs officer that was running the booth.

"Are you visiting New Rhodesia for business or pleasure?" it asked me.

"Business."

"The nature of your business?"

"I am a duly licensed private investigator," I replied. "I don't believe I'm required to tell you more than that."

"Will you require a copy of our constitution and penal code so that you may study what is and is not permitted in the pursuit of your business?"

"That won't be necessary."

"How long do you plan to stay on New Rhodesia?"

"One day, two at the most."

"I have given you a three-day visa," said the robot, handing me back my disk. "It will vanish from your passport at that time, and if you are still on New Rhodesia and have not filed for an extension, you will be in violation of our laws."

"I understand."

"Our standard currency is the New Rhodesia shilling, but Democracy credits and Maria Theresa dollars are also accepted. If you have other human currencies, you may exchange them at any of the three banks within the spaceport." It paused as if waiting for a question, but I didn't have any. "Our atmosphere is 21 percent oxygen, 77 percent nitrogen, and 2 percent inert gasses that are harmless to carbon-based life-forms. Our gravity is 96 percent Standard, and our day is 27.23 Standard hours."

"Thanks," I said. "May I pass through now?"

"I must check to make sure you have sufficient funds to purchase passage away from New Rhodesia," it replied, as it transmitted my thumbprint to the Master Computer back on Deluros VIII. I tensed, because while I'd just deposited the money Mrs. Vanderwycke had given me, my credit history was what they call spotty. "Checking . . . satisfactory. You may enter the main body of the spaceport, Jacob Masters."

I walked straight to an information computer and asked where the Benzagari Carnival and Sideshow was performing. It gave me an address than didn't mean a thing, so I took it to the Transport Depot and hired an aircar to take me there.

It was about ten miles out of town, a series of tents and torch-lit kiosks that were meticulous recreations of the ones that had plied their trade on Earth before Man had reached the stars, with the added advantage that they were climate-controlled and a cyclone couldn't have blown them away. There were games of every variety, games for humans, games for aliens, even races for the ugly little six-legged creatures that passed for pets on New Rhodesia. The barkers and shills were everywhere—Men, Canphorites, Lodinites, Mollutei, Atrians, even a couple of Belargans.

The din was deafening. There were grunts and growls, trills and shrill whistles, snorts and clicks, and here and there even some words I could understand. The standard language in the galaxy is Terran since Men are the dominant race, and usually the other races wear T-packs— translating mechanisms that are programmed to work in Terran and their native tongues—but someone had decided the carnival would have a more exotic flavor if the T-packs weren't used, and I have to admit they had a point: it certainly felt different from anything I'd ever encountered.

Except for the frigid, methane-breathing Atrians who had to wear protective suits, all the other aliens were warm-blooded oxygen breathers, and they were all more-or-less humanoid. There were half a dozen races I'd never seen before, ranging from a ten-foot-tall biped that looked like an animated tent pole to a short, burly, three-legged being covered with what seemed to be dull purple feathers.

Finally I walked up to one of the human barkers and asked him to point out a Gromite to me. He looked around for a moment, then turned back to me.

"I don't see any right now, but they're all over the place," he said.

"What do they look like?"

"Maybe a foot shorter than you, rich red skin, two arms, two legs, too damned many fingers and toes. They don't wear clothes. I know this is supposed to be a sexual galaxy, but if they've got genders, they keep it to themselves." Suddenly he pointed. "There's the boss, making his collections."

I looked, and decided I'd never mistake a Gromite for anything else. The legs had an extra joint, the elbows seemed to bend in both directions, there was no nose but just a narrow slit above a broad mouth, the eyes were orange and were faceted like an insect's, and if he had any genitals they sure as hell weren't external.

"Maybe he doesn't need pants," said the barker, "but he sure as hell could use a money belt. We're really raking it in tonight."

"Have you been with the show long?" I asked.

"A year, give or take."

"Do you know if there's a Gromite called Crozchziim working here?"

"Beats the hell out of me," he said. "It's not a name I'd remember." Then: "Who'd he kill?"

"Why do you think he killed anyone?"

"Why else would you be looking for him?"

"He's no killer. I just need to talk to him. I'm told that he's a juggler, or some kind of entertainer."

"Well, there's your answer. He'd be in the big tent, and I work the Midway. We could both work the show for a year and never meet."

"This particular Gromite might be traveling with a young human."

"Bully for him," said the barker, losing interest. "You got any other questions, or do you mind if I go back to work?"

I left him and headed over to Benzagari. I flashed my credentials at him and he came to a stop.

"We're breaking no laws," he said. "If you have any complaints, please speak to Lieutenant James Ngoma."

"I'm not here to arrest you or shake you down," I said. "I just need some information." He didn't say anything, so I continued. "I'm looking for a young human named Andy Vanderwycke. He's probably traveling with a Gromite named Crozchziim."

"I have never heard of either of them."

Birds of a feather. I already knew that he'd been Crozchziim's partner in an act years ago, so he was obviously protecting a fellow Gromite. I considered explaining that I didn't want the damned Gromite, that I was after the Man, but he had no reason to believe me and aliens don't sell out their brothers to humans.

I left him and headed for the main tent. It was packed, split just about evenly between humans and everything else. New Rhodesia was a human world, but it was also a center of commerce, and it had a large Alien Quarter. The Men still outnumbered the aliens three or four to one, but Men had a lot of things to do with their evenings, and obviously the aliens didn't.

There were a trio of Lodinite tumblers in the center, and a couple of human clowns were walking the perimeter of the ring, entertaining some of the kids of all species who couldn't work up much enthusiasm for alien acrobats. They were just finishing up their act when I got there, and a minute later a human knife thrower entered the ring. A pretty, scantily clad girl was tied to a huge spinning wheel, the wheel was set in motion, and the man hurled his first knife. There was an audible gasp as the knife buried itself in the woman's stomach and she uttered a shrill scream. The man released four more knives in quick succession, and each one failed to miss the girl, whose screams grew weaker each time. Then, just before the audience could charge the ring to dismember the knife thrower, the wheel came to a stop, the shackles came loose, and the "dying" girl walked briskly to the center of the ring, pulled all five knives from her body, politely handed them back to the thrower, and bowed to the audience.

"Nice trick," I said to a human who was walking down the aisle, hawking candies and the wriggling little wormlike things that the Mollutei eat for snacks.

"That's no trick," he said. "Those are real knives. If he throws one into you, you die."

"Then why didn't she die?"

"Mutant. Her blood coagulates instantly, and her skin heals by the next morning—and he really *is* a good aim. He always misses her vital organs."

"That doesn't explain why the shock and pain doesn't kill her."

"She had all her pain receptors surgically disconnected."

"Are you guessing, or do you know that for a fact?"

He smiled. "She's my sister."

I bought a candy bar from him to cement our friendship, then asked another question. "I'm looking for a Gromite who might be working here as a juggler. Have you seen one?"

"Sure. You want Crunchtime."

"Crunchtime?" I repeated.

"That's not his name, but it's as close as I can come to pronouncing it, and he answers to it. Most everyone calls him that now."

"Is he traveling with a human, a young man maybe nineteen or twenty years old, kind of slender, maybe two or three inches over six feet?"

"Never saw him in the act, and I don't mix with aliens when I'm on my own time."

"When is Crunchtime due to appear?"

He glanced at the ring, where a Canphorite was putting some huge forty-ton creature through its paces, tossing it a ball, making it stand on its back four legs, climbing into its huge maw.

"Soon as this guy and his pet are done."

"Some pet," I remarked.

"Yeah, I know, it looks like it could eat half the audience for breakfast, but it's really a herbivore. Friendliest damned monster you ever saw. It loves everybody."

You live and learn. The deadliest killer I ever came across looked like a Milquetoast who'd faint if you just frowned at him.

I waited until the Canphorite and his pet left the ring, and then a trio of jugglers entered—one human, one Lodinite, and one Gromite. And since the Gromite I sought had been a juggler and a guy who had a difficult time with alien names had dubbed this Gromite Crunchtime, I was pretty sure I'd found Crozchziim.

I have to admit he was damned good at what he did. He kept six or seven objects of different shapes and weights going at once, then tossed them even higher and got an even dozen in motion. I'd assumed that sooner or later the three of them would start juggling things back and forth, but none of them even acknowledged the others' existence until they all took their bows a few minutes later.

When they left the ring I handed the candy bar to a little girl, then walked to the exit they'd used and was soon just a few steps behind the Gromite.

"Hey, Crunchtime!" I called.

He stopped and turned to face me.

"Do I know you?" he asked in perfect Terran.

"Not yet," I said. "My name's Jake Masters."

"Mine is Crozchziim."

"I know. Will you settle for Crunchtime? It's a hell of a lot easier for me to pronounce."

He nodded his head, which startled me. The way he was put together, it looked like it was about to fall off. "What do you want of me, Mr. Masters?"

"I just want to ask you a few questions," I said. "You used to work for Beatrice Vanderwycke, right?"

"That is correct."

"You left in kind of a hurry."

"She doesn't want me back," he said, "and she is not the type to send you all this way to present me with my vacation pay—so why are you here?"

I pulled out my card. "Can you read Terran?" He nodded again, and I handed it to him. "I've been hired to find her son."

"And do what?"

"Bring him back."

"Why?"

"That's not my concern," I said.

"It should be," said Crunchtime.

"Why do you think so?"

"Before you disrupt an innocent young man's life, don't you think you should know why you're doing it?"

"She's his mother and she's worried about him," I said.

He stared at me, and when he was done I knew what a sneer of contempt and disbelief from a Gromite looked like.

Finally he spoke. "Tell Mrs. Vanderwycke he is safe and healthy and she has nothing to worry about. Now your job is done. Good-bye, Mr. Masters."

"Let him tell me," I said.

"He has no desire to see anyone connected with his mother," said the Gromite.

"His father's concerned too."

"His father had seen him a total of twenty-seven days since he was born. It is difficult to believe that he is suddenly concerned about the boy's well-being."

"So nobody cares about him except you?"

"Melanie Grimes does," said Crunchtime. "But you already know that. Who else would have given you my name?"

"She trusted me enough to tell me that Andy was probably traveling with you. Why can't you trust me enough to tell me where he is?"

"I have my reasons, and Andy has his."

"Why not make things easy on both of us and cooperate with me?" I said reasonably. "You know I'm going to find him with or without your help."

"Without." He paused and stared at me for a long minute. "You may think you know what this is about, Mr. Masters, but I assure you that you have no idea whatsoever."

"Enlighten me."

"Keep out of matters that don't concern you," said Crunchtime. "If you find him and take him back before he's ready, you will be responsible for whatever happens."

"Before he's ready for what?" I demanded. "And what do you expect to happen?"

"I have said enough. I will speak no further. This interview is over."

He turned and walked away. I considered following him, but decided it was a waste of time. The kid had to know his mother would send someone after him; he probably had a prearranged set of signals with Crunchtime to warn him when anyone showed up.

I spent the rest of the night wandering through the sideshow, searching for Andy Vanderwycke. I had his holo with me, but I never had a chance to use it, because I never saw a young man of his height and build. As the crowds thinned out I began looking behind the kiosks. I turned up a couple half my age having sex behind a shooting gallery, three men and two aliens who were so zoned out on booze or drugs that nothing was going to wake them before morning, and ten or twelve hucksters of all races selling contraband items, some of which made no sense to me.

One bedraggled man approached me with some truly unique pornography—an animated deck of cards with a queen of hearts I still dream about—and another tried to sell me a pair of hallucinogenic alphanella seeds, which are illegal on just about every world in the Democracy. I asked each of them if they had seen anyone answering to Andy's description, but once they saw I wasn't about to buy their goods they muttered their negatives and went looking for some other sucker.

When an Andrican hooker who looked like a four-foot-tall Tinker Bell, complete with wings and a voice that sounded like gentle chimes, hinted at what she would like to do for or to me, I pulled out a fifty-credit note and told her I wasn't interested in what she was selling but I'd give her the money if she could tell me where to find Andy Vanderwycke. She explained that she didn't know any human male called Andy, but if I was after male companionship her uncle was available.

Finally I stumbled upon Prospero the Living Encyclopedia, a humanoid alien. To this day I don't know what race he belonged to; from a distance he could pass for a man, but when you got close to him you noticed the lidless eyes with the slit pupils, the third nostril, and the hair that was constantly weaving itself into new patterns.

Prospero's booth was at the far end of the midway, and he offered a prize of one hundred New Rhodesia shillings to anyone who asked him a question that he couldn't answer. He was really remarkable: he knew the time for the fastest mile ever run on Greenveldt, the gross planetary product of Far London, and the copyright date of the Canphorite poet Tanblixt's first book.

Finally I stepped up and faced him.

"Greetings, my good sir," he said in sibilant Terran, and now that I was standing right in front of him I saw that his tongue was forked, not like a snake's but like a real fork, with four distinct tines. "And what question do you wish the magnificent Prospero to answer?"

"I'm looking for a human named Andy Vanderwycke," I said. "Is he with the carnival?"

"Yes."

"Where can I find him?"

"Only one question to a customer, good sir," said Prospero with a very alien smile.

"I'll just get back in line and ask again," I told him.

"That is your privilege."

So I went to the back of the line, waited half an hour to reach the front again, and walked up to him.

"Remember me?" I said.

"The all-seeing and all-knowing Prospero remembers everything. What is your question, good sir?"

"Where can I find Andy Vanderwycke?"

"At the Benzagari Carnival and Sideshow."

"Where at the carnival?"

"I'm sorry, good sir, but each patron is limited to only one question."

"I can keep this up as long as you can," I said irritably. "And I can get a lot nastier about it. Why don't you make it easy on both of us?"

"Good sir, you are causing a disturbance," said Prospero. "Please do not force me to call for Security."

The line was shorter this time, and I was facing him again in another seven or eight minutes.

"Consider your question very carefully, good sir," he said when I confronted him. "The show will be shutting down in another five minutes."

"Okay, this is my question: No matter how often I ask or how I word it, you're not going to tell me what I want to know, are you?"

"No, good sir, I am not. Next?"

I stepped aside, considered waiting for him to leave his booth, and decided against it. Carnies always stuck together against outsiders. It was possible that I could beat the information out of him—but if I couldn't, then by morning not a single member of the carnival would ever speak to me again, and that's assuming I wasn't arrested for assault.

Within half an hour the entire show was shut down. I was about to hunt up someplace to spend the night when I saw them starting to break down the tents.

"What's going on?" I asked the insectoid alien who seemed to be in charge of the work crew.

"We open on Aristides IV in two days, and it will take a day to set up there," he squeaked at me.

"But you've only been on New Rhodesia for two nights," I said.

"We're only here because we were thrown off of Brutus II," was his answer. "Our next scheduled playdate is Aristides."

I considered trying to hitch a ride with the carny, but I knew Crunchtime would have alerted Benzagari about my snooping around, and there was no way I could go with them except as a stowaway. So, since all my expenses were being paid, I went back to the spaceport and booked passage to Aristides IV, then rented a room at the attached hotel. The ship didn't leave until midday, and when I showed up they told me that the carny's chartered ship left at dawn, so Andy Vander-wycke was going to have half a day to hide before I got there.

When the ship touched down and I'd cleared Customs, I asked an information computer where the carnival was setting up shop, and was informed that they'd be playing at the local indoor stadium.

I didn't like that at all. If they'd taken their tents out into the countryside, the crew would be staying with the show, and I'd at least know where to start looking. But if they hadn't unpacked the tents, that meant they'd be staying in hotels.

Aristides IV was like most Democracy worlds—Men lived where they wanted, and all the other races were confined to the Alien Quarter. Maybe Andy was new at being on the run but most members of a carny have spent their entire lives avoiding spouses, bill collectors, or the police, and they'd have given him a quick education in laying low. And the first thing they'd have told him was not to stay where they stayed. They could misdirect me and protect him out in the countryside, but not in a hotel on a strange world. It would be too easy for me to bribe a desk clerk or bartender, too easy for an experienced detective to crack any computer lock on any door.

So if he had half a brain, he wouldn't be where I could pay a few credits or let myself into a few rooms to find him. If it was me and I was traveling with a Gromite, I'd be hiding with him in the Alien Quarter until I had to show up for work, and I granted the kid enough smarts or access to enough advice to do the same.

In one way, it made my job more difficult, because aliens stick together the way carnies do, and they don't like Men walking through the little piece of each city that's reserved for them. On the other hand, a six-foot three-inch human would be a lot easier to spot in the Alien Quarter than in a string of hotels and restaurants populated by nothing but Men.

I took the slidewalk out of the spaceport, moved over to the expresswalk, and found myself at the edge of the Quarter a few minutes later. A Lodinite patrolled the gate, and gave me the standard warning about how no one could be held responsible for anything that happened to me once I left the human section of the city and entered the Alien Quarter. He recited the usual liturgy about how aliens were justifiably resentful of their status on human worlds, and that even though I was doubtless in no way responsible I nonetheless represented the race of Man and they might be inclined to take out their frustration on me. When I answered that I knew all that and told him to cut the lecture short, he glared at me and then announced that the gate's sensors had detected a weapon that was hidden from sight.

I pulled my burner out and showed it to him.

"This is a Stern and Mason laser pistol, Model ZQ, purchased on Odysseus, registration number 362LV5413. If you'll check my passport, you'll see that I'm licensed to carry it."

He ran a microscanner across my passport disk, then deactivated it.

"I would recommend that you keep it concealed," he said stiffly. "No other race is allowed to own or carry weapons on Aristides, and displaying it would just create resentment, which is present already."

"I wasn't displaying it when your sensor spotted it," I pointed out.

He had no response to that, so he waited another minute just to annoy me, and then let me pass through the gate.

I was a block into the Alien Quarter before the smell hit me. It was kind of a cross between rotting flesh and raw sewage, and it got stronger the farther I proceeded.

The squalor was almost unbelievable. Alien waste washed slowly along the street gutters, exposed to the air, going God knew where. Everything was in a state of decay, doors and windows were rotting or missing, dead animals and the occasional dead alien lay on the streets and slidewalks. Here and there undernourished alien children, most of them naked or nearly so, played incomprehensible games. When they saw me every last one of them rushed up, hand or paw or tentacle extended, begging for food or money.

I tried to ignore them, but they wouldn't go away and fell into step behind me. Finally I figured I might as well see if I could make some use of them, so I stopped, turned, and asked if any of them knew where the performers from the carnival were staying. I got nothing but blank looks, and I realized that none of them were wearing T-packs, so they couldn't understand me.

After another block I came upon an ancient Triskargi who had a tarnished T-pack hanging around his neck. He looked like he wanted to hop away on his froglike legs as I approached him, but when he saw all the children he seemed reassured that I wasn't out to harm him and he stayed where he was.

"Hi," I said. "None of the kids can understand me."

"They have no T-packs," he said.

"I know. But there are a couple of Triskargi kids among them. You can speak to them, and most of them seem to understand each other, so they've probably developed some sort of lingua franca to communicate with each other. I want you to ask them if they know where the carnival performers are staying."

It took a few minutes, because the old Triskargi had no idea what a carnival was, but finally he understood and relayed the question. One of the Canphorite kids—I never remember which ones come from Canphor VI and which from Canphor VII—said he could lead me to some of them. He wanted seventeen trillion credits for his services. We negotiated, and I talked him down to twenty credits.

"Have him tell his friends not to follow us," I told the Triskargi. "If they hear us all coming, they'll have time to hide."

"They are entertainers," he said. "Why should they hide?"

"Just tell him."

He did as I asked, and the Canphorite child and I set out to the west. The planet's four moons were all out in midafternoon, casting strange flickering shadows across the Quarter. I was going to ask my guide for the names of the moons, but then I remembered he couldn't understand me, so I just followed him in silence.

Finally we stopped at a deep burrow, and the child turned and looked at me.

"Is this it?" I asked.

He couldn't understand my words, but he knew what I was asking. He pointed into the burrow.

I thanked him, tipped him another ten credits, watched him race back toward his playmates, and then I entered the burrow. The tunnels, which were about ten feet high and almost as wide, descended at about a twenty-degree angle, twisting and winding, occasionally broadening into what passed for a room. It was almost an underground city. A number of aliens saw me, but no one greeted me or tried to stop me. They simply stared in silence, as if this intrusion was just one more humiliation they were being forced to suffer.

At last the ground began to level out, and I came to a tall, heavily muscled Sett who was wearing a T-pack.

"I'm looking for a Gromite and a Man," I said. "They would have arrived this morning."

He stared at me without speaking.

"They were traveling with a carnival." Silence. "Have you seen them?"

"They are not here."

"That wasn't my question. Have you seen them?"

"Yes."

"Where are they now?"

"I do not know."

"Who does?"

"No one in this burrow knows. When they heard that you had entered the Quarter, they left. We asked them not to tell us their destination, so that you cannot torture it out of us."

"I don't torture people."

"Then you are a most unusual Man." He paused. "Go back where you belong, Jake Masters."

They'd been there, all right. No one else in the Quarter knew my name. And if they had friends watching me, they were going to be able to stay one step ahead of me in the Alien Quarter. There was no sense wasting any more time there, so I retraced my steps, and an hour later I checked into the Regal Arms, which wasn't regal and didn't have any arms, but it was where the carny's human contingent was staying.

I hung around the bar, and bought half a dozen of them drinks at various points in the evening. I didn't get the resentment here that I did when I spoke to the aliens, but I didn't get any information either. When money couldn't pry any answers loose, I tried invoking Hatchet Ben Jeffries's name. He was looking for his son, I explained, and he could get pretty deadly when he didn't get what he wanted. It didn't help. Maybe they knew where Andy was, maybe they didn't, but carnies have this code, and they don't break it.

I have a code, too. It has to do with earning my pay, and I wasn't going to let a wall of silence get in the way. I went up to my room a couple of hours after midnight, slept in until noon, and wandered down to the hotel's restaurant for some breakfast. The whole meal was composed of soya products, but they were well disguised and it wasn't too difficult to pretend I was eating eggs from Silverblue or Prateep VI and coffee imported from Earth itself.

I'd learned the night before that because of some city ordinance the carny's games couldn't open until dusk, and since there was no sense drawing a crowd if they couldn't be bilked, the entertainment wouldn't start for another hour or so after that.

I showed up while they were still setting up, and found out where the performers' dressing rooms were located. The aliens were segregated, so I figured I wouldn't find the kid there. I went to the human dressing rooms and checked out their occupants, but there was no one who matched the holo I was carrying around.

I walked up and down the games and booths, checking out the barkers, the shills, everyone who might be remotely connected to the carnival. No luck. I entered the main auditorium, studied all the ushers and candy butchers. Nothing.

I finally decided that my best bet was just to keep an eye on Crunchtime. Sooner or later he had to make contact with Andy Vanderwycke, had to let his guard down, and I planned to be there when he did.

I grabbed a seat in the front row and settled back to wait for the Gromite. As the crowd filed in, a trio of clowns, two human, one Lodinite, began doing some ancient routines and pratfalls to warm them up. The kids loved it; after all, it wasn't ancient to them.

Then came the wire walker, and the intricate flight patterns of the winged aliens from far Shibati, and the dinosaur trainer (or the whatever-the-hell-it-was trainer), and the magician, and some tumblers, and finally Crunchtime and the other two jugglers entered the ring. I waited until his performance was over, then followed him out.

A young woman approached him and handed him something, I couldn't see what. He studied it for a moment and gave it back to her, and then she walked away. I followed her, made a mental note of the office she entered, and then returned to Crunchtime.

"Feel like talking yet?" I asked.

"You came looking for me in the Alien Quarter," he said. "That was very unwise."

"I like sightseeing."

"You are wasting your time, Mr. Masters."

"I'm being paid for it," I told him. "And I plan to follow you night and day until I find Andy or you tell me where he is."

"That is your right," he replied. "And it is my right not to tell you."

"A Mexican standoff."

"What is a Mexican?"

"Beats me," I admitted. "It's an ancient expression."

"I am going into my dressing room now," he said. "Unless you have an insatiable curiosity to observe how a Gromite passes the food he has digested, you will not accompany me."

With that, he turned on what passed for his heel and entered the room, and I went over to the woman's office. The concrete floor could have used a carpet, the whitewashed walls could have used some paintings or holographs, and the coffee pot could have used some coffee. She was sitting in a chair that was probably a decade older than she was, studying holos cast by her computer. I know she heard me come in, but she didn't bother to look up.

"Hi," I said. "My name is Jake Masters. I'd like to ask you a question."

"The answer is no."

"You haven't heard the question."

"I don't have to. You're Jake Masters, and you're harassing Crozchziim. Go away and leave him alone."

"Word gets around pretty fast."

"This is a carnival," she said as if that explained everything.

"I admire your loyalty, but I'm not here for the Gromite. I just need some information."

"Read an encyclopedia."

"I talked to one last night," I said wryly. "It didn't help."

"Life is full of disappointments."

"Just show me what you showed the Gromite."

"It's been atomized."

"I don't believe you. Let me take a look and I'm out of here."

She finally looked up at me. "Go, stay, what you do doesn't interest me."

I decided to take a different tack. "The games are crooked, and the carny has broken maybe thirty laws already tonight," I said. "I could tell the authorities."

She actually smiled. "Go ahead. Do you think you can pay them more than we already did?"

I smiled back. "Okay, lady, you win this round. But I'm going to find the young man I'm looking for."

"Maybe you will, maybe you won't, but you're not going to do it with my help." She went back to staring at her computer's array of images, and I finally left the office.

I went up and down the rows of games and attractions again, trying to spot a tall nineteen-year-old who looked anything like the holo of Andy Vanderwycke, but with no luck. I went through the lighting booth, the prop room, the performers' cafeteria, all the back-stage rooms, got a pleasant eyefull in the ladies' dressing room, but couldn't see any sign of the kid.

It was driving me crazy. He had to be there. Crunchtime had as much as admitted it. So had the alien in the burrow. So had the lady with the computer. It wasn't that damned big a carnival—so why couldn't I spot him?

It was time for the next show, and I went back into the main audi-torium, trying to figure out what I was overlooking. The crowd began getting restless, and the clowns came out to amuse them again—and suddenly I knew where Andy Vanderwycke was hiding. I watched the whole damned show again, then walked out the performers' exit. Crunchtime went past me and seemed surprised that I didn't stop him to ask more questions. I stepped aside as the dinosaur lumbered past, smiled at a couple of good-looking girls in tights, and finally the person I was waiting for appeared.

"Hi, Andy," I said.

He stopped cold and stared at me.

"Nice disguise," I said.

He took off his red bulbous nose and green fright wig. "I thought so until now."

"Really, it is," I said. "Who'd ever look twice at Bonzo the Clown?"

"How did you spot me?" he asked.

"Mostly it was a process of elimination."

I handed him my card.

"What happens now?" said Andy. "You're not going to kill me in front of all these people. And if I yell for help, my friends will tear you apart no matter what you do to me."

"I'm not here to kill you," I said, surprised. "I was hired to take you back to Odysseus."

"Same thing," he said.

"Your mother's very worried about you."

He smiled ruefully. "I'll just bet she is."

"One way or another you're coming back to Odysseus," I said, "so why not do it peacefully?"

"Oh, I'll go back to Odysseus," he replied. "But I'm not ready yet."

It was the same thing Crunchtime had said, and I offered the same response. "Ready for what?"

He stared long and hard at me, as if trying to make up his mind. Finally he shrugged. "What the hell. I might as well tell you. If you're lying and you're here to kill me, you're going to do it anyway. If you're telling the truth, maybe what I say will make a difference—though my guess is that my mother paid you so much that it won't matter."

"You talk, I'll listen."

"Let's find Crozchziim first," said Andy.

"What do you need him for?"

"We're due to leave the planet in a couple of hours, and he knows the ticket codes."

So now I knew what the girl had shown Crunchtime—the codes he'd need to get them aboard the ship.

"Forget it," I said. "Your pal can come or go as he pleases, but you're not running away."

"I'm not running away," he said. "I'm running *to* something."

"To what?"

"When we find Crozchziim." He paused. "He can corroborate everything I'm going to tell you."

We walked to Crunchtime's dressing room. Andy was about to enter it when I grabbed his arm.

"Have someone else tell him to come out," I said. "You're staying with me."

He spoke to a Canphorite who was walking by. The Canphorite entered the room, and a moment later Crunchtime emerged.

"So you found him," he said tonelessly.

"Yeah, I found him," I answered. "I told you I would."

"And this time you will kill him."

"This time?" I repeated, confused. "What are you talking about?"

"It is time to drop all the pretenses, Mr. Masters—if that is your real name," said Crunchtime. "You have been stalking Andy for six days. You came close to killing him on Brookmandor II. Now you have changed your tactics and are impersonating a detective, trying to enlist the help of others, but you are still a killer."

"I'm a detective," I said firmly. "I work out of Odysseus, and I was hired five days ago by Beatrice Vanderwycke. The first time I ever saw you or Andy was when I arrived on Aristides yesterday. If someone's stalking the kid, it isn't me."

They exchanged looks, and finally Andy spoke up. "All right, Mr. Masters. I believe you. Now let's go somewhere private and see if you can return the favor."

"Lead the way," I said. "And don't run."

He led me to a deserted office. "Benzagari's working out of this room while we're here. He's checking the take on the midway, and then he's got to pay off the police, so he won't be back for at least half an hour."

I sat down on a sofa. "All right, I'm listening," I said. Andy sat on the edge of a desk, and Crunchtime, who wasn't built to fit in or on any human furniture, stood near Andy. "Start with why I shouldn't believe you bought passage off Aristides tonight expressly to get away from me."

"Because it's true," he said. "I have to go to Port Samarkand."

"Never heard of it."

"It's about seventy light-years from here."

"What's on Port Samarkand?"

"Duristan."

"What's Duristan?" I said.

"Duristan is a who, not a what . . . and my life depends on my reaching him."

I looked from one to the other. "Keep talking."

"What, exactly, did my mother tell you about me?"

"That you ran away and she wants you back."

"What did she say about me?" he repeated. "You can tell me. I won't take offense."

"That you were emotionally unstable and had been in therapy. I saw your father, too. He confirmed that you've been troubled since you were a child."

"He's right," said Andy. "Something happened when I was six, something that made me lose almost a whole year of my life. They tell me I was catatonic and it took them almost a year to snap me out of it. Did he tell you that?"

"Yes, he did."

He stared at me for a moment. "Did he tell you anything about my mother?"

"He doesn't think too much of her."

"You're being coy, Mr. Masters, and we have no time for that. My ship leaves in an hour, and I have to be on it. What did he tell you about her?"

"He said she was an extremely dangerous woman."

"He's right." He paused. "I'm legally of age, Mr. Masters. I've been living on Crozchziim's savings until I got my first paycheck two nights ago. I didn't take a single credit with me when I left, and I've asked nothing of her, indeed had no contact with her, since then. Why do you think she wants me back?"

"Why should I play guessing games when you're going to tell me?" I said.

"During the two months before I left home I had increasingly violent nightmares," said Andy. "Terrible images of blood and carnage."

"Lots of people do," I said, though most of my dreams were about ripe naked women I was never going to have and bill collectors I was never going to avoid.

"This was different. It was the same dream every night. I couldn't make out exactly what was happening, but it was terrifying." He paused. "Do you know what I think?"

"Probably, but why don't you tell me anyway?"

"I think she did something when I was six years old, something I wasn't supposed to see, something so terrible that after I saw it I couldn't face the truth of it and became catatonic for a year. When I came back to my senses, I couldn't remember anything. I still can't." He paused. "I don't know if this recurring nightmare is what I saw when I saw six, trying to burst into my consciousness—but *she* thinks it is. When I mentioned that I kept having this dream night after night, things began happening. I got what seemed like ptomaine poisoning from spoiled food—but she ate the same meal and was fine. I found a pill that didn't belong among my prescriptions. And every day she would ask about my dreams. I knew if I stayed there she'd find a way to kill me, so I took off."

"I had remained in Mrs. Vanderwycke's service only because of Andy," added Crunchtime, "and when he explained the situation, I agreed that he could not remain on Odysseus. As it is, there has already been an attempt on his life on Brookmandor II, just before we joined the carnival."

"It's not that hard to spot a tall skinny kid and a Gromite traveling together," I said. "I came in cold, and it only took me two days, even with his makeup. What ever gave you the idea that you could hide out in a carnival? Hell, you didn't even change your name, and Hatchet Ben Jeffries knew you'd been a juggler."

"Benzagari is an old friend," replied Crunchtime. "And we had to perform here to get our bona fides before traveling to Port Samarkand."

"You were making sense right up until now," I said.

"We must make contact with Duristan."

"This is where I came in," I said. "Who is Duristan?"

"He's a Rabolian," said Andy.

I frowned. "I know something about Rabolians, but I'll be damned if I can remember what it is."

"They're mentalists."

"That's right," I said, as it suddenly came back to me. "They're one of the few telepathic races."

"They're more than telepaths," said Andy. "A telepath can just read what I'm thinking. A true mentalist, a Rabolian, can dig out things I didn't even know were in my mind."

"And you think he's going to be able to tell you what you saw?"

"That's right."

"Then what?"

"It'll be my insurance policy. I'll write up the details, swear to it, store it in half a dozen locations, and let her know that if anything happens to me it'll be made public." He paused. "You look dubious, Mr. Masters."

"Call me Jake. And I *am* dubious."

"You think I'm lying to you, Jake?"

"Nobody could think up a lie like that," I said. "No, I believe you."

"Well, then?"

"Maybe your mother had nothing to do with what you saw. Maybe you went a little haywire and dissected your pet puppy. Maybe you saw a couple of kids making whoopee and were scared by all the forbidden activity and noise. There are aliens whose appearance would give anyone nightmares; maybe you bumped into one. Or maybe it was something else."

"It was her!" he snapped. "Why else would she be trying to kill me?"

"I don't know that she *is* trying to kill you," I said. "But even if you're right, are you sure you want to go through with this? When we bury things so deep it takes a Rabolian to dig them out, they're probably better left alone."

"I've got to do it. It's the only way I'll ever get her to leave me alone. And . . ."

"And?"

"I've got to know."

"Okay, I've got another question. Why are you pretending to be carnies?

"Duristan works for a carnival," explained Crunchtime. "Mrs. Vanderwycke is no fool. She knows Andy's best defense against her is the knowledge of what he saw all those years ago, and she knows that the most likely person to unlock that information is a Rabolian."

"All I've heard so far is that Duristan works for a carnival," I said. "Why not just walk up and pay him to do whatever it is that he does?"

"When someone tried to kill Andy on Brookmandor II, we decided that he couldn't continue to travel without a disguise, and I imposed upon an old friendship with a fellow Gromite to get us jobs here. Andy never takes off his clown makeup, not in public, not backstage. We felt that we would attract no undue attention if we went to Port Samarkand as performers."

I sighed deeply. One of the problems with novices in any line of work is that the ideas they think are new and unique are usually old enough to have long white whiskers.

"So where do you stand, Mr. Masters?" asked Andy. "Are you going to stop us?"

"Jake," I corrected him. "And I'm thinking about it."

"Think fast. We're running out of time."

"I'll make you a deal," I said at last.

"What kind of deal?" asked Andy suspiciously.

"I'll go with you to Port Samarkand," I said. "If this whole thing is a false alarm and you don't know anything that would make your mother want to kill you, you agree to come back to Odysseus with me. I don't give a damn if you just walk in the door, say 'Hi, Mom,' and walk right back out. I'm being paid to take you back, not to make sure that you stay."

"And if I *do* know something?"

"We'll play it by ear," I said. "No promises. That's my deal. Take it, or we go back to Odysseus on the next ship bound for Iliad system."

Andy looked at Crunchtime, as if expecting the Gromite to say something, but the alien kept his mouth shut, and finally the kid nodded his agreement.

"Okay, Jake, you've got a deal. Now let's get the hell out of here."

The three of us took an express aircar to the spaceport. Crunchtime had boarding codes for both of them, so they boarded immediately. I had to buy my passage, but the flight was half empty and since we were late, they let me board and pay the robot host once we'd taken off.

Crunchtime had to sit in the alien section, so Andy and I sat together toward the front of the ship. The kid was still in his clown makeup, which attracted some stares. One guy wasn't laughing, just staring, and I thought I'd seen him before.

I nudged Andy with an elbow.

"What is it?" he asked.

"Don't make a production of it, but take a look at the guy across the aisle, maybe three rows back. He's wearing a brown tunic, and he's got a scar on his chin. Tell me if you recognize him."

"Yes," he said a moment later. "He was at the carnival every night."

"Is he the guy who tried to kill you on Brookmandor II?"

"I don't know. It was dark, and he was too far away."

"But he was definitely hanging around the carny?"

"Yes." He looked nervous. "What do you do about him?"

"Nothing—yet."

"Are you going to wait until he shoots me?" demanded Andy.

"He has every right to be on the ship," I said. "At least now I know what he looks like, so I can spot him on Port Samarkand."

"What if he shoots me right at the spaceport? I mean, you're carrying a gun, so why shouldn't he have one too?"

"My gun is sealed," I explained. "And it'll stay that way until they automatically deactivate the seal as we leave the Port Samarkand spaceport. That's the rules, kid. The only thing I can use it for is a club. If he's got one, it's in the same condition. Besides, no one's going to try to kill you at a spaceport. They've got more security there than anywhere else on the planet."

"I hope you're right," he said dubiously.

"I am," I said. And added silently: *I hope.*

We braked to sub-light speeds four hours into the voyage, and touched down on Port Samarkand a few minutes later. Before we left the ship we got the usual information about atmospheric content, climate, gravity, time zones, the whole deal. Humans sit at the front and exit first, and once we got off we waited at Customs for Crunchtime to catch up with us.

"Maybe I'd better go wash this makeup off before I pass through Customs," suggested Andy.

"Why bother?" I asked. "Your passport says you're an entertainer. Nobody will stop you. If the clerk asks, just say you're late for a performance."

"It'll never work," he said, but of course it did. Nobody questioned him, and we passed through Customs without any problems.

We stopped at an information computer to find out where Duristan's carnival was playing, but even before I posed the question I saw the guy in the brown tunic head off for the men's room.

"You take care of this," I said to Andy. "I'll be back in a minute."

The guy was standing in front of a sink when I got there.

"Warm," he muttered, and warm water poured out. "Soap." When he was done he said "Dry," and a burst of warm air blew across his hands. He saw me in the mirror, but didn't even bother to turn and face me while he was drying his hands.

"I figured we'd talk sooner or later, Mr. Masters," he said.

"How do you know my name?"

"My employer told me you'd be traveling with the kid."

"So she's paying you to kill him while I take the fall?" I said.

"Be a little more discreet, Mr. Masters," he said easily. "There are security monitors everywhere." Suddenly he smiled. "And I work for *him*, not her."

"Him?" I repeated.

"The father," he said, making sure he didn't mention Ben Jeffries's name aloud. "I'm here to make sure nothing happens to his son."

"Then that wasn't you on Brookmandor?"

"Not the way you think."

"I don't follow you."

"I was on Brookmandor, but I didn't try to kill him. The only reason he made it to Aristides is because I"—he remembered the camera—"*hindered* the man who was after him."

My guess was that he hindered him right into the morgue.

"So the kid's father is paying you to be his guardian angel," I said. "He offered the same job to me." I frowned. "Why? He doesn't even like him."

"There's an outstanding warrant for my employer on Odysseus," said the man.

"Yeah, I know. For murder."

"That's right." He paused. "He's committed a lot of crimes,

including his share of murders—but that wasn't one of them. He wants to go back to Odysseus, but he can't set foot on the planet while that warrant's in effect. If this Rabolian can unlock information that the mother did it, they'll drop the warrant."

"What's on Odysseus that's so important?"

"I don't know and I don't care. Maybe it's loot he hid there twenty years ago, maybe it's something else. My job is just to make sure no harm comes to the kid until he reaches this Rabolian telepath." He paused again. "I'm glad we're on the same side. I wasn't sure when you showed up. I was afraid you were going to take him back, and then I'd have had to kill you." He didn't choose his words for the security monitors this time; they don't arrest you for what you might have done under other circumstances.

He could have sounded aggressive or arrogant, but he said it so matter-of-factly that I realized killing me would have been nothing personal. It was just business to him. He didn't care whether I lived or died, he didn't care what reason Jeffries had for wanting to return to Odysseus, he probably didn't care what was buried in Andy's memory. He just did his job and never got involved. Hard to like a guy like that, but equally hard to hate him. He was just another fact of Nature, like a refreshing breeze that might or might not turn into a hurricane. You may get out of its way, but there's no sense getting mad at it.

"Okay, we're allies, at least for the time being," I said. "You got a name?"

"Lots of 'em."

"None of which you want to share?"

"What purpose would it serve?"

And that way no one could beat it out of me.

"I've got to call you something. How's Boris?"

"As good as any other."

We had nothing further to say, so Boris went back into the main lobby of the spaceport. I waited another couple of minutes, then followed him. I didn't want anyone to see us together. I couldn't hide the fact that I was traveling with Andy, but if anyone was watching us, I didn't want them to know Boris was part of the team.

"We found Duristan," said Andy as I walked up to him and Crunchtime. "He's about ten minutes from here." He sneaked a look at Boris. "Did you find out who he is?"

"Don't worry about him," I said. "He's on our side."

"What!" It was more an exclamation than a question.

"He works for your father," I answered. "He's the guy who saved your ass back on Brookmandor."

I thought the kid was going to walk over and thank him, so I grabbed his arm. "Just ignore him," I said. "He'll be a lot more effective if it doesn't look like we all know each other."

The three of us walked to an aircar and told it to take us to the carnival where Duristan was working. As we glided a foot or two above the ground, I turned to Andy.

"I'm going to get out maybe four hundred yards from the carny and walk the rest of the way," I told him.

"Why?"

"You're supposed to be a clown and a juggler, remember? What am I—your agent?"

"I hadn't thought of that," he admitted. "We'll apply for the jobs, and then—"

"Why bother?" I said. "You've seen how fast acts come and go at these shows. Just walk around like you belong. If anyone stops you, then play dumb and say you're looking for work."

"That makes sense," he agreed.

"All right," I said. "I'll find out where Duristan hangs out when he's not performing and meet you there."

"Okay," he said as the carnival came into view and I ordered the aircar to stop.

"Remember," I said as I climbed out. "If you see Boris—that's your father's man—don't stare at him or try to talk to him."

Then I was on the street and the aircar shot ahead. I walked up to the ticket booth, paid for my admission with cash in case my name had shown up on any computers, and entered the show.

Duristan didn't figure to be in the main arena—everyone knew that Rabolians were telepaths, and most people didn't want Duristan or any other Rabolian having a little fun at their expense by revealing some of their more embarrassing secrets to the audience. He figured to set up shop as a fortune teller or something similar, so I went to the rows of games and exhibits, looking for him.

He was there all right, sitting all alone in a glittering turban and a satin robe covered with the symbols of the zodiac. That outfit would have looked mildly silly on a human; it looked positively ludicrous on a tripodal Rabolian who was as wide as he was tall.

There was no sign of Andy and Crunchtime, so I went to the next booth, picked up a toy pulse gun, and began shooting at images of alien predators that seemed to be leaping through the air at me. I hit the first two. When I missed the third the creature smiled and informed me in exquisite Terran that I was lunch, and once he digested me—it would take about three seconds—I could play again for another twenty credits. I decided not to.

I killed a little more time walking up and down the rows of games—they looked exactly like the games I'd seen on Aristides and in every other carnival I'd ever been to—and then headed back toward Duristan's booth. I saw Andy and Crunchtime approaching it, and then I heard Boris yell "Duck!"

The flare from a pulse gun nailed Andy in the right shoulder and spun him around. Boris jumped into sight, screecher in hand, and fired a blast of solid sound at the man with the pulse gun. He dropped like a rock, but then Boris fell backward, a black smoking hole in his belly. I spotted the guy who'd done it and downed him with my laser pistol. Then I raced up to Andy, who had dropped to one knee.

"Are you okay, kid?" I asked.

He nodded, and I went over to Boris. One look and I knew he wasn't going to make it to the hospital.

"Did I get him?" he whispered as I kneeled down beside him.

"You got one of them. I got another. How many were there?"

"Only two, I hope," he said with a weak grin. "I never saw the second one."

"I'll tell Jeffries what happened. If you have any family, does he know how to contact them?"

"No family," Boris grated. His hand reached up and clawed my shoulder. "You're his guardian angel now," he said, and died.

I walked back to Andy and helped him to his feet. "Can you stand on your own?" I asked.

He didn't answer. At first I thought he was too weak, or had lost too much blood. Then I saw him staring at something, and I followed his gaze.

Duristan had fallen out of his booth and lay sprawled on the ground, dead. A wild shot from the pulse gun had taken the top of his head off.

"Shit!" I muttered. "Come on, let's get you out of here."

But the local security team had shown up by then, and held us until we could be turned over to the police. The police surgeon treated Andy's wound and gave him something for the pain.

They kept us most of the night, but the few people who'd been on the scene verified our stories and they finally let us go about six hours later. They'd probably have kept me until the inquest, but there were so many warrants out for the two dead men that they figured I'd done them a favor.

"What now?" asked Andy as we walked out of the station. "Are you taking me back?"

"Eventually," I replied. "Let me get to a subspace radio first."

We found one in a local hotel, and I contacted Jeffries back on Corvus II. I told him what had happened and that Boris was dead, then waited about three minutes for him to receive the message and for his reply to get back to me.

"Where are you going next?" he asked.

"I'm being paid to return him to Odysseus, and that's what I plan to do," I said. "But if you'll pay our passage, we'll stop at Rabol on the way." I'd have paid it if he said no, but I didn't see any reason to tell him that.

"It's a deal. By the time you get to the spaceport the tickets will be waiting for you."

"There are three of us," I said. "Don't forget the Gromite."

"Right."

He broke the connection, I told Andy and Crunchtime what he'd said, and we had the hotel summon an aircar.

The spaceport wasn't crowded, but every face looked like a potential assassin. I went to the men's room with Andy while he removed his makeup—there was no sense pretending to be a clown any longer—and then we went to the waiting area. Crunchtime was already sitting in the aliens' section when we got there.

A pretty young redhead in a spaceport uniform walked up to the passengers, asking each if they wanted anything to drink while they waited to board the ship. Andy asked for a local fruit drink, and I requested a cup of coffee. She returned a few minutes later, passing out drinks and pocketing payments and tips. Finally she approached Andy and me.

"Your drinks," she announced, handing us each what we had ordered.

"Thank you," I said. I grabbed her wrist as she turned to go. "Andy, don't touch it."

I could see puzzlement in his eyes and fear in hers.

"Whatever they paid you for this, it wasn't enough," I told her. "Who hired you?"

"Please!" she said. "You're hurting me!"

"I'll do a lot more than hurt you if I don't get an answer."

"Security will be here any second!"

"Then Andy will give them his drink, they'll analyze it, and you'll be about seventy-five years old before you see the outside of a prison again," I said. "Now, who are you working for?"

"I don't know! It was a man I'd never seen before! He said it was a joke—that it would get the young man drunk and acting silly! I swear it!"

"What was his name?"

"I don't know! I never saw him before! He gave me fifty credits. It was a joke!"

The speaker system announced that our ship was ready for boarding.

"I'm going to let you go," I said. "Just walk away like nothing's happened. We're taking the drink onboard with us. You say a word to anyone, we give the drink to the police and tell them where we got it. Do you understand me?"

She nodded her head and I let her go. She walked away as fast as she could without breaking into a run, and was soon out of sight.

"How did you know?" whispered Andy, his eyes wide.

"She collected money from every other customer before she gave them their drinks, but she was so anxious for you to down yours that she never asked us to pay her."

"That's an awfully little thing to go on," he said.

"Wait for big things in this business and you don't celebrate too many birthdays." I stood up. "Let's get on the ship."

I took the drink from him as he stood up. We passed a row of potted plants on the way to the hatch, and I dumped the contents into the last of them.

"That was our evidence!" he said.

"Do you want to go to Rabol, or do you want to stick around and press charges?" I asked. "Besides, they won't let you take an opened drink onto a ship. The jump to light speeds does strange things to it, even in a pressurized cabin. If she really worked here, she'd have known I was bluffing."

As we took our seats, he still looked disturbed. "Maybe we should have stuck around long enough to see her put in jail."

"She's just a dupe," I said. "And don't forget—there's still someone on Aristides who wants you dead."

"Maybe she lied," he persisted. "Maybe she knew it was poison. Maybe she poisoned it herself."

"I doubt it, but even if you're right we've seen the last of her. She knows we can identify her."

"But—"

"Look, kid," I said firmly, "I'm not a cop anymore. I'm being paid to get you home in one piece, not to put all the bad guys in jail."

He finally shut up. The trip was uneventful—almost all trips are uneventful these days—and we touched down on Rabol sixteen hours later.

The air was thin, the sun was so far away that it seemed like twilight even though it was midday, and the gravity was 1.23 Standard, which meant that you felt like you were carrying a forty-pound rock on your back.

There were a few humans in the spaceport, as well as some Mollutei and a tall, long-legged Domarian, but mostly there were hundreds of little round Rabolians scurrying all over the place.

As we approached the Customs booth, I pulled out my passport disk.

"Put it away, Jacob Masters," said the Rabolian working the booth. "Your passport is in order, but you have no business on Rabol. You will remain here while Andrew Vanderwycke is allowed to pass through Customs. The Gromite Crozchziim will stay here with you."

"You got all that out of my mind in five seconds?" I said.

"Yes," he replied. "I apologize for not reading it faster, but I am being bombarded by thoughts from the Customs booths on each side of me."

"If you're that good, why don't you just tell Andy what he needs to know right now, and we'll get back on the ship before it can take off again."

"I would do irrepairable harm to his mind if I were to probe as deeply as required," answered the Customs officer. "He must go to an expert who can extract the necessary information without damaging him."

"Who do I see?" asked Andy, who was standing behind me.

"I have already made the appointment," came the answer. "Please pass through, and you will find an escort waiting to take you there."

The kid did as he was told, and Crunchtime and I went to a waiting area. Since this wasn't a Democracy planet, humans and non-humans weren't segregated, and we sat down together.

"How long do you think this will take?" he asked.

"I don't know. But given how fast this guy read our minds, it could be just a few minutes." I looked back at the Customs official. "I'm surprised he was so polite."

"Why should that surprise you?"

"Because on a world of telepaths, why would anyone learn manners or white lies or any of the social graces when everyone knows exactly what you're really thinking?" I replied. "I'll bet it's probably just a courtesy for off-worlders. They probably insulted the first few, read their minds, and figured out what was required."

"Why would Duristan leave Rabol to take a job in a sideshow?" mused Crunchtime.

"Maybe Mrs. Duristan didn't like what he was thinking every time a pretty young Rabolian twiched by," I said. "Maybe he had an urge to cheat at poker. Maybe he just wondered what the rest of the galaxy looked like; after all, a traveling carnival sees an awful lot of it." I got to my feet. "Wait here."

"Where are you going?" he asked.

"To the subspace sending station."

When I got there I fed Beatrice Vanderwycke's code into the machine, and a couple of minutes later her holograph appeared before me. It kept trying to break up but somehow preserved its integrity.

"Mr. Masters," she said to my image. "You were supposed to report to me at regular intervals."

"Every fourth or fifth day," I said smoothly. "And here I am."

"I want a progress report."

"I've got him."

"Excellent. How soon can you have him here?"

"Five days, maybe four," I said. "It depends on what kind of connections I can make."

"Why so long?"

"It's very complicated. I'll explain when we get there."

"I'll see you then."

She broke the connection.

"He's in fine health," I said sardonically to the spot where her image had been. "I was sure you'd be concerned."

I returned to Crunchtime and sat down next to him.

"You'll be pleased to know that Mrs. Vanderwycke expressed no interest in you whatsoever," I said. "She never even mentioned your name."

"You contacted her?" he said, surprised.

"Just now."

"But she's been trying to have Andy killed!" he said. "Now she'll be prepared for him when he returns to Odysseus!"

"I told her we'd be there in four or five days," I explained. "After I checked the flight schedule. If Andy can get back here in the next hour, we can get on a ship to Pollux IV, transfer to one bound for the Iliad system, and be there in less than a day. If she's setting up a trap, she's going to be three days late."

"I see," he said, his eyes widening. "It's probably just as well that we remain isolated from the Rabolian population. If telepaths cannot lie, observing the way your brain works might drive them all mad."

"I assume that's a compliment," I said dryly.

He was silent for so long that I began wondering if it really *was* a compliment after all. Then he nudged me and pointed across the spaceport huge lobby. "Here he comes."

The kid was walking toward us, accompanied by a Rabolian, who left him at the entrance to the waiting area. Andy came over and sat down, his face an expressionless mask.

"How did it go?" I asked.

"It was an . . . unusual . . . experience," he said. "I hope I never undergo anything like it again."

"Did it hurt much?"

"Not the way you mean," he said. "I learned what I needed to learn." He shuddered. "I also learned things no one should have to know about themselves."

He refused to say any more about it, and we soon boarded the ship to the Pollux system. We had a four-hour layover there, and I realized I hadn't eaten since we'd left Aristides, so we stopped at a restaurant in the spaceport. They didn't mind that Crunchtime was with us, but the chairs couldn't accomodate him, so he waited outside. I wanted a big, thick steak, but when I saw the prices—even mutated cattle couldn't metabolize the stuff that passed for grass on Pollux IV, and all their beef was imported—I settled for a soya substitute instead. I kept telling myself that it tasted just like grade-A prime beef, but my stomach knew I was lying. Andy just wanted water, and when they insisted that he had to order something if he was going to sit there, I told him to order a beer and I drank it when it arrived.

Then we waited for the boarding call, and finally clambered onto the ship that would take us back to Odysseus. After we'd been traveling for a couple of hours, I turned to Andy. A cartoon holo was running on his entertainment center, but he was staring through it, not at it.

"Are you going to be okay, kid?" I asked.

"Yes, I'm fine."

"We don't have to go right to your home," I continued. "We could go to the the police first, maybe bring some of them along."

"We'll have all the backup we need," said Andy. "You don't think my father is going to let anyone kill me before I prove he didn't commit that murder on Odysseus, do you?"

"No, I don't."

"I know he doesn't give a damn about me," he continued. "The only reason he wants me alive is to clear him so he can go back to Odysseus and pick up whatever he left behind from some robbery."

"How come he never asked you to get it and bring it to him?" I asked.

"He doesn't trust me," said the kid. "He doesn't trust anyone." He paused. "Before we touch down, I'll have my pocket computer prepare a cube proving that my father was innocent, that my mother committed the murder he's wanted for and a lot worse crimes as well. But—"

"I know," I interrupted. "I won't turn it over to your dad until after you see your mother, or he won't have any reason to protect you."

He looked relieved that we were on the same page. "Right."

"How are you holding up, kid?" I asked him.

"I'm not afraid," he said calmly. "For the first time in my life, I'm not afraid of her. Besides," he added, "you saved my life at the carnival on Port Samarkand, and again at the spaceport. You'll save it on Odysseus if you have to."

I wanted to deny it, but I knew deep down he was right. Maybe I wasn't a cop any longer, but I still had an urge to see justice done. I'd do whatever I could to keep him alive, regardless of the risk. I began to really resent the guardian angel business.

He stopped talking, and I closed my eyes. I was just going to rest them for a moment, but the next thing I knew he was nudging me and telling me that we'd entered Odysseus's stratosphere.

"Here," he said, slipping a cube into my pocket. "I trust you to know when and how to use it."

"I appreciate your trust, but weren't you going to make half a dozen copies and ship them to various lock boxes around the Democracy?" I asked.

"I've been thinking about it," he said. "The information the cube contains is my insurance only while it's a threat, something to hold over her. If someone actually releases it, she'll go to jail, but she's vindictive enough to put a hit out on me. One cube's as good as twenty to make her leave me alone, and it's probably safer for me."

"That's some family you got yourself, kid," I said.

"My father's not so bad," he replied.

Hatchet Ben Jeffries, extortionist and bank robber and murderer, Hatchet Ben who considered his son a useless weakling worth keeping alive only until he could get his hands on whatever he'd left behind on Odysseus, wasn't so bad compared to his mother. It made me understand why he didn't have any friends, why the only thing he trusted was an alien with an unpronounceable name.

The ship touched down in a few more minutes, and I turned to the kid as we got off. "We're not going to your mother's house," I said. "It's too dangerous."

"Why?" he replied. "She's not going to do a thing until she finds out what I know and who I've told."

"Just the same, I want to meet her on neutral ground. She may have ways of extracting the information in private."

"A restaurant?" he suggested.

I considered it. "No, too easy for her to pay off the owner, or plant her men at every nearby table." I looked at the big Welcome to Odysseus screen that greeted newcomers with a list of the day's major events. "Okay," I said, "there's a murderball game going on right now in the stadium. That's about two miles from here. I'll tell her to meet us outside the box office in"—I checked the starting time—"about an hour. The game figures to be over by then, and there'll be thousands of people streaming out."

"You really think I need this kind of protection?" he asked.

"Kid, I don't even know if *this* will be adequate, but it's better than going to your home."

"All right," he consented. "You're the boss—at least, until I see her face-to-face."

I went to a vidphone booth and called Beatrice Vanderwycke. When she recognized me her image registered surprise.

"Mr. Masters," she said. "I hadn't expected to hear from you for three more days. Where are you?"

"At the Odysseus spaceport."

"Excellent! How soon can I expect you here?"

"There's been a change of plans," I said. "We're not coming to the house."

"I am paying you to find my son and deliver him to me, Mr. Masters. That was our agreement."

"I found him, and I'm going to deliver him," I replied. "But there was nothing in our agreement that stipulated I had to return him to your home."

"Where will you deliver him?"

"The box office at the murderball stadium, one hour from now," I said. "And Mrs. Vanderwycke?"

"Yes?"

"I want to be paid in cash."

She gave me a look that said she'd rather pay me in red-hot pokers. "I'll be there," she said, and broke the connection.

Since we had an hour, we began walking to the stadium. I stopped when we were about a quarter-mile away from it.

"What now?" asked Andy.

"No crowd," I pointed out. "The game hasn't let out yet. We'd be sitting ducks if we went there now."

We ducked into a coffee shop. They wouldn't serve Crunchtime at our table, but there was an alien section, and he sat there.

"I don't see anyone," said Andy, staring at the stadium through a window.

"Neither do I."

"You look disappointed."

"I am. Not surprised, just disappointed."

"Why to both?"

"I assume any men your mother hired are too good to be spotted, and I know your dad's got nothing but professionals on his payroll. So I'm not surprised that I can't find them—but I wish I knew where they were. Your mother's muscle may not be here yet—after all, she just found out we were on the planet forty-five minutes ago—but I have to assume your father has had some men tailing us since we came through Customs. I just want to know where everyone is so I know when and where to duck."

"Maybe being in a crowd will scare them off," he said.

"Kid, the safest place to kill someone is in the middle of a crowd," I told him. "They'll give the cops a hundred different descriptions of you, and that's if they don't start accusing each other first."

"I never thought of that."

"You never had to. And the best way to kill someone in a crowd or anywhere else is to crack his head open with a blunt instrument. Not much ballistics can do with a club or a hammer."

"So much for all those locked-room mysteries I used to watch," he said with a smile.

"They're good entertainment," I said. "But mighty few murders are committed by left-handed tightrope-walking midgets. They're committed by professionals who do it for a living and know all the angles."

Suddenly we could hear a huge roar, and then, about a minute later, the first people began leaving the stadium. Soon there were more and more, a veritable flood of Men and aliens.

"Okay," I said, getting to my feet. "Let me make a pit stop and then we'll go."

I entered the men's room, pulled Andy's cube out of my pocket, and hid it inside a ventilation shaft where the wall joined the ceiling. If Beatrice Vanderwycke's men got the drop on me, they weren't going to find it when they frisked me.

I returned to the table, left some money on it, told Andy to get up, and signaled Crunchtime to join us. The three of us left the restaurant and approached the stadium. Making any progress against all those people who were in such a hurry to get home was like swimming upstream against a raging river, but we finally made it.

"I don't see her," said Andy as he stood in front of a ticket booth.

"She'll be here," I said with absolute certainty.

"Maybe she can't see us where we're standing," he said.

"Then she'll find us. Stay right where you are, with your back against the booth. If anything's going to happen, let's make sure it happens in front of us."

And then, suddenly, she was there. I never saw her approaching us, but she was standing maybe six feet away, staring coldly at the kid.

"You've put me to a lot of trouble, Andrew," she said.

"You put me to more," he answered. "Years and years of it." His voice quavered just a bit. He was still scared of her, but he wasn't going to back off. I was proud of him. "But it's over now," he continued. "My nightmares are gone"—he forced a smile—"and yours are about to begin."

"I'm sure I don't know what you're talking about, Andrew," she said. "You're back, and that's all that matters. Your room is ready for you. Let's go home."

The crowd was getting thicker. It was difficult to hear over the noise. A man in a gray outfit jostled against me and apologized.

"It won't work, Mother," he said. "I *know*."

"What do you think you know?" she asked, her face reflecting her contempt for him.

"I know who you killed, I know how you made it look like Father did it, I know where you hid the body, and I know that even after all these years there's enough DNA evidence to convict you."

"That's a very dangerous thing to say, even to a loving mother," replied Beatrice Vanderwycke.

"Are you threatening me, Mother?" said Andy. "Because if you are, you should know that if anything happens to me, Jake will turn everything over to the police."

She caught it instantly.

You damned fool! I thought. *You just told her that you and I are the only ones with the proof!*

She turned to the man in the gray outfit, who was still standing near us.

"Kill them," she said calmly.

He pulled a pulse gun, but before he could fire it a laser beam caught him in the chest and hurled him backward. I looked around. It was the small guy from Jeffries's house. Before I could nod a thanks he keeled over, and suddenly there was a small firefight going on between her men and Jeffries's men.

People in the crowd started screaming and running. A couple of kids got knocked down, and one got trampled pretty badly. So did an old man. There was confusion everywhere—and suddenly there was a small screecher in her hand, and it was aimed at me.

"No!" cried Andy. He dove for the weapon, but she was already pressing the firing mechanism, and he got the full force of the solid sound on his left temple.

He dropped like a brick, and she turned to fire at me, but I had my burner out, and I put a black bubbling hole right between her cold hate-filled eyes.

The instant Andy and his mother fell to the ground the firefight stopped. No matter which side they were on, they seemed to know that everything was over. If they worked for Jeffries, they'd failed to save his son, and if they worked for Beatrice Vanderwycke, they hadn't been able to protect her.

Andy twitched feebly, and I knelt down next to him.

"Crunchtime, he's alive!" I yelled. "Get some help!"

There was no answer. I turned to look for him, and saw the Gromite lying on the ground in a pool of pink blood. He'd stopped a shot that was meant for mother or son, it no longer mattered which.

The police showed up a few minutes later. They raced Andy off to the hospital, and I spent the next four hours telling my story over and over again. Finally enough eyewitnesses testified that I'd shot Beatrice Vanderwycke in self-defense that they had to let me go.

I rushed to the hospital to see how the kid was doing. He was in surgery, and six hours later they guided the airsled out. It was two days before he woke up, and he wasn't the same Andy Vanderwycke I'd been traveling with. His eyes were dull, his face expressionless, and he didn't speak.

I asked his doctor how long it would be before he recovered.

"He took the full force of a sonic pistol in his head at a range of perhaps two feet," said the doctor. "It's burned out half his neural circuits."

"When will he be himself again?"

"Quite possibly never."

"He's just going to lie there and stare for the rest of his life?" I asked.

"In time he'll respond to his name, and be able to locomote and feed himself. Eventually he'll comprehend about thirty words. There's always a chance that he'll recover, of course, but the odds are not in favor of it. You have to understand, Mr. Masters—he's lucky to be alive."

I stared at the kid. "I wouldn't call *this* luck," I said bitterly.

I had one last stop to make, one loose end to take care of. I went to the coffee shop by the stadium, waited until the men's room was empty, and made sure the cube was still there. I had every intention of turning it over to Ben Jeffies, but first I wanted to make sure Andy would be taken care of once he got his hands on it.

I caught the next ship to the Corvus system, and a few hours later they passed me through the security checkpoints on the Jeffries estate and ushered me into the mansion.`

I cooled my heels for a few minutes in a library that was filled with unread books and unwatched cubes, and then was summoned to the study. Jeffries, all steel and gray, was waiting for me.

"I heard you had some trouble on Odysseus," he said. "I lost three men there."

"Yeah, it got messy." I paused. "I'm afraid I've got some bad news for you."

"You don't have what I need?"

I blinked. "I'm talking about your son. He took a shot meant for me. There's every likelihood that he's going to be a vegetable for the rest of his life."

"I don't give a shit about that!" he snapped. "I need to get that murder warrant quashed so I can get to Odysseus! Do you have any idea what he learned on Rabol?"

You son of a bitch, I thought. *Your kid has been turned into a potted plant getting the proof you need, and all you care about is picking up some loot you left on Odysseus twenty years ago.*

It was time, I decided, for the guardian angel to perform one last duty.

"He said he could prove that you were innocent of the murder on Odysseus," I said. "But he was shot before he could tell me the details or make any record of them."

"So I'll talk to him and find out."

I shook my head. "He won't know you or understand you. His neural circuits are blown."

"Is there any chance he'll come out of it?"

I shrugged. "Who knows? There's always a chance."

"All right, Jake," he said, pulling out a wad of bills. "I told you I'd pay you if Betty didn't. This will cover your time and expenses. Our business is done."

His men escorted me back to the spaceport and stayed with me until the ship took off. By the time I'd reached Odysseus Andy Vanderwycke had already been transferred to the most expensive, most exclusive facility on Deluros VIII.

That was three years ago. I haven't seen or spoken to the kid since they took him away. I stop by the coffee shop every few months to make sure the cube is still there. If the medical team on Deluros VIII can fix Andy, I'll turn it over to his father. And if not . . . well, one of these days I'll take the kid on a little trip to Rabol and see if they can straighten out all the crooked wiring and fuse some loose connections. I'll also remind them that there are a couple of areas that are better left alone.

Who knows? Maybe one team or the other can pull it off. After all, aren't angels the harbingers of miracles?

Old MacDonald Had a Farm

We were driving around, going from the post office to the supermarket or some such, and Carol kept humming the opening two lines of an old nursery song. Endlessly. She wasn't even aware that she was doing it, until I rather irritably pointed it out to her and suggested that she hum some *other* nursery rhyme before the repetitions drove me crazy. Which one did I want, she asked. I don't know, I said; maybe "Old MacDonald Had a Farm," which was the only one I could think of on the spur of the moment.

And since I'm a science fiction writer, the second I said it I began wondering what kind of a farm Old MacDonald would have maybe two hundred years from now. I had the story plotted out before we got home, and I wrote it that night. (I always write at night, never during the day. A lot of writers seem to share that vampirish tendancy.)

"Old MacDonald Had a Farm" was a Hugo nominee in 2002, won the Asimov's Readers Poll, and won a Spanish award the following year.

I came to praise Caesar, not to bury him.

Hell, we all did.

The farm spread out before us, green and rolling, dotted with paddocks and water troughs. It looked like the kind of place you wish your parents had taken you when you were a kid and the world was still full of wonders.

Well, the world may not have been full of wonders any longer, but the farm was. Problem was, they weren't exactly the kind you used to dream of—unless you were coming down from a *really* bad acid trip.

The farm was the brainchild of Caesar Claudius MacDonald. He'd finally knuckled under to public pressure and agreed to show the place off to the press. That's where I came in.

My name's McNair. I used to have a first name, but I dumped it when I decided a one-word byline was more memorable. I work for the *SunTrib*, the biggest newstape in the Chicago area. I'd just broken the story that put Billy Cheever away after the cops had been after him for years. What I wanted for my efforts was my own syndicated column; what I got was a trip to the farm.

For a guy no one knew much about, one who almost never appeared in public, MacDonald had managed to make his name a household word in something less than two years. Even though one of his corporations owned our publishing company, we didn't have much on him in our files, just what all the other news bureaus had: he'd earned a couple of PhDs, he was a widower who by all accounts had been faithful to his wife, he'd inherited a bundle and then made a lot more on his own.

MacDonald was a Colorado native who emigrated to New Zealand's South Island, bought a 40,000-hectare farm, and hired a lot of technicians over the years. If anyone wondered why a huge South Island farm didn't have any sheep, they probably just figured he had worked out some kind of tax dodge.

Hell, that's what I thought too. I mean, why else would someone with his money bury himself on the underside of the globe for half a lifetime?

Then, a week after his sixty-sixth birthday, MacDonald made the Announcement. That's the year they had food riots in Calcutta and Rio and Manila, when the world was finding out that it was easier to produce eleven billion living human beings than to feed them.

Some people say he created a new life-form. Some say he produced a hybrid (though not a single geneticist agrees with that). Some—I used to snicker at them—say that he had delved into mysteries that Man Was Not Meant to Know.

According to the glowing little computer cube they handed out, MacDonald and his crew spent close to three decades manipulating DNA molecules in ways no one had ever thought of before. He did a lot of trial and error work with embryos, until he finally came up with the prototype he sought. Then he spent a few more years making certain that it would breed true. And finally he announced his triumph to the world.

Caesar MacDonald's masterpiece was the Butterball, a meat animal that matured at six months of age and could reproduce at eight months, with a four-week gestation period. It weighed four hundred pounds at maturity, and every portion of its body could be consumed by Earth's starving masses, even the bones.

That in itself was a work of scientific brilliance—but to me the true stroke of genius was the astonishing efficiency of the Butterballs' digestive systems. An elephant, back when elephants still existed, would eat about six hundred pounds of vegetation per day, but could only use about forty percent of it, and passed the rest as dung. Cattle and pigs, the most common meat animals prior to the Butterballs, were somewhat more efficient, but they, too, wasted a lot of expensive feed.

The Butterballs, on the other hand, utilized one hundred percent of what they were fed. Every pellet of food they ingested went right into building meat that was meticulously bioengineered to please almost every palate. Anyway, that's what the endless series of P.R. releases said.

MacDonald had finally consented to allow a handful of pool reporters to come see for themselves.

We were hoping for a look at MacDonald too, maybe even an interview with the Great Man. But when we got there, we learned that he had been in seclusion for months. Turned out he was suffering from depression, which I would have thought would be the last thing to affect humanity's latest savior, but who knows what depresses a genius? Maybe, like Alexander, he wanted more worlds to conquer, or maybe he was sorry that Butterballs didn't weigh eight hundred pounds. Hell, maybe he had just worked too hard for too long, or maybe he realized that he was a lot closer to the end of life than the beginning and didn't like it much. Most likely, he just didn't consider us important enough to bother with.

Whatever the reason, we were greeted not by MacDonald himself, but by a flack named Judson Cotter. I figured he had to work in P.R.; his hair was a little too perfect, his suit too up-to-the-minute, his hands too soft for him to have been anything else but a pitchman.

After he apologized for MacDonald's absence, he launched into a worshipful biography of his boss, not deviating one iota from the holobio they'd shown us on the plane trip.

"But I suspect you're here to see the farm," he concluded after paraphrasing the bio for five minutes.

"No," muttered Julie Balch from *NyVid*, "we came all this way to stand in this cold wet breeze and admire your clothes."

A few of us laughed, and Cotter looked just a bit annoyed. I made a mental note to buy her a drink when the tour was done.

"Now let me see a show of hands," said Cotter. "Has anyone here ever seen a live Butterball?"

Where did they find you? I thought. *If we'd seen one, do you really think we'd have flown all the way to hell and gone just to see another?*

I looked around. No one had raised a hand. Which figured. To the best of my knowledge, nobody who didn't work for MacDonald had ever seen a Butterball in the flesh, and only a handful of photos and holos had made it out to the general public. There was even a rumor that all of MacDonald's employees had to sign a secrecy oath.

"There's a reason, of course," continued Cotter smoothly. "Until the international courts verified Mr. MacDonald's patent, there was always a chance that some unscrupulous individual or even a rogue nation would try to duplicate the Butterball. For that reason, while we have shipped and sold its meat all over the world, always with the inspection and approval of the local food and health authorities, we have not allowed anyone to see or examine the animals themselves. But now that the courts have ruled in our favor, we have opened our doors to the press." *Screaming bloody murder every step of the way*, I thought.

"You represent the first group of journalists to tour the farm, but there will be many more, and we will even allow Sir Richard Perigrine to make one of his holographic documentaries here at the farm." He paused. "We plan to open it to public tours in the next two or three years."

Suddenly a bunch of bullshit alarms began going off inside my head.

"Why not sooner, now that you've won your case?" asked Julie, who looked like she was hearing the same alarms.

"We'd rather that *you* bring the initial stories and holos of the Butterballs to the public," answered Cotter.

"That's very generous of you," she persisted. "But you still haven't told us why."

"We have our reasons," he said. "They will be made apparent to you before the tour is over."

My old friend Jake Monfried of the *SeattleDisk* sidled over to me. "I hope I can stay awake that long," he said sardonically. "It's all rubbish anyway."

"I know," I said. "Their rivals don't even need the damned holos.

Any high school kid could take a hunk of Butterball steak and come up with a clone."

"So why haven't they?" asked Julie.

"Because MacDonald's got fifty lawyers on his payroll for every scientist," answered Jake. He paused, his expression troubled. "Still, this guy's lying to us—and it's a stupid lie, and he doesn't look *that* stupid. I wonder what the hell he's hiding?"

We were going to have to wait to find out, because Cotter began leading us across a rolling green plain toward a barn. We circled a couple of ponds, where a few dozen birds were wading and drinking. The whole setting looked like something out of a Norman Rockwell or a Grandma Moses painting, it was so wholesome and innocent—and yet every instinct I had screamed at me that something was wrong here, that nothing could be as peaceful and tranquil as it appeared.

"To appreciate what Mr. MacDonald has done here," said Cotter as we walked toward a large barn on a hillside, "you have to understand the challenge he faced. More than five billion men, women, and children have serious protein deficiencies. Three billion of them are quite literally starving to death. And of course the price of meat—*any* meat—had skyrocketed to the point where only the very wealthy can afford it. So what he had to do was not only create an animal as totally, completely nutritious as the Butterball, but he had to also create one that could mature and breed fast enough to meet mankind's needs now and in the future."

He stopped until a couple of laggards caught up with the group. "His initial work took the form of computer simulations. Then he hired a bevy of scientists and technicians who, guided by his genius, actually manipulated DNA to the point where the Butterballs existed not just on the screen and in Mr. MacDonald's mind, but in the flesh.

"It took a few generations for them to breed true, but fortunately a Butterball generation is considerably less than a year. Mr. MacDonald then had his staff spend some years mass-producing Butterballs. They were designed to have multiple births, not single offspring, and average ten to twelve per litter—and all of our specimens were bred and bred again so that when we finally introduced the Butterball to the world two years ago, we felt confident that we could keep up with the demand without running out of Butterballs."

"How many Butterballs have you got here?" asked the guy from *Eurocom International*, looking out across the rolling pastures and empty fields.

"We have more than two million at this facility," came the answer. "Mr. MacDonald owns some twenty-seven farms here and in Australia, each as large or larger than this one and each devoted to the breeding of Butterballs. Every farm has its own processing plant. We're proud to note that while we have supplied food for billions, we've also created jobs for more than eighty thousand men and women." He paused to make sure we had recorded that number or were jotting it down.

"That many?" mused Julie.

"I know it seems like we sneaked up on the world," said Cotter with a smile. "But for legal reasons we were compelled to keep the very existence of the Butterballs secret until we were ready to market them—and once we *did* go public, we were processing, shipping, and selling hundreds of tons from each farm every month right from the start. We had to have all our people in place to do that."

"If they give him the Nobel, he can afford to turn the money down," Jake said wryly.

"I believe Mr. MacDonald is prepared to donate the money to charity should that happy event come to pass," responded Cotter. He turned and began walking toward the barn, then stopped about eighty feet from of it.

"I must prepare you for what you're going to—"

"We've already seen the holos," interrupted the French reporter.

Cotter stared at him for a moment, then began again. "As I was saying, I must prepare you for what you're going to *hear*."

"Hear?" I repeated, puzzled.

"It was a fluke," he explained, trying to look unconcerned and not quite pulling it off. "An accident. An anomaly. But the fact of the matter is that the Butterballs can articulate a few words, just as a parrot can. We could have eliminated that ability, of course, but that would have taken more experimentation and more time, and the world's hungry masses couldn't wait."

"So what do they say?" asked Melissa.

Cotter smiled what I'm sure he thought was a comforting smile. "They simply repeat what they hear. There's no intelligence behind it. None of them has a vocabulary of more than a dozen words. Mostly they articulate their most basic needs."

He turned to the barn and nodded to a man who stood by the door. The man pushed a button, and the door slid back.

The first big surprise was the total silence that greeted us from within the barn. Then, as they heard us approaching—we weren't speaking, but coins jingle and feet scuff the ground—a voice, then a hundred, then a thousand, began calling out:

"Feed me!"

It was a cacophony of sound, not quite human, the words repeated again and again and again: *"Feed me!"*

We entered the barn, and finally got our first glimpse of the Butterballs. Just as in their holos, they were huge and roly-poly, almost laughably cute, looking more like oversized bright pink balloons than anything else. They had four tiny feet, good for balance but barely capable of locomotion. There were no necks to speak of, just a small pink balloon that swiveled atop the larger one. They had large round eyes with wide pupils, ears the size of small coins, two slits for nostrils, and generous mouths without any visible teeth.

"The eyes are the only part of the Butterball that aren't marketable," said Cotter, "and that is really for aesthetic reasons. I'm told they are quite edible."

The nearest one walked to the edge of its stall.

"*Pet me!*" it squeaked.

Cotter reached in and rubbed its forehead, and it squealed in delight.

"I'll give you a few minutes to wander around the barn, and then I'll meet you outside, where I'll answer your questions."

He had a point. With a couple of thousand Butterballs screaming "*Feed me!*" more and more frantically, it was almost impossible to think in there. We went up and down the rows of small stalls, captured the place on film and tape and disk and cube, then went back outside.

"That was impressive," I admitted when we'd all gathered around Cotter again. "But I didn't see any two million Butterballs in there. Where are the rest of them?"

"There are more than three hundred barns and other enclosures on the farm," answered Cotter. "Furthermore, close to half a million are outside in pastures."

"I don't see anything but empty fields," remarked Jake, waving a hand toward the pristine enclosures.

"We're a huge farm, and we prefer to keep the Butterballs away from prying eyes. In fact, this barn was built only a month ago, when we finally decided to allow visitors on the premises. It is the only building that's as close as a mile to any of our boundary lines."

"You said that some of them were in pastures," said Julie. "What do they eat?"

"Not grass," answered Cotter. "They're only outside because they're multiplying so fast that we're actually short of barns at the moment." He paused. "If you looked carefully at them, you noticed that grazing is quite beyond their capabilities." He held up a small golden pellet for us to see. "This is what they eat. It is totally artificial, created entirely from chemicals. Mr. MacDonald was adamant that no Butterball should ever eat any product that might nourish a human being. Their digestive systems were engineered to utilize this particular feed, which can provide nourishment to no other species on Earth."

"As long as you tinkered with their digestive systems, why didn't you make them shit-eaters?" asked Jake, only half-jokingly. "They could have served two purposes at once."

"I assume that was meant in jest," said Cotter, "but in point of fact, Mr. MacDonald considered it at one time. After all, some nourishiment *does* remain in excrement—but alas, not enough. He wanted an animal that could utilize one hundred percent of what we fed it."

"How smart are they?" asked one of the Brits. "When I was a child, I had a dog that always wanted me to feed it or pet it, but it never told me so."

"Yes it did," said Cotter. "It just didn't use words."

"Point taken," said the Brit. "But I'd still like to know . . ."

"These are dumb farm animals," said Cotter. "They do not think, they do not dream, they have no hopes or aspirations, they do not wish to become archbishop. They just happen to be able to articulate a few words, not unlike many birds. Surely you don't think Mr. MacDonald would create a sentient meat animal."

"No, of course not," interjected Julie. "But hearing them speak is still a bit of a shock."

"I know," said Cotter. "And that's the *real* reason we've invited you here, why we're inviting so many other press pools—to prepare the public."

"That's going to take a lot of preparation," I said dubiously.

"We have to start somewhere," said Cotter. "We have to let the people know about this particular anomoly. Men love to anthropomorphize, and a talking animal makes doing so that much easier. The consumers must be made to understand, beyond any shadow of a doubt, that these are unintelligent meat animals, that they do not know what their words mean, that they have no names and aren't pets, that they do not mourn the loss of their neighbors any more than a cow or a goat does. They are humanity's last chance—note that I did not even say humanity's last *best* chance—and we cannot let the protestors and pick-eters we know will demonstrate against us go unanswered. No one will believe *our* answers, but they should believe the answers of the unbiased world press."

"Yeah," I said under my breath to Jake. "And if kids didn't want to eat Bambi, or Henry the Turkey, or Penelope Pig, how is anyone going to make them dig into Talky the Butterball, who actually exists?"

"I heard that," said Cotter sharply, "and I must point out that the children who will survive because of the Butterballs will almost certainly never have been exposed to Bambi or Henry or any of the others."

"Maybe not for a year or two," I replied, unimpressed. "But before long you'll be selling Butterburgers on every street corner in the States."

"Not until we've fulfilled our mission among the less fortunate peoples of the world—and by that time the people you refer to should be prepared to accept the Butterballs."

"Well, you can hope," I said.

"If it never comes to that, it doesn't really matter," said Cotter with an elaborate shrug. "Our mission is to feed Earth's undernourished billions."

We both knew it would come to that, and sooner than anyone planned, but if he didn't want to argue it, that was fine with me. I was just here to collect a story.

"Before I show you the processing plant, are there any further questions?" asked Cotter.

"You mean the slaughterhouse, right?" said Jake.

"I mean the processing plant," said Cotter severely. "Certain words are not in our lexicon."

"You're actually going to show us Butterballs being . . . *processed?*" asked Julie distastefully.

"Certainly not," answered Cotter. "I'm just going to show you the plant. The process is painless and efficient, but I see no value in your being able to report that you watched our animals being prepared for market."

"Good!" said Julie with obvious relief.

Cotter gestured to an open bus that was parked a few hundred meters away, and it soon pulled up. After everybody was seated, he climbed on and stood next to the driver, facing us.

"The plant is about five miles away, at almost the exact center of the farm, insulated from curious eyes and ears."

"*Ears?*" Meilssa jumped on the word. "Do they scream?"

Cotter smiled. "No, that was just an expression. We are quite humane, far more so than any meat packing plant that existed before us."

The bus hit a couple of bumps that almost sent him flying, but he hung on like a trooper and continued bombarding us with information, about three-quarters of it too technical or too self-serving to be of any use.

"Here we are," he announced as the bus came to a stop in front of the processing plant, which dwarfed the barn we had just left. "Everyone out, please."

We got off the bus. I sniffed the air for the odor of fresh blood, not that I knew what it smelled like, but of course I couldn't detect any. No blood, no rotting flesh, nothing but clean, fresh air. I was almost disappointed.

There were a number of small pens nearby, each holding perhaps a dozen Butterballs.

"You have perhaps noticed that we have no vehicles capable of moving the hundreds and thousands of units we have to process each day?" asked Cotter, though it came out more as a statement than a question.

"I assume they are elsewhere," said the lady from India.

"They were inefficient," replied Cotter. "We got rid of them."

"Then how do you move the Butterballs?"

Cotter smiled. "Why clutter all our roads with vehicles when they aren't necessary?" he asked, tapping out a design on his pocket computer. The main door to the processing plant slid open, and I noticed that the Butterballs were literally jumping up and down with excitement.

Cotter walked over to the nearest pen. "Who wants to go to heaven?" he asked.

"*Go to heaven!*" squeaked a Butterball.

"*Go to heaven!*" rasped another.

Soon all twelve were repeating it almost as if it were a chant, and I suddenly felt like I was trapped inside some strange surrealistic play.

Finally Cotter unlocked their pen and they hopped—I hadn't seen any locomote at the other barn—up to the door and into the plant.

"It's as simple as that," said Cotter. "The money we save on vehicles, fuel, and maintenance allows us to—"

"There's nothing simple about it!" snapped Julie. "This is somewhere between blasphemy and obscenity! And while we're at it," she added suspiciously, "how can a dumb animal possibly know what heaven is?"

"I repeat, they are not sentient," said Cotter. "Just as you have code words for your pet dog or cat, we have them for the Butterballs. Ask your dog if he wants a treat, and he'll bark or sit up or do whatever you have conditioned him to do. We have conditioned the Butterballs in precisely the same way. They don't know the meaning of the word 'heaven' any more than your pet knows the meaning of the word 'treat,' but we've conditioned them to associate the word with good feelings and with entry into the processing plant. They will happily march miles through a driving rain to 'go to heaven.'"

"But heaven is such a . . . a *philosophical* concept," persisted the Indian woman. "Even to use it seems—"

"Your dog knows when he's been good," interrupted Cotter, "because you tell him so, and he believes you implicitly. And he knows when he's been bad, because you show him what he's done to displease you and you call him a bad dog. But do you think he understands the abstract philosophical concepts of good and bad?"

"All right," said Julie. "You've made your point. But if you don't mind, I'd rather not see the inside of the slaughterhouse."

"The processing plant," he corrected her. "And of course you don't have to enter it if it will make you uncomfortable."

"I'll stay out here, too," I said. "I've seen enough killing down in Paraguay and Uraguay."

"We're not killing anything," explained Cotter irritably. "I am simply showing you—"

"I'll stay here anyway," I cut him off.

He shrugged. "As you wish."

"If you have no vehicles to bring them to the plant," asked the Brit, approaching the entrance, "how do you move the . . . uh, the finished product out?"

"Through a very efficient system of underground conveyers," said Cotter. "The meat is stored in subterranean freezers near the perimeter of the property until it is shipped. And now . . ." He opened a second pen, offered them heaven, and got pretty much the same response.

Poor bastards, I thought as I watched them hop and waddle to the door of the plant. *In times gone by, sheep would be enticed into the slaughterhouse by a trained ram that they blindly followed. But leave it to us to come up with an even better reward for happily walking up to the butcher block: heaven itself.*

The Butterballs followed the first dozen into the belly of the building, and the rest of the pool followed Cotter in much the same way. There was a parallel to be drawn there, but I wasn't interested enough to draw it.

I saw Julie walking toward one of the pens. She looked like she didn't want any company, so I headed off for a pen in the opposite direction. When I got there, four or five of the Butterballs pressed up against the fence next to me.

"*Feed me!*"

"*Feed me!*"

"*Pet me!*"

"*Feed me!*"

Since I didn't have any food, I settled for petting the one who was more interested in being petted than being fed.

"Feel good?" I asked idly.

"*Feel good!*" it said.

I almost did a double take at that.

"You're a hell of a mimic, you know that?" I said.

No reply.

"Can you say what I say?" I asked.

Silence.

"Then how the hell did you learn to say it feels good, if you didn't learn it just now from me?"

"*Pet me!*"

"Okay, okay," I said, scratching it behind a tiny ear.

"*Very good!*"

I pulled my hand back as if I'd had an electric shock. "I never said the word 'very.' Where did you learn it?" *And more to the point, how did you learn to partner it with 'good'?*

Silence.

For the next ten minutes I tried to get it to say something different. I wasn't sure what I was reaching for, but the best I got was a "*Pet me!*" and a pair of "*Good's.*"

"All right," I said at last. "I give up. Go play with your friends, and don't go to heaven too soon."

"*Go to heaven!*" it said, hopping up and down. "*Go to heaven!*"

"Don't get so excited," I said. "It's not what it's cracked up to be."

"*See Mama!*" it squealed.

"What?"

"*See God! See Mama!*"

Suddenly I knew why MacDonald was being treated for depression. I didn't blame him at all.

I hurried back to the slaughterhouse, and when Cotter emerged alone a moment later I walked up to him.

"We have to talk," I said, grabbing him by the arm.

"Your colleagues are all inside inspecting the premises," he said, trying to pull himself loose from my grip. "Are you sure you wouldn't care to join them?"

"Shut up and listen to me!" I said. "I just had a talk with one of your Butterballs."

"He told you to feed him?"

"He told me that he would see God when he went to heaven."

Cotter swallowed hard. "Oh, shit—another one!"

"Another one of *what*?" I demanded. "Another sentient one?"

"No, of course not," said Cotter. "But as often as we impress the need for absolute silence among our staff, they continue to speak to each other in front of the Butterballs, or even to the Butterballs themselves. Obviously this one heard someone saying that God lives in heaven. It has no concept of God, of course; it probably thinks God is something good to eat."

"He thinks he's going to see his mother, too," I said.

"He's a *mimic!*" said Cotter severely. "Surely you don't think he can have any memory of his mother? For Christ's sake, he was weaned at five weeks!"

"I'm just telling you what he said," I replied. "Like it or not, you've got a hell of a P.R. problem: Just how many people do you want him saying it to?"

"Point him out to me," said Cotter, looking panicky. "We'll process him at once."

"You think he's the only one with a vocabulary?" I asked.

"One of the very few, I'm sure," said Cotter.

"Don't be *that* sure," said Julie, who had joined us while I was talking to Cotter. She had an odd expression on her face, like someone who's just undergone a religious experience and wishes she hadn't. "Mine looked at me with those soft brown eyes and asked me, very gently and very shyly, not to eat it."

I thought Cotter would shit in his expensive suit. "That's impossible!"

"The hell it is," she shot back.

"They are *not* sentient," he said stubbornly. "They are *mimics*. They do not think. They do not know what they are saying." He stared at her. "Are you sure he didn't say '*feed*'? It sounds a lot like '*eat*.' You've got to be mistaken."

It made sense. I hoped he was right.

"'Don't feed me?'" repeated Julie. "The only unhungry Butterball on the farm?"

"Some of them speak better than others. He could have been clearing his throat, or trying to say something that came out wrong. I've even come across one that stutters." It occurred to me that Cotter was trying as hard to convince himself as he was to convince her. "We've tested them a hundred different ways. They're not sentient. They're *not!*"

"But—"

"Consider the facts," said Cotter. "I've explained that the words sounds alike. I've explained that the Butterballs are not all equally skilled at articulation. I've explained that after endless lab experiements the top animal behavioral scientists in the world have concluded that they are not sentient. All that is on one side. On the other is that you *think* you may have heard something that is so impossible that any other explanation makes more sense."

"I don't know," she hedged. "It sounded exactly like . . ."

"I'm sure it did," said Cotter soothingly. "You were simply mistaken."

"No one else has ever heard anything like that?" she asked.

"No one. But if you'd like to point out which of them said it . . ."

She turned toward the pen. "They all look alike."

I tagged along as the two of them walked over to the Butterballs. We spent about five minutes there, but none of them said anything but "*Feed me!*" and "*Pet me!*" and finally Julie sighed in resignation.

"All right," she said wearily. "Maybe I was wrong."

"What do you think, Mr. McNair?" asked Cotter.

My first thought was: what the hell are you asking *me* for? Then I looked into his eyes, which were almost laying out the terms of our agreement, and I knew.

"Now that I've had a few minutes to think about it, I guess we were mistaken," I said. "Your scientists know a lot more about it than we do."

I turned to see Julie's reaction.

"Yeah," she said at last. "I suppose so." She looked at the Butterballs. "Besides, MacDonald may be a zillionaire and a recluse, but I don't think he's a monster, and only a monster could do something like . . . well . . . yes, I must have been mistaken."

And that's the story. We were not only the first pool of journalists to visit the farm. We were also the last.

The others didn't know what had happened, and of course Cotter wasn't about to tell them. They reported what they saw, told the world that its prayers were answered, and only three of them even mentioned the Butterballs' special talent.

I thought about the Butterballs all during the long flight home. Every expert said they weren't sentient, that they were just mimics. And I suppose my Butterball could very well have heard someone say that God lived in heaven, just as he could have heard someone use the word "very." It was a stretch, but I could buy it if I had to.

But where did Julie Balch's Butterball ever hear a man begging not to be eaten? I've been trying to come up with an answer to that since I left the farm. I haven't got one yet—but I *do* have a syndicated column, courtesy of the conglomerate that owns the publishing company.

So am I going to use it to tell the world?

That's my other problem: Tell it *what?* That three billion kids can go back to starving to death? Because whether Cotter was telling the truth or lying through his teeth, if it comes down to a choice between Butterballs and humans, I know which side I have to come down on.

There are things I can control and things I can't, things I know and things I am trying my damnedest not to know. I'm just one man, and I'm not responsible for saving the world.

But I *am* responsible for me—and from the day I left the farm, I've been a vegetarian. It's a small step, but you've got to start somewhere.

The Amorous Broom

A JOHN JUSTIN MALLORY STORY

One day my friend Bill Fawcett phoned me and asked me if I'd like to contribute a story to *Masters of Fantasy*, an original anthology he was assembling. The only stipulation was that I had to use a continuing fantasy character I had created.

I have lots of continuing science fiction characters, but the only continuing fantasy character I have is John Justin Mallory. So I unretired him for the fifth time, and here he is again.

John Justin Mallory, his feet up on his desk, his battered fedora worn at an angle, was studying the *Racing Form*.

"You know," he announced, "I think I just may take a run out to the track this afternoon."

"Oh my God!" breathed Winnifred Carruthers, his pudgy, pink-faced, gray-haired partner. "That poor creature is entered again, isn't he?"

"How did you guess?" asked Mallory.

"It's the only time you ever go to the track—when Flyaway's running."

"'Running' is an overstatement," said the not-quite-human creature perched atop the refrigerator in the next room. "Flyaway plods."

"When I want advice from the office cat," said Mallory irritably, "rest assured I'll ask for it."

"That's what Flyaway does," continued Felina from atop the refrigerator. "He rests assured."

"If you ever leave here," said Mallory, "don't apply for a job as a comedian."

"Why should I leave here?" purred Felina. "It's warm and dry and you feed me."

"How many races has Flyaway lost in a row now, John Justin?" asked Winnifred.

"Fifty-three."

"Doesn't that suggest something to you?" she persisted.

"That it's past time for him to win."

"You are the finest detective in this Manhattan," continued Winnifred. "How can you be so stupid?"

"Oh, ye of little faith," said Mallory.

"You have solved a lot of tricky cases, and put yourself in harm's way at least half a dozen times. Did you do it solely so you could keep losing your money on Flyaway?"

"When I go out on a case, my function is to detect," replied Mallory. "When I go to the track, my function is to bet. Why do you have such a problem with that? Mallory & Carruthers is paying its bills. This is discretionary income."

"I don't have a problem with betting," shot back Winnifred. "But betting involves an element of chance. Putting your money on Flyaway doesn't."

"You're going to look mighty silly when he finally wins one," said Mallory.

"Well said!" cried a voice. "You tell 'em, John Justin Mallory!"

Mallory was on his feet in an instant. "Who said that?" he demanded.

Felina leaped catlike to the floor and bounded into the office. She grinned, extended a shining claw at the end of her forefinger, and pointed it toward a broom that was leaning against a wall in the far corner.

"Come on," said Mallory. "Brooms don't talk."

"I most certainly do," said the broom.

Mallory stared at the broom for a moment, then looked at Winnifred. "Yours?" he asked.

"I never saw it before," she said.

"Then what's it doing here?"

"Why not ask it?" suggested Winnifred.

"I've never spoken to a broom before. How does one address it?"

"You may call me Hecate," said the broom.

"Isn't that a witch's name?" asked Winnifred.

"She was my first owner."

"All right, Hecate," said Mallory. "Who and what are you, and more to the point, what are you doing in my office?"

"I want to be near you, John Justin Mallory," said Hecate.

"Why?"

"The Grundy hates you. Isn't that enough?"

"Okay, he's behind this, right?"

"No, he doesn't know I'm here," said the broom.

"It's pretty hard to keep a secret from the most powerful demon on the East Coast," said Mallory. He paused. "Where does the Grundy *think* you are?"

"Hanging on his wall with his other magical trophies."

"Why aren't you there?"

"He's mean and cruel and unfeeling," complained the broom. "He put me there a year ago and hasn't let me down since. I made up my mind to escape months ago, but I didn't know where to find sanctuary until he started complaining about you. Mallory did this, and Mallory did that, and Mallory thwarted him again—so I knew that you were the one person who could protect me from the Grundy." Hecate paused. "He was wrong about you. You're beautiful, John Justin Mallory."

Mallory turned to Winnifred. "Call a cab."

"What are you going to do?" asked Hecate apprehensively.

"I'm going to return you to your owner before he rips my office apart looking for you."

"But you can't! He'll just hang me on that wall again!"

"We all have problems," said Mallory, walking across the room toward the broom. "Yours will have to be resolved without my help."

He picked up the broom and began carrying it to the front door.

It squealed.

"Oh, my! What strong, manly hands you have, John Justin Mallory!"

"Where the hell's your voice coming from?" asked Mallory.

"Why?"

"I want to shut you up. I thought I'd put some tape over your mouth."

"I'll never tell!"

Mallory opened the door, then looked back over his shoulder. "Tell them I'll pay double if the cabbie doesn't ask any questions."

"Right," said Winnifred.

It took Mallory twenty minutes to drive to the Grundy's Gothic Baptist castle at the north end of Central Park. He handed the broom to one of the Grundy's trolls, then walked back across the drawbridge, climbed into the cab, and had it drive him home.

When he entered the office the broom was propped against his desk, waiting for him.

"I forgive you, John Justin Mallory," it said.

"How the hell did you get back ahead of me?"

"I'm a magic broom. I can fly. My original mistress and I used to fly everywhere. She loved the loop-the-loop, before my arthritis made it too difficult."

"Forget all that," said Mallory. "You don't seem to understand the situation here. You belong to my mortal enemy, a being who can bring freezing weather to the whole damned city just by blowing on it. He touches things and they die. If he finds you here, he's going to think—"

"Think what?" interrupted a familiar voice.

"*Oh, shit!*" muttered Mallory, turning to face his newest visitor. "Doesn't anyone ever knock or even use a door anymore?"

The creature facing Mallory was tall, a few inches over six feet, with two prominent horns protruding from his hairless head. His eyes were a burning yellow, his nose sharp and aquiline, his teeth white and gleaming, his skin a bright red. His shirt and pants were crushed velvet, his cloak satin, his collar and cuffs made of the fur of some white polar animal. He wore gleaming black gloves and boots, and he had two mystic rubies suspended from his neck on a golden chain. When he exhaled, small clouds of vapor emanated from his mouth and nostrils.

"Why should I knock?" replied the Grundy. "Did you knock when you stole my broom from me?"

"I didn't steal it," said Mallory. "Hell, I just drove across the city to return it."

"Yet here it is," said the Grundy, pointing to Hecate.

"Take it," said Mallory. "I didn't ask for it and I don't want it. It's yours."

"How can you say that after all we've been to each other?" demanded the broom.

"We haven't been a thing to each other, and we're never going to see each other again!" snapped Mallory. He picked the broom up and thrust it into the Grundy's hands. "Take it and get the hell out of here."

"You still have no fear of me, have you?" asked the Grundy curiously.

"Let's say I have a healthy respect for what you can do," answered Mallory.

"But no fear."

"Not today. I didn't steal the damned thing, and you must know it. It's not *my* fault that your broom has a crush on me." He paused thoughtfully. "Maybe you should introduce it to a nice, masculine mop."

"No!" cried the broom. "It's *you* that I love!"

Mallory and the Grundy exchanged looks, and for the first time since arriving in this Manhattan from his own, the detective actually felt a surge of sympathy for the demon. What could one, even a demon, do in the face of such earnest if misdirected passion?

"Mallory!" screamed the broom, as the Grundy secured his grip on it. "Aren't you going to say anything?"

"We'll always have Paris," answered Mallory.

And then the Grundy and the broom blinked out of sight, all trace of them gone in the smallest fraction of a second.

"Well," said Mallory, "what did you think of that?"

"I felt sorry for it," said Winnifred.

"We've got Felina. One freeloader is enough."

"But to spend the rest of its life hanging on a wall . . ."

"It's a *broom*, for God's sake!" said Mallory irritably. "It doesn't *have* a life."

"It feels and it thinks," insisted Winnifred stubbornly.

"It feels foolishly and it thinks irrationally," replied Mallory.

"So says the man who's about to bet on Flyaway again."

"Maybe I'll just go to the Emerald Isle Pub and hang one on," muttered Mallory. "I've got to get away from this place."

"I'll go with you," said a voice.

"Shit! You're back *again*?" growled Mallory, looking around the room until he finally spotted the broom leaning against the fireplace. "Didn't the Grundy just take you away about two minutes ago?"

"He adjusts Time for his own convenience," said the broom. "I've been back at the castle for almost three days of subjective time. I had to wait until the room was empty of trolls, goblins, and leprechauns before I made my escape."

"You know that I'm just going to send you back," said Mallory wearily.

"No!" cried the broom. "You can't send me back to a life of humiliation and degradation. Everyone looks at me as if I'm . . . I'm some kind of *object*."

"I don't know how to tell you this gently," said Mallory, "but you *are* an object."

"No! I'm a living entity, with hopes and dreams and fears and sexual needs!"

"I don't think I want to hear about this," said Mallory.

"You *can't* send me back! I beg of you, Mallory—I live only for you! Let me come out and catch criminals with you!"

"I'm not a cop. I don't go out and walk a beat and catch criminals. I'm a detective. I wait until someone hires me."

"You need management. Advertising. Let me write your phone book ads." It lowered its voice to a whisper. "And lose the fat broad. I'm all you'll ever need."

"Well, I like *that*!" snorted Winnifred.

"Have you any other requests?" asked Mallory sardonically.

"Make sure the cat thing doesn't sharpen her claws on me."

"That's all?"

"That's all—except that I'm dying to see you work. When do you expect to be tailing a villain up a dark alley?"

"Not for at least five or ten minutes," said Mallory sardonically.

"Then I'll just stay right here and admire you," said the broom. "You're beautiful, John Justin Mallory. Exquisite. Perfection personified."

"Thank you," said Mallory in bored tones.

"I'll bet you'd be hell in a heart-shaped waterbed with a mirror on the ceiling."

"Goddammit!" snapped Mallory. "I've been in this Manhattan for almost two years now, and every time I think I'm starting to really understand it, someone says something like that!"

"*I* understand it," offered Felina. "It's filled with people who were put here to scratch me and feed me." She sidled over to Mallory. "Ask it if it drinks milk."

"You want to share your milk with it?" asked Mallory, surprised.

"If it says it does, I'll scratch it until it's nothing but a pile of wood shavings."

"I heard that!" said the broom sternly. "What kind of monsters do you keep in your office, Mallory?"

The detective sighed. "The kind that won't go away."

"In answer to the cat thing's question, I don't drink milk."

"Just out of curiosity, what *do* you eat and drink?" asked Mallory, still wondering where its mouth was.

"It's been so long since I've eaten, I can't remember," said the broom. "Not all of us lead a life of privilege. Some of us undergo endless privation while the object of our affection continues to ignore us."

"I've been the object of your affection for about ten minutes, tops," said Mallory.

"Not so. I've loved you from afar for years."

"Years?" demanded Mallory.

"Well, weeks, anyway," said the broom. "Why must you insist on precision, John Justin Mallory? Why don't you just sweep me up in your arms and tell me you return my love?"

"You want a list of reasons?"

"My God, you know how to hurt a person!" moaned the broom. "This is so humiliating—especially in front of the fat broad and the cat creature."

"I'm sure they both appreciate your sensitivity."

"How could they? They're still here!"

"They belong here. You don't."

"How can you say that to me?" demanded the broom. "Who else loves you so completely and unselfishly? Who else hears heavenly music at the sound of your voice? This is the passion of the eons! How can you be so blind to it?"

"I have cataracts," said Mallory dryly.

"I pour my heart out in front of these two unwanted hangers-on, and you make puny little jokes. Do you enjoy causing me such pain?"

"I hadn't really thought about it," admitted Mallory. "But now that you mention it, somehow I don't feel guilty at all."

The broom screamed in agony. "Cut me to the quick! Spit on my love! See if I care!"

"This has gone on long enough," said Mallory. He picked up his phone and dialed the letters G, R, U, N, D, and Y in succession. An instant later the Grundy materialized in front of the detective's desk.

"Will you please take your emotionally unstable broom back?" asked Mallory.

The Grundy stared at the broom for a long moment, then turned back to the detective. "This broom is proving to be more trouble than it is worth. I hereby give it to you."

"I don't want it."

The broom moaned.

"What you want doesn't interest me," said the Grundy. "The broom is yours."

"You're all heart, Grundy," said Mallory.

"Save your sarcasm, Mallory," said the Grundy. "You will need it for comfort when I am slowly and painfully disemboweling you."

"Were you planning on doing that sometime soon?"

"Soon, late, what is the difference? Death always wins in the end."

"I don't know why you're so anxious to kill me," said Mallory. "I'm the only person you know who's never lied to you."

"Why do you think you're still alive?" asked the demon, and vanished.

"Everyone comes and goes so fast here," said Mallory sarcastically. "Somehow, I don't think we're in Kansas any more, Toto."

"My name is Hecate, not Toto," said the broom. "And now we can be together forever and ever. Isn't it wonderful?"

Mallory looked across the room at Winnifred. "You know, I could really grow to hate that goddamned demon."

"What do you plan to do about . . . well, you know?"

"The broom?" he said. "Well, it's here and it's ours. We may as well put it to work."

"I don't do dishes or windows," said the broom.

"You're magic. You have powers. I was thinking of taking you on a case and seeing what you can do."

"You and me? Together? Stalking super-villains to their lairs? Breaking up international espionage gangs?"

"We got a lady goblin who thinks her husband is cheating on her," said Mallory. "I've got to follow him until I find out if she's right or wrong."

"How mundane!"

"They give you medals for tracking down super-villains," explained Mallory. "They give you money for tracking down straying husbands. We're running a business."

"It makes no difference," said the broom after a moment's consideration. "As long as I can be with you . . . uh . . . can I call you Darling?"

"I'd rather you didn't."

"Okay, Sweetie," said the broom. "Let's go tracking unfaithful goblins."

Monday night—the first case:

They had followed the goblin to the corner of Lust and Despair. Then it took a sharp turn down Lust Street.

"We've got the goods on him!" cried the broom excitedly. "He's going to patronize a brothel!"

The goblin turned at the sound of the broom's voice, peered into the darkness until it saw Mallory, and then took off like a bat out of hell.

"Thanks a heap," muttered Mallory.

Wednesday night—the second case:

They stood in the shadows near the Kringleman Arms hotel, watching one ersatz Santa Claus after another enter the place with a pot of money in hand.

"So how do you know which ones are legitimate and which are keeping the money themselves?" asked the broom in its normal speaking voice.

Three Santas instantly emerged from the lobby and began firing Saturday Night Specials into the shadows. Mallory could almost feel the bullets whistle by as he raced around the corner and dove for safety behind a pair of trash cans.

"Whatever would I do without you?" said Mallory, checking to make sure he still possessed all the requisite arms and legs.

Saturday night—the third case:

An old man, his hair white and thinning, sparse whiskers on his chin, his eyes hidden by a pair of sunglasses, walked down Broadway, beggar's cup in one hand, an ancient cane in the other.

Behind the shades, Mallory was concentrating his gaze on Creepy Conrad's Bazaar of the Exotic, where he was certain that Conrad was showing his client prints of some very revealing, if inartistic, photos prior to blackmailing him.

A woman stopped to toss a few coins into Mallory's cup. She inadvertently brushed against him as she walked by, and to keep in character he pretended to momentarily lose his balance. The woman instantly stopped and helped him regain his equilibrium.

"Take your hands off the man I love!" roared the broom.

Creepy Conrad looked out at the distraction, stared long and hard at Mallory, grinned as he finally recognized him, and quickly substituted some photos of Tassle-Twirling Tessie Twinkle, the lizard girl who shed her skin four times a night at the Rialto Burlesque, for the blackmail shots.

"Well?" asked Winnifred, looking up from her paperwork as Mallory shuffled into the office.

"If I take that damned broom on two or three more cases, we'll be looking for a new line of work."

"Where is Hecate now?"

"Down at the corner, getting some coffee and a donut."

"Why didn't she just—?"

"She doesn't want me to know where her mouth is," interrupted Mallory. "Right now I'm more interested in locating her jugular."

"So what are we going to do?"

"I've been giving it some thought," said Mallory. "After all, we're detectives. Our job isn't necessarily catching crooks or preventing crimes, it's solving problems . . . so I think it's time we solved our own."

"How?"

"I've got an idea, but I can't do it myself. That damned broom'll never let me out of its sight long enough." He pulled a roll of bills out of his pocket and stared mournfully at it. "This was what I was going to bet on Flyaway the night Hecate showed up."

"What do you want me to do, John Justin?"

He tossed the roll to her. "Buy a gallon of glue, and a few bottles of glitter, and then go over to Morgan the Gorgon's hardware store and . . ."

"What's going on here?" demanded Hecate.

"Business as usual," said Mallory. "Why?"

"There's nothing usual about this!" said the broom.

"Oh, you mean *these?*" said Mallory, gesturing to twenty brand-new brooms lined up on the wall, each totally covered with gold and silver glitter.

"Yes, I mean these!" snapped the broom. "They weren't here before! What's going on, Mallory?"

"You were so helpful the last few nights that I decided we could use even more brooms," said Mallory. "And as long as I'm going to be spending all my time with them, why not surround myself with beauty?"

"But . . . but—" sputtered Hecate.

Mallory picked up a broom at random. "Isn't this one gorgeous?" he asked, stroking it lovingly. "I'll never be bored on a stakeout again."

"You ingrate!" screamed Hecate. "You heathen! You ungrateful swine! How dare you forsake me for another broom!"

"Another twenty brooms," Mallory corrected it pleasantly.

"And I would have married you!" said the broom. It began weeping copiously. "I'm going back to where I was appreciated. Maybe the Grundy didn't spend much time with me, but I was well cared for and people stopped by to admire me every day and . . ." Its voice tailed off.

"You can stay here," said Mallory. "I promise to take you out of the broom closet at least twice a year, for exceptionally easy cases. And think of all the fun you can have hanging around with all these truly beautiful brooms. Who knows? Some of their elegance might rub off."

"My mother was right!" cried the broom. "Never trust a man!"

And then, with one final heart-wrenching sob, it vanished as quickly and completely as the Grundy ever had.

"Well, you got rid of it, John Justin," said Winnifred.

"I feel like shit," said Mallory grimly. "Still, it had to be done."

"Don't feel bad," said Felina. "*I* certainly won't feel bad when I desert you under duress."

"Thanks," said Mallory ironically. "I take enormous comfort in that."

Felina smiled happily. "I knew you would."

"Remind me to check on the broom in a few months and make sure it's doing okay," said Mallory.

"I will, John Justin," said Winnifred.

"Good." He pulled out a tissue, blew his nose, and tossed it into the waste basket next to his desk. "When did you buy that?"

"Buy what, John Justin?"

"The waste basket with the fancy trim," he said. "I don't remember seeing it before."

"I didn't buy any waste basket," said Winnifred.

The waste basket approached Mallory and rubbed gently against his leg.

"I think I'm in love with you," it said.

Hothouse Flowers

My father lived to the ripe old age of eighty-nine. He spent his last two years in a full-care facility. Whenever I visited him, I was impressed by the nursing staff, at how hard they worked to keep their patients comfortable and happy (and, yes, alive).

Back when they established Social Security, the average American's life span was sixty-four years. These days it's nearing eighty. Extrapolate another century's worth of medical progress and there's no telling how long we may be expected to live. But that has nothing to do with the quality of life, merely the length of it. I combined that notion with my observations of the nursing staff and came up with "Hothouse Flowers," which was a Hugo nominee in 2000.

I test the temperature. It is eighty-three degrees, warm but not hot. Just right.

I spend the next hour puttering around, checking medications, adjusting the humidity, cleaning one of the life stations. Then Superintendent Bailey stops by on his way out to dinner.

"How are your charges doing?" he asks. "Any problems today?"

"No, sir, everything's fine," I answer.

"Good," he says. "We wouldn't want any problems, especially not with the celebration coming up."

The celebration is the turn of the century, although there is some debate about that, because we are all preparing to celebrate the instant the clock hits midnight and 2200 A.D. begins, but some spoilsport scientists (or maybe they're mathematicians) have told the press that the new century *really* begins a year later, when we enter 2201.

Not that my charges know the difference, but I'm glad we're celebrating it this year, because it means that we'll decorate the place with bright colors—and if we like it, why, we'll do it again in 2201.

I have been married to Felicia for seventeen years, and I hardly ever regret it. She was a little bit pudgy when we met, and she has gotten pudgier over the years so that now she is honest-to-goodness fat and there is simply no other word for it. Her hair, which used to be brown, is streaked with gray now, and she's lost whatever physical grace she once had. But she is a good life partner. Her taste in holos is similar to mine, so we almost never fight about what to watch after dinner, and of course we both love our work.

As we eat dinner, the topic turns to our gardens, as always.

"I'm worried about Rex," she confides.

Rex is *Begonia rex*, her hanging basket.

"Oh?" I say. "What's wrong with him?"

She shakes her head in puzzlement. "I don't know. Perhaps I've been letting him get *too* much sun. His leaves are yellowing, and his roots could be in better shape."

"Have you spoken to one of the botonists?"

"No. They're totally absorbed in cloning that new species of *Aglaonema crispum*."

"Still?"

She shrugs. "They say it's important."

"The damned plant's been around for centuries," I say. "I can't see what's so important about it."

"I told you: they engineered an exciting mutation. It actually glows in the dark, as if it's been dusted with phosphorescent silver paint."

"It's not going to put the energy company out of business."

"I know. But it's important to *them*."

"It seems unfair," I say for the hundredth, or maybe the thousandth, time. "They get all the fame and money for creating a new species, and you get paid the same old salary for keeping it alive."

"I don't mind," she replies. "I love my work. I don't know what I'd do without my greenhouse."

"I know," I say soothingly. "I feel the same way."

"So how is *your* Rex today?" she asks.

It's my turn to shrug. "About the same as usual." Suddenly I laugh.

"What's so funny?" asks Felicia.

"You think your Rex is getting too much sun. I decided *my* Rex wasn't getting enough, so this afternoon I moved him closer to a window."

"Will it make a difference, do you think?" she asks.

I sigh deeply. "Does it ever?"

I walk up to the Major and smile at him. "How are we today?" I ask.

The Major looks at me through unfocused eyes. There is a little drool running out the side of his mouth, and I wipe it off.

"It's a lovely morning," I say. "It's a pity you can't be outside to enjoy it." I pause, waiting for the reaction that never comes. "Still," I continue, "you've seen more than your share of them, so missing a few won't hurt." I check the screen at his life station, find his birthdate, and dope it out. "Well, I'll be damned! You've actually seen 60,573 mornings!"

Of course, he's been here for almost half of them: 29,882 to be exact. If he ever did count them, he stopped a long time ago.

I clean and sterilize his feeding tubes and his medication tubes and his breathing tubes, examine him for bedsores, wash him, take his temperature and blood pressure, and check to make sure his cholesterol hasn't gone above the 350 level. (They want it lower, of course, but he can't exercise and they've been feeding him intravenously for more than half a century, so they won't do anything about changing his diet. After all, it hasn't killed him so far, and altering it just might do so.)

I elevate his withered body just long enough to change the bedding, then gently lower him back down. (That used to take ten minutes, and at least one helper, before they developed the anti-grav beam. Now it's just a matter of a few seconds, and I like to think it causes less discomfort, though of course the Major is in no condition to tell me.)

Then it's on to Rex. Felicia has problems with her Rex, and I have problems with mine.

"Good morning, Rex," I say.

He mumbles something incomprehensible at me.

I look down at him. His right eye is bloodshot and tearing heavily.

"Rex, what am I going to do with you?" I say. "You know you're not supposed to stare at the sun."

He doesn't really know it. I doubt that he even knows his name is Rex. But cleansing his eye and medicating it is going to put me behind schedule, and I have to blame *someone*. Rex doesn't mind being blamed. He doesn't mind burning out his retina. He doesn't even mind lying motionless for decades. If there is anything he *does* mind, nobody's found it yet.

I spill some medication on him while fixing his eye, so I decide that rather than just change his diaper I might as well go all the way and give him a DryChem bath. I marvel, as always, at the sheer number of surgical scars that crisscross his torso: the first new heart, the second, the new kidneys, the new spleen, the new left lung. There's a tiny, ancient scar on his lower belly which I think was from the removal of a burst appendix, but I can't find any record of it on the computer and he's been past talking about it for almost a century.

Then I move on to Mr. Spinoza. He's laying there, mouth agape, eyes open, head at an awkward angle. I can tell even before I reach him that he's not breathing. My first inclination is to call Emergency, but I realize that his life station will have reported his condition already, and sure enough, just seconds later the Resurrection Team arrives and sets up a curtain around him (as if any of his roommates could see or care), and within ten minutes they've got the old gentleman going again.

This is the fifth time Mr. Spinoza has died this year. All this dying has to be hard on his system, and I worry that one of these days it's going to be permanent.

"So how was your Major today?" asks Felicia at dinner.

"Same as usual," I say. "How's yours?"

Her Major is the *Browallia speciosa majorus*. "Ditto," she says. "Old, but hanging on." She frowns. "We may not get any blossoms this year, though. The roots are a little ropey."

"I'm sorry to hear it."

"It happens." She pauses. "How was the rest of your day?"

"We had some excitement," I reply.

"Oh?"

"Mr. Spinoza died again."

"That's the fourth time, isn't it?" she asks.

"The fifth," I correct her. "The Resurrection Team revived him."

"The Resuscitation Team," she corrects me.

"You have your word for them, I have mine," I say. "Mine's better. Resurrection is what they do."

"So you've only lost one this week," says Felicia, if not changing the subject at least moving on a tangent away from it.

"Right. Mr. Lazlo. He was 193 years old."

"193," she muses, and then shrugs. "I guess he was entitled."

"You mentioned that you lost one too," I note.

"My *cymbidium*."

"That's an orchid, right?" I say. "The one they nicknamed Peter Pan?"
She nods.

"Silly name for an orchid," I remark.

"It stayed young forever, or so it seemed," she replies. "It had the most exquisite blooms. I'm really going to miss it. I'd had it for almost twenty years." She smiles sadly, and a single tear begins to roll down her cheek. "I worked so hard over it, sometimes I felt like its mother." She looks at me. "That sounds ludicrous, doesn't it?"

"Not at all," I say, sincerely touched by her grief.

"It's all right," she says. Then she stares at my face. "Don't be so concerned. It was just a flower."

"It's called empathy," I answer, and she lets it drop . . . but I *am* troubled, and by the oddest thought: *Shouldn't I feel worse about losing a person than she feels about losing an orchid?*

But I don't.

I don't know when it began. Probably with the first caveman who made a sling for a broken arm or forced water out of a drowned companion's lungs. But somewhere back in the dim and distant past man invented medicine. It had its good centuries and its bad centuries, but by the end of the last millennium it was curing so many diseases and extending so many lives that things got out of hand.

More than half the people who were alive in 2050 were still alive in 2150. And almost 90 percent of the people who were alive in 2100 will be alive in 2200. Medical science had doubled and then trebled man's life span. Immortality was within our grasp. Life everlasting beckoned.

We were so busy increasing the length of life that no one gave much thought to the *quality* of those extended lives.

And then we woke up one day to find that there were a lot more of them than there were of us.

His name is Bernard Goldmeier. They carry him in on an airsled, then transfer him to Mr. Lazlo's old life station.

After I clean the Major's tubes and change his bedding and medicate Rex's eye, I call up Mr. Goldmeier's medical history on the holoscreen at his life station.

"This place stinks!" rasps a dry voice.

I jump, startled, then turn to see who spoke. There is no one in the room except me and my charges.

"Who said that?" I demand.

"I did," replies Mr. Goldmeier.

I look closely at him. The skin hangs loose and brown-spotted on his bald head. His cheeks are covered by miscolored flesh and his nose has oxygen tubes inserted into it—but his eyes, sunken deep in his head, are clear and he is staring at me.

"You really spoke!" I exclaim.

"You never heard an inmate speak before?"

"Not that I remember."

Which is another unhappy truth. By age 100, one out of every two people has some form of senile dementia. By 125, it's four out of five. By 150, it's ninety-nine out of one hundred. Mr. Goldmeier is 153 years old; the odds against his retaining anything close to normal mental capacities are better than one hundred to one.

"I should add," I say, "that the proper term is 'charge,' not 'patient' and certainly not 'inmate.'"

"A zombie by any other name . . ."

I decide there is no sense arguing with him. "How do you feel?" I ask.

"Look at me," he says disgustedly. "How would *you* feel?"

"If you're in any discomfort . . ." I begin.

"I told you: this place stinks. It reeks of shit and urine."

"Some of our charges are incontinent," I explain. "We have to show them understanding and compassion."

"Why?" he rasps. "What do they show us in exchange?"

"Try to be a little more tolerant," I say.

"*You* try!" he snaps. "I'm busy!"

I can't help but ask: "Busy doing what?"

"Hanging on to reality!"

I smile. "Is that so difficult?"

"Why don't you ask some of your other inmates?" He sniffs the air and makes a face. "Goddamnit! Another one's crapping all over himself! What the hell am I doing here anyway? I'm not a fucking vegetable yet!"

I check all the notations on the screen.

"You're here, Mr. Goldmeier," I say, not without some satisfaction at what I'm about to tell him, "because no other ward will have you. You've offended every attendant and orderly in the entire complex."

"Where do I go when I offend you?"

"This is your last stop. You're here for better or worse."

Lucky me. I turn back to the holoscreen and begin punching in the standard questions.

"What are you doing now?" he demands. He tries to boost himself up on a scrawny, miscolored elbow to watch me, but he's too weak.

"Checking to see if I'm to medicate you for any diseases," I reply.

"I haven't been out of bed in forty years," he rasps. "If I have a disease, I got it from one of you goons."

I ignore his answer and continue staring at the screen. "You have a history of cancer."

"Big deal," he says. "As quick as I get it, you bastards cure it." He pauses. "Seventeen cancers. You cut five out, burned three out, and drowned the other nine in your chemicals."

I keep reading the screen. "I see you still have your original heart," I note with some surprise. Most hearts are replaced by the time the patient is 120 years old, the lungs and kidneys even sooner.

"Are you offering me yours?" he replies sarcastically.

Okay, so he's an arrogant, hostile bastard—but he's also my only charge who's capable of speech, so I force a smile and try again.

"You're a lucky man," I begin.

He glares at me. "You want to explain that?"

"You've retained your mental acuity. Very few manage that at your advanced age."

"And you think that's lucky, do you?"

"Certainly."

"Then you're a fool," said Mr. Goldmeier.

I sigh. "I'm trying very hard to be your friend. You're not making it easy."

His emaciated face contracts in a look of disgust. "Why in hell should you want to be my friend?"

"I want to be friends with all my charges."

"*Them?*" he says contemptuously, scanning the room. "You'd probably get more action from a bunch of potted plants." It's not dissimilar from what Felicia says on occasion.

"Look," I say. "You're going to be here for a very long time. So am I. Why don't we at least try to cultivate the illusion of civility?"

"That's a disgusting thought."

"Being civil?" I ask, wondering what kind of creature they have delivered to my ward.

"That, too," he says. "But I meant being here for a very long time." He exhales deeply, and I hear a rattling in his chest and make a mental note to tell the doctors about his congestion. Then he adds: "Being *anywhere* for a very long time."

"What makes you so bitter?" I ask.

"I've seen terrible things, things no man should ever have to see."

"We've had our share," I agree. "The war with Brazil. The meteor that hit Mozambique. The revolution in Canada."

"Fool!" he snaps. "Those were *diversions*."

"Diversions?" I repeat incredulously. "Just what hellholes have you been to?"

"The worst," he answers. "I've been to places where men begged for death, and slowly went mad when it didn't come."

"I don't remember reading or hearing about anything like that," I say. "Where was this?"

He stares unblinking at me for a long moment before he answers. "Right here, in the wards."

Felicia looks up from her plate. "His name's Bernard Goldmeier?" she asks.

"That's right."

"I don't have any Bernards," she says. "It's not the kind of name they give to flowers."

"It doesn't matter."

Suddenly her face brightens. "I do have a gold flower, though—a *Mesembryanthemum criniflorum*. I can call it Goldie, or even Goldmeier."

"It's not important."

"But it is," she insists. "For years it's been how we compare our days." She smiles. "It makes me feel closer to you, caring for flowers with the same names."

"Fine," I say. "Call it whatever you want."

"You seem"—she searches for the word—"upset."

"He troubles me."

"Oh? Why?"

"I love my work," I begin.

"I know you do."

"And it's meaningful work," I continue, trying to keep the resentment from my voice. "Maybe I'm not a doctor, but I stand guard over them and hold Death at bay. That's important, isn't it?"

"Of course it is," she says soothingly.

"He belittles it."

"That doesn't mean a thing," says Felicia, reaching across the table and taking my hand. "You know how they get when they're that old."

Yes, I know how they get. But he's not like them. He sounds—I don't know—normal, like me; that's the upsetting part.

"He doesn't seem irrational," I say aloud. "Just bitter."

"Enough bitterness will make anyone irrational."

"I know," I say. "But . . ."

"But what?"

"Well, it's going to sound juvenile and selfish . . ."

"You're the least selfish man I know," says Felicia. "Tell me what's bothering you."

"It's just that . . . well, I always thought that if my charges could speak to me, they'd tell me how grateful they were, how much my efforts meant to them." I pause and think about it. "Does that make me selfish?"

"Certainly not," she replies. "I think they *ought* to be grateful." She pats my hand. "A lot of people in that place are just earning salaries; you're there because you care."

"Anyway, here I've finally got someone who *could* thank me, could tell me that I'm appreciated, and instead he's furious because I'm going to do everything within my power to keep him alive."

She coos and purrs and making soothing noises, but she doesn't actually *say* anything, and finally I change the subject and ask her about her garden. A moment later she is rapturously describing the new buds on the *Aphelandra squarrosa*, and telling me that she thinks she will have to divide the *Scilla sibirica*, and I listen gratefully and do not think about Mr. Goldmeier, lying motionless in his bed and cursing the darkness, until I arrive at work in the morning.

"Are you feeling any better today?" I ask as I approach Mr. Goldmeier's life station.

"No, I'm not feeling better today," he says nastily. "God's fresh out of miracles."

"Are you at least adjusting to your new surroundings?"

"Hell, no."

"You will."

"I damned well better not!"

I stare at him. "You're not leaving here."

"I know."

"Then you might as well get used to the place."

"Never!"

"I don't understand you at all," I say.

"That's because you're a fool!" he snaps. "Look at me! I have no money and no family. I can't feed myself or even sit up."

"That's no reason to be so hostile," I say placatingly. I am about to tell him that his condition is no different from most of my charges, but he speaks first.

"All I have left is my rage. I won't let you take it away; it's all that separates me from the vegetables here."

I look at him and shake my head sadly. "I don't know what made you like this."

"153 years made me like this," he says.

I continue staring at him, at the atrophied legs that will never walk again, at the shriveled arms and skeletal fingers, at the deathmask skull with its burning, sunken eyes, and I think: *Maybe—just maybe— senility is Nature's way of making life in such a body tolerable. Maybe you're not as lucky as I thought.*

The Major's chin is wet with drool, and I walk over to him and wipe it off.

"There," I say. "Clean as a whistle."

Okay, I think, staring down at him. *You're not grateful, but at least you don't hate me for doing what you can no longer do for yourself. Why can't they all be like you?*

"Why don't you ask for a transfer to another ward if he's bothering you that much?" asks Felicia.

"What would I say?" I reply. "That this old man who can't even roll over without help is driving me away?"

"Just tell them you want a change."

I shake my head. "My work is important to me. My *charges* are important to me. I can't turn my back on them just because he makes my life miserable."

"Maybe you should sit down and figure out *why* he upsets you."

"He makes me think uncomfortable thoughts."

"What kind of uncomfortable thoughts?"

"I don't want to talk about it," I reply. But what I really mean is: *I don't want to think about it.*

I just wish I could get my brain to listen to me.

Superintendent Bailey enters the ward and approaches me.

"I'm going to need you to work a little overtime today," he informs me.

"Oh?" I reply. "What's the problem?"

"There must be some virus going around," he says. "A third of the staff has called in sick."

"All right. I'll just have to let Felicia know I'll be late for dinner. Where do you want me to go when I'm through here?"

"Ward 87."

"Isn't that a woman's ward?" I ask.

"Yes."

"I'd rather have a different assignment, sir."

"And I'd rather have a full staff!" he snaps. "We're both doomed to be disappointed today."

He turns and leaves the ward.

"What have you got against women?" croaks Mr. Goldmeier. I had thought he was asleep, but he's been lying there, motionless, with his eyes (and his ears) wide open.

"Nothing," I answer. "I just don't think I should bathe them."

"Why the hell not?"

"It's a matter of respecting their dignity."

"Their dignity?" he snorts derisively.

"Their modesty, if you prefer."

"Dignity? Modesty? What the fuck are you talking about?"

"They're human beings," I answer with dignity of my own.

"Not any more," he replies contemptuously. "They're a bunch of vegetables that don't give a damn who bathes them." He closes his eyes. "You're a blind, sentimental fool."

I hate it when he says things like that, because I want to explain that I am *not* a blind, sentimental fool. But that requires me to prove he is wrong, and I can't—I've tried.

All human beings have modesty and dignity. If they haven't any, then they're not human beings any more—and if they're not human beings, why are we keeping them alive? Therefore, they *must* have modesty and dignity.

Then I think of those shriveled bodies and atrophied limbs and uncomprehending eyes, and I start getting another migraine.

Two days have passed, and I am not eating or sleeping any better than Mr. Goldmeier.

"What did he say this time?" says Felicia wearily, staring across the dining room table at me.

"I'm not sure," I answer. "He kept talking about youth in Asia, so finally I looked them up in the encyclopedia. All it says is that there are a lot of them and they're starving." I pause, frowning. "But as far as I can tell, he's never been to Asia. I don't know why he kept talking about them."

"Who knows?" says Felicia with a shrug. "He's an old man. They don't always make sense."

"He makes *too* goddamned much sense," I mutter bitterly.

"Could you have misunderstood the words?" she asks. "Old men mumble a lot."

"I doubt it. I understand everything else he says, so why not this?"

"Let's find out for sure," she says, activating the dining room computer. It glows with life. "Computer, find synonyms for the term 'youth in Asia.'"

The computer begins rattling them off. "Young people in Asia. Adolescents in Asia. Children in Asia. Teenagers in—"

"Stop!" commands Felicia. "Synonym was the wrong term. Computer, are there any homonyms for the term 'youth in Asia'?"

"A homonym is an exact match," answers the computer, "and there is no exact match."

"Are there any close approximations?"

"One. The word euthanasia."

"Ah," says Felicia triumphantly. "And what does it mean?"

"It is an archaic word, no longer in use. I can find no definition of it in my memory bank."

"Eu-tha-na-sia," says Mr. Goldmeier, articulating each syllable. "How the hell can the dictionaries and encyclopedias not list it any longer?"

"They list it," I explain. "They just don't define it."

"Figures," he says disgustedly. As I wait patiently for him to tell me what the word means, he changes the subject. "How long have you worked here?"

"Almost fourteen years."

"Seen a lot of patients come and go?"

"Of course I have."

"Where do they go when they leave here?"

"They don't, except when they're transferred to another ward."

"So they come to this place, and then they die?"

"You make it sound like it happens overnight," I reply. "We've kept some of them alive for more than a century," I add proudly. "A *lot* of them, in fact."

He stares at me. I recognize that particular stare; it means I'm not going to like what he says next.

"You could save a lot of time and effort by killing them right away."

"That would be contrary to civil and moral law!" I reply angrily. "It's our job to keep every patient alive."

"Have you ever asked them if they *want* to be kept alive?"

"No one wants to die."

"Right. It's against all civil and moral law." He coughs and tries to clear his lungs. "Well, that's why you won't find it in the dictionary."

"Find what?" I ask, confused.

"*Euthanasia*," he says.

"I don't understand you."

"That's what we were talking about, isn't it?" he says. "It means mercy killing."

"Mercy killing?"

"You've heard both words before. Figure it out."

I am still wondering why anyone would think it was merciful to kill another human being when my shift ends and I go home.

"Why would someone want to die?" I ask Felicia.

She rolls her eyes. "Goldmeier again?"

"Yes."

"Somehow I'm not surprised," she says in annoyed tones. She shakes her head sadly. "I don't know where that man gets his ideas. No one wants to die." She paused. "Look at it logically. If someone's in pain, he can go on medication. If he's lost a limb, he can get a prosthesis. If he's too feeble even to feed himself —well, that's what trained people like you are there for."

"What if he's just tired of living?"

"You know better than that," replied Felicia with unshakable certainty. "Every living organism fights to stay alive. That's the first law of Nature."

"Yes, I suppose so," I agree.

"He's a nasty old man. Did he say anything else?"

"No, not really." I toy with my food. Somehow my appetite has vanished. "How were things at the greenhouse?"

"They finally got exactly the shade of phosphorescent silver they want for the *Aglaonema crispum*," she says. "I think they're going to call it the 'Silver Charm.'"

"Cute name."

"Yes, I rather like it. They tell me there was once a famous race-horse, centuries ago, with that name." She pauses. "Of course, it means some extra work for me."

"Potting them?"

"They're all potted. No, the problem is making room for them. I think we'll have to get rid of the *Browallia speciosa majorus*."

"But those are your Majors!" I protest. "I know how you love them!"

"I do," she admits. "They have exquisite blossoms. But they've got some kind of exotic root rot disease." She sighs deeply. "I saw some miscoloration, some slimy residue . . . but I didn't identify it in time. It's my fault they're dying."

"Why not bring them home?" I suggest.

"If you want Majors, I'll bring some young, healthy ones that will flower in the spring. But I'm just going to dump the old ones in the garbage. The disease won."

I'm grasping for something, but I'm not quite sure what. "Didn't you just tell me that every living thing fights to stay alive?"

"The Majors don't want to die," said Felicia. "They're infected, so I'm taking that decision out of their hands before the disease can spread to other plants."

"But if—"

"Don't go getting philosophical with me," she says. "They're only flowers. It's not as if they feel any pain."

Later that night I find myself wondering when was the last time Rex or the Major or Mr. Spinoza or any of the others felt any pain.

Fifty years? Seventy-five? One hundred? More?

Then I realize that that's what Mr. Goldmeier *wants* me to think. He sees the weak and he wants them dead.

But they're not his targets at all. They never were.

I finally know who he is trying to infect.

I show up early for work and enter my ward. Everyone is sleeping.

I look at my charges, and a warm glow comes over me. *We are a team, you and I. I give you life and you give me satisfaction and a sense of purpose. I pledge to you that I will never let anyone destroy the bond between us.*

When I think about it, there is really very little difference between Felicia's job and my own. She has to protect her flowers; I have to protect mine.

I fill a syringe and walk silently over to Mr. Goldmeier's life station.

It is time to start weeding my garden.

His Award-Winning Science Fiction Story

The late Robert Sheckley was more than my friend (and, on a recent story, my collaborator). When I was a teenager and young man, preparing to be a writer, he, more than anyone else, was my role model, not for what he wrote (which was brilliant) but for the accessibility of his prose (which was even more brilliant).

Years later, after he'd tried his hand at absurdist science fiction, I decided to try an absurdist story myself, just to see if I could do it. This is the result. I consider it a strange, cute, and decidedly minor story. So why is it included here? Because a few months before we went to press, Thousand Beauty Films actually optioned it. I invite you to read the story and see if you can figure out how anyone can possibly make a movie out of it.

Chapter 1

Call me Ishmael.

Chapter 2

Lance Stalwart and Conan Kinnison sat at the controls of their tiny two-man scout ship, a good dozen parsecs in advance of the main body of the Terran Fleet, debating their possible courses of action, reviewing all their options.

One moment they had been all alone in the Universe, or so it had seemed; then all space was filled with the Arcturian navy, millions upon millions of ships, some short and squat, a few saucer-shaped, a handful piercing the void like glowing silver needles, all made of an impenetrable titanium alloy, well over half of them equipped for hyperspatial jumps, all girded for warfare, each and every one manned by a crew of malicious, malignant, hate-filled Arcs, each of whom had been schooled in spacial warfare since earliest infancy, each a precisely functioning cog in the vast, seemingly impervious and unconquerable Arc war machine that had smashed its way to victory after victory against the under-manned Terrans and was even now plunging toward the Terran home system in a drive that was not to be denied unless Stalwart and Kinnison managed to pull a couple of magical rabbits out of their tactical hat.

"Jesus H. Christ!" muttered Stalwart disgustedly. "If I'd ever written a sentence like that they'd have thrown me out of school."

"I'd sure love to have the purple prose concession on this guy's word processor," agreed Kinnison.

"And here we are, risking our asses in the middle of God knows where, and we don't even know what a goddamned Arc looks like," complained Stalwart. "If *I* were writing this story, that's the very first thing I'd put in."

Chapter 2

It walked in the woods.

It was never born. It existed. Under the pine needles the fires burn, deep and smokeless in the mold. In heat and in darkness and decay there is growth. It grew, but it was not alive. It walked unbreathing through the woods, and thought and saw and was hideous and strong, and it was not born and it did not live. And—perhaps it could not be destroyed.

"No good!" snapped Kinnison. "It's not enough that you're going to get sued over my name. Now you've gone and swiped an entire opening from Theodore Sturgeon. You'd better go back right now and describe an Arc properly."

"Right," said Resnick.

Chapter 2

He walked in the woods.

He was never born. *He* existed. *He* grew, but *he* was not alive. *He* walked unbreathing through the woods, and thought and saw and was hideous and strong, and *he* was not born and *he* did not live. And—

"You are not exactly the swiftest learner I ever came across," said Kinnison.

"I've had it with this crap!" snapped Stalwart. "Screw you, Resnick! I'm going up to Chapter 20. Maybe things will get a little better by then."

He set off at a slow trot, vanishing into the distant haze.

"That's funny," mused Kinnison. "I always thought Chapter 20 was more to the left."

"Only if you're writing in Arabic," said his companion.

"Who the hell are you?" demanded Kinnison.

"Harvey Wallbanger," said Harvey Wallbanger.

"Should I know you?"

"I'm from the Space Opera Stock Character Replacement Center," said Wallbanger. He stretched vigorously. "Ah, it feels good to be back in harness! I've been sitting on the sidelines for years. I would have preferred a Hawk Carse reprint, but my agent says that the main thing for a Stock Character is to keep working."

"I suppose so," said Kinnison, eyeing him warily.

"By the way," said Wallbanger, "why are you eyeing me warily?"

"Oh, no reason," said Kinnison, averting his eyes.

"Go ahead, tell me," urged Wallbanger. "I won't be offended. Really I won't."

"You don't have any facial features," said Kinnison.

"I don't need them," answered Wallbanger. "I'm just here so you won't have to talk to yourself."

"This is crazy!" snapped Kinnison. "I don't know who I'm fighting, or why they're mad at me, or what they look like, and my shipmate is doing God knows what in Chapter 20, and now they've given me a faceless assistant, and I'm going on strike."

"What?" said Wallbanger, fulfilling his literary function to perfection.

"This just doesn't make any sense," said Kinnison, "and I'm not going back to work until I've got some motivation."

Suddenly a cloud of dust arose in the Altair sector. The sound of hoofbeats grew louder and louder until a magnificent coal black stallion galloped into view, steam rising in little clouds from his heavily lathered body.

The Great Masked Writer of the Planes dismounted and approached Kinnison and Wallbanger. He was tall, debonaire, handsome in a masculine, ruddy sort of way, incredibly erudite, and unquestionably the world's greatest lay. He

HA!

"What the hell was that?" asked Kinnison.

"Just my wife, dusting the computer keyboard," said Resnick. "It certainly shouldn't be construed as an editorial comment."

I REPEAT: HA!

"At least tell her to use lowercase letters," whined Kinnison. "She's giving me a headache." He paused. "What are you doing here, anyway? It's really most irregular."

Resnick patted the stallion's beautifully arched neck. "Steady there, big fella," he said in tones that inspired instant confidence. He turned back to Kinnison. "He'll give you a half mile in forty-seven seconds any time you ask for it. He performs best with blinkers and a run-out bit, and he doesn't like muddy tracks."

"Why are you telling me all this?" asked Kinnison.

"Because he's yours now," said Resnick, handing over the reins. "Take him."

"What's his name?"

"Motivation."

"But he's a horse!"

"Look—you asked for Motivation, I'm giving you Motivation. Now, do you want him or not?"

"I'm terribly confused," said Kinnison. "Maybe we ought to go back to the beginning and see if it works out any better this time."

Chapter 1

Call me Ishmael.

Chapter 2

"You've lost me already," complained Kinnison, scratching his shaggy head. "I mean, like, who the hell is Ishmael?"

"It's a sure-fire beginning," said Resnick, shoving Wallbanger into the murky background. "Every great American novel begins with 'Call me Ishmael.'"

"How many novels is that, at a rough guess?" asked Kinnison.

"Well, the downstate returns aren't all in yet," replied Resnick, "but so far, rounded off, it comes to one."

"Hah!" snapped Kinnison. "And how the hell many Ishmaels do you know?"

"One," said Resnick, delighted at how neatly it was all working out.

"Who?"

"Ishmael Valenzuela," said Resnick, who may have overstated the case originally, but was unquestionably the greatest lay in the sovereign state of Ohio.

HA!

"Who the hell is Ishmael Valenzuela?" demanded Kinnison.

"A jockey," answered Resnick. "He rode Kelso and Tim Tam and Mister Gus."

"What's he got to do with this story?"

"I thought he might ride Motivation in the Prix de l'Arc de Triomphe," explained Resnick. "It's the biggest race in Europe. Then I'll have an Ishmael and an Arc all in the same place, and it'll make it much easier to tie up all the loose ends."

"It'll never work," said Kinnison. "What if they call it the Prix instead of the Arc?"

"They wouldn't dare! This is a G-rated story."

"Still, it would make me very happy if you'd go back to the beginning and get rid of Ishmael."

"I don't know . . ."

"Come on," urged Kinnison. "After all, you got in your dirty pun, bad as it was."

"Yeah," said Resnick. "But that was five sentences ago. We could have used a little something right here."

Chapter 1

And call me Conrad.

Chapter 2

"I don't think I'm getting through to you at all," complained Kinnison. "Now you've ripped off a Roger Zelazny title."

"Boy, nothing pleases you!" muttered Resnick.

Chapter 1

Call me Ishmael.

Chapter 2

"You sure as hell haven't gotten very far," said Lance Stalwart, strolling in from the northeast.

"Are you back already?" asked Kinnison, startled.

"There's nothing much happening up ahead. Resnick makes it with Loni Anderson thirty or forty times between Chapter 12 and Chapter 18, but that's about it. I'm still trying to figure out what she's doing in a science fiction story."

"I've always been a Goldie Hawn man myself," said Kinnison, apropos of nothing.

"No way," said Resnick. "Loni Anderson has two insurmountable advantages."

"You can't keep making filthy jokes like that!" roared Kinnison. "This is supposed to be a serious space opera, and here you are talking about Loni Anderson's boobs, for Christ's sake!"

"Yeah!" chimed in Stalwart. "You can't go around talking about her tits in print! Don't you know kids are going to be reading this, you stupid fucking bastard?"

"This chapter," said Kinnison, "is turning into an udder disaster."

Chapter 1

Call me Ishmael.

Chapter 2

Conan Kinnison, a retarded Albanian dwarf, hobbled over to Lance Stalwart, whose wrought-iron lung had stopped functioning. The ship's temperature had risen to forty-four degrees Centigrade, the oxygen content was down to six percent, and all the toilets were backing up.

"Is it too late to apologize?" rasped Kinnison through his hideously deformed lips.

The most fantastic bed partner in Hamilton County, Ohio

HA!

nodded his acquiescence, mercy being one of his many unadvertised virtues.

Chapter 1

Call me Ishmael.

Chapter 2

"Ahh, that's better!" said Lance Stalwart, stretching his bronzed, muscular, six-foot seven-inch frame. "You know, I think the problem may be that you don't know where this story is going. It really hasn't got much direction."

"It's got Motivation, though," said Resnick sulkily.

"Maybe what it needs is a title," offered Kinnison. "Most of the stories I've read have had titles."

"Why bother?" asked Resnick wearily. "The editors always change them anyway."

"Only if they make sense," said Kinnison.

Chapter 3: The Search for a Title

"The floor is now open for suggestions," said the most skillful lover living at 1409 Throop Street in Cincinnati, Ohio.

WHAT ABOUT THE GARDENER?

Chapter 3: The Search for a Title

"The floor is now open for suggestions," said the most skillful lover (possibly excepting the gardener) living at 1409 Throop Street in Cincinnati, Ohio.

BIG DEAL.

"It's got to sound science-fictional, grip the reader, and give me a little direction," continued Resnick. "I will now entertain recommendations."

"*The Mote in God's Thigh*," said Loni Anderson.

"*Buckets of Gor*," suggested John Norman.

"*Call Me Ishmael*," said Valenzuela.

"*Tarzan Stripes Forever*," said Edgar Rice Burroughs.

"I don't like any of them," said Kinnison.

"Me neither," agreed Stalwart. "It is my considered opinion that the title ought to be: *His Award-Winning Science Fiction Story*. That way, when Resnick's next collection comes out, the editor can put a blurb on the cover stating that the volume includes His Award-Winning Science Fiction Story."

"I *like* that idea!" said Resnick enthusiastically.

"Then it's settled," said Kinnison with a sigh of relief. "I feel like a new man."

"Me, too!" said Loni Anderson. "Where's the gardener?"

Chapter 2

"You know," said Kinnison wearily, "if you'd spend a little less time watching the Bengals' defense blow one lead after another and a little more time trying to write this goddamned story, I'd be willing to meet you halfway. But as things stand now, I don't have the energy for a whole novel. I keep getting this sense of deja vu."

"Me, too," said John Carter, who had wandered over from the Barsoom set. "Only it's spelled *Dejah vu*."

"Why not make a short story out of it?" continued Kinnison.

"Well, it's not really an *Omni* or *Playboy* type of story," responded Resnick, "and no one else pays very well."

"How about selling it to Harlan Ellison for *The Last Dangerous Visions?*" suggested Kinnison. "Word has it that it'll be coming out in another ten years or so."

"Hah! Call that stuff dangerous visions?" snorted Stalwart contemptuously. "I've got an uncle who can't see a redwood tree at ten paces, and he drives a school bus. Now, *that's* what I call dangerous vision!"

"Well, I was saving it for a smash ending," said Resnick, "but if we've all decided that this is a short story, I might as well bring it out now."

So saying, he produced a little gadget which could blow up approximately half the known universe. The patents on the various parts were held by Murray Leinster, Jack Williamson, Edmund Hamilton, and E. E. Smith (who also invented half of Conan Kinnison, but I can't say which half because this is a G-rated story).

"I think I've seen one of those before," said Lance Stalwart. "What do you call it?"

"This," explained Resnick, "is a pocket frammistan, guaranteed to get you out of any jams you may get into, except for those requiring massive doses of penicillin."

"It's a nice idea," said Kinnison, "but we can't use it."

"Why not?" demanded Resnick.

"We can't use a pocket frammistan," explained Kinnison patiently, "because none of us has any pockets. In fact, until you insert a few descriptive paragraphs into this story, none of us is even wearing any pants."

"You'd better solve this one quick," warned Stalwart, "or you stand in considerable danger of having this damned thing turn into a novelette."

"Let's backtrack a little," suggested Resnick, "and see if there is anything we missed."

Chapter 1

Call me Ishmael.

Chapter 2

"Ah, here it is!" said Resnick, picking up a crumpled piece of paper off the floor.

"What is it?" asked Kinnison, peeking over his shoulder.

"Our salvation," said Resnick, uncrumpling the paper. On it was scribbled a single word: *Laskowski*.

"It's just an old piece of correspondence," said Kinnison despondently.

"Not any more," said Resnick.

"But what does it mean?" asked Stalwart.

"That's the beauty of it," said Resnick. "This is a science fiction story, so we can make it do or mean anything we want."

"Not quite anything," said Kinnison fussily. "Unless, of course, you want this to wind up as a fantasy story."

"I'll keep that in mind," said Resnick, who was anxious to get on with the show and move ahead to Chapters 12 through 18.

"Give us an idea how it works," said Stalwart.

"Right," said Kinnison. "If we're going to have to depend on a laskowski, we at least deserve some say in its function."

"Fair enough," agreed Resnick, walking to the blackboard.

Chapter 3: The Creation of the Laskowski

Students will be allowed forty minutes, no more and no less, and must mark their papers with a Number One Lead Pencil. Anyone disobeying the honor system will have bamboo splints driven under his fingernails, or maybe be forced to read *Dhalgren*.

What Laskowski Means to Me:

A) "Your Highness, may I present Arx Kreegah, the Grand Laskowski of the star system of . . ."

B) "Hey, Harry, get a load of the laskowskis on that babe, willya?"

C) Kinnison touched the button once, and the dread Laskowski Ray shot out, destroying all life in its path, except for one pathetic little flower . . .

D) "Ah, Earthman, just because I have two laskowskis where Terran females have but one, does that make me any less a woman?"

E) "The rare eight-legged laskowski mosquito, though seemingly harmless, can, when engorged with the blood of a left-handed Turkish rabbi . . ."

F) "They're closing on us fast!" cried Stalwart. "If we don't get the Laskowski Drive working in the next ten seconds, we're up Paddle Creek without a . . ."

G) "Chess is fine for children," said Pooorht Knish, waving a tentacle disdainfully, "but out here we play a *real* game: laskowski."

H) "No, thanks," panted Kinnison. "I couldn't laskowski again for hours!"

I) None of the above.

Chapter 4

"Well, how did it come out?" asked Stalwart.

"We've got six votes for None of the Above, two didn't understand the question, and seventeen voted for Harold Stassen," said Resnick grimly.

"Then we're back where we started?" asked Kinnison, choking back a manly little sob.

"Not quite," said Resnick. "We got all the way up to Chapter 4 this time."

"While you guys have been talking, I've been reading some market reports," said Wallbanger, "and I've come to the conclusion that a short story is just about the hardest thing to sell."

"So what do you suggest?" asked Resnick.

"A vignette."

"A what?"

"You know—a short-short story," replied Wallbanger. "They get rejected much faster. Why, you could get a rejection every four days with a vignette, whereas a short story might not be bounced more than once a month. As for a novel"—he shrugged disdainfully—"hell, it could take ten years to get turned down by everyone."

"I don't know," said Resnick unhappily. "I sort of had my heart set on a rip-roaring space opera, with about thirty-five chapters, glittering with wit and action and a subtle sense of poetic tragedy."

"Couldn't you condense it all into a vignette?" said Kinnison. "I'm exhausted. I don't think I could go through all this again."

"Or maybe even a poem," suggested Stalwart hopefully.

"Or a nasty book review," added Wallbanger. "There's a huge market for them, especially if you misuse a lot of five-syllable words."

"No," said Kinnison decisively. "Let him stick with what he does best."

"Right," said Resnick, sitting down at the word processor.

Chapter 1

Call me Ishmael.

(for my friend and long-suffering editor, George Laskowski)

For I Have Touched the Sky

Of the stories I've written at novelette length (7,500 to 17,500 words), this is my favorite. It occurred to me during a 1987 trip to Kenya. Until that point, almost all I'd ever gotten out of Africa were ideas for novels—but I had just completed "Kirinyaga," which was destined to win me my first Hugo, a few weeks earlier—and suddenly, everywhere I looked, there were more Kirinyaga stories begging to be written. I had this one titled and plotted before I'd been there for two days. I started writing it the night I got home, finished it the next evening, and sold it to *The Magazine of Fantasy and Science Fiction* the following week.

"For I Have Touched the Sky" was nominated for both the Nebula and the Hugo in 1990 and won Japan's Hayakawa Award and Poland's SFinks Award.

There was a time when men had wings.

Ngai, who sits alone on His throne atop Kirinyaga, which is now called Mount Kenya, gave men the gift of flight, so that they might reach the succulent fruits on the highest branches of the trees. But one man, a son of

Gikuyu, who was himself the first man, saw the eagle and the vulture riding high upon the winds, and spreading his wings, he joined them. He circled higher and higher, and soon he soared far above all other flying things.

Then, suddenly, the hand of Ngai reached out and grabbed the son of Gikuyu.

"What have I done that you should grab me thus?" asked the son of Gikuyu.

"I live atop Kirinyaga because it is the top of the world," answered Ngai, "and no one's head may be higher than my own."

And so saying, Ngai plucked the wings from the son of Gikuyu, and then took the wings away from *all* men, so that no man could ever again rise higher than His head.

And that is why all of Gikuyu's descendants look at the birds with a sense of loss and envy, and why they no longer eat the succulent fruits from the highest branches of the trees.

We have many birds on the world of Kirinyaga, which was named for the holy mountain where Ngai dwells. We brought them along with our other animals when we received our charter from the Eutopian Council and departed from a Kenya that no longer had any meaning for true members of the Kikuyu tribe. Our new world is home to the maribou and the vulture, the ostrich and the fish eagle, the weaver and the heron, and many other species. Even I, Koriba, who am the *mundu-mugu*—the witch doctor—delight in their many colors and find solace in their music. I have spent many afternoons seated in front of my *boma*, my back propped up against an ancient acacia tree, watching the profusion of colors and listening to the melodic songs as the birds come to slake their thirst in the river that winds through our village.

It was on one such afternoon that Kamari, a young girl who was not yet of circumcision age, walked up the long, winding path that separates my *boma* from the village, holding something small and gray in her hands.

"*Jambo*, Koriba," she greeted me.

"*Jambo*, Kamari," I answered her. "What have you brought to me, child?"

"This," she said, holding out a young pygmy falcon that struggled weakly to escape her grasp. "I found him in my family's *shamba*. He cannot fly."

"He looks fully fledged," I noted, getting to my feet. Then I saw that one of his wings was held at an awkward angle. "Ah!" I said. "He has broken his wing."

"Can you make him well, *mundumugu*?" asked Kamari.

I examined the wing briefly, while she held the young falcon's head away from me. Then I stepped back.

"I can make him well, Kamari," I said. "But I cannot make him fly. The wing will heal, but it will never be strong enough to bear his weight again. I think we will destroy him."

"No!" she exclaimed, pulling the falcon back. "You will make him live, and I will care for him!"

I stared at the bird for a moment, then shook my head. "He will not wish to live," I said at last.

"Why not?"

"Because he has ridden high upon the warm winds."

"I do not understand," said Kamiri, frowning.

"Once a bird has touched the sky," I explained, "he can never be content to spend his days on the ground."

"I will *make* him content," she said with determination. "You will heal him and I will care for him, and he will live."

"I will heal him and you will care for him," I said. "But," I added, "he will not live."

"What is your fee, Koriba?" she asked, suddenly businesslike.

"I do not charge children," I answered. "I will visit your father tomorrow, and he will pay me."

She shook her head adamantly. "This is *my* bird. *I* will pay the fee."

"Very well," I said, admiring her spirit, for most children—and *all* adults—are terrified of their *mundumugu*, and would never openly contradict or disagree with him. "For one month you will clean my *boma* every morning and every afternoon. You will lay out my sleeping blankets and keep my water gourd filled, and you will see that I have kindling for my fire."

"That is fair," she said after a moment's consideration. Then she added: "What if the bird dies before the month is over?"

"Then you will learn that a *mundumugu* knows more than a little Kikuyu girl," I said.

She set her jaw. "He will not die." She paused. "Will you fix his wing now?"

"Yes."

"I will help."

I shook my head. "You will build a cage in which to confine him, for if he tries to move his wing too soon, he will break it again and then I will surely have to destroy him."

She handed the bird to me. "I will be back soon," she promised, racing off toward her *shamba*.

I took the falcon into my hut. He was too weak to struggle very much, and he allowed me to tie his beak shut. Then I began the slow task of splinting his broken wing and binding it against his body to keep it motionless. He shrieked in pain as I manipulated the bones together, but otherwise he simply stared unblinking at me, and within ten minutes the job was finished.

Kamari returned an hour later, holding a small wooden cage in her hands.

"Is this large enough, Koriba?" she asked.

I held it up and examined it.

"It is almost too large," I replied. "He must not be able to move his wing until it has healed."

"He won't," she promised. "I will watch him all day long, every day."

"You will watch him all day long, every day?" I repeated, amused.

"Yes."

"Then who will clean my hut and my *boma*, and who will fill my gourd with water?"

"I will carry his cage with me when I come," she replied.

"The cage will be much heavier when the bird is in it," I pointed out.

"When I am a woman, I will carry far heavier loads on my back, for I shall have to till the fields and gather the firewood for my husband's *boma*," she said. "This will be good practice." She paused. "Why do you smile at me, Koriba?"

"I am not used to being lectured to by uncircumcised children," I replied with a smile.

"I was not lecturing," she answered with dignity. "I was *explaining*."

I held a hand up to shade my eyes from the afternoon sun.

"Are you not afraid of me, little Kamari?" I asked.

"Why should I be?"

"Because I am the *mundumugu*."

"That just means you are smarter than the others," she said with a shrug. She threw a stone at a chicken that was approaching her cage, and it raced away, squawking its annoyance. "Someday I shall be as smart as you are."

"Oh?"

She nodded confidently. "Already I can count higher than my father, and I can remember many things."

"What kind of things?" I asked, turning slightly as a hot breeze blew a swirl of dust about us.

"Do you remember the story of the honey bird that you told to the children of the village before the long rains?"

I nodded.

"I can repeat it," she said.

"You mean you can remember it."

She shook her head vigorously. "I can repeat every word that you said."

I sat down and crossed my legs. "Let me hear," I said, staring off into the distance and idly watching a pair of young men tending their cattle.

She hunched her shoulders, so that she would appear as bent with age as I myself am, and then, in a voice that sounded like a youthful replica of my own, she began to speak, mimicking my gestures.

"There is a little brown honey bird," she began. "He is very much like a sparrow, and as friendly. He will come to your *boma* and call to you, and as you approach him he will fly up and lead you to a hive, and then wait while you gather grass and set fire to it and smoke out the bees. But you must *always*"—she emphasized the word, just as I had done—"leave some honey for him, for if you take it all, the next time he will lead you into the jaws of *fisi*, the hyena, or perhaps into the desert where there is no water and you will die of thirst." Her story finished, she stood upright and smiled at me. "You see?" she said proudly.

"I see," I said, brushing away a large fly that had lit on my cheek.

"Did I do it right?" she asked.

"You did it right."

She stared at me thoughtfully. "Perhaps when you die, I will become the *mundumugu*."

"Do I seem that close to death?" I asked.

"Well," she answered, "you are very old and bent and wrinkled, and you sleep too much. But I will be just as happy if you do not die right away."

"I shall try to make you just as happy," I said ironically. "Now take your falcon home."

I was about to instruct her concerning his needs, but she spoke first.

"He will not want to eat today. But starting tomorrow, I will give him large insects, and at least one lizard every day. And he must always have water."

"You are very observant, Kamari."

She smiled at me again, and then ran off toward her *boma*.

She was back at dawn the next morning, carrying the cage with her. She placed it in the shade, then filled a small container with water from one of my gourds and set it inside the cage.

"How is your bird this morning?" I asked, sitting close to my fire, for even though the planetary engineers of the Eutopian Council had given Kirinyaga a climate identical to Kenya's, the sun had not yet warmed the morning air.

Kamari frowned. "He has not eaten yet."

"He will, when he gets hungry enough," I said, pulling my blanket more tightly around my shoulders. "He is used to swooping down on his prey from the sky."

"He drinks his water, though," she noted.

"That is a good sign."

"Can you not cast a spell that will heal him all at once?"

"The price would be too high," I said, for I had forseen her question. "This way is better."

"How high?"

"*Too* high," I repeated, closing the subject. "Now, do you not have work to do?"

"Yes, Koriba."

She spent the next few minutes gathering kindling for my fire and filling my gourd from the river. Then she went into my hut to clean it and straighten my sleeping blankets. She emerged a moment later with a book in her hand.

"What is this, Koriba?" she asked.

"Who told you that you could touch your *mundumugu's* possessions?" I asked sternly.

"How can I clean them without touching them?" she replied with no show of fear. "What is it?"

"It is a book."

"What is a book, Koriba?"

"It is not for you to know," I said. "Put it back."

"Shall I tell you what I think it is?" she asked.

"Tell me," I said, curious to hear her answer.

"Do you know how you draw signs on the ground when you cast the bones to bring the rains? I think that a book is a collection of signs."

"You are a very bright little girl, Kamari."

"I *told* you that I was," she said, annoyed that I had not accepted her statement as a self-evident truth. She looked at the book for a moment, then held it up. "What do the signs mean?"

"Different things," I said.

"*What* things?"

"It is not necessary for the Kikuyu to know."

"But *you* know."

"I am the *mundumugu*."

"Can anyone else on Kirinyaga read the signs?"

"Your own chief, Koinnage, and two other chiefs can read the signs," I answered, sorry now that she had charmed me into this conversation, for I could foresee its direction.

"But you are all old men," she said. "You should teach me, so when you all die someone can read the signs."

"These signs are not important," I said. "They were created by the Europeans. The Kikuyu had no need for books before the Europeans came to Kenya; we have no need for them on Kirinyaga, which is our own world. When Koinnage and the other chiefs die, everything will be as it was long ago."

"Are they evil signs, then?" she asked.

"No," I said. "They are not evil. They just have no meaning for the Kikuyu. They are the white man's signs."

She handed the book to me. "Would you read me one of the signs?"

"Why?"

"I am curious to know what kind of signs the white men made."

I stared at her for a long minute, trying to make up my mind. Finally I nodded my assent.

"Just this once," I said. "Never again."

"Just this once," she agreed.

I thumbed through the book, which was a Swahili translation of Shakespeare's poems, selected one at random, and read it to her:

Live with me, and be my love,
And we will all the pleasures prove
That hills and valleys, dales and fields,
And all the craggy mountains yields.
There will we sit upon the rocks,
And see the shepherds feed their flocks,
By shallow rivers, by whose falls
Melodious birds sing madrigals.
There will I make thee a bed of roses,
With a thousand fragrant posies,
A cap of flowers, and a kirtle
Embroider'd all with leaves of myrtle.
A bed of straw and ivy buds,
With coral clasps and amber studs;
And if these pleasures may thee move,
Then live with me and be my love.

Kamari frowned. "I do not understand."

"I told you that you would not," I said. "Now put the book away and finish cleaning my hut. You must still work in your father's *shamba*, along with your duties here."

She nodded and disappeared into my hut, only to burst forth excitedly a few minutes later.

"It is a *story!*" she exclaimed.

"What is?"

"The sign you read! I do not understand many of the words, but it is a story about a warrior who asks a maiden to marry him!" She paused. "*You* would tell it better, Koriba. The sign doesn't even mention *fisi*, the hyena, and *mamba*, the crocodile, who dwell by the river and would eat the warrior and his wife. Still, it is a story! I had thought it would be a spell for *mundumugus*."

"You are very wise to know that it is a story," I said.

"Read another to me!" she said enthusiastically.

I shook my head. "Do you not remember our agreement? Just that once, and never again."

She lowered her head in thought, then looked up brightly. "Then teach *me* to read the signs."

"That is against the law of the Kikuyu," I said. "No woman is permitted to read."

"Why?"

"It is a woman's duty to till the fields and pound the grain and make the fires and weave the fabrics and bear her husband's children," I answered.

"But I am not a woman," she pointed out. "I am just a little girl."

"But you will become a woman," I said, "and a woman may not read."

"Teach me now, and I will forget how when I become a woman."

"Does the eagle forget how to fly, or the hyena to kill?"

"It is not fair."

"No," I said. "But it is just."

"I do not understand."

"Then I will explain it to you," I said. "Sit down, Kamari."

She sat down on the dirt opposite me and leaned forward intently.

"Many years ago," I began, "the Kikuyu lived in the shadow of Kirinyaga, the mountain upon which Ngai dwells."

"I know," she said. "Then the Europeans came and built their cities."

"You are interrupting," I said.

"I am sorry, Koriba," she answered. "But I already know this story."

"You do not know all of it," I replied. "Before the Europeans came, we lived in harmony with the land. We tended our cattle and plowed our fields, we produced just enough children to replace those who died of old age and disease, and those who died in our wars against the Maasai and the Wakamba and the Nandi. Our lives were simple but fulfilling."

"And *then* the Europeans came!" she said.

"Then the Europeans came," I agreed, "and they brought new ways with them."

"Evil ways."

I shook my head. "They were not evil ways for the Europeans," I replied. "I know, for I have studied in European schools. But they were not good ways for the Kikuyu and the Maasai and the Wakamba and the Embu and the Kisi and all the other tribes. We saw the clothes they wore and the buildings they erected and the machines they used, and we tried to become like Europeans. But we are not Europeans, and their ways are not our ways, and they do not work for us. Our cities became overcrowded and polluted, and our land grew barren, and our animals died, and our water became poisoned, and finally, when the Eutopian Council allowed us to move to the world of Kirinyaga, we left Kenya behind and came here to live according to the old ways, the ways that are good for the Kikuyu." I paused. "Long ago the Kikuyu had no written language, and did not know how to read, and since we are trying to create a Kikuyu world here on Kirinyaga, it is only fitting that our people do not learn to read or write."

"But what is good about not knowing how to read?" she asked. "Just because we didn't do it before the Europeans came doesn't make it bad."

"Reading will make you aware of other ways of thinking and living, and then you will be discontented with your life on Kirinyaga."

"But *you* read, and you are not discontented."

"I am the *mundumugu*," I said. "I am wise enough to know that what I read are lies."

"But lies are not always bad," she persisted. "You tell them all the time."

"The *mundumugu* does not lie to his people," I replied sternly.

"You call them stories, like the story of the lion and the hare, or the tale of how the rainbow came to be, but they are lies."

"They are parables," I said.

"What is a parable?"

"A type of story."

"Is it a true story?"

"In a way."

"If it is true in a way, then it is also a lie in a way, is it not?" she replied, and then continued before I could answer her. "And if I can listen to a lie, why can I not read one?"

"I have already explained it to you."

"It is not fair," she repeated.

"No," I agreed. "But it is true, and in the long run it is for the good of the Kikuyu."

"I still don't understand why it is good," she complained.

"Because we are all that remain. Once before the Kikuyu tried to become something that they were not, and we became not city-dwelling Kikuyu, or bad Kikuyu, or unhappy Kikuyu, but an entirely new tribe called Kenyans. Those of us who came to Kirinyaga came here to preserve the old ways—and if women start reading, some of them will become discontented, and they will leave, and the none day there will be no Kikuyu left."

"But I don't want to leave Kirinyaga!" she protested. "I want to become circumcised, and bear many children for my husband, and till the fields of his *shamba*, and someday be cared for by my grandchildren."

"That is the way you are supposed to feel."

"But I also want to read about other worlds and other times."

I shook my head. "No."

"But—"

"I will hear no more of this today," I said. "The sun grows high in the sky, and you have not yet finished your tasks here, and you must still work in your father's *shamba* and come back again this afternoon."

She arose without another word and went about her duties. When she finished, she picked up the cage and began walking back to her *boma*.

I watched her walk away, then returned to my hut and activated my computer to discuss a minor orbital adjustment with Maintenance, for it had been hot and dry for almost a month. They gave their consent, and a few moments later I walked down the long winding path into the center of the village. Lowering myself gently to the ground, I spread my pouchful of bones and charms out before me and invoked Ngai to cool Kirinyaga with a mild rain, which Maintenance had agreed to supply later in the afternoon.

Then the children gathered about me, as they always did when I came down from my *boma* on the hill and entered the village.

"*Jambo*, Koriba!" they cried.

"*Jambo*, my brave young warriors," I replied, still seated on the ground.

"Why have you come to the village this morning, Koriba?" asked Ndemi, the boldest of the young boys.

"I have come here to ask Ngai to water our fields with His tears of compassion," I said, "for we have had no rain this month, and the crops are thirsty."

"Now that you have finished speaking to Ngai, will you tell us a story?" asked Ndemi.

I looked up at the sun, estimating the time of day.

"I have time for just one," I replied. "Then I must walk through the fields and place new charms on the scarecrows, that they may continue to protect your crops."

"What story will you tell us, Koriba?" asked another of the boys.

I looked around and saw that Kamari was standing among the girls.

"I think I shall tell you the story of the Leopard and the Shrike," I said.

"I have not heard that one before," said Ndemi.

"Am I such an old man that I have no new stories to tell?" I demanded, and he dropped his gaze to the ground. I waited until I had everyone's attention, and then I began:

"Once there was a very bright young shrike, and because he was very bright, he was always asking questions of his father.

"'Why do we eat insects?' he asked one day.

"'Because we are shrikes, and that is what shrikes do,' answered his father.

"'But we are also birds,' said the shrike. 'And do not birds such as the eagle eat fish?'

"'Ngai did not mean for shrikes to eat fish,' said his father, 'and even if you were strong enough to catch and kill a fish, eating it would make you sick.'

"'Have you ever eaten a fish?' asked the young shrike.

"'No,' said his father.

"'Then how do you know?' said the young shrike, and that afternoon he flew over the river, and found a tiny fish. He caught it and ate it, and he was sick for a whole week.

"'Have you learned your lesson now?' asked the shrike's father, when the young shrike was well again.

"'I have learned not to eat fish,' said the shrike. 'But I have another question.'

"'What is your question?' asked his father.

"'Why are shrikes the most cowardly of birds?' asked the shrike. 'Whenever the lion or the leopard appears, we flee to the highest branches of the trees and wait for them to go away.'

"'Lions and leopards would eat us if they could,' said the shrike's father. 'Therefore, we must flee from them.'

"'But they do not eat the ostrich, and the ostrich is a bird,' said the bright young shrike. 'If they attack the ostrich, he kills them with his kick.'

"'You are not an ostrich,' said his father, tired of listening to him.

"'But I am a bird, and the ostrich is a bird, and I will learn to kick as the ostrich kicks,' said the young shrike, and he spend the next week practicing kicking any insects and twigs that were in his way.

"Then one day he came across *chui*, the leopard, and as the leopard approached him, the bright young shrike did not fly to the highest branches of the tree, but bravely stood his ground.

"'You have great courage to face me thus,' said the leopard.

"'I am a very bright bird, and I not afraid of you,' said the shrike. 'I have practiced kicking as the ostrich does, and if you come any closer, I will kick you and you will die.'

"'I am an old leopard, and cannot hunt any longer,' said the leopard. 'I am ready to die. Come kick me, and put me out of my misery.'

"The young shrike walked up to the leopard and kicked him full in the face. The leopard simply laughed, opened his mouth, and swallowed the bright young shrike.

"'What a silly bird,' laughed the leopard, 'to pretend to be something that he was not! If he had flown away like a shrike, I would have gone hungry today—but by trying to be what he was never meant to be, all he did was fill my stomach. I guess he was not a very bright bird after all.'"

I stopped and stared straight at Kamari.

"Is that the end?" asked one of the other girls.

"That is the end," I said.

"Why did the shrike think he could be an ostrich?" asked one of the smaller boys.

"Perhaps Kamari can tell you," I said.

All the children turned to Kamari, who paused for a moment and then answered.

"There is a difference between wanting to be an ostrich, and wanting to know what an ostrich knows," she said, looking directly into my eyes. "It was not wrong for the shrike to want to know things. It was wrong for him to think he could become an ostrich."

There was a momentary silence while the children considered her answer.

"Is that true, Koriba?" asked Ndemi at last.

"No," I said, "for once the shrike knew what the ostrich knew, it forgot that it was a shrike. You must always remember who you are, and knowing too many things can make you forget."

"Will you tell us another story?" asked a young girl.

"Not this morning," I said, getting to my feet. "But when I come to the village tonight to drink *pombe* and watch the dancing, perhaps I will tell you the story about the bull elephant and the wise little Kikuyu boy. Now," I added, "do none of you have chores to do?"

The children dispersed, returning to their *shambas* and their cattle pastures, and I stopped by Juma's hut to give him an ointment for his joints, which always bothered him just before it rained. I visited Koinnage and drank *pombe* with him, and then discussed the affairs of the village with the Council of Elders. Finally I returned to my own *boma*, for I always take a nap during the heat of the day, and the rain was not due for another few hours.

Kamari was there when I arrived. She had gathered more wood and water, and was filling the grain buckets for my goats as I entered my *boma*.

"How is your bird this afternoon?" I asked, looking at the pygmy falcon, whose cage had been carefully placed in the shade of my hut.

"He drinks, but he will not eat," she said in worried tones. "He spends all his time looking at the sky."

"There are things that are more important to him than eating," I said.

"I am finished now," she said. "May I go home, Koriba?"

I nodded, and she left as I was arranging my sleeping blanket inside my hut.

She came every morning and every afternoon for the next week. Then, on the eighth day, she announced with tears in her eyes that the pygmy falcon had died.

"I told you that this would happen," I said gently. "Once a bird has ridden upon the winds, he cannot live on the ground."

"Do all birds die when they can no longer fly?" she asked.

"Most do," I said. "A few like the security of the cage, but most die of broken hearts, for having touched the sky they cannot bear to lose the gift of flight."

"Why do we make cages, then, if they do not make the birds feel better?"

"Because they make *us* feel better," I answered.

She paused, and then said: "I will keep my word and clean your hut and your *boma*, and fetch your water and kindling, even though the bird is dead."

I nodded. "That was our agreement," I said.

True to her word, she came back twice a day for the next three weeks. Then, at noon on the twenty-ninth day, after she had completed her morning chores and returned to her family's *shamba*, her father, Njoro, walked up the path to my *boma*.

"*Jambo*, Koriba," he greeted me, a worried expression on his face.

"*Jambo*, Njoro," I said without getting to my feet. "Why have you come to my *boma*?"

"I am a poor man, Koriba," he said, squatting down next to me. "I have only one wife, and she has produced no sons and only two daughters. I do not own as large a *shamba* as most men in the village, and the hyenas killed three of my cows this past year."

I could not understand his point, so I merely stared at him, waiting for him to continue.

"As poor as I am," he went on, "I took comfort in the thought that at least I would have the bride prices from my two daughters in my old age." He paused. "I have been a good man, Koriba. Surely I deserve that much."

"I have not said otherwise," I replied.

"Then why are you training Kamari to be a *mundumugu?*" he demanded. "It is well known that the *mundumugu* never marries."

"Has Kamari told you that she is to become a *mundumugu?*" I asked.

He shook his head. "No. She does not speak to her mother or myself at all since she has been coming here to clean your *boma.*"

"Then you are mistaken," I said. "No woman may be a *mundumugu.* What made you think that I am training her?"

He dug into the folds of his *kikoi* and withdrew a piece of cured wildebeest hide. Scrawled on it in charcoal was the following inscription:

I AM KAMARI
I AM TWELVE YEARS OLD
I AM A GIRL

"This is writing," he said accusingly. "Women cannot write. Only the *mundumugu* and great chiefs like Koinnage can write."

"Leave this with me, Njoro," I said, taking the hide, "and send Kamari to my *boma.*"

"I need her to work on my *shamba* until this afternoon."

"Now," I said.

He sighed and nodded. "I will send her, Koriba." He paused. "You are certain that she is not to be a *mundumugu?*"

"You have my word," I said, spitting on my hands to show my sincerity.

He seemed relieved, and went off to his *boma.* Kamari came up the path a few minutes later.

"*Jambo,* Koriba," she said.

"*Jambo*, Kamari," I replied. "I am very displeased with you."

"Did I not gather enough kindling this morning?" she asked.

"You gathered enough kindling."

"Were the gourds not filled with water?"

"The gourds were filled."

"Then what did I do wrong?" she asked, absently pushing one of my goats aside as it approached her.

"You broke your promise to me."

"That is not true," she said. "I have come every morning and every afternoon, even though the bird is dead."

"You promised not to look at another book," I said.

"I have not looked at another book since the day you told me that I was forbidden to."

"Then explain *this*," I said, holding up the hide with her writing on it.

"There is nothing to explain," she said with a shrug. "I wrote it."

"And if you have not looked at books, how did you learn to write?" I demanded.

"From your magic box," she said. "You never told me not to look at *it*."

"My magic box?" I asked, frowning.

"The box that hums with life and has many colors."

"You mean my computer?" I said, surprised.

"Your magic box," she repeated.

"And it taught you how to read and write?"

"*I* taught me—but only a little," she said unhappily. "I am like the shrike in your story—I am not as bright as I thought. Reading and writing is very difficult."

"I told you that you must not learn to read," I said, resisting the urge to comment on her remarkable accomplishment, for she had clearly broken the law.

Kamari shook her head.

"You told me I must not look at your books," she replied stubbornly.

"I told you that women must not read," I said. "You have disobeyed me. For this you must be punished." I paused. "You will continue your chores here for three more months, and you must bring me two hares and two rodents, which you must catch yourself. Do you understand?"

"I understand."

"Now come into my hut with me, that you may understand one thing more."

She followed me into the hut.

"Computer," I said. "Activate."

"Activated," said the computer's mechanical voice.

"Computer, scan the hut and tell me who is here with me."

The lens of the computer's sensor glowed briefly.

"The girl, Kamari wa Njoro, is here with you," replied the computer.

"Will you recognize her if you see her again?"

"Yes."

"This is a Priority Order," I said. "Never again may you converse with Kamari wa Njoro verbally or in any known language."

"Understood and logged," said the computer.

"Deactivate." I turned to Kamari. "Do you understand what I have done, Kamari?"

"Yes," she said, "and it is not fair. I did not disobey you."

"It is the law that women may not read," I said, "and you have broken it. You will not break it again. Now go back to your *shamba*."

She left, head held high, youthful back stiff with defiance, and I went about my duties, instructing the young boys on the decoration of their bodies for their forthcoming circumcision ceremony, casting a counterspell for old Siboki (for he had found hyena dung within his *shamba*, which is one of the surest signs of a *thahu*, or curse), instructing Maintenance to make another minor orbital adjustment that would bring cooler weather to the western plains.

By the time I returned to my hut for my afternoon nap, Kamari had come and gone again, and everything was in order.

For the next two months, life in the village went its placid way. The crops were harvested, old Koinnage took another wife and we had a two-day festival with much dancing and *pombe*-drinking to celebrate the event, the short rains arrived on schedule, and three children were born to the village. Even the Eutopian Council, which had complained about our custom of leaving the old and the infirm out for the hyenas, left us completely alone. We found the lair of a family of hyenas and killed three whelps, then slew the mother when she returned. At each full moon I slaughtered a cow—not merely a goat, but a large, fat cow—to thank Ngai for His generosity, for truly He had graced Kirinyaga with abundance.

During this period I rarely saw Kamari. She came in the mornings when I was in the village, casting the bones to bring forth the weather, and she came in the afternoons when I was giving charms to the sick and conversing with the Elders—but I always knew she had been there, for my hut and my *boma* were immaculate, and I never lacked for water or kindling.

Then, on the afternoon after the second full moon, I returned to my *boma* after advising Koinnage about how he might best settle an argument over a disputed plot of land, and as I entered my hut I noticed that the computer screen was alive and glowing, covered with strange symbols. When I had taken my degrees in England and America I had learned English and French and Spanish, and of course I knew Kikuyu and Swahili, but these symbols represented no known language, nor, although they used numerals as well as letters and punctuation marks, were they mathematical formulas.

"Computer, I distinctly remember deactivating you this morning," I said, frowning. "Why does your screen glow with life?"

"Kamari activated me."

"And she forgot to deactivate you when she left?"

"That is correct."

"I thought as much," I said grimly. "Does she activate you every day?"

"Yes."

"Did I not give you a Priority Order never to communicate with her in any known language?" I asked, puzzled.

"You did, Koriba."

"Can you then explain why you have disobeyed my directive?"

"I have not disobeyed your directive, Koriba," said the computer. "My programming makes me incapable of disobeying a Priority Order."

"Then what is this that I see upon your screen?"

"This is the Language of Kamari," replied the computer. "It is not among the 1,732 languages and dialects in my memory banks, and hence does not fall under the aegis of your directive."

"Did you create this language?"

"No, Koriba. Kamari created it."

"Did you assist her in any way?"

"No, Koriba, I did not."

"Is it a true language?" I asked. "Can you understand it?"

"It is a true language. I can understand it."

"If she were to ask you a question in the Language of Kamari, could you reply to it?"

"Yes, if the question were simple enough. It is a very limited language."

"And if that reply required you to translate the answer from a known language to the Language of Kamari, would doing so be contrary to my directive?"

"No, Koriba, it would not."

"Have you in fact answered questions put to you by Kamari?"

"Yes, Koriba, I have," replied the computer.

"I see," I said. "Stand by for a new directive."

"Waiting . . ."

I lowered my head in thought, contemplating the problem. That Kamari was brilliant and gifted was obvious: she had not only taught herself to read and write, but had actually created a coherent and logical language that the computer could understand and in which it could respond. I had given orders, and without directly disobeying them she had managed to circumvent them. She had no malice within her, and wanted only to learn, which in itself was an admirable goal. All that was on the one hand.

On the other hand was the threat to the social order we had labored so dilligently to establish on Kirinyaga. Men and women knew their responsibilities and accepted them happily. Ngai had given the Maasai the spear, and He had given the Wakamba the arrow, and He had given the Europeans the machine and the printing press, but to the Kikuyu He had given the digging stick and the fertile land surrounding the sacred fig tree on the slopes of Kirinyaga.

Once before we had lived in harmony with the land, many long years ago. Then had come the printed word. It turned us first into slaves, and then into Christians, and then into soldiers and factory workers and mechanics and politicians, into everything that the Kikuyu were never meant to be. It had happened before; it could happen again.

We had come to the world of Kirinyaga to create a perfect Kikuyu society, a Kikuyu Utopia. Could one gifted little girl carry within her the seeds of our destruction? I could not be sure, but it was a fact that gifted children grew up. They became Jesus, and Mohammed, and Jomo Kenyata—but they also became Tippoo Tib, the greatest slaver of all, and Idi Amin, butcher of his own people. Or, more often, they became Frederich Neitzsche and Karl Marx, brilliant men in their own right, but who influenced less brilliant, less capable men. Did I have the right to stand aside and hope that her influence upon our society would be benign when all history suggested that the opposite was more likely to be true?

My decision was painful, but it was not a difficult one.

"Computer," I said at last, "I have a new Priority Order that supercedes my previous directive. You are no longer allowed to communicate with Kamari under any circumstances whatsoever. Should she activate you, you are to tell her that Koriba has forbidden you to have any contact with her, and you are then to deactivate immediately. Do you understand?"

"Understood and logged."

"Good," I said. "Now deactivate."

When I returned from the village the next morning, I found my water gourds empty, my blanket unfolded, my *boma* filled with the dung of my goats.

The *mundumugu* is all-powerful among the Kikuyu, but he is not without compassion. I decided to forgive this childish display of temper, and so I did not visit Kamari's father, nor did I tell the other children to avoid her.

She did not come again in the afternoon. I know, because I waited beside my hut to explain my decision to her. Finally, when twilight came, I sent for the boy, Ndemi, to fill my gourds and clean my *boma*, and although such chores are woman's work, he did not dare disobey his *mundumugu*, although his every gesture displayed contempt for the tasks I had set for him.

When two more days had passed with no sign of Kamari, I summoned Njoro, her father.

"Kamari has broken her word to me," I said when he arrived. "If she does not come to clean my *boma* this afternoon, I will be forced to place a *thahu* upon her."

He looked puzzled. "She says that you have already placed a curse on her, Koriba. I was going to ask you if we should turn her out of our *boma*."

I shook my head. "No," I said. "Do not turn her out of your *boma*. I have placed no *thahu* on her yet—but she must come to work this afternoon."

"I do not know if she is strong enough," said Njoro. "She has had neither food nor water for three days, and she sits motionless in my wife's hut." He paused. "*Someone* has placed a *thahu* on her. If it was not you, perhaps you can cast a spell to remove it."

"She has gone three days without eating or drinking?" I repeated.

He nodded.

"I will see her," I said, getting to my feet and following him down the winding path to the village. When we reached Njoro's *boma* he led me to his wife's hut, then called Kamari's worried mother out and stood aside as I entered. Kamari sat at the farthest point from the door, her back propped against a wall, her knees drawn up to her chin, her arms encircling her thin legs.

"*Jambo*, Kamari," I said.

She stared at me but said nothing.

"Your mother worries for you, and your father tells me that you no longer eat or drink."

She made no answer.

"You also have not kept your promise to tend my *boma*."

Silence.

"Have you forgotten how to speak?" I asked.

"Kikuyu women do not speak," she said bitterly. "They do not think. All they do is bear babies and cook food and gather firewood and till the fields. They do not have to speak or think to do that."

"Are you that unhappy?"

She did not answer.

"Listen to my words, Kamari," I said slowly. "I made my decision for the good of Kirinyaga, and I will not recant it. As a Kikuyu woman, you must live the life that has been ordained for you." I paused. "However, neither the Kikuyu nor the Eutopian Council are without compassion for the individual. Any member of our society may leave if he wishes. According to the charter we signed when we claimed this world, you need only walk to that area known as Haven, and a Maintenence ship will pick you up and transport you to the location of your choice."

"All I know is Kirinyaga," she said. "How am I to choose a new home if I am forbidden to learn about other places?"

"I do not know," I admitted.

"I don't *want* to leave Kirinyaga!" she continued. "This is my home. These are my people. I am a Kikuyu girl, not a Maasai girl or a European girl. I will bear my husband's children and till his *shamba*, I will gather his wood and cook his meals and weave his garments, I will leave my parents' *shamba* and live with my husband's family. I will do all this without complaint, Koriba, if you will just let me learn to read and write!"

"I cannot," I said sadly.

"Buy *why*?"

"Who is the wisest man you know, Kamari?" I asked.

"The *mundumugu* is always the wisest man in the village."

"Then you must trust to my wisdom."

"But I feel like the pygmy falcon," she said, her misery reflected in her voice. "He spent his life dreaming of soaring high upon the winds. I dream of seeing words upon the computer screen."

"You are not like the falcon at all," I said. "He was prevented from being what he was meant to be. You are prevented from being what you are not meant to be."

"You are not an evil man, Koriba," she said solemnly. "But you are wrong."

"If that is so, then I shall have to live with it," I said.

"But you are asking *me* to live with it," she said, "and that is your crime."

"If you call me a criminal again," I said sternly, for no one may speak thus to the *mundumugu*, "I shall surely place a *thahu* on you."

"What more can you do?" she asked bitterly.

"I can turn you into a hyena, an unclean eater of human flesh who prowls only in the darkness. I can fill your belly with thorns, so that your every movement will be agony. I can—"

"You are just a man," she said wearily, "and you have already done your worst."

"I will hear no more of this," I said. "I order you to eat and drink what your mother brings to you, and I expect to see you at my *boma* this afternoon."

I walked out of the hut and told Kamari's mother to bring her banana mash and water, then stopped by old Benima's *shamba*. Buffalo had stampeded through his fields, destroying his crops, and I sacrificed a goat to remove the *thahu* that had fallen upon his land.

When I was finished I stopped at Koinnage's *boma*, where he offered me some freshly brewed *pombe* and began complaining about Kibo, his newest wife, who kept taking sides with Shumi, his second wife, against Wambu, his senior wife.

"You can always divorce her and return her to her family's *shamba*," I suggested.

"She cost twenty cows and five goats!" he complained. "Will her family return them?"

"No, they will not."

"Then I will not send her back."

"As you wish," I said with a shrug.

"Besides, she is very strong and very lovely," he continued. "I just wish she would stop fighting with Wambu."

"What do they fight about?" I asked.

"They fight about who will fetch the water, and who will mend my garments, and who will repair the thatch on my hut." He paused. "They even argue about whose hut I should visit at night, as if I had no choice in the matter."

"Do they ever fight about ideas?" I asked.

"Ideas?" he repeated blankly.

"Such as you might find in books."

He laughed. "They are *women*, Koriba. What need have they for ideas?" He paused. "In fact, what need have any of us for them?"

"I do not know," I said. "I was merely curious."

"You look disturbed," he noted.

"It must be the *pombe*," I said. "I am an old man, and perhaps it is too strong."

"That is because Kibo will not listen when Wambu tells her how to brew it. I really should send her away"—he looked at Kibo as she carried a load of wood on her strong, young back—"but she is so young and so lovely." Suddenly his gaze went beyond his newest wife to the village. "Ah!" he said. "I see that old Siboki has finally died."

"How do you know?" I asked.

He pointed to a thin column of smoke. "They are burning his hut."

I stared off in the direction he indicated. "That is not Siboki's hut," I said. "His *boma* is more to the west."

"Who else is old and infirm and due to die?" asked Koinnage.

And suddenly I knew, as surely as I knew that Ngai sits on His throne atop the holy mountain, that Kamari was dead.

I walked to Njoro's *shamba* as quickly as I could. When I arrived, Kamari's mother and sister and grandmother were already wailing the death chant, tears streaming down their faces.

"What happened?" I demanded, walking up to Njoro.

"Why do you ask, when it is you who destroyed her?" he replied bitterly.

"I did not destroy her," I said.

"Did you not threaten to place a *thahu* on her just this morning?" he persisted. "You did so, and now she is dead, and I have but one daughter to bring the bride price, and I have had to burn Kamari's hut."

"Stop worrying about bride prices and huts and tell me what happened, or you shall learn what it means to be cursed by a *mundumugu*!" I snapped.

"She hung herself in her hut with a length of buffalo hide."

Five women from the neighboring *shamba* arrived and took up the death chant.

"She hung herself in her hut?" I repeated.

He nodded. "She could at least have hung herself from a tree, so that her hut would not be unclean and I would not have to burn it."

"Be quiet!" I said, trying to collect my thoughts.

"She was not a bad daughter," he continued. "Why did you curse her, Koriba?"

"I did not place a *thahu* upon her," I said, wondering if I spoke the truth. "I wished only to save her."

"Who has stronger medicine than you?" he asked fearfully.

"She broke the law of Ngai," I answered.

"And now Ngai has taken His vengeance!" moaned Njoro fearfully. "Which member of my family will He strike down next?"

"None of you," I said. "Only Kamari broke the law."

"I am a poor man," said Njoro cautiously, "even poorer now than before. How much must I pay you to ask Ngai to receive Kamari's spirit with compassion and forgiveness?"

"I will do that whether you pay me or not," I answered.

"You will not charge me?" he asked.

"I will not charge you."

"Thank you, Koriba!" he said fervently.

I stood and stared at the blazing hut, trying not to think of the smoldering body of the little girl inside it.

"Koriba?" said Njoro after a lengthy silence.

"What now?" I asked irritably.

"We did not know what to do with the buffalo hide, for it bore the mark of your *thahu*, and we were afraid to burn it. Now I know that the marks were made by Ngai and not you, and I am afraid even to touch it. Will you take it away?"

"What marks?" I said. "What are you talking about?"

He took me by the arm and led me around to the front of the burning hut. There, on the ground, some ten paces from the entrance, lay the strip of tanned hide with which Kamari had hanged herself, and scrawled upon it were more of the strange symbols I had seen on my computer screen three days earlier.

I reached down and picked up the hide, then turned to Njoro. "If indeed there is a curse on your *shamba*," I said, "I will remove it and take it upon myself, by taking Ngai's marks with me."

"Thank you, Koriba!" he said, obviously much relieved.

"I must leave to prepare my magic," I said abruptly, and began the long walk back to my *boma*. When I arrived I took the strip of buffalo hide into my hut.

"Computer," I said. "Activate."

"Activated."

I held the strip up to its scanning lens.

"Do you recognize this language?" I asked.

The lens glowed briefly.

"Yes, Koriba. It is the Language of Kamari."

"What does it say?"

"It is a couplet:

I know why the caged birds die —
For, like them, I have touched the sky."

The entire village came to Njoro's *shamba* in the afternoon, and the women wailed the death chant all night and all of the next day, but before long Kamari was forgotten, for life goes on and she was just a little Kikuyu girl.

Since that day, whenever I have found a bird with a broken wing I have attempted to nurse it back to health. It always dies, and I always bury it next to the mound of earth that marks where Kamari's hut had been.

It is on those days, when I place the birds in the ground, that I find myself thinking of her again, and wishing that I was just a simple man, tending my cattle and worrying about my crops and thinking the thoughts of simple men, rather than a *mundumugu* who must live with the consequences of his wisdom.

Unsafe at Any Speed

ANOTHER SERIOUS PEDANTIC ESSAY BY MIKE RESNICK

I had sold a tongue-in-cheek article titled "Why Martians Are Attracted to Big-Breasted Women" to *Analog*, with the subtitle "A Serious Pedantic Essay." When it came time to write another Serious Pedantic Essay, I remembered the wonderfully funny article Larry Niven had written about the potentially tragic consequences of Superman's love life ("Man of Steel, Woman of Kleenex") and felt sure he wouldn't mind my examining another problem that befalls any visitor from Krypton who goes around with a big red *S* on his chest.

He's faster than a speeding bullet. He's able to leap tall buildings in a single bound. He can even exceed the speed of light when he feels like it.

So why does Superman find himself taking the bus to the scene of the crime more and more often?

The answer, of course, lies in the dynamics that allow him to fly. The man doesn't have an antigravity device, and he isn't a hollow-boned creature like a hawk that can simply ride the warm thermals until he sees a likely place to swoop down and confront a villain.

No, Superman "flies" the way normal men and women jump: by pushing off from the ground. Now, if you're an average, everyday kind of guy, that doesn't amount to much. Even if you're Michael Jordan, you're only soaring 44 inches above the ground for a maximum of 3.247 seconds. But if you're Superman, the force required to reach escape velocity—he doesn't limit himself to Metropolis, but frequently flies to other worlds—or the push needed to approximate light speeds for distant emergencies is sufficient to send the Earth careening out of orbit and into the Sun. When they sing "There'll be a hot time in the old town tonight" they won't be kidding.

But let's say that old Superdupe has friends with the combined brainpower of Doc Smith, John Campbell, and Isaac Asimov to help him find a way around that. You know what? He's *still* going to take public or private transportation to the scene of the crime.

Consider the following:

— If he reaches 660 miles per hour velocity, he will create an endless series of sonic booms. The plate glass industry will love him, but the insurance companies will refuse to cover property in any area where he's likely to appear—and there is no question that the good citizens of Metropolis would rather do without Superman than without house insurance, especially with Luthor on the loose with one of those neat Destructo rays he invented in the prison machine shop.

— Most of the time, crises requiring Superman's brand of powerful aid arise without warning. That means that he almost never files a flight plan, and that in turn makes him a serious menace to aerial navigation. Even if the local police are delighted to see him come racing to their aid, you can bet that the Federal Aviation Authority will be less than thrilled and will fine him for each unauthorized flight.

— Greenpeace will march against him and picket him, as his tail draft is precisely the kind that neither the spotted owl nor the condor can overcome. At the very minimum, he will be forbidden to fly over the Pacific Northwest (and any other area, anywhere in the world, with endangered avian species).

— He won't fare much better in the Northeast, as the wake of his tail wind will dredge up almost all the garbage that Manhattan pays New Jersey to haul off that overcrowded, overconsuming island.

— He plays havoc with bird migration patterns, since current research shows their homing instincts are a mixture of visual cues, wind patterns, and magnetic fields, all of which he constantly disrupts.

— He screws up weather patterns, and even such a respected conservative scientist as Al Gore has concluded that he is responsible for El Niño.

— There is every likelihood that when he flies he is a primary cause of tornadoes, cyclones, and hurricanes.

Then, of course, there are the unanswered questions, such as the legalities. Superman is a law-abiding citizen. So which name does he use on his passport—his true-blue 100 percent American name of Clark Kent, his unregistered nickname of Superman, or his alien name of Kal-El (and if the latter, has he applied for citizenship)?

Does he require a visa every time he flies over another country's air space?

When a transcontinental or interstellar adventure is done, must he clear Customs before he can return to his home in Metropolis?

Must he go through quarantine whenever he returns from another planet—or whenever he visits California from a neighboring state?

And let's consider some of the consequences of flying over other nations' air space—not just our enemies, but our friends, too.

Can Great Britain's early warning system tell that he's just a man cruising at an altitude of 40,000 feet, approaching London at 3,500 miles per hour—or does it identify him as an incoming missile wrapped, for unknown reasons, in a red cape?

When Iraq's radar spots him, will Saddam Hussein assume that the United States has launched a nuclear attack and respond in kind—by which I mean, of course, will he launch a SCUD attack on Israel?

What about the countries that *can* respond in kind—those that are using the latest, most up-to-date American weapons systems, such as, say, the Chinese?

And while all this is going on, does the Hubble telescope lock onto him and spend days tracking him as a Close Solar Object, rather than concentrating on incoming asteroids, comets, and other Close and Potentially Dangerous Solar Objects?

But I think I've made my point. Superman, poor fellow, is a captive of his own abilities, and can only fly in formation with F-16 fighter jets during military air shows on selected national holidays.

He even has to watch his diet. Not to put too fine a point on it, having super strength does not mean that he has a super intestinal tract. Pardon my bluntness, but the mere act of breaking wind could send him thousands of miles off course, while severely affecting the Earth's rotation.

This would seem to limit him to ground travel—he is, after all, faster than a speeding bullet—but alas, even land travel is too fraught with danger for him to use his abilities:

— A speeding bullet travels well in excess of 500 miles per hour. The wear and tear on our nation's roads would run into billions of dollars every year.

— The wear and tear where Superman has run is nothing compared to the damage when he skids to a stop.

— About a tenth of a second after Superman stops, the twenty million (or so) insects caught up in his draft will stop too—mashed to an unsightly pulp on his back and cape.

— As pointed out, Superman is subject to our laws, and of course willingly obeys them. But even with the best will in the world, he cannot, when traveling in excess of 500 miles an hour, manage to stop at every light that turns red as he is approaching it. His traffic citations would be so numerous that he simply could not pay even a small percentage of them on a journalist's salary.

— Also, after three major speeding violations in a two-year period, drivers have to surrender their licenses. I am not aware that Superman has a running license. When considering alternative punishments, I think it highly unlikely that the authorities will remove his legs, and simply taking away his boots seems somehow ineffective.

The man's superlative gifts have proven to be counterproductive. Just as he must always pull his punches for fear of killing an opponent, just as he must never yield to his instinct to crush Lois Lane to him for fear of literally turning her into jelly, he cannot race to the scene of the crime at top speed, but must go in slow, moderate stages.

So the next time you're walking along the streets of Metropolis, and you hear someone say, "Look up in the sky!" followed by "It's a bird!" and then "It's a plane!" just keep walking.

The odds, alas, are thousands to one that one of those observers was right.

The Pale Thin God

I have written perhaps nine science fiction novels and twenty science fiction short stories about Africa, either set there or extrapolated from things African. It's a continent I find fascinating, one Carol and I keep returning to whenever we can scrape together the time and the money. When I write about it, I try to do so with respect, and this includes respect for their non-Western religious beliefs.

One day a young man I'd never met before approached me at a science fiction convention and explained rather forcefully that I was doing a disservice to Jesus, who was a greater god than the pantheon of African gods, and that I should make that clear in one of my stories.

I took him at his word and wrote "The Pale Thin God." I've never seen him again, but I sincerely hope he was unhappy with the story, thought it proved exactly what he wanted me to prove. (It became, I believe, the shortest story ever to make the Nebula Preliminary Ballot.)

He stood quietly before us, the pale thin god who had invaded our land, and waited to hear the charges.

The first of us to speak was Mulungu, the god of the Yao people.

290

"There was a time, many eons ago, when I lived happily upon the earth with my animals. But then men appeared. They made fire and set the land ablaze. They found my animals and began killing them. They devised weapons and went to war with each other. I could not tolerate such behavior, so I had a spider spin a thread up to heaven, and I ascended it, never to return. And yet *you* have sacrificed yourself for these very same creatures."

Mulungu pointed a long forefinger at the pale thin god. "I accuse you of the crime of Love."

He sat down, and immediately Nyambe, the god of the Koko people, arose.

"I once lived among men," he said, "and there was no such thing as death in the world, because I had given them a magic tree. When men grew old and wrinkled, they went and lived under the tree for nine days, and it made them young again. But as the years went by men began taking me for granted, and stopped worshiping me and making sacrifices to me, so I uprooted my tree and carried it up to heaven with me, and without its magic, men finally began to die."

He stared balefully at the pale thin god. "And now you have taught men that they may triumph over death. I charge you with the crime of Life."

Next Ogun, the god of the Yoruba people, stepped forward.

"When the gods lived on Earth, they found their way barred by impenetrable thorn bushes. I created a *panga* and cleared the way for them, and this *panga* I turned over to men, who use it not only for breaking trails but for the glory of war. And yet you, who claim to be a god, tell your worshipers to disdain weapons and never to raise a hand in anger. I accuse you of the crime of Peace."

As Ogun sat down, Muluku, god of the Zambezi, rose to his feet.

"I made the earth," he said. "I dug two holes, and from one came a man, and from the other a woman. I gave them land and tools and seeds and clay pots, and told them to plant the seeds, to build a house, and to cook their food in the pots. But the man and the woman ate the raw seeds, broke the pots, and left the tools by the side of a trail. Therefore, I summoned two monkeys, and made the same gifts to them. The two monkeys dug the earth, built a house, harvested their grain, and cooked it in their pots." He paused. "So I cut off the monkeys' tails and stuck them on the two men, decreeing that from that day forth they would be monkeys and the monkeys would be men."

He pointed at the pale thin god. "And yet, far from punishing men, you forgive them their mistakes. I charge you with the crime of Compassion."

En-kai, the god of the Maasai, spoke next.

"I created the first warrior, Le-eyo, and gave him a magic chant to recite over dead children that would bring them back to life and make them immortal. But Le-eyo did not utter the chant until his own son had died. I told him that it was too late, that the chant would no longer work, and that because of his selfishness, Death will always have power over men. He begged me to relent, but because I am a god and a god cannot be wrong, I did not do so."

He paused for a moment, then stared coldly at the pale thin god. "You would allow men to live again, even if only in heaven. I accuse you of the crime of Mercy."

Finally Huveane, god of the Basuto people, arose.

"I, too, lived among men in eons past. But their pettiness offended me, and so I hammered some pegs into the sky and climbed up to heaven, where men would never see me again." He faced the pale thin god. "And now, belatedly, you have come to our land, and you teach that men may ascend to heaven, that they may even sit at your right hand. I charge you with the crime of Hope."

The six fearsome gods turned to me.

"We have spoken," they said. "It is your turn now, Anubis. Of what crime do you charge him?"

"I do not make accusations, only judgments," I replied.

"And how do you judge him?" they demanded.

"I will hear him speak, and then I will tell you," I said. I turned to the pale thin god. "You have been accused of the crimes of Peace, Life, Mercy, Compassion, Love, and Hope. What have you to say in your defense?"

The pale thin god looked at us, his accusers.

"I have been accused of Peace," he said, never raising his voice, "and yet more Holy Wars have been fought in my name than in the names of all other gods combined. The earth has turned red with the blood of those who died for my Peace.

"I have been accused of Life," he continued, "yet in my name, the Spaniards have baptized Aztec infants and dashed out their brains against rocks so they might ascend to heaven without living to become warriors.

"I have been accused of Mercy, but the Inquisition was held in my name, and the number of men who were tortured to death is beyond calculation.

"I have been accused of Compassion, yet not a single man who worships me has ever lived a life without pain, without fear, and without misery.

"I have been accused of Love, yet I have not ended suffering, or disease, or death, and he who leads the most blameless and saintly life will be visited by all of my grim horsemen just as surely as he who rejects me.

"Finally, I have been accused of Hope," he said, and now the stigmata on his hands and feet and neck began to glow a brilliant red, "and yet since I have come to your land, I have brought famine to the north, genocide to the west, drought to the south, and disease to the east. And everywhere, where there was Hope, there is only poverty and ignorance and war and death.

"So it has been wherever I have gone, so shall it always be.

"Thus do I answer your charges."

They turned to me, the six great and terrible deities, to ask for my judgment. But I had already dropped to my knees before the greatest god of us all.

Mwalimu in the Squared Circle

A few years ago I was editing an anthology titled *Alternate Warriors*. The title tells the theme: take some famed proponent of non-violence—Gandhi, Jesus, Martin Luther King—and put him in a situation where he must either advocate violence or actually take up the battle in person.

I have always had enormous admiration for the late Julius Nyerere, Tanzania's first president, and when it came time to write my own story for the book, I remembered the challenge from Idi Amin that leads off the story. I knew Nyerere and Amin weren't as famous as most of the people in the anthology, but on the other hand I had a lot of clout with the editor and I knew he'd approve.

The first time through, I found myself telling a humorous story—after all, it's based on a pretty ludicrous proposition. But then, when I was about halfway through it and feeling vaguely dissatisfied, Editor Resnick realized that there was a much more meaningful story to be told, and sent Author Resnick back to the drawing board to do it right.

"Mwalimu in the Squared Circle" was a Hugo nominee in 1994.

While this effort was being made, Amin postured: "I challenge President Nyerere in the boxing ring to fight it out there rather than that soldiers lose their lives on the field of battle . . . Mohammed Ali would be an ideal referee for the bout."

—George Ivan Smith
GHOSTS OF KAMPALA (1980)

As the Tanzanians began to counterattack, Amin suggested a crazy solution to the dispute. He declared that the matter should be settled in the boxing ring. "I am keeping fit so that I can challenge President Nyerere in the boxing ring and fight it out there, rather than having the soldiers lose their lives on the field of battle." Amin added that Mohammed Ali would be an ideal referee for the bout, and that he, Amin, as the former Uganda heavyweight champ, would give the small, white-haired Nyerere a sporting chance by fighting with one arm tied behind his back, and his legs shackled with weights.

—Dan Wooding and Ray Barnett
UGANDA HOLOCAUST (1980)

Nyerere looks up through the haze of blood masking his vision and sees the huge man standing over him, laughing. He looks into the man's eyes and seems to see the dark heart of Africa, savage and untamed.

He cannot remember quite what he is doing here. Nothing hurts, but as he tries to move, nothing works, either. A black man in a white shirt, a man with a familiar face, seems to be pushing the huge man away, maneuvering him into a corner. Chuckling and posturing to people that Nyerere cannot see, the huge man backs away, and now the man in the white shirt returns and begins shouting.

"*Four!*"

Nyerere blinks and tries to clear his mind. Who is he, and why is he on his back, half-naked, and who are these other two men?

"*Five!*"

"Stay down, Mwalimu!" yells a voice from behind him, and now it begins to come back to him. *He* is Mwalimu.

"*Six!*"

He blinks again and sees the huge electronic clock above him. It is one minute and fifty-eight seconds into the first round. He is Mwalimu, and if he doesn't get up, his bankrupt country has lost the war.

"*Seven!*"

He cannot recall the last minute and fifty-eight seconds. In fact, he cannot recall anything since he entered the ring. He can taste his blood, can feel it running down over his eyes and cheeks, but he cannot remember how he came to be bleeding, or laying on his back. It is a mystery.

"*Eight!*"

Finally his legs are working again, and he gathers them beneath him. He does not know if they will bear his weight, but they must be doing so, for Mohammed Ali—that is his name! Ali—is cleaning his gloves off and staring into his eyes.

"You should have stayed down," whispers Ali.

Nyerere grunts an answer. He is glad that the mouthpiece is impeding his speech, for he has no idea what he is trying to say.

"I can stop it if you want," says Ali.

Nyerere grunts again, and Ali shrugs and stands aside as the huge man shuffles across the ring toward him, still chuckling.

It began as a joke. Nobody ever took anything Amin said seriously, except for his victims.

He had launched a surprise bombing raid in the north of Tanzania. No one knew why, for despite what they did in their own countries, despite what genocide they might commit, the one thing all African leaders had adhered to since Independence was the sanctity of national borders.

So Julius Nyerere, the Mwalimu, the Teacher, the President of Tanzania, had mobilized his forces and pushed Amin's army back into Uganda. Not a single African nation had offered military assistance; not a single Western nation had offered to underwrite so much as the cost of a bullet. Amin had expediently converted to Islam, and now Libya's crazed but opportunistic Quaddafi was pouring money and weapons into Uganda.

Still, Nyerere's soldiers, with their tattered uniforms and ancient rifles, were marching toward Kampala, and it seemed only a matter of time before Amin was overthrown and the war would be ended, and Milton Obote would be restored to the Presidency of Uganda. It was a moral crusade, and Nyerere was convinced that Amin's soldiers were throwing down their weapons and fleeing because they, too, knew that Right was on Tanzania's side.

But while Right may have favored Nyerere, Time did not. He knew what the Western press and even the Tanzanian army did not know: that within three weeks, not only could his bankrupt nation no longer supply its men with weapons, but it could not even afford to bring them back out of Uganda.

"I challenge President Nyerere in the boxing ring to fight it out there rather than that soldiers lose their lives on the field of battle . . ."

The challenge made every newspaper in the Western world, as columnist after columnist laughed over the image of the 330-pound Amin, former heavyweight champion of the Kenyan army, stepping into the ring to duke it out with the five-foot one-inch, 112-pound, fifty-seven-year-old Nyerere.

Only one man did not laugh: Mwalimu.

"You're crazy, you know that?"

Nyerere stares calmly at the tall, well-built man standing before his desk. It is a hot, humid day, typical of Dar es Salaam, and the man is already sweating profusely.

"I did not ask you here to judge my sanity," answers Nyerere. "But to tell me how to defeat him."

"It can't be done. You're spotting him two hundred pounds and twenty years. My job as referee is to keep him from out-and-out killing you."

"You frequently defeated men who were bigger and stronger than you," notes Nyerere gently. "And, in the latter portion of your career, younger than you as well."

"You float like a butterfly and sting like a bee," answers Ali. "But fifty-seven-year-old presidents don't float, and little bitty guys don't sting. I've been a boxer all my life. Have you ever fought anyone?"

"When I was younger," says Nyerere.

"How much younger?"

Nyerere thinks back to the sunlit day, some forty-eight years ago, when he pummeled his brother, though he can no longer remember the reason for it. In his mind's eye, both of them are small and thin and ill nourished, and the beating amounted to two punches, delivered with barely enough force to stun a fly. The next week he acquired the gift of literacy, and he has never raised a hand in anger again. Words are far more powerful.

Nyerere sighs. "*Much* younger," he admits.

"Ain't no way," says Ali, and then repeats, "Ain't no way. This guy is not just a boxer, he's crazy, and crazy people don't feel no pain."

"How would *you* fight him?" asks Nyerere.

"Me?" says Ali. He starts jabbing the air with his left fist. "Stick and run, stick and run. Take him dancing till he drops. Man's got a lot of blubber on that frame." He holds his arms up before his face. "He catches up with me, I go into the rope-a-dope. I lean back, I take his punches on my forearms, I let him wear himself out." Suddenly he straightens up and turns back to Nyerere. "But it won't work for you. He'll break your arms if you try to protect yourself with them."

"He'll only have one arm free," Nyerere points out.

"That's all he'll need," answers Ali. "Your only shot is to keep moving, to tire him out." He frowns. "But . . ."

"But?"

"But I ain't never seen a fifty-seven-year-old man that could tire out a man in his thirties."

"Well," says Nyerere with an unhappy shrug, "I'll have to think of something."

"Think of letting your soldiers beat the shit out of *his* soldiers," says Ali.

"That is impossible."

"I thought they were winning," said Ali.

"In fourteen days they will be out of ammunition and gasoline," answers Nyerere. "They will be unable to defend themselves and unable to retreat."

"Then give them what they need."

Nyerere shakes his head. "You do not understand. My nation is bankrupt. There is no money to pay for ammunition."

"Hell, I'll loan it to you myself," says Ali. "This Amin is a crazy man. He's giving blacks all over the world a bad name."

"That is out of the question," says Nyerere.

"You think I ain't got it?" says Ali pugnaciously.

"I am sure you are a very wealthy man, and that your offer is sincere," answers Nyerere. "But even if you gave us the money, by the time we converted it and purchased what we needed it would be too late. This is the only way to save my army."

"By letting a crazy man tear you apart?"

"By defeating him in the ring before he realizes that he can defeat my men in the field."

"I've seen a lot of things go down in the squared circle," says Ali, shaking his head in disbelief, "but this is the strangest."

"You cannot do this," says Maria when she finally finds out.

"It is done," answers Nyerere.

They are in their bedroom, and he is staring out at the reflection of the moon on the Indian Ocean. As the light dances on the water, he tries to forget the darkness to the west.

"You are not a prizefighter," she says. "You are Mwalimu. No one expects you to meet this madman. The press treats it as a joke."

"I would be happy to exchange doctoral theses with him, but he insists on exchanging blows," says Nyerere wryly.

"He is illiterate," said Maria. "And the people will not allow it. You are the man who brought us independence and who has led us ever since. The people look to you for wisdom, not pugilism."

"I have never sought to live any life but that of the intellect," he admits. "And what has it brought us? While Kenyatta and Mobutu and even Kaunda have stolen hundreds of millions of dollars, we are as poor now as the day we were wed." He shakes his head sadly. "I stand up to oppose Amin, and only Sir Seretse Khama of Botswana, secure in his British knighthood, stands with me." He pauses again, trying to sort it out. "Perhaps the old *mzee* of Kenya was right. Grab what you can while you can. Could our army be any more ill-equipped if I had funneled aid into a Swiss account? Could I be any worse off than now, as I prepare to face this madman in"—he cannot hide his distaste—"a boxing ring?"

"You must *not* face him," insists Maria.

"I must, or the army will perish."

"Do you think he will let the army live after he has beaten you?" she asks.

Nyerere has not thought that far ahead, and now a troubled frown crosses his face.

He had come to the office with such high hopes, such dreams and ambitions. Let Kenyatta play lackey to the capitalist West. Let Machal sell his country to the Russians. Tanzania would be different, a proving ground for African socialism.

It was a dry, barren country without much to offer. There were the great game parks, the Serengeti and the Ngorongoro Crater in the north, but four-fifths of the land was infested with the tsetse fly, there were no minerals beneath the surface, Nairobi was already the capital city of East Africa, and no amount of modernization to Dar es Salaam could make it competitive. There was precious little grazing land and even less water. None of this fazed Nyerere; they were just more challenges to overcome, and he had no doubt that he could shape them to his vision.

But before industrialization, before prosperity, before anything else, came education. He had gone from the bush to the presidency in a single lifetime, had translated the entire body of Shakespeare's work into Swahili, had given form and structure to his country's constitution, and he knew that before everything came literacy. While his people lived in grass huts, other men had harnessed the atom, had reached the Moon, had obliterated hundreds of diseases, all because of the written word. And so while Kenyatta became the *Mzee*, the Wise Old Man, he himself became *Mwalimu*. Not the President, not the Leader, not the Chief of Chiefs, but the Teacher.

He would teach them to turn away from the dark heart and reach for the sunlight. He created the *ujamaa* villages, based on the Israeli *kibbutzim*, and issued the Arusha Declaration, and channeled more than half his country's aid money into the schools. His people's bellies might not be filled, their bodies might not be covered, but they could read, and everything would follow from that.

But what followed was drought, and famine, and disease, and more drought, and more famine, and more disease. He went abroad and described his vision and pleaded for money; what he got were ten thousand students who arrived overflowing with idealism but devoid of funds. They meant well and they worked hard, but they had to be fed, and housed, and medicated, and when they could not mold the country into his utopia in the space of a year or two, they departed.

And then came the madman, the final nail in Tanzania's financial coffin. Nyerere labeled him for what he was and found himself conspicuously alone on the continent. African leaders simply didn't criticize one another, and suddenly it was the Mwalimu who was the pariah, not the bloodthirsty butcher of Uganda. The East African Union, a fragile thing at best, fell apart, and while Nyerere was trying to save it, Kenyatta, the true capitalist, appropriated all three countries' funds and began printing his own money. Tanzania, already near bankruptcy, was left with money that was not honored anywhere beyond its borders.

Still, he struggled to meet the challenge. If that was the way the *Mzee* wanted to play the game, that was fine with him. He closed the border to Kenya. If tourists wanted to see his game parks, they would have to stay in *his* country; there would be no more round trips from Nairobi. If Amin wanted to slaughter his people, so be it; he would cut off all diplomatic relations, and to hell with what his neighbors thought. Perhaps it was better this way; now, with no outside influences, he could concentrate entirely on creating his utopia. It would be a little more difficult, it would take a little longer, but in the end, the accomplishment would be that much more satisfying.

And then Amin's air force dropped its bombs on Tanzania.

The insanity of it.

Nyerere ducks a roundhouse right, Amin guffaws and winks to the crowd, Ali stands back and wishes he were somewhere else.

Nyerere's vision has cleared, but blood keeps running into his left eye. The fight is barely two minutes old, and already he is gasping for breath. He can feel every beat of his heart, as if a tiny man with a hammer and chisel is imprisoned inside his chest, trying to get out.

The weights attached to Amin's ankles should be slowing him down, but somehow Nyerere finds that he is cornered against the ropes. Amin fakes a punch, Nyerere ducks, then straightens up just in time to feel the full power of the madman's fist as it smashes into his face.

He is down on one knee again, fifty-seven years old and gasping for breath. Suddenly he realizes that no air is coming in, that he is suffocating, and he thinks his heart has stopped . . . but no, he can feel it, still pounding. Then he understands: his nose is broken, and he is trying to breathe through his mouth and the mouthpiece is preventing it. He spits the mouthpiece out and is mildly surprised to see that it is not covered with blood.

"Three!"

Amin, who has been standing at the far side of the ring,

approaches, laughing uproariously, and Ali stops the count and slowly escorts him back to the neutral corner.

The pen is mightier than the sword. The words come, unbidden, into Nyerere's mind, and he wants to laugh. A horrible, retching sound escapes his lips, a sound so alien that he cannot believe it came from him.

Ali slowly returns to him and resumes the count.

"*Four!*" Stay down, you old fool, Ali's eyes seem to say.

Nyerere grabs a rope and tries to pull himself up.

"*Five!*" I bought you all the time I could, say the eyes, but I can't protect you if you get up again.

Nyerere gathers himself for the most difficult physical effort of his life.

"*Six!*" You're as crazy as *he* is.

Nyerere stands up. He hopes Maria will be proud of him, but somehow he knows that she won't.

Amin, mugging to the crowd in a grotesque imitation of Ali, moves in the for kill.

When he was a young man, the president of his class at Uganda's Makerere University, already tabbed as a future leader by his teachers and his classmates, his fraternity entered a track meet, and he was chosen to run the four-hundred-meter race.

I am no athlete, he said; I am a student. I have exams to worry about, a scholarship to obtain. I have no time for such foolishness. But they entered his name anyway, and the race was the final event of the day, and just before it began his brothers came up to him and told him that if he did not beat at least one of his five rivals, his fraternity, which held a narrow lead after all the other events, would lose.

Then you will lose, said Nyerere with a shrug.

If we do, it will be your fault, they told him.

It is just a race, he said.

But it is important to *us*, they said.

So he allowed himself to be led to the starting line, and the pistol was fired, and all six young men began running, and he found himself trailing the field, and he remained in last place all the way around the track, and when he crossed the finish wire, he found that his brothers had turned away from him.

But it was only a game, he protested later. What difference does it make who is the faster? We are here to study laws and vectors and constitutions, not to run in circles.

It is not that you came in last, answered one of them, but that you represented us and you did not try.

It was many days before they spoke to him again. He took to running a mile every morning and every evening, and when the next track meet took place, he volunteered for the four-hundred-meter race again. He was beaten by almost thirty meters, but he came in fourth, and collapsed of exhaustion ten meters past the finish line, and the following morning he was reelected president of his fraternity by acclamation.

There are forty-three seconds left in the first round, and his arms are too heavy to lift. Amin swings a roundhouse that he ducks, but it catches him on the shoulder and knocks him halfway across the ring. The shoulder goes numb, but it has bought him another ten seconds, for the madman cannot move fast with the weights on his ankles, probably could not move fast even without them. Besides, he is enjoying himself, joking with the crowd, talking to Ali, mugging for all the cameras at ringside.

Ali finds himself between the two men, takes an extra few seconds awkwardly extricating himself—Ali, who has never taken a false or awkward step in his life—and buys Nyerere almost five more seconds. Nyerere looks up at the clock and sees there is just under half a minute remaining.

Amin bellows and swings a blow that will crush his skull if it lands, but it doesn't; the huge Ugandan cannot balance properly with one hand tied behind his back, and he misses and almost falls through the ropes.

"Hit him now!" come the yells from Nyerere's corner.

"Kill him, Mwalimu!"

But Nyerere can barely catch his breath, can no longer lift his arms. He blinks to clear the blood from his eyes, then staggers to the far side of the ring. Maybe it will take Amin twelve or thirteen seconds to get up, spot him, reach him. If he goes down again then, he can be saved by the bell. He will have survived the round. He will have run the race.

Vectors. Angles. The square of the hypotenuse. It's all very intriguing, but it won't help him become a leader. He opts for law, for history, for philosophy.

How was he to know that in the long run they were the same?

He sits in his corner, his nostrils propped open, his cut man working on his eye. Ali comes over and peers intently at him.

"He knocks you down once more, I gotta stop it," he says.

Nyerere tries to answer through battered lips. It is unintelligible. Just as well; for all he knows, he was trying to say, "Please do."

Ali leans closer and lowers his voice.

"It's not just a sport, you know. It's a science, too."

Nyerere utters a questioning croak.

"You run, he's gonna catch you," continues Ali. "A ring ain't a big enough place to hide in."

Nyerere stares at him dully. What is the man trying to say?

"You gotta close with him, grab him. Don't give him room to swing. You do that, maybe I won't have to go to your funeral tomorrow."

Vectors, angles, philosophy, all the same when you're the Mwalimu and you're fighting for your life.

·⫶⫶·

The lion, some four hundred pounds of tawny fury, pulls down the one-ton buffalo.

The one-hundred-pound hyena runs him off his kill.

The twenty-pound jackal winds up eating it.

And Nyerere clinches with the madman, hangs on for dear life, feels the heavy blows raining down on his back and shoulders, grabs tighter. Ali separates them, positions himself near Amin's right hand so that he can't release the roundhouse, and Nyerere grabs the giant again.

His head is finally clear. The fourth round is coming up, and he hasn't been down since the first. He still can't catch his breath, his legs will barely carry him to the center of the ring, and the blood is once again trickling into his eye. He looks at the madman, who is screaming imprecations to his seconds, his chest and belly rising and falling.

Is Amin tiring? Does it matter? Nyerere still hasn't landed a single blow. Could even a hundred blows bring the Ugandan to his knees? He doubts it.

Perhaps he should have bet on the fight. The odds were thousands to one that he wouldn't make it this far. He could have supplied his army with the winnings, and died honorably.

It is not the same, he decides, as they rub his shoulders, grease his cheeks, apply ice to the swelling beneath his eye. He has survived the fourth round, has done his best, but it is not the same. He could finish fourth out of six in a foot race and be reelected, but if he finishes second tonight, he will not have a country left to reelect him. This is the real world, and surviving, it seems, is not as important as winning.

Ali tells him to hold on, his corner tells him to retreat, the cut man tells him to protect his eye, but no one tells him how to *win*, and he realizes that he will have to find out on his own.

Goliath fell to a child. Even Achilles had his weakness. What must he do to bring the madman down?

He is crazy, this Amin. He revels in torture. He murders his wives. Rumor has it that he has even killed and eaten his infant son. How do you find weakness in a barbarian like that?

And suddenly, Nyerere understands, you do it by realizing that he *is* a barbarian—ignorant, illiterate, superstitious.

There is no time now, but he will hold that thought, he will survive one more round of clinching and grabbing, of stifling closeness to the giant whose very presence he finds degrading.

Three more minutes of the sword, and then he will apply the pen.

He almost doesn't make it. Halfway through the round Amin shakes him off like a fly, then lands a right to the head as he tries to clinch again.

Consciousness begins to ebb from him, but by sheer force of will he refuses to relinquish it. He shakes his head, spits blood on the floor of the ring, and stands up once more. Amin lunges at him, and once again he wraps his small, spindly arms around the giant.

"A snake," he mumbles, barely able to make himself understood.

"A snake?" asks the cornerman.

"Draw it on my glove," he says, forcing the words out with an excruciating effort.

"Now?"

"Now," mutters Nyerere.

He comes out for the seventh round, his face a mask of raw, bleeding tissue. As Amin approaches him, he spits out his mouthpiece.

"As I strike, so strikes this snake," he whispers. "Protect your heart, madman." He repeats it in his native Zanake dialect, which the giant thinks is a curse.

Amin's eyes go wide with terror, and he hits the giant on the left breast.

It is the first punch he has thrown in the entire fight, and Amin drops to his knees, screaming.

"*One!*"

Amin looks down at his unblemished chest and pendulous belly, and seems surprised to find himself still alive and breathing.

"*Two!*"

Amin blinks once, then chuckles.

"*Three!*"

The giant gets to his feet, and approaches Nyerere.

"Try again," he says, loud enough for ringside to hear. "Your snake has no fangs."

He puts his hand on his hips, braces his legs, and waits.

Nyerere stares at him for an instant. So the pen is *not* mightier than the sword. Shakespeare might have told him so.

"I'm waiting!" bellows the giant, mugging once more for the crowd.

Nyerere realizes that it is over, that he will die in the ring this night, that he can no more save his army with his fists than with his depleted treasury. He has fought the good fight, has fought it longer than anyone thought he could. At least, before it is over, he will have one small satisfaction. He feints with his left shoulder, then puts all of his strength into one final effort, and delivers a right to the madman's groin.

The air rushes out of Amin's mouth with a *woosh!* and he doubles over, then drops to his knees.

Ali pushes Nyerere into a neutral corner, then instructs the judges to take away a point from him on their scorecards.

They can take away a point, Nyerere thinks, but they can't take away the fact that I met him on the field of battle, that I lasted more than six rounds, that the giant went down twice. Once before the pen, once before the sword.

And both were ineffective.

Even a Mwalimu can learn one last lesson, he decides, and it is that sometimes even vectors and philosophy aren't enough. We must find another way to conquer Africa's dark heart, the madness that pervades this troubled land. I have shown those who will follow me the first step; I have stood up to it, faced it without flinching. It will be up to someone else, a wiser Mwalimu than myself, to learn how to overcome it. I have done my best, I have given my all, I have made the first dent in its armor. Rationality cannot always triumph over madness, but it must stand up and be counted, as I have stood up. They cannot ask any more of me.

Finally at peace with himself, he prepares for the giant's final assault.

Here's Looking at You, Kid

I love old black-and-white Warner Brothers movies. If I were to name my favorite actor, it'd be pretty much of a tie between Humphrey Bogart and the team that has been affectionately called the Mutt and Jeff of international crime, Sydney Greenstreet and Peter Lorre. They only made three movies together, and while I prefer *The Maltese Falcon*, if only because it gives Sydney and Peter their juiciest parts, *Casablanca* is universally considered to be one of the two or three greatest movies of all time.

In retrospect this story certainly doesn't look difficult to write. To this day I don't know why it was. I'd wanted to write it for years. I must have made half a dozen false starts over a ten-year period, but it just never jelled. Each time I'd put it aside for a year or more, then try again, and decide I still didn't like it. And then one day in 2002 I sat down, tried again, finished it in about ninety minutes, and decided I'd finally done it right—or as close to right as I was capable of doing.

"I came to Casablanca for the waters."

Renault almost guffaws. "Waters? What waters? We're in the desert."

I shrug. "I was misinformed," I say.

Renault gives me a look.

Okay, pal, I think, *I'm keeping my end of the bargain, I gave you a hell of a line, one they'll be quoting for months. Just remember that when* she *shows up.*

Then Renault lays it on me: he's making an arrest tonight. At Rick's. Okay, so he knows about Ugarte. Big deal. He acts like he's doing me a favor, as if we need the publicity.

"We know there are many exit visas sold in this cafe," he continues, "but we know you have never sold one. That is the reason we permit you to remain open."

"I thought it was because we let you win at roulette." *Oh, I'm in rare form tonight. There's another quotable line for you. Now just remember who your friends are.*

"That is another reason," agrees Renault amiably.

Then comes The Moment. He mentions Victor Lazlo. I act impressed. I'm doing my job, playing my role, piling up points. Why admit that I hate the son of a bitch, that he's got the brains of a flea and the personal magnetism of a fire hydrant, that he speaks only in platitudes?

I start wondering: how can I score a bonus point? Then the perfect solution hits me, and I offer to bet that Lazlo escapes.

I can see in Renault's eyes that he knows that Lazlo can never be confined to Casablanca, that he'll find a way to leave, but he's got his agenda and his priorities, just as I have mine, and he takes the bet.

Then he goes off to arrest Ugarte. Poor little bastard with the poached-egg eyes and the high nasal whine. He wasn't a bad guy, not when you compare him to the rest of the scum that inhabit this god-forsaken city in the sand. Sure, he lied and he cheated and he took what didn't belong to him—but show me a resident of Casablanca who doesn't do the same thing. Hell, Ferrari buys and sells human beings, and Renault buys and sells the favors of half the human race. All Ugarte did was kill and rob some Nazis.

He runs up to me, the doomed little man in his sweat-stained white suit, the gendarmes hot on his tail, and begs me to help him, hide him, do *something* for him. I can't, of course; there are twenty French cops waving their guns at us . . . but it gives me a chance to add to the persona I've been building so carefully. I push Ugarte away, right into the arms of Renault's men, and brush myself off, uttering some crowd-pleasing drivel about how I stick my neck out for no one. The trick is to say it with insincere sincerity, so that everyone knows I'm going to stick my neck out for someone sooner or later.

I let Renault introduce me to the head Kraut and the obsequeous Kraut and the pizza-eater who can't stop talking, and then Sam starts playing The Song and I know Ilsa's here. I pretend I don't, I walk up to him and start demanding that he quit playing, and then I see her. She's a big girl, taller than I remember, and I'm glad they've got me wearing lifts; it wouldn't do to have her tower over me. Her perfume is as sweet and delicate as I remember, her eyes are as blue, her cheekbones as high, her skin as smooth. It still surprises me how such a large woman can be so feminine.

Our eyes meet, and that old feeling is still there. Suddenly I don't care that she deserted me in Paris, I'd sell everything I've got to Ferrari or anyone else if she'd agree to go away with me; hell, I'd even toss Sam into the bargain. She left me once, but it won't happen again, not this time. I've done everything asked of me. I started the casino, I've come up with line after line that people will quote, I've created a persona that men will want to emulate and women will want to seduce. I'm five feet seven, I smoke like a chimney, I'm starting to go bald— and I'm a romantic hero. Now fair is fair. This time she's got to stay with me, this time we have a happy ending. *You owe me that, pal, and I expect you to pay your debts.* Maybe you can even clean things up so we can go back to the States. If not, then Australia, or maybe Rio or Bahia—someplace, *any* place that this goddamned war hasn't reached.

I look at her again, and I remember the way she melted in my arms, the smell and taste and feel of her when I kissed her. And I think of our last morning in Paris. She wore blue, the Germans wore guns. I like the sound of it, but at the last moment *He* jerks me around and changes it. "The Germans wore gray," I find myself saying. "You wore blue." *Okay*, I admit, *it's better your way. But I'm trying, damn it; surely you can see that I'm trying.*

Then she hits me between the eyes with it—she's married to Lazlo.

"That sexless speechmaker?" I want to say. "I'll bet he hasn't touched you in six months." But I don't; I manage to look shocked. And I'm thinking, *That was a low blow, pal. I'm walking the line for you, I'm pulling my weight, and* this *is how you thank me? You'd better get your act together quick, or I'm not the only one who will suffer. I don't have to be cynical and sardonic, you know; I can keep my mouth shut just as easily—and don't you forget it.*

She walks off with the King of the Platitudes, and I stay behind to brood. Sam closes the place up and starts playing The Song, while I wonder aloud why out of all the gin joints in all the towns in all the world she walked into mine—and the second the words leave my mouth, I know I've given him another line that he'll be taking bows for five years from now.

I'm making you famous, I think. *I've never been better than I am tonight. You want to thank me? Give me the girl, and this time let me keep her.*

Ilsa stops by to pay me a secret visit and tell me why she married Lazlo, as if I give a damn. So she's lived with him for the past year. Who cares? There aren't any virgins left in the world, not in the middle of all this killing. We all have flings, and the dumb ones marry them. All I care about is that she's back, and I have to make sure that this time she stays.

I lie and tell her that Ugarte only gave me one letter of transit, not two. I can get Lazlo out of the country, but she'll have to stay until I can figure a way to get us out together. It doesn't seem to bother her.

She left me once, she says, and she hasn't the strength to do it again. Just the words I want to hear.

I know I can take her to bed right now, and it's been a long time, but *He* says No, not yet, we have to build more tension, Lazlo's only a block away and Strasser's goons might break in at any moment, and even Renault could sell you out for the right price.

So we just talk. I'm so pissed that I go out of my way to speak in monosyllables. *No more quotes for you, pal, not until you meet me halfway.*

An hour before dawn I send her back to Lazlo, half-hoping she'll walk in on him with one of the bimbos who set up shop under the gas lamps along the street . . . but I know it won't happen: this guy's too much in love with himself to waste his attentions on anyone else. Then, when the sun comes up, I walk over to the Blue Parrot and offer to sell out to Ferrari. He practically drools at the chance to buy Rick's.

I tell him he's got to keep Sam, and he agrees. Then I decide to do my good deed for the day—I don't figure stealing Lazlo's wife really counts as one—so I tell him that Sam gets a quarter of the profits. He grins and tells me he knows Sam gets only 10 percent, but he's worth a quarter and a quarter's what he'll get. I grimace. He agreed too fast. That means with Ferrari doing the books Rick's won't show a profit for the next ten years, and poor Sam will be working his ass off for twenty bucks a week and tips—but I haven't got time to worry about that, because I'm trying to get all my ducks in a row before the grand climax.

Before long I'm at the airport with Renault. I've told Ilsa to get Lazlo here, to tell him there are two letters of transit and they're for the pair of them. It's going to be interesting to see his face when he finds out we're putting him on the plane all by himself. My guess is that as soon as he figures out that he'll still be able to spout off in front of an audience he won't argue, he'll just grab his letter, kiss Ilsa good-bye, and go.

I still don't know which side Renault's on—the one with the most willing women, probably—so I take his gun away and turn mine on him. He seems more amused than frightened.

Suddenly Ilsa and Lazlo appear out of the fog, just as the plane to Lisbon begins warming up its engines. I hand him an envelope with one letter, and he doesn't even look at it, he just thanks me and tells me this time our side will win.

I want to sneer and say, "I ain't on your side, sweetheart!" but something—some*one*—stops me. He goes off to check the luggage, and I turn to Ilsa.

"We're together forever now, baby." That's what I *want* to say. But what comes out is some speech about how the problems of three people don't come to a hill of beans, and that he needs her for his work.

I check my pocket. The other letter of transit is gone, and I know with a sinking feeling in the pit of my stomach that Lazlo has both of them.

No! I want to scream. *I did my job! I played my part, I gave you all the quotes you can handle, I let Ugarte go down the tubes and I'm arranging for Lalzo to get out in one piece. I won, damn it! I deserve her!*

Ilsa looks at me with tears in her eyes. "And I said I would never leave you!" she says.

Then don't! I try to say. *I hope you don't think I'm doing all this for the bozo you married.* But the words catch in my throat, and instead I'm telling her that we'll always have Paris.

She's about to say something else, but I just give her a loving smile and find myself saying, "Here's looking at you, kid."

Great. The dumbest thing I've said in years, and it's the one everyone will remember.

Then they're on the plane, and I turn around and Major Strasser's there. He's got no reason in the world to be at the airport except to make me look even more heroic. *Fuck you, pal,* I say silently. *If I don't get the girl, you don't get a John Wayne gunfight.* I shoot Strasser down in cold blood just as the plane takes off.

It's obvious that we need a memorable line, something to break the tension.

Think of your own line. I'm not playing any more.

Finally Renault says, "Round up the usual suspects."

Not bad. I'd have done better, but not bad.

There's nothing left to do. We start walking off into the fog. He says something about going to Brazzaville. Just what I always wanted: a garrison with no electricity, no running water, and no women except for the ones who wear those huge plates in their lips.

Give me a break, I try to say. What comes out is, "Louis, I think this is the beginning of a beautiful friendship."

Then it's over, and I'm in limbo. I analyze what I did, what I said, what I could have done better, or at least differently. I've got to prepare, to think of subtle ways to manipulate Him as He manipulates me. I've got a little time to get ready: there'll be the newsreel, and a couple of cartoons, and the coming attractions, and then we start it all over again.

Only this time I'll get the girl.

The Burning Spear at Twilight

When Harry Turtledove invited me to write a story for *Alternate Generals III*, I decided to take another African leader I admired as much as Julius Nyerere (whom you've already encountered if you're reading this book in order). He was Jomo Kenyatta, the *Mzee* (Wise Old Man) of Kenya, the country's first president, and the purported-but-never-proven leader of the Mau Mau.

The Mau Mau rebellion (officially termed "The Emergency" by the British government) lasted from 1952 to 1956. It was as brutal a battle as has ever been seen, filled with killings and torture and mutilations—but public perceptions to the contrary, it was unsuccessful. Fifteen thousand Kikuyu were killed; less than one hundred white colonists died. And when it was over, the British still governed Kenya for another seven years, when they finally proclaimed Independence for political and economic, not military, reasons.

Kenyatta spent the years of the Emergency in a tiny jail cell in the desert town of Maralal. But since this was an alternate history, I decided to see how the Mau Mau would have fared had he actually been the general the British thought he was.

J omo Kenyatta paces his cell.

It is seven feet by nine feet. There is a barred window, something less than two feet on a side. Along one wall is a metal cot with a thin ripped mattress. In a corner is a rusted pail, filled with his urine and excrement. He has worn the same clothes for seventeen days; laundry day won't come for another two weeks.

It is ninety-seven degrees out, a cool day for Kenya's Northern Frontier District. The flies are out in force; usually even the insects lie up in the shade during the heat of the day.

Kenyatta has been in the cell in Maralal for just over a year. He has six years yet to serve. He wonders how much of his sentence he will manage to survive before he dies. His British guards, those who speak to him, are betting he doesn't live for half his sentence, but he will fool them. He is a tough old bird; he will serve well over half his time, perhaps even five years, before he succumbs.

He thinks back to the trial. Someday, when Kenya is finally free of the British, they will print the transcript, and the world will see that he was railroaded on a trumped-up charge. King of the Mau Mau indeed! To this day, he does not even know what "Mau Mau" means, or what language it represents.

Suddenly his door opens, and he realizes through the haze of heat that almost melts the mind that it is Sunday already, and that it is time for the one weekly visitor he is allowed. This time it is James Thuku, a friend of his from the old days.

Thuku waits until the door locks behind him, then places his hands together and bows as a British guard watches his every move.

"Greetings, O Burning Spear," he says. "I trust all is well with you?"

"You may call me Jomo, or even Johnston," replies Kenyatta, for before he was Jomo Kenyatta he was Johnston Kamau. "And I am as well as can be expected."

"Let me shake your hand in the tradition of the white man, that I may feel your strength," says Thuku.

Kenyatta frowns. The Kikuyu do not shake hands. But there is something in Thuku's expression that tells him that today they do, and he extends his hand. Thuku grabs it, squeezes it, and when they part, Kenyatta is holding a folded note in his huge hand.

"How do my people fare?" he asks, pocketing the note until he is no longer under close observation through the little window in the door.

Thuku's face says, *How do you think they fare?* but his voice answers, "They miss you, Burning Spear, and every day they ask the British to release you."

"Please thank them for their efforts on my behalf," says Kenyatta. Then: "Are they well fed and fairly treated?"

"Well, they are not in prison," answers Thuku. "At least, not all of them."

Stupid, thinks Kenyatta. *Here I give you an opportunity to say what the British wish to hear, and instead you tell me this. I doubt that they will allow you back here again.*

"More farms have been attacked?" asks Kenyatta.

Thuku nods. He doesn't care if the British hear. After all, it is in all the papers. "Yes, and they have killed and mutilated hundreds of cattle and goats belonging to the British."

"They are foolish," said Kenyatta in a clear voice, loud enough to be heard beyond the cell. "The British are not evil, merely misinformed. They are not our enemies, and mark my words, someday they will even be our allies."

Thuku looks at him as if he has gone mad.

"They are a handsome race," continues Kenyatta. "They have strong faces and straight backs." He switches from English to Kikuyu, which is much more complex and difficult to learn than Swahili, and—he hopes—beyond the abilities of the guards to understand. "And they have large ears," he concludes.

A look of dawning comprehension crosses James Thuku's face, and the next ten minutes consist of nothing but a discussion of the weather, the harvest, the marriages and births and deaths of the people Kenyatta knows.

Finally Thuku goes to the door. "Let me out," he says. "I am done here."

The door opens, and Thuku turns to Kenyatta. "I will be back next week, Burning Spear."

"I wouldn't bet on that," remarks one of the guards.

Neither would I, agrees Kenyatta silently.

He waits until the evening meal is done and the new guards have replaced the old. Then, while there is still enough light to read, he unfolds the message and reads it:

It has begun! Tonight we spill the blood of the British!

The news is slow to trickle in. For six months after Thuku leaves, Kenyatta is allowed no visitors at all. Finally he learns what has happened, not from the Kikuyu, but from the British commander.

Kenyatta has requested an audience with him daily since he learned that he has been denied any visitors, and finally it is granted.

The black man with the gray beard is brought, in chains, to the commander's office. The commandant sits as his desk, fanning himself in a futile attempt to gain some slight degree of comfort in the hot, still air.

"You wished to see me?" he demands

"I wish to know why I have not been allowed to have any visitors," says Kenyatta.

"We're not about to let them report on their missions to you, or receive new orders," says the commander.

"I don't know what you are talking about," says Kenyatta.

"I'm talking about your goddamned Mau Mau, and the massacre they committed at Lari!" yells the commander, pounding the desk with a fist. "We're not going to let you black heathens get away with this, and when we catch Deedan Kimathi—and we will—I will take great pleasure in incarcerating him in the cell next to yours. I won't even care about your exchanging information with him, since you're both going to be here until you rot!"

And with that, Kenyatta is escorted back to his cell.

"What happened at Lari?" he asks his guard.

"You ought to know. You were in charge of it."

"I am a prisoner who is not even in charge of his own life. How can I possibly know what happened?"

"What happened is that your savages went out and butchered ninety-three loyal Kikuyu in the town on Lari," says the guard. "Chopped them to bits."

"Loyal Kikuyu," repeats Kenyatta.

"That's right."

"Loyal to who?"

The guard curses and shoves the black man into his cell.

Kenyatta knows what will come next. It will not happen to him. He's probably safer in his cell than any of the Mau Mau are in their hideouts. But the British cannot tolerate this. They will strike back, and in force. He has to get word to his people, to warn them—but how is he to do so when he is allowed no visitors?

He begins smoking, begging an occasional cigarette from the guards. One day, months later, a guard gives him two, and he thanks him profusely, lights one, and explains that he's keeping the second one for the evening. Then, when the guards have changed, he unwraps the cigarette and scrawls *You must get me out of here!* in Swahili on the paper. He doesn't dare write it in English for fear the guards may find it, and by the same token he can't write it in Kikuyu for he is sure that the prison doesn't employ any members of the Kikuyu tribe now that they are at war with each other.

Day in and day out he stands by his window, watching and waiting with the patience of a leopard. Finally, almost two weeks after he has written his message and carefully folded it up, a black groundskeeper is trimming the bushes near his window. The man is a Samburu, and the Samburu and Kikuyu have never been allies, but he has no choice other than to hope the man realizes that the British are the blood enemy of both races. He coughs to catch the man's attention, then tosses the folded note out through the bars.

The Samburu picks it up, unfolds it, stares at it.

Can you even read? wonders Kenyatta. *And if you can, will you take it to my people, or to the guards?*

The Samburu stares expressionlessly at him for a long moment, then walks away.

Kenyatta waits, and waits, and waits some more. He has not seen the Samburu again, and he has been given nothing else to write on. Burning day follows freezing night, and he tries futilely to exercise in his nine-by-seven-foot universe. He begs for tidbits of information, but the guards have been instructed not to speak to him. He thinks it has been two years since James Thuku passed him the note, but he could be wrong: it could be eighteen months, it could even be three years. It is hard enough to keep his sanity without worrying about the passage of time.

And then one night he hears it: the sound of bare feet on the uneven ground outside his window. There are more sounds, sounds he cannot identify, then a crash! and a thud! and suddenly four Kikuyu men, their faces painted for war, are in his cell, helping him to his feet. One of them strips off his prison clothes and wraps him in a red kikoi. Another brings his trademark flyswatter, a third his leopardskin cap. They gently help him walk out the door.

"Where is your car?" asks Kenyatta, looking around. "I am too weak to walk all the way to Kikuyuland."

"A car would be searched, Burning Spear," says one of them. "We have brought an ox wagon. You will hide in the back, under a pile of blankets and skins."

"Skins?" says Kenyatta, frowning. "The British will stop you, and once they see the skins, they will search the wagon."

Another warrior smiles. "The British are too busy fighting for their lives, Burning Spear. The Nandi or the Wakamba will stop us, and if we let them take the skins, they will look no farther."

And it is as the warrior has predicted.

Kenyatta asks them not to announce that he is free. He will go to his village, regain some of his strength, some of the weight he has lost, and try to learn what has been happening.

"I do not know if we can spare you that long, Burning Spear," says one of the warriors. "The war does not go well."

"Of course it doesn't," says Kenyatta.

"They bomb the holy mountain daily, and some fifteen thousand of us are captives in the camps along Langata Road."

"Are you surprised?" asks Kenyatta.

"Did not you yourself tell us that we could not lose, that freedom was within our grasp?"

"It was. I only hope that the Mau Mau has not pissed it away for all time to come."

They stare at the old man, dumbfounded, and then at each other, and their expressions seem to say: *Can this be the Burning Spear we have worshipped all these years? What have the British done to him?*

Deedan Kimathi stands with his back to the cave wall, high in the Aberdare Mountains, and faces the assembled warriors. They are truly a ragtag army, not half a dozen pair of shoes between them, most armed only with spears and clubs.

If I only had a real army, he thinks. *If only we had the weapons the British have.*

Still, he is prepared to fight to the bitter end with what he has, and he has pinpointed the one way in which they might still defeat the British who are crawling all over the Aberdares and the holy mountain of Kirinyaga itself.

"We have suffered minor defeats," he says, shrugging off an increasing number of military disasters in a sentence fragment, "but now the time has come to assert ourselves."

"How?" asks General China. (Kimathi tries not to wince at the ridiculous names his generals have chosen for themselves.) "Every day the British planes drop bombs on us. Even the elephants and the buffalo have deserted the holy mountain. If we have proved anything, it is that we cannot fight them with sticks and stones."

"We will fight them with a weapon they are unprepared to deal with," says Kimathi with all the confidence he can project. "We will fight them with a weapon they do not have in their arsenal." He sees stirrings of interest in his audience. "We will fight them with barbarism and savagery."

"We already have," says General China. "And what good has it done?"

"This time will be different," promises Kimathi. "We will attack their women and their children, we will make Nairobi itself a place of unspeakable horror, we will kill and torture and mutilate, and against such an onslaught even the British will have to concede defeat and go home."

"Nairobi?" asks a dubious voice.

"Wherever they think they are safe, wherever they hide their most precious possessions—their women and their children and their elderly. We have been making a mistake. They brought them all in from the farms to the city, and yet we continued to attack the farms. This is *our* land, and we do not have to fight by British rules. They bring an army to the White Highlands, and we meet them in battle with spears against rifles. We have learned our lesson. We must go where their army isn't, must do our killing when there is no chance of retribution. When they finally realize that we are slaughtering them in Nairobi and move their army there, we will attack them in Mombasa, and when they come to Mombasa, they will find we are butchering their children in Lamu and Naivasha."

"That is the path to disaster," says a strong voice, and all eyes turn to the mouth of the cave, where Jomo Kenyatta is standing, surrounded by a small force of painted Kikuyu.

"Burning Spear!" exclaims Kimathi, surprised. "I did not know you were free!"

"It is not something the British wish to publicize," says Kenyatta as he walks forward. "But it was essential that I escape and join you, because this battle cannot be won by the methods you described."

"Then we will make them pay in blood for every Kikuyu they kill!" says Kimathi passionately.

"There are far more British than Kikuyu," says Kenyatta. "Is that really what you want—to trade a Kikuyu life for a British life until one side or the other runs out of lives, for I can tell you which side will run out of lives first."

"What have they done to you?" demands Kimathi. "You were the first to advocate independence!"

"And I still do."

"Then we must drive the British from our land!"

"I agree."

Kimathi frowns. "What are you saying?"

"The day of our hoped-for independence began in sunshine and fair weather—but we have already reached the twilight, and this Mau Mau war, these atrocities, have done nothing but guarantee that the British will not leave. Soon it will be dark, and the rays of hope will vanish as surely as the rays of sunshine."

"How would *you* get them to leave?" asks General China. "Ask them politely?"

Kenyatta shakes his head. "They will not go because *I* ask them. They will not go because *you* ask them. But when the right people ask them, they will go." He holds a book up above his head. "Does anyone know what this is?"

"A book," replies a warrior.

"Ah, but what book?"

"A British Bible?" guesses the warrior.

"It is a novel called *Something of Value*, written by an American named Robert Ruark. Even as we stand here, it is the best-selling book in the English-speaking world."

"What is that to us?" demands Kimathi, aggressively hiding the fact that he cannot read.

"It is about the Mau Mau. It depicts us as savages, not fit to rule ourselves. In this book we do nothing but maim and torture and mutilate."

"Good!" says Kimathi. "That should frighten them."

Kenyatta sighs deeply and shakes his head. "I have lived in England. They will never abandon their colonists to face such savagery as this book has convinced them that we will commit. You keep expecting the Americans, who fought the British to gain independence, to help us—but I tell you that no American will help the Kikuyu that are depicted in this book."

"Then what would you have us do?" asks Kimathi. "I swore a blood oath: I will never call a white man Bwana again. I will never rest while the penalty for killing a white man is death and the penalty for killing a Kikuyu is a twenty-five-pound fine. I will never pay a hut tax to the British, who force us to work on their farms—*their* farms on *our* homeland!" He pulls himself up to his full height and thrusts his jaw forward. "*Never!*" he roars.

"Never!" yell a number of the assembled Kikuyu.

"I agree," says Kenyatta. "I have been fined and beaten and jailed for my beliefs. They have not changed. But because I know how the world works, and you have lived all your lives in Kikuyuland, which in turn is only a very small portion of Kenya, you lack the experience to deal with the British."

"All your experience got you was a jail sentence!" says General Burma.

"Use your brain," says Kenyatta, suddenly annoyed that no one can intuit what he is trying to say, that he must carefully explain it step by step as if to a roomful of children. "Why do you think that I was the only one they jailed before Mau Mau? All your other leaders were fined, but only I have been kept away from you." He pauses. "It is because only I know how to drive the British from our land."

"We will not bow and beg," says Kimathi stubbornly.

"No one is asking you to."

"Then what?"

"You must trust me," says Kenyatta. "I know how our enemy thinks, how he reacts. I can still lead you to independence, but time is running out and you must do exactly what I say."

"*I* am the leader of Mau Mau!" says Kimathi. "We will do it my way!"

"I put it to you," says Kenyatta to the Kikuyu. "You have done it Deedan Kimathi's way for three long years and where has it gotten you? Twenty thousand Kikuyu, those loyal to us and those loyal to the British, are dead, and less than one hundred British have died. Once we owned the White Highlands, and our tribal lands extended to Nairobi in the south and the Rift Valley to the west. Now we hide in caves atop the Aberdares and the holy mountain, and that is all we have left. Will you continue to follow Deedan Kimathi, or will you follow me?"

As one, the Kikuyu jump to their feet and pledge their loyalty to the Burning Spear.

Kimathi turns to Kenyatta. "You have won," he says bitterly. "The army is yours."

Kenyatta shakes his head. "We are in the midst of a war, and the army needs a leader. It is yours."

Kimathi frowns. "Then I don't understand . . ."

"The army," says Kenyatta with a smile, "will respond to the commands of one general—you. And *you* will respond to the commands of one general—*me*."

"I hope you know what you are doing."

"I know exactly what I am doing," says Kenyatta. He raises his voice for all to hear. "I am not just the Spear, I am the Burning Spear—and what does a burning spear do?"

"It stabs!" cry a number of warriors.

"And what else?"

There is a puzzled silence.

Kenyatta smiles a confident smile. "It illuminates."

Kenyatta has set up his headquarters in the densest part of the forest on Kirinyaga, at an altitude of about nine thousand feet. He knows he would be safer in Mombasa, or even on the Loita Plains in Maasailand, but he thinks it is important that his warriors be able to see that he is here with them, and he understands the importance of symbolism, which is why he is on the holy mountain rather than in the nearby Aberdares, which cover far more territory.

He is sitting on a wooden stool—he finds he no longer has the energy he had before his incarceration, and can no longer stand for hours on end—and one of his generals, this one a General Tibet (Kenyatta is sure the man has no idea where Tibet is located), is reporting the latest disaster: a squadron of British commandos has ambushed twenty Mau Mau warriors and killed every last one of them. It occurred near the Gura Falls, about thirteen thousand feet up in the Aberdares.

Kenyatta sighs deeply. "It begins," he says.

"I do not understand, Burning Spear," says General Tibet.

"The first true step toward independence," says Kenyatta.

"But our men were slaughtered. We did not kill a single white man."

"If you had killed ten of them, it would make no difference," replies Kenyatta. "There are fifty million more where they came from."

He pauses. "Listen carefully, and do exactly as I say. After darkness falls, take five men that you trust to Gura."

"And bring back the bodies?" asks General Tibet.

Kenyatta shakes his head. "No. Arm them with sharp pangas, and when you arrive, cut the arms and legs from the bodies."

"We cannot do this!" protests General Tibet. "They are Kikuyu, not British!"

"They are dead. They will not mind." Kenyatta stares at him. "If you cannot do this, tell me now, and I will get someone who can."

"I will do it," says General Tibet, frowning. "But I do not know *why* I am doing it."

"Trust me, and it will all become clear," says Kenyatta.

General Tibet leaves, and Kenyatta turns to an aid. "Bring them to me now."

Four white men and two white women, all blindfolded, are ushered into Kenyatta's presence.

"You may remove your blindfolds now," says Kenyatta in English. They do so.

"Well, I'll be damned!" mutters one of them. "So the rumors are true!"

Kenyatta surveys them. The reporters and photographers are from the *New York Times*, *Newsweek*, the *Chicago Daily News*, two more from the British tabloids, and a documentary filmmaker.

"Welcome to Kikuyuland," says Kenyatta at last. "I apologize for the blindfolds, but I'm sure you understand why they were necessary."

"Okay, we're here," says one of the Americans. "Now what?"

"I promised you exclusive interviews when my emissary made secret contact with you, and you shall have them," answers Kenyatta. "I will give each of you half an hour. Then we will have dinner, and you will spend the night. Tomorrow morning you will be taken to observe the battlefield, such as it is." He pauses. "You are free to wander around my camp here, but please do not take any photographs that might help the British to identify our location. Also, do not overexert yourself until you have adjusted to the altitude. I do not want the British reporting that we kill journalists."

One by one, Kenyatta gives his interviews. He is the voice of reason, only too happy to cease the hostilities if the British would stop slaughtering his people and give them back their country.

While the journalists are fed their dinner, Kenyatta retires to his cave to catch up on the day's news. His spies have little to report: the British seem to have melted into the forests and vanished. They are getting to know the Aberdares and the holy mountain as well as the Kikuyu themselves do.

"We have killed no British today?" asks Kenyatta.

"We have not killed any this week, Burning Spear," says an aide.

"Just as well. When it has been dark for three hours, and the journalists are all asleep, take two men out with you. Find a clearing within a mile of here, and dig three shallow graves. Then fill them in, and put a cross at the head of each."

"But we have no one to bury in them," says the aide, puzzled.

Kenyatta smiles. "I won't tell them if you don't."

"I do not understand any of this," says Deedan Kimathi, and for the first time Kenyatta sees that his second-in-command is sitting at the back of the cave.

"You will."

"Why do you allow these journalists to see our camp?" persists Kimathi. "Even if they take no photographs, they will remember enough landmarks to lead the British to this very cave."

"But they won't," says Kenyatta.

"How do you know?" demands Kimathi.

"Because I have lived among the white man and you haven't. I know it is difficult for you to believe, but there is an entire segment of white men who are predisposed to believe only the worst of their own race and only the best of ours, and these journalists represent the publications that they read, that mold their opinions. When they see the mutilated bodies of our men in the morning, they will not ask who mutilated them; they will assume it was the British, because they have been taught to assume that their own race is morally flawed. And when they see the graves with the crosses, they will not dig them up to see if British soldiers are really buried there. They will see that we treat their dead with respect, that we mark their graves with the cross of the Christians, and they will never doubt the evidence of their eyes."

"But this is foolish!" says Kimathi. "*I* would not believe it!"

"You are not a white journalist who is searching for a story that fits his prejudices," said Kenyatta.

Within a week, the photos of the limbless Kikuyu corpses have appeared in every major newspaper and magazine in the Western world. Three Pulitzer Prizes are eventually awarded for photos and articles cataloging the descent of well-trained British soldiers into total savagery.

Kenyatta has chewed the *qat* leaves for two hours. He feels his consciousness slipping away. It is almost as if he has broken free of his old, weakened body, and is looking down on it from a great height.

"You are sure, Burning Spear?" asks the *mundumugu*, the witch doctor.

"I am sure."

"If I hear you cry out, I will stop."

"If you stop, I will order you put to death," said Kenyatta placidly. The *mundumugu* cannot tell if it is the Burning Spear speaking, or the *qat* leaves.

Five minutes later Kenyatta is so far gone into his trancelike state that he can no longer respond to questions. The *mundumugu* rolls him onto his belly and picks up the leather whip.

"May Ngai forgive me," he mutters as he brings the whip down on the old man's back. Tears roll down his face as he whips the man he worships again and again.

·⫻⫻⫻·

"I was treated fairly by my captors," Kenyatta is saying to four British journalists.

"That's not the way I heard it," replies one of the journalists.

"I have never said otherwise," protests Kenyatta.

"But a couple of your men say we tortured you."

"You are British," says Kenyatta. "Would you torture a middle-aged man who did not have the power to do you any harm?"

"No . . . but I'm not in the military."

"I have no complaints about my treatment."

"They *never* beat you?" persists another journalist, whose face practically begs him to contradict her.

"If they did, I'm sure they had their reasons."

"Then they *did* beat you!"

"You are putting words in my mouth," says Kenyatta. "If I were beaten, then surely I would bear the scars." He spreads his arms out. "Can you see any?"

"Would you take your shirt off?"

"Are you calling me a liar?" asks Kenyatta with no show of anger.

"No, sir," answers the journalist quickly. "But I would like to report to my readers that I have seen you shirtless and that you bear no scars."

"And then what?" asks Kenyatta with an amused smile. "Will you ask me to remove my pants as well?"

"No," says the journalist, returning his smile. "I'm sure just the shirt will be enough."

"As you wish," says Kenyatta, getting to his feet and starting to fumble with his shirt. "But I want you all to remember that I told you I have no complaints about my treatment at the hands of the British. I bear them no malice. The day will come when England will be Kenya's greatest friend and ally."

As he speaks, he removes his shirt.

"You see?" he says, facing them.

"Would you turn around please?"

Kenyatta turns his back to them. He is glad they cannot see his grin of triumph as their gasps of shock and horror come to his ears.

In the coming months he invites *National Geographic* to see the death throes of elephants, rhinos, and buffalo that have been crippled and torn apart by the British bombs. A ten-week-old lion cub with one foreleg blown away makes the cover of *Life*.

Every Kikuyu child who receives a wound from anything—a thorn bush, a jackal, a stray British bullet—is gathered into a single medical facility (it is too primitive to dignify it by calling it a hospital), and an endless parade of Western aid workers and journalists is ushered through it.

Each Kikuyu who dies from a British bullet is mutilated and photographed. Any British soldiers killed by the Kikuyu—and a number who never existed—are buried and their graves marked with crosses.

The King's African Rifles and the British army deny all the press's charges, but the journalists know better: they have seen the carnage with their own eyes. They know the British are extracting a terrible, barbaric revenge against the Mau Mau up in the forested mountains, they know that the Kikuyu are treating the dead of the enemy with honor, they know that the old Burning Spear has been tortured in a British prison, and they know that hundreds of innocent Kikuyu children have become victims of a British army gone mad.

Within six months the American government is pressuring the British to grant Kenya its independence. The French, the Germans, and the Italians follow suit within weeks. Even the SPCA has publicly condemned the United Kingdom.

"I cannot believe it!" exclaims Kimathi as word comes to them that the British have declared a cease-fire and are withdrawing from the holy mountain. "We have killed only four of them in ten months, and they have killed thousands of us, and yet *we* are winning the war!"

"Different times call for different methods," replies Kenyatta, who is unsurprised by this turn of events. "There is a sentence in their Bible that says the meek shall inherit the earth. They should have read it more carefully."

Two months later the meek have inherited Kenya. It is a foregone conclusion that Kenyatta will become the first president; an election seems a waste of time and money, but of course they will hold it.

At the ceremony that makes independence official, Malcolm Mac-Donald, the last British governor of Kenya, introduces Kenyatta to Prince Philip, who formally invites him into the Commonwealth.

"It is a new era, and hence a time for new names," declares the prince. "Just as Kenya Colony has become simply Kenya, I think it is time to cast aside the sobriquet of Burning Spear"—he waits until a murmur of disapproval from the crowd dies down, then continues— "and replace it with *M'zee*, the Wise Old Man. Certainly," he adds with a rueful smile, "he is wiser than we were."

Kenyatta silently agrees that the name suits him better these days. He decides to keep it.

The Kemosabee

When Piers Anthony and Richard Gilliam invited me to contribute to *Tales of the Great Turtle*, an anthology of science fiction and fantasy stories about American Indians, I was a little hesitant. After all, I was sure all the major Indian figures like Geronimo and Sitting Bull and Crazy Horse would be taken, and the only fictional Indian I could remember was Tonto.

Then, a few days later, while channel-flipping between sports events, I came to the scene in the movie *Cat Ballou* where Cat's father explains that the Indians are one of the twelve lost tribes of Israel.

I ran right to the computer and knocked out "The Kemosabee" in a little over an hour. I think it's one of the two or three funniest short stories I've ever written—and I've written a *lot* of funny stories.

So me and the Masked Man, we decide to hook up and bring evil-doers to justice, which is a pretty full-time occupation considering just how many of these *momzers* there are wandering the West. Of course, I don't work on Saturdays, but this is never a problem, since he's usually sleeping off Friday night's binge and isn't ready to get back in the saddle until about half past Monday.

We get along pretty well, though we don't talk much to each

other—my English is a little rusty, and his Yiddish is nonexistent—but we share our food when times are tough, and we're always saving each other's life, just like it says in the dime novels.

Now, you'd think two guys who spend a whole year riding together wouldn't have any secrets from each other, but actually that's not the case. We respect each other's privacy, and it is almost twelve months to the day after we form a team that we find ourselves answering a call of Nature at the very same time, and I look over at him, and I am so surprised I could just *plotz*, you know what I mean?

It's then that I start calling him Kemosabee, and finally one day he asks me what it means, and I tell him that it means "uncircumcized goy," and he kind of frowns and tells me that he doesn't know what *either* word means, so I sit him down and explain that Indians are one of the lost Hebrew tribes, only we aren't as lost as we're supposed to be, because Custer and the rest of those *meshugginah* soldiers keep finding us and blowing us to smithereens. And the Kemosabee, he asks if Hebrew is a suburb of Hebron, and right away I see we've got an enormous cultural gap to overcome.

But what the hell, we're pardners, and we're doing a pretty fair job of ridding the West of horse thieves and stage robbers and other varmints, so I say, "Look, Kemosabee, you're a *mensch* and I'm proud to ride with you, and if you wanna get drunk and *shtup* a bunch of *shikses* whenever we go into town, that's your business and who am I to tell you what to do? But Butch Cavendish and his gang are giving me enough *tsouris* this month, so if we stop off at any Indian villages, let's let this be our little secret, okay?"

And the Kemosabee, who is frankly a lot quicker with his guns than his brain, just kind of frowns and looks hazy and finally nods his head, though I'm sure he doesn't know what he's nodding about.

Well, we ride on for another day or two, and finally reach his secret silver mine, and he melts some of it down and shoves it into his shells, and like always I ride off and hunt up Reb Running Bear and have him say Kaddish over the bullets, and when I hunt up the Masked Man again I find he has had the *chutzpah* to take on the whole Cavendish gang single-handed, and since they know he never shoots to kill and they ain't got any such compunctions, they leave him lying there for dead with a couple of new *pupiks* in his belly.

So I make a sled and hook it to the back of his horse, which he calls Silver but which he really ought to call White, or at least White with the Ugly Brown Blotch on His Belly, and I hop up my pony, and pretty soon we're in front of Reb Running Bear's tent, and he comes out and looks at the Masked Man lying there with his ten-gallon stetson for a long moment, and then he turns to me and says, "You know, that has got to be the ugliest *yarmulkah* I've ever seen."

"This is my pardner," I say. "Some goniffs dry-gulched him. You got to make him well."

Reb Running Bear frowns. "He doesn't look like one of the Chosen People to me. Where was he *bar mitzvahed?*"

"He wasn't," I say. "But he's one of the Good Guys. He and I are cleaning up the West."

"Six years in Hebrew school and you settle for being a janitor?" he says.

"Don't give me a hard time," I said. "We got bad guys to shoot and wrongs to right. Just save the Kemosabee's life."

"The Kemosabee?" he repeats. "Would I be very far off track if I surmised that he doesn't keep kosher?"

"Look," I say, deciding that it's time to play hardball, "I hadn't wanted to bring this up, but I know what you and Mrs. Screaming Hawk were doing last time I visited this place."

"Keep your voice down or that *yenta* I married will make my life hell!" he whispers, glancing back toward his teepee. Then he grimaces. "Mrs. Screaming Hawk. Serves me right for taking her to Echo Canyon. *Feh!*"

I stare at him. "So *nu?*"

"All right, all right, Jehovah and I will nurse the Kemosabee back to health."

"Good," I say.

He glares at me. "But just this one time. Then I pass the word to all the other Rabbis: we don't cure no more *goys*. What have they ever done for us?"

Well, I am all prepared to argue the point, because I'm a pretty open-minded kind of guy, but just then the Kemosabee starts moaning and I realize that if I argue for more than a couple of minutes we could all be sitting *shivah* for him before dinnertime, so I wander off and pay a visit to Mrs. Rutting Elk to console her on the sudden passing of her husband and see if there is anything I can do to cheer her up, and Reb Running Bear gets to work, and lo and behold, in less than a week the Masked Man is up and around and getting impatient to go out after desperados, so we thank Reb Running Bear for his services, and he loads my pardner down with a few canteens of chicken soup, and we say a fond *shalom* to the village.

I am hoping we have a few weeks for the Kemosabee to regain his strength, of which I think he is still missing an awful lot, but as Fate would have it, we are riding for less than two hours when we come across the Cavendish gang's trail.

"Aha!" he says, studying the hoofprints. "All thirty of them! This is our chance for revenge!"

My first thought is to say something like, "What do you mean *we*, mackerel eater?"—but then I remember that Good Guys never back down from a challenge, so I simply say "Ugh!" which is my opinion of taking on thirty guys at once, but which he insists on interpreting as an affirmative.

We follow the trail all day, and when it's too dark to follow it any longer, we make camp on a small hill.

"We should catch up with them just after sunrise," says the Masked Man, and I can see that his trigger finger is getting itchy.

"Ugh," I say.

"We'll meet them on the open plain, where nobody can hide."

"Double ugh with cherries on it," I say.

"You look very grim, old friend," he says.

"Funny you should mention it," I say, but before I can suggest that we just forget the whole thing, he speaks again.

"You can have the other twenty-nine, but Cavendish is mine."

"You're all heart, Kemosabee," I say.

He stands up, stretches, and walks over to his bedroll. "Well, we've got a hard day's bloodletting ahead of us. We'd best get some sleep."

He lays down, and ten seconds later he's snoring like all get-out, and I sit there staring at him, and I just know he's not gonna come through this unscathed, and I remember Reb Running Bear's promise that no medicine man would ever again treat a *goy*.

And the more I think about it, the more I think that it's up to me, the loyal sidekick, to do something about it. And finally it occurs to me just what I have to do, because if I can't save him from the Cavendish gang, the least I can do is save him from himself.

So I go over to my bedroll, pull out a bottle of Mogen David, pour a little on my hunting knife, and try to remember the exact words the medicine man recites during the *bris*, and I know that someday, when he calms down, he'll thank me for this.

In the meantime, I'm gonna have to find a new nickname for my pardner.

The 43 Antarean Dynasties

We were in Cairo in 1989 and had a guide named Iman. He was a very pleasant and highly intelligent fellow, who explained that he had previously taught at the university, but he had a family to feed and found that he could make more money from tourists' tips. He explained that you couldn't even apply for a job as a guide until you had the equivalent of a master's degree in Egyptian history and spoke at least four languages fluently—which meant that he was far better-educated than 99 percent of the people he guided.

So here was this man, whose race had built pyramids and temples on an unbelievably vast scale when our ancestors were living in mud huts, showing off the lost glories of his people to the newest set of conquerors. For tips. And I remember that at one point he told us how pleased he was to have attentive listeners, because his previous group got annoyed with him for interrupting their discussion of the point spread in the upcoming Steelers-Rams game.

I took some notes, thought about it for eight years—some stories take longer to coalesce than others—and wrote "The 43 Antarean Dynasties."

It won the 1998 Hugo for Best Short Story
and picked up the Ignotus Award (the Spanish
Hugo) a couple of years later.

*T*o thank the Maker of All Things for the birth of his first male offspring, the Emperor Maloth IV ordered his architects to build a temple that would forever dwarf all other buildings on the planet. It was to be made entirely of crystal, and the spire-covered roof, which looked like a million glistening spear-points aimed at the sun, would be supported by 217 columns, to honor his 217 forebears. When struck, each column would sound a musical note that could be heard for kilometers, calling the faithful to prayer.

The structure would be known as the Temple of the Honored Sun, for his heir had been born exactly at midday, when the sun was highest in the sky. The temple took twenty-seven Standard years to complete, and although races from all across the galaxy would come to Antares III to marvel at it, Maloth further decreed that no aliens or nonbelievers would ever be allowed to enter it and desecrate its sacred corridors with their presence . . .

A man, a woman, and a child emerge from the Temple of the Honored Sun. The woman holds a camera to her eye, capturing the same image from a dozen unimaginative angles. The child, his lip sparsely covered with hair that is supposed to imply maturity, never sees beyond the game he is playing on his pocket computer. The man looks around to make sure no one is watching him, grinds out a smokeless cigar beneath his heel, and then increases his pace until he joins them.

They approach me, and I will myself to become one with my surroundings, to insinuate myself into the marble walls and stone walkways before they can speak to me.

I am invisible. You cannot see me. You will pass me by.

"Hey, fella—we're looking for a guide," says the man. "You interested?"

I stifle a sigh and bow deeply. "I am honored," I say, glad that they do not understand the subtleties of Antarean inflection.

"Wow!" exclaims the woman, aiming her camera at me. "I never saw anything like that! It's almost as if you folded your torso in half! Can you do it again?"

I am reminded of an ancient legend, possibly aprocryphal though I choose to believe it. An ambassador, who was equally fascinated by the way the Antarean body is jointed, once asked Komarith I, the founder of the 38th Dynasty, to bow a second time. Komarith merely stared at him without moving until the embarrassed ambassador slunk away. He went on to rule for twenty-nine years and was never known to bow again.

It has been a long time since Komarith, almost seven millennia now, and Antares and the universe have changed. I bow for the woman while she snaps her holographs.

"What's your name?" asks the man.

"You could not pronounce it," I reply. "When I conduct members of your race, I choose the name Hermes."

"Herman, eh?"

"Hermes," I correct him.

"Right. Herman."

The boy finally looks up. "He said Hermes, Dad."

The man shrugs. "Whatever." He looks at his timepiece. "Well, let's get started."

"Yeah," chimes in the child. "They're piping in the game from Roosevelt III this afternoon. I've got to get back for it."

"You can watch sports anytime," says the woman. "This may be your only chance to see Antares."

"I should be so lucky," he mutters, returning his attention to his computer.

I recite my introductory speech almost by rote. "Allow me to welcome you to Antares III, and to its capital city of Kalimetra, known throughout the galaxy as the City of a Million Spires."

"I didn't see any million spires when we took the shuttle in from the spaceport," says the child, whom I could have sworn was not listening. "A thousand or two, maybe."

"There was a time when there were a million," I explain. "Today only 16,304 remain. Each is made of quartz or crystal. In late afternoon, when the sun sinks low in the sky, they act as a prism for its rays, creating a flood of exotic colors that stretches across the thoroughfares of the city. Races have come from halfway across the galaxy to experience the effect."

"Sixteen thousand," murmurs the woman. "I wonder what happened to the rest?"

No one knew why Antareans found the spires so aesthetically pleasing. They towered above the cities, casting their shadows and their shifting colors across the landscape. Tall, delicate, exquisite, they reflected a unique grandness of vision and sensitivity of spirit. The rulers of Antares III spent almost thirty-eight thousand years constructing their million spires.

During the Second Invasion, it took the Canphorite armada less than two weeks to destroy all but 16,304 of them . . .

The woman is still admiring the spires that she can see in the distance. Finally she asks who built them, as if they are too beautiful to have been created by Antareans.

"The artisans and craftsmen of my race built everything you will see today," I answer.

"All by yourselves?"

"Is it so difficult for you to believe?" I ask gently.

"No," she says defensively. "Of course not. It's just that there's so *much . . .*"

"Kalimetra was not created in a day or a year, or even a millennium," I point out. "It is the cumulative achievement of 43 Antarean Dynasties."

"So we're in the 43rd Dynasty now?" she asks.

·⧗⧙Ⅲⅉⵘ·

It was Zelorean IX who officially declared Kalimetra to be the Eternal City. Neither war nor insurrection had ever threatened its stability, and even the towering temples of his forefathers gave every promise of lasting for all eternity. It was a Golden Age, and he could see no reason why it should not go on forever . . .

"The last absolute ruler of the 43rd Dynasty has been dust for almost three thousand years," I explain. "Since then we have been governed by a series of conquerers, each alien race superceding the last."

"Thank goodness they didn't destroy your buildings," says the woman, turning to admire a water fountain, which for some reason appears to her to be a mystical alien artifact. She is about to take a holo when the child restrains her.

"It's just a goddamned water bubbler, Ma," he says.

"But it's fascinating," she says. "Imagine what kind of beings used it in ages past."

"Thirsty ones," says the bored child.

She ignores him and turns back to me. "As I was saying, it must be criminal to rob the galaxy of such treasures."

"Yeah, well *somebody* destroyed some buildings around here," interjects the child, who seems intent on proving someone wrong about something. "Remember the hole in the ground we saw over that way?" He points in the direction of the Footprint. "Looks like a bomb crater to me."

"You are mistaken," I explain, leading them over to it. "It has always been there."

"It's just a big sinkhole," says the man, totally unimpressed.

"It is worshipped by my people as the Footprint of God," I explain. "Once, many eons ago, Kalimetra was in the throes of a years-long drought. Finally Jorvash, our greatest priest, offered his own life if God would bring the rains. God replied that it would not rain until He wept again, and we had not yet suffered enough to bring forth His tears of compassion. But He promised that He would strike a bargain with Jorvash." I pause for effect, but the man is lighting another cigar and the child is concentrating on his pocket computer. "The next morning Jorvash was found dead inside his temple, while God had created this depression with His foot and filled it with water. It sustained us until He finally wept again."

The woman seems flustered. "Um . . . I hate to ask," she finally says, "but could you repeat that story? My recorder wasn't on."

The man looks uncomfortable. "She's always forgetting to turn the damned thing on," he explains, and flips me a coin. "For your trouble."

Lobilia was the greatest poet in the history of Antares III. Although he died during the 23rd Dynasty, most of his work survived him. But his masterpiece, "The Long Night of the Exile"— the epic of Bagata's Exile and his triumphant Return—was lost forever.

Though he was his race's most famous bard, Lobilia himself was illiterate, unable even to write his own name. He created his poetry extemporaneously, embellishing upon it with each retelling. He recited his epic just once, and was so satisfied with its form that he refused to repeat it for the scribes who were waiting for a final version and hadn't written it down.

"Thank you," says the woman, deactivating the recorder after I finish. She pauses. "Can I buy a book with some more of your quaint folk legends?"

I decide not to explain the difference between a folk legend and an article of belief. "They are for sale in the gift shop of your hotel," I reply.

"You don't have enough books?" mutters the man.

She glares at him, but says nothing, and I lead them to the Tomb, which always impresses visitors.

"This is the Tomb of Bedorian V, the greatest ruler of the 37th Dynasty," I say. "Bedorian was a commoner, a simple farmer who deposed the notorious Maelastri XII, himself a mighty warrior who was the last ruler of the 36th Dynasty. It was Bedorian who decreed universal education for all Antareans."

"What did you have before that?"

"Our females were not allowed the privilege of literacy until Bedorian's reign."

"How did this guy finally die?" asks the man, who doesn't really care but is unwilling to let the woman ask all the questions.

"Bedorian was assassinated by one of his followers," I reply.

"A male, no doubt," says the woman wryly.

"Before he died," I continue, "he united three warring states without fighting a single battle, decreed that all Antareans should use a common language, and outlawed the worship of *kreneks*."

"What are *kreneks*?"

"They are poisonous reptiles. They killed many worshippers in nameless, obscene ceremonies before Bedorian IV came to power."

"Yeah?" says the child, alert again. "What were they like?"

"What is obscene to one being is simply boring to another," I say. "Terrans find them dull." Which is not true, but I have no desire to watch the child snicker as I describe the rituals.

"What a shame," says the woman, though her voice sounds relieved. "Still, you certainly seem to know your history."

I want to answer that I just make up the stories. But I am afraid if I say it, she will believe it.

"Where did you learn all this stuff?" she continues.

"To become a licensed guide," I reply, "an Antarean must undergo fourteen years of study, and must also speak a minimum of four alien languages fluently. Terran is always one of the four."

"That's some set of credentials," comments the man. "I made it through one year of dental school and quit."

And yet, it is you who are paying me.

"I'm surprised you don't work at one of the local universities," he continues.

"I did once."

Which is true. But I have my family to feed—and tourists' tips, however small and grudgingly given, are still greater than my salary as a teacher.

A *rapu*—an Antarean child—insinuates his way between myself and my clients. Scarcely more than an infant, he is dressed in rags, and his face is smudged with dirt. There are open sores on the reticulated plates of his skin, and his golden eyes water constantly. He begs plaintively for credits in his native tongue. When there is no response, he extends his hand in what has become a universal gesture that says: *You are rich. I am poor and hungry. Give me money.*

"Yours?" asks the man, frowning, as his wife takes half a dozen holos in quick succession.

"No, he is not mine."

"What is he doing here?"

"He lives in the street," I answer, my compassion for the *rapu* alternating with my humilation at having to explain his presence and situation. "He is asking for coins so that he and his mother will not go hungry tonight."

I look at the *rapu* and think sadly: *Timing is everything. Once, long ago, we strode across our world like gods. You would not have gone hungry in any of the 43 Dynasties.*

The human child looks at his Antarean counterpart. I wonder if he realizes how fortunate he is. His face gives no reflection of his thoughts; perhaps he has none. Finally he picks his nose and goes back to manipulating his computer.

The man stares at the *rapu* for a moment, then flips him a two-credit coin. The *rapu* catches it, bows and blesses the man, and runs off. We watch him go. He raises the coin above his head, yelling happily—and a moment later, we are surrounded by twenty more street urchins, all filthy, all hungry, all begging for coins.

"Enough's enough!" says the man irritably. "Tell them to get the hell out of here and go home, Herman."

"They live here," I explain gently.

"Right here?" demands the man. He stomps the ground with his foot, and the nearest *rapus* jump back in fright. "On this spot? Okay, then tell them to stay here where they live and not follow us."

I explain to the *rapus* in our own tongue that these tourists will not give them coins.

"Then we will go to the ugly pink hotel where all the Men stay and rob their rooms."

"That is none of my concern," I say. "But if you are caught, it will go hard with you."

The oldest of the urchins smiles at my warning.

"If we are caught, they will lock us up, and because it is a jail they will have to feed us, and we will be protected from the rain and the cold—it is far better than being here."

I have no answer for *rapus* whose only ambition is to be warm and dry and well fed, but merely shrug. They run off, laughing and singing, as if they are human children off to play some game.

"Damned aliens!" mutters the man.

"That is incorrect," I say.

"Oh?"

"A matter of semantics," I point out gently. "*They* are indigenous. *You* are the aliens."

"Well, they could do with some lessons in behavior from us aliens, then," he growls.

We walk up the long ramp to the Tomb and are about to enter it, when the woman stops.

"I'd like a holo of the three of you standing in the entrance," she announces. She smiles at me. "Just to prove to our friends we were here, and that we met a real Antarean."

The man walks over and stands on one side of me. The child reluctantly moves to my other side.

"Now put your arm around Herman," says the woman.

The child steps back, and I see a mixture of contempt and disgust on his face. "I'll pose with it, but I won't *touch* it!"

"You do what your mother says!" snaps the man.

"No way!" says the child, stalking sulkily back down the ramp. "You want to hug him, you go ahead!"

"You listen to me, young man!" says the man, but the child does not stop or give any indication that he has heard, and soon he disappears behind a temple.

It was Tcharock, the founder of the 30th Dynasty, who decreed that the person of the Emperor was sacrosanct and could not be touched by any being other than his medics and his concubines, and then only with his consent.

His greatest advisor was Chaluba, who extended Tcharock's rule to more than 80 percent of the planet and halted the hyperinflation that had been the 29th Dynasty's legacy to him.

One night, during a state function, Chaluba inadvertently brushed against Tcharock while introducing him to the Ambassador from far Domar.

The next morning Tcharock regretfully gave the signal to the executioner, and Chaluba was beheaded. Despite this unfortunate beginning, the 30th Dynasty survived for 1,062 Standard years.

The woman, embarrassed, begins apologizing to me. But I notice that she, too, avoids touching me. The man goes off after the child, and a few moments later the two of them return—which is just as well, for the woman has begun repeating herself.

The man pushes the child toward me, and he sullenly utters an apology. The man takes an ominous step toward him, and he reluctantly reaches out his hand. I take it briefly—the contact is no more pleasant for me than for him—and then we enter the Tomb. Two other groups are there, but they are hundreds of meters away, and we cannot hear what their guides are saying.

"How high is the ceiling?" asks the woman, training her camera on the exquisite carvings overhead.

"Thirty-eight meters," I say. "The Tomb itself is 203 meters long and 67 meters wide. The body of Beldorian V is in a large vault beneath the floor." I pause, thinking as always of past glories. "On the Day of Mourning, the day the Tomb was completed, a million Antareans stood patiently in line outside the Tomb to pay their last respects."

"I don't mean to ask a silly question," says the woman, "but why are all the buildings so *enormous?*"

"Ego," suggests the man, confident in his wisdom.

"The Maker of All Things is huge," I explain. "So my people felt that any monument to Him should be as large as possible, so that He might be comfortable inside it."

"You think your God can't find or fit into a small building?" asks the man with a condescending smile.

"He is everyone's God," I answer. "And while He can of course find a small temple, why should we force Him to live in one?"

"Did Beldorian have a wife?" asks the woman, her mind back to smaller considerations.

"He had five of them," I answer. "The tomb next to this one is known as The Place of Beldorian's Queens."

"He was a polygamist?"

I shake my head. "No. Beldorian simply outlived his first four queens."

"He must have died a very old man," says the woman.

"He did not," I answer. "There is a belief among my people that those who achieve public greatness are doomed to private misery. Such was Beldorian's fate." I turn to the child, who has been silent since returning, and ask him if he has any questions, but he merely glares at me without speaking.

"How long ago was this place built?" asks the man.

"Beldorian V died 6,302 Standard years ago. It took another 17 years to build and prepare the Tomb."

"6,302 years," he muses. "That's a long time."

"We are an ancient race," I reply proudly. "A human anthropologist has suggested that our 3rd Dynasty commenced before your ancestors crossed over the evolutionary barrier into sentience."

"Maybe we spent a long time living in the trees," says the man, clearly unimpressed and just a bit defensive. "But look how quickly we passed you once we climbed down."

"If you say so," I answer noncommittally.

"In fact, everybody passed you," he persists. "Look at the record: How many times has Antares been conquered?"

"I am not sure," I lie, for I find it humiliating to speak of it.

When the Antareans learned that Man's Republic wished to annex their world, they gathered their army in Zanthu and then marched out onto the battlefield, 300,000 strong. They were the cream of the planet's young warriors, gold of eye, the reticulated plates of their skin glistening in the morning sun, prepared to defend their homeworld.

The Republic sent a single ship that flew high overhead and dropped a single bomb, and in less than a second there was no longer an Antarean army, or a city of Zanthu, or a Great Library of Cthstoka.

Over the millennia Antares was conquered four times by Man, twice by the Canphor Twins, and once each by Lodin XI, Emra, Ramor, and the Sett Empire. It was said that the parched ground had finally quenched its thirst by drinking a lake of Antarean blood.

As we leave the Tomb, we come to a small, skinny *rapu*. He sits on a rock, staring at us with his large, golden eyes, his expression rapt in contemplation.

The human child pointedly ignores him and continues walking toward the next temple, but the adults stop.

"What a cute little thing!" enthuses the woman. "And he looks so hungry." She digs into her shoulder bag and withdraws a sweet that she has kept from breakfast. "Here," she says, holding it up. "Would you like it?"

The *rapu* never moves. This is unique not only in the woman's experience, but also in mine, for he is obviously undernourished.

"Maybe he can't metabolize it," suggests the man. He pulls a coin out, steps over to the *rapu*, and extends his hand. "Here you go, kid."

The *rapu*, his face frozen in contemplation, makes no attempt to grab the coin.

And suddenly I am thinking excitedly: *You disdain their food when you are hungry, and their money when you are poor. Could you possibly be the One we have awaited for so many millennia, the One who will give us back our former glory and initiate the 44th Dynasty?*

I study him intently, and my excitement fades just as quickly as it came upon me. The *rapu* does not disdain their food and their money. His golden eyes are clouded over. Life in the streets has so weakened him that he has become blind, and of course he does not understand what they are saying. His seeming arrogance comes not from pride or some inner light, but because he is not aware of their offerings.

"Please," I say, gently taking the sweet from the woman without coming into actual contact with her fingers. I walk over and place it in the *rapu's* hand. He sniffs it, then gulps it down hungrily and extends his hand, blindly begging for more.

"It breaks your heart," says the woman.

"Oh, it's no worse than what we saw on Bareimus V," responds the man. "They were every bit as poor—and remember that awful skin disease that they all had?"

The woman considers, and her face reflects the unpleasantness of the memory. "I suppose you're right at that." She shrugs, and I can tell that even though the child is still in front of us, hand outstretched, she has already put him from her mind.

I lead them through the Garden of the Vanished Princes, with its tormented history of sacrifice and intrigue, and suddenly the man stops.

"What happened here?" he asks, pointing to a number of empty pedestals.

"History happened," I explain. "Or avarice, for sometimes they are the same thing." He seems confused, so I continue: "If any of our conquerers could find a way to transport a treasure back to his home planet, he did. Anything small enough to be plundered *was* plundered."

"And these statues that have been defaced?" he says, pointing to them. "Did you do it yourselves so they would be worthless to occupying armies?"

"No," I answer.

"Well, whoever did *that*"—he points to a headless statue— "ought to be strung up and whipped."

"What's the fuss?" asks the child in a bored voice. "They're just statues of aliens."

"Actually, the human who did that was rewarded with the governorship of Antares III," I inform them.

"What are you talking about?" asks the man.

"The second human conquest of the Antares system was led by Commander Lois Kiboko," I begin. "She defaced or destroyed more than three thousand statues. Many were physical representations of our deity, and since she and her crew were devout believers in one of your religions, she felt that these were false idols and must be destroyed."

"Well," the man replies with a shrug, "it's a small price to pay for her saving you from the Lodinites."

"Perhaps," I say. "The problem is that we had to pay a greater price for each successive savior."

He stares at me, and there is an awkward silence. Finally I suggest that we visit the Palace of the Supreme Tyrant.

"You seem such a docile race," she says awkwardly. "I mean, so civilized and unaggressive. How did your gene pool ever create a real, honest-to-goodness tyrant?"

The truth is that our gene pool was considerably more aggressive before a seemingly endless series of alien conquests decimated it. But I know that this answer would make them uncomfortable, and could affect the size of my tip, so I lie to them instead. (I am ashamed to admit that lying to aliens becomes easier with each passing day. Indeed, I am sometimes amazed at the facility with which I can create falsehoods.)

"Every now and then each race produces a genetic sport," I say, and I can see she believes it, "and we Antareans are so docile, to use your expression, that this particular one had no difficulty achieving power."

"What was his name?"

"I do not know."

"I thought you took fourteen years' worth of history courses," she says accusingly, and I can tell she thinks I am lying to her, whereas every time I have actually lied she has believed me.

"Our language has many dialects, and they have all evolved and changed over thirty-six thousand years," I point out. "Some we have deciphered, but to this day many of them remain unsolved mysteries. In fact, right at this moment a team of human archaeologists is hard at work trying to uncover the Tyrant's name."

"If it's a dead language, how are they going to manage that?"

"In the days when your race was still planetbound, there was an artifact called the Rosetta Stone that helped you translate an ancient language. We have something similar—ours is known as the Bosperi Scroll—that comes from the Great Tyrant's era."

"Where is it?" asks the woman, looking around.

"I regret to inform you that both the archaeologists and the Bosperi Scroll are currently in a museum on Deluros VIII."

"Smart," says the man. "They can protect it better on Deluros."

"From who?" asks the woman.

"From anyone who wants to steal it, of course," he says, as if explaining it to a child.

"But I mean, who would want to steal the key to a dead language?"

"Do you know what it would be worth to a collector?" answers the man. "Or a thief who wanted to ransom it?"

They discuss it further, but the simple truth is that it is on Deluros because it was small enough to carry, and for no other reason. When they are through arguing, I tell her that it is because they have devices on Deluros that will bring back the faded script, and she nods her head thoughtfully.

We walk another four hundred meters and come to the immense Palace of the Kings. It is made entirely of gold, and becomes so hot from the rays of the sun that one can touch the outer surface only at night. This was the building in which all the rulers of the 7th through the 12th Dynasties resided. It was from here that my race received the Nine Proclamations of Ascendency, and the Charter of Universal Rights, and our most revered document, the Mabelian Declaration.

It was a wondrous time to have lived, when we had never tasted defeat and all problems were capable of solution, when stately caravans plied their trade across secure boundaries and monarchs were just and wise, when each day brought new triumphs and the future held infinite promise.

I point to the broken and defaced stone chair. "Once there were 246 jewels and precious stones embedded in the throne."

The child walks over to the throne, then looks at me accusingly. "Where are they?" he demands.

"They were all stolen over the millennia," I reply.

"By conquerers, of course," offers the woman with absolute certainty.

"Yes," I say, but again I am lying. They were stolen by my own people, who traded them to various occupying armies for food or the release of captive loved ones.

We spend a few more minutes examining the vanished glory of the Palace of the Kings, then walk out the door and approach the next crumbling structure. It is the Hall of the Thinkers, revered to this day by all Antareans, but I know they will not understand why a race would create such an edificace to scholarship, and I haven't the energy to explain, so I tell them that it is the Palace of the Concubines, and of course they believe me. At one point the child, making no attempt to mask his disappointment, asks why there are no statues or carvings showing the concubines, and I think very quickly and explain that Lois Kiboko's religious beliefs were offended by the sexual frankness of the artifacts and she had them all destroyed.

I feel guilty about this lie, for it is against the Code of Just Behavior to suggest that a visitor's race may have offended in any way. Ironically, while the child voices his disappointment, I notice that none of the three seems to have a problem accepting that another human would destroy millennia-old artwork that upset his sensibilities. I decide that since they feel no guilt, this one time I shall feel none, either. (But I still do. Tradition is a difficult thing to transcend.)

I see the man anxiously walking around, looking into corners and behind pedestals, and I ask him if something is wrong.

"Where's the can?" he says.

"I beg your pardon?"

"The can. The bathroom. The lavatory." He frowns. "Didn't any of these goddamned concubines ever have to take a crap?"

I finally discern what he wants and direct him to a human facility that has been constructed just beyond the Western Door.

He returns a few minutes later, and I lead them all outside, past the towering Onyx Obelisk that marked the beginning of the almost-forgotten 4th Dynasty. We stop briefly at the Temple of the River of Light, which was constructed *over* the river, so that the sacred waters flow through the temple itself.

We leave and turn a corner, and suddenly a single structure completely dominates the landscape.

"What's *that*?" asks the woman.

"That is the Spiral Ramp to Heaven," I answer.

"What a fabulous name!" she enthuses. "I just know a fabulous story goes with it!" She turns to me expectantly.

"There was a time, before our scientists knew better, that people thought you could reach heaven if you simply built a tall enough ramp."

The child guffaws.

"It is true," I continue. "Construction was begun during the 2nd Dyntasy, and continued for more than seven hundred years until midway through the 3rd. It looks as if you can see the top from here, but you actually are looking only at the bottom half of it. The rest is obscured by clouds."

"How high does it go?" asked the woman.

"More than nine kilometers," I say. "Three kilometers higher than our tallest mountain."

"Amazing!" she exclaims.

"Perhaps you would like a closer look at it?" I suggest. "You might even wish to climb the first kilometer. It is a very gentle ascent until you reach the fifth kilometer."

"Yes," she replies happily. "I think I'd like that very much."

"I'm not climbing anything," says the man.

"Oh, come on," she urges him. "It'll be fun!"

"The air's too thin and the gravity's too heavy and it's too damned much like work. One of these days *I'm* going to choose our itinerary, and I promise you it won't involve so goddamned much walking."

"Can we go back and watch the game?" asks the child eagerly.

The man takes one more look at the Spiral Ramp to Heaven. "Yeah," he says. "I've seen enough. Let's go back."

"We really should finish the tour," says the woman. "We'll probably never be in this sector of the galaxy again."

"So what? It's just another backwater world," replies the man. "Don't tell your friends about the Stairway to the Stars or whatever the hell it's called and they'll never know you missed it."

Then the woman comes up with what she imagines will be the clinching argument. "But you've already agreed to pay for the tour."

"So we'll cut it short and pay him half as much," says the man. "Big deal."

The man pulls a wad of credits out of his pocket and peels off three ten-credits notes. Then he pauses, looks at me, pockets them, and presses a fifty-credit note into my hand instead.

"Ah, hell, you kept your end of the bargain, Herman," he says. Then he and the woman and child begin walking back to the hotel.

The first aliens ever to visit Antares were rude and ill-mannered barbarians, but Perganian II, the greatest Emperor of the 31st Dynasty, decreed that they must be treated with the utmost courtesy. When the day of their departure finally arrived, the aliens exchanged farewells with Perganian, and one of them thrust a large, flawless blue diamond into the Emperor's hand in payment for his hospitality.

After the aliens left the courtyard, Perganian let the diamond drop to the ground, declaring that no Antarean could be purchased for any price.

The diamond lay where it had fallen for three generations, becoming a holy symbol of Antarean dignity and independence. It finally vanished during a dust storm and was never seen again.

Keepsakes

If you were to rob my house (and please don't), I'd just report the theft of the car, the jewelry, the stereo, and the other expensive stuff you're most likely to take, and wait for the insurance company to send me a check. But you could also steal three or four things that have no cash value whatsoever, and I'd be morose and depressed over their loss for years. It's all a matter of relative values.

It's a theme I always wanted to address, and when Robert Silverberg invited me to write a novella for *Between Worlds*, I realized that I could structure a story to deal with those—and other—concerns within the editorial restrictions of the anthology.

(This is one of the few times I've agreed to a title change after handing in a story. My original title was "The Star Gypsies," but Silverberg's *Star of Gypsies* was being reprinted within a month of the anthology's release, and we didn't want to cause any confusioin. I don't know if "Keepsakes" is quite as evocative a title, but it's certainly every bit as accurate.)

They came like a plague, blown on the galactic winds.

No one knew where they came from, no one knew where they were going, no one even knew for sure if they were human. One day they would appear and offer their services, and sometime later they would leave, their coffers filled to overflowing with broken dreams and shattered hopes. Oh, they were paid in currency, lots of it—but what they really traded in was misery.

They had many names, some of their own devising, some not. The one that stuck was the Star Gypsies.

It was my job to hunt them down. Of course, no one told me what to do when I caught them, because they usually hadn't broken any laws. Hearts, yes; dreams, absolutely. But laws? Not often, if at all.

They gave me an assistant. Well, actually, they gave me a lot of assistants, but the one I'm referring to was Jebediah Burke, because he's the one this story is about.

He was a young man, was Jebediah, young and handsome and eager to make a name for himself, to right wrongs and rescue damsels in distress, to make the galaxy a better place, to do all the things you really think are possible before Life starts peeling away your romantic illusions. He had a thick shock of wavy brown hair that never stayed in place but always looked like the wind was blowing through it. He was tall and lanky, but he moved gracefully. His eyes were a pale blue; I know you can't characterize a pair of eyes, but to me they always seemed to be open and trusting. Now that I think of it, I can't remember him ever blinking.

I don't know why he joined the service. He'd been to school and graduated with honors. There were a hundred other things he could have done, more lucrative and certainly less frustrating, but like I said, he had a young man's thirst to see new worlds, and a young man's urge to make a difference. He was such a friendly, decent young man that the old hands refrained from telling him that none of us would ever make a difference, that Man had spent quite a few thousand years trying to protect his neighbors from themselves, and we sure as hell didn't have much to show for it except some resentful neighbors.

I still remember his first day on the job. He'd already found his desk in the huge office when I showed up, and was pouring over all the material we had accumulated on the Star Gypsies. He had pulled up holographic interviews with victims, transcripts, financial records, anything he could access.

We got the introductions over with, and I left him to study the face of the enemy. Except, of course, that he couldn't find it. Finally he walked over to me.

"Excuse me, sir," he began.

"Forget the sir," I said. "I'm just Gabe."

"I feel awkward calling you by your first name, sir," he said.

"Get over it. The last thing I need if we're on an undercover assignment is someone calling me sir."

"I'll try to remember that, sir . . . I mean Gabe."

"It shouldn't be hard," I said. "It's a biblical name, just like yours."

"Jebediah isn't biblical, Gabe."

"Okay," I said. "One's biblical and one sounds biblical. That's close enough. Now, what's your problem?"

"The Star Gypsies."

"They're the whole department's problem," I noted wryly. "Just what particular facet of them is bothering you?"

He frowned. "I must be asking the computer the wrong questions," he said. "I can find out everything they've done—well, everything that's been reported, anyway—but I can't find any hard information on them. I can't even find out what they look like."

I couldn't resist a smile. "Now you know why we welcomed you with open arms."

"You mean *nobody* knows?" he said in disbelief. "How can that be? Surely the victims gave you descriptions!"

"We have more descriptions than we know what to do with," I said. "They're not worth the powder to blow them to hell."

"I don't understand, sir."

"Gabe."

"Gabe," he amended.

"To humans, they look like men. To the inhabitants of Komornos, they look like Komornans. To a Mollutei, they look like Mollutes."

"They're shape-changers?"

"We don't know what the hell they are," I admitted. "They've been around for close to ninety years, and we still don't have any idea." I sighed. "They were here before I got here, and they'll be here after you and I are both in the grave. Welcome to the service; at least you're not lacking job security."

He seemed to stare right through me at some fixed point in space only he could see. For a moment I thought he'd actually gone into some kind of trance, or perhaps that he was seriously reconsidering his choice of careers, but then he relaxed and rejoined the here and now.

"Ninety years, and we've never captured one," he said. "Now *that's* a challenge."

"That's a pit of quicksand," I corrected him.

"Maybe you just need fresh eyes, Gabe."

"Fresh eyes?" I repeated, wondering what the hell he was talking about.

"Maybe you just need someone who looks at the problem from a different angle."

I didn't want to discourage him his first morning on the job, so I allowed that maybe a pair of fresh eyes could spot what we'd all been missing. Then I went back to reading the day's reports, while he returned to his desk and learned what more he could about the Star Gypsies, most of it second-, third-, and even fourth-hand accounts and tall tales.

At noon I stopped by and invited him out to lunch.

"I think I'd be better off staying here and learning what I can," he said.

"Come on," I said. "They've been around longer than we've both been alive. Another hour won't hurt."

He shrugged, deactivated his computer, got to his feet, and followed me out the door. We took the slidewalk to the corner, stepped onto a crosswalk, and let it carry us to Romeo's, which is the restaurant most of our people hang out at when they're on the planet.

"It's amazing," said Jebediah as we sat down at a table in the corner and the holographic menu suddenly appeared in midair, rotating gently so we could both read it.

"Romeo's?" I repeated. "It's just a lunch shop."

"No," he said, looking around. "I mean, any one of them could be a Star Gypsy."

"They could," I agreed. "But most of them are your coworkers."

He frowned disapprovingly. "They're all humans. Everyone I saw in the office this morning was human."

"The department is only about 40 percent human," I explained. "But most of the nonhumans can't metabolize our food, so they eat at their own restaurants."

"We should probably join them every now and then to show solidarity."

I shook my head. "You wouldn't want to go back to work for a day or two after seeing what they eat."

"I didn't notice any of them in the office."

"They're in the building," I said. "We try to accommodate their needs, whether it's chlorine or methane or two hundred degrees Farenheit."

"I'd like to speak to some of them, to get their take on the Star Gypsies."

"It's all there in the computer," I told him.

"I'd rather do it face-to-face," he said, "unless you have some objection to that."

"Be my guest," I said. "I suppose two-thirds of them actually have faces, and you'll figure out where the rest are hiding their ears and mouths."

He was silent for a moment. "Do you think you've ever seen one, Gabe?"

"An alien? Every day."

"I mean a Star Gypsy."

"Probably. I really couldn't say."

"What do you suppose they really want?" he asked.

"Most days I think they want to drive me crazy."

"That was a serious question," said Jebediah.

"That was an almost-serious answer," I replied. "Beyond that, I don't know what the hell they want. Why does their only goal seem to be making people miserable? Why don't they just rob some banks and be done with it? If they're going to walk away with everything a man holds dear, why not finish the job and kill him?" I sighed. "You start questioning motivations and you could run smack-dab into Eternity."

He shook his head. "Every sentient being has a motivation," he said with conviction.

"Figure theirs out and we just might make you the head of the department the next morning," I said.

"Maybe I will," he half promised.

I looked at the temperature. It was twenty-eight degrees Celsius. And getting warmer.

"Maybe it'll snow tomorrow, too," I said.

Well, it didn't snow, but there was a change. Not in the weather; the weather on Goldenrod never changes. But we got word that the Star Gypsies had been on New Rhodesia, and had made off with "the usual."

I figured Jebediah might as well see what we were up against, so I gave him a couple of hours to pack and meet me at the spaceport. He was waiting for me when I got there.

"I tried to find New Rhodesia on a star map, and I couldn't," he announced as we walked out to the ship.

"Officially it's Beta Draconis IV," I said. "But the inhabitants call it New Rhodesia, and that's good enough for me."

"Are they human?"

"The colonists are. There are some remnants of the native race, but I gather we won't be running into them."

"Shy?"

"Decimated," I replied. "Not every world welcomed us with open arms."

He looked his disapproval. I wanted to explain to him that you can't be a hero if you don't have some enemies to conquer, and that actually the enemies in this star cluster had proven a little easier to conquer than most, but I decided not to. Young idealists have enough disillusionments in store for them; why rush the revelations?

We reached the ship and stopped.

"This is it?" said Jebediah, hands on hips, studying it.

"This is it."

"We're not going to keep our identities secret in this thing," he said. "Maybe we should get one that doesn't display all the departmental insignia."

"We don't have any," I said. "Besides, there won't be anyone there to frighten away. If the Star Gypsies aren't gone yet, I guarantee they'll be gone by the time we get there."

"How do you know?" asked Jebediah.

"Because they always are."

We took the airlift up to the ship's hatch. I set the navigational computer for the Beta Draconis system and ordered it to alert me when we got within half a light-year, and then, since it would be a dull twenty-hour trip even at light speeds, Jebediah and I lay down in pods in the Deepsleep Chamber.

It awakened us eighteen hours later, as programmed. I was famished, as I always am when I come out of Deepsleep, and so was Jebediah. We made our way to the galley, ordered up a couple of meals, and ate in silence.

Then Jebediah got up and carefully inspected every inch of the ship. He never said a word, never touched a thing, just looked and mentally cataloged. I decided that it was a shame his thoroughness was wasted on our particular quest.

Finally he sat back down.

"Tell me what we know about the situation," he said. I noticed that "Please," "Gabe," and even "sir" had vanished from his vocabulary, but of course he was now an old-timer in his second full day on the job.

"New Rhodesia's a farming world," I said. "It supplies food to eleven nearby planets, most of them mining worlds, plus a couple of scientific outposts out in the Horatius system's asteroid belt."

"What's New Rhodesia's population?"

"Humans, maybe eight thousand. Natives, and I have no idea what they call themselves or what we call them, about four hundred thousand, maybe a little more."

"Eight thousand," he repeated. "I'm surprised the Star Gypsies had even heard of it."

"That's the kind of place they specialize in," I said.

"What happened there?"

"They had their wettest season on record," I answered. "The ground got saturated, the harvesting machines couldn't work because they kept sinking into the mud, and the crops were in danger of rotting where they stood. Most of the colonists are mortgaged up to the hilt, and they couldn't make it through a single season without a harvest." I paused and lit a smokeless cigar. "Then one day the Star Gypsies showed up and offered to work the fields—for a price, of course."

"And did they?"

"Oh, yes," I said. "They always deliver on their promises. From what I can tell, they worked in shifts, around the clock, day in and day out, until every last field was harvested."

"And then?"

"And then they took their payment and left—or if they haven't left yet, they'll be gone before we show up."

"What kind of payment?"

"That's the question no one ever asks up front," I said ruefully. "Oh, they'll have demanded money, of course, and the farmer will be happy to pay it—and if that's all they wanted, we could disband the department and go catch murderers and extortionists."

"What do you think they got along with the money?" persisted Jebediah.

"Why guess?" I said. "We'll be there in a few hours, and then we'll know."

He fell silent, and I could tell from his expression that something was still troubling him, so I asked him about it.

"I don't understand any of this," he said. "They don't steal anything. They don't physically harm anyone. Whatever they got paid, people have agreed to their terms in advance. So why are we chasing after them? What laws have they broken?"

"None."

"Then—"

"When you go to war, do you do it because someone has broken a law?" I asked. "No, you do it because a force of the enemy, however large or small, has committed actions that are detrimental to the people you are charged with protecting. This is pretty much the same thing."

It didn't sound all that convincing even to me, and he sure as hell didn't look convinced.

"Look, kid," I said, "they trade in heartbreak and misery. I don't really care if it's legal or not, and neither do the people who pay us. Our job is to stop them by any means available."

"Even if they're not breaking any laws?"

"Even so."

He shook his head. "There's got to be more to it than that. You don't spend the resources of an entire governmental department tracking them down just because you disapprove of them."

"Disapprove is an understatement," I responded.

"I'm trying to understand, Gabe," he said. "I've heard rumors and old wives' tales about the Star Gypsies, but I couldn't find any justification in our files for going after them. They do what they promise to do; they don't rob anyone. Are you sure the complaints aren't cases of biter-bit?"

"Biter-bit?" I repeated, puzzled. It wasn't an expression I'd heard before.

"People who thought they'd outwitted them, who thought they were getting the better of a bargain, and then found out they hadn't."

"There's a lot of biting that goes on," I acknowledged. "And the Star Gypsies do all of it."

"I'm not trying to start am argument, Gabe," he said. "But if I'm going to devote a goodly portion of my life to hunting down the Star Gypsies, I want to be sure I'm on the right side—and so far I'm not convinced."

"Tell you what," I said. "Talk face-to-face with some of their victims, and then if you want a transfer, I'll agree to it and sign the papers. Fair enough?"

"Yes, that's fair enough."

He didn't say another word until we touched down on New Rhodesia nine hours later. He just sat and stared at the various screens and panels around the ship, and I could tell he was wondering what this had to do with making the galaxy a better place. I almost wished for his sake that he wasn't about to find out.

New Rhodesia was like a giant mudball. It had been raining for three months solid, and it was still raining when we touched down at the tiny spaceport. The air was thick with moisture, and the proximity of the yellow sun made the world uncomfortably warm.

The department made sure there was an airbus waiting for us. We hopped in, grateful for the air-cooled and dehumidified compartment. The bus levitated a couple of feet above the ground and the robot driver's head swiveled 180 degrees until it was facing us.

"May I have your destination, please?" it asked in a dull grating monotone.

"Yeah," I said. "Jacob Ellsworth's farm. Do you know where it is, or do you need coordinates?"

"All human locations are entered in my data banks," it said.

"Good. We want the farmhouse. If there's more than one dwelling, take us to the largest one."

"We shall arrive in eleven minutes and twenty-three seconds," announced the robot as the airbus raced forward.

"I know you don't have to watch the road, that the vehicle has dozens of sensors, and that you're just an extension of it," I said. "But I'd still feel a lot more comfortable if you turned your head around and watched the road."

The robot swiveled its head back without another word.

"Jacob Ellsworth," said Jebediah. "He's the one who filed the complaint?"

"Indirectly," I said.

"Indirectly?"

"You'll see."

We drove past a couple of huge farms that hadn't been harvested. The smell of the rotting vegetation even penetrated our compartment, and you could see the stuff bent in half from its own water-burdened weight, with mold starting to spread all over what remained of it.

Then we came to a neat flat field, maybe four thousand hectares, everything picked clean, fresh furrows in the ground, and I knew we'd reached the Ellsworth farm.

"How come only this one was harvested?" asked Jebediah.

"Maybe the other farmers knew better than to deal with the Star

Gypsies," I said. "Or maybe there were only enough of them to work a few farms this time. They don't all travel together, you know. In fact, I hear they've started showing up in the Albion and Quinellus Clusters in the past few months."

We drove alongside a pasture filled with mutated cattle, huge but placid animals standing some twelve feet at the shoulder, chewing their cud and staring at us with lackluster eyes. Off in the distance I could see some other animals, not from Terran stock, in a pair of smaller pastures.

And then we were at the house. I wasn't surprised to see a police vehicle in front of it. Nearby was a medical vehicle; the two robot attendants stood motionless at its doors, not bothering to acknowledge our—or even New Rhodesia's—existence.

Jebediah and I got out of the airbus and walked up to the front door. It scanned our retinas, and since it had no record of us it refused to open but immediately informed any occupants of our presence. A moment later a uniformed officer ordered the door to dilate and let us in. He was short and stocky, starting to lose his hair, and there were sweat stains all over his shirt, possibly due to exertion, more likely just from the heat and the humidity. He looked familiar, but I couldn't place him.

"Hi, Gabe," he said, extending his hand. "It's been a long time."

"It sure has," I said, shaking his hand and wondering who he was.

"Ben Paulson," he said when he realized I couldn't come up with his name. "You were my first boss."

"Oh, sure," I said. "Now I remember. You used to have a little more hair and a little less stomach. Meet Jebediah Burke, your replacement ten or fifteen times removed."

"Please to meet you, Jebediah," he said. "Been on the job long?"

"Just a couple of days," said Jebediah.

"Good luck," said Paulson. "You're going to need it. Not everyone can last as long as Gabe." He laughed humorlessly. "Not anyone, now that I think of it."

"You're the one who discovered him?" I asked.

"Yeah," said Paulson. "Isn't that a bitch? Quit the department, move out to the boonies where I'll never have to deal with the Star Gypsies again, and the bastards pick *my* planet." He snorted disgustedly. "I should have kept working for you—it paid better." He paused for a moment, remembering the old days. "Nah. They'd have locked me away in an asylum by now."

"I take it Ellsworth was dead when you found him?" I said.

He nodded an affirmative. "At least I didn't have to watch," said Paulson. "The medical robot says he'd been dead for almost a day before anyone noticed he wasn't answering his messages. I'll get a precise time of death back at the infirmary—we're too small a world to have a real bona fide hospital—but I've kept him here in case you want to look at him."

"No, that won't be necessary," I said.

"I'd like to see him," interjected Jebediah.

"Help yourself," said Paulson. "He's in the vehicle out front—the one with the two robots."

"Is there a code word?" asked Jebediah as he reached the door.

"No, just climb in and see what you need to see. They're not programmed to stop you."

Jebediah went out, and Paulson turned to me. "He's very young."

"We all were once."

"These damned Star Gypsies can age you fast." He shook his head sadly. "Too bad, an earnest young man like that."

"You might as well wait until he gets back. Then you won't have to repeat everything."

"Won't he take your word for it?"

"Not this week," I said.

"He will soon," said Paulson knowingly.

"Is there anything to drink in the kitchen?" I asked.

"No booze in the entire house," he said. "I put on some coffee about half an hour ago, if that's your style."

"This guy, this Ellsworth, he left a bubble, right?"

"Right."

"Well, I'd rather see it with some alcohol, but I suppose coffee's better than nothing."

I followed him into the kitchen and had just ordered the machine to pour my coffee when Jebediah came back into the house and entered the kitchen. It was all he could do to keep from saluting.

"A single wound to the temple," he announced. "I'd say death was instantaneous."

"It was," agreed Paulson.

"It looks self-inflicted," continued Jebediah, "but we can't be sure at this point."

"Yes, we can," said Paulson. "Follow me, gentlemen."

He led is to the main parlor, opened up a small case with his official insignia on it, and withdrew a translucent bubble about an inch in diameter.

"This was rigged to begin playing the minute someone walked into this room," he said. "You can examine it when we're done, but I need it back. It's evidence."

I nodded. "Okay, play it."

He activated the globe, and suddenly a full-sized three-dimensional Ellsworth stood facing a recording device that no one could see.

"I am Jacob Ellsworth," said the simulacron, and you didn't have to be a genius to see that the man was obviously distraught. "I just want to leave a record so someone will know what happened." He started to say something, the words wouldn't come out, he cleared his throat, and began again.

"My crops were rotting in the field when they came. I don't know if they were human or not. They looked like men. They said they'd heard about our problems here on New Rhodesia and had come to help. I explained the situation, that the ground was so wet we couldn't work it. They offered to harvest our crops by hand, mine and Hiram

Morton's. Hiram said no, that he wouldn't have any truck with them, but I was desperate. Last year's crop wasn't that good, and I had a pair of notes due on the farm."

He'd been going pretty good there for a moment, but now he started choking off his words again.

"They asked me how much I owed on the notes, and I told them. Then they asked what the crop would be worth if I could get it to market, and I told them that, too. And they named a price that would even allow me a small profit after I paid off my debts. The only other thing they wanted in addition to the money we'd agreed upon was a single keepsake of their time on New Rhodesia, a book of their choosing from my house. I couldn't see anything wrong with that, and I agreed."

And now the tears began running down his scrawny cheeks.

"Tell Hiram Morton I should have listened to him." He stared at the lens. "They did what they said they'd do, and I paid them. And then they took their keepsake."

He paused, struggling to put together the words.

"I'm not like most farmers. I'm not tied to the land. I don't love the soil. The only thing in my life I've ever loved was Elizabeth, my wife. We were married for forty-three years. She died six years ago."

And now he glared furiously into the lens.

"They took the only book of holographs of her that I owned! I told them that they couldn't have it, that they could have anything else in the house. But they said this was the only book they wanted. I tried to stop them, but I'm an old man and they threw me down and ripped it from my hands and left with it."

The tears began again.

"And now I'll never see her again. Already I'm having trouble remembering exactly what the lines and curves of her face were like, the color of her eyes, the shape of her lips. In another week or another month it'll be completely gone. Those bastards stole the only memory I want, the only thing I ever loved!"

He raised a laser pistol to his left temple.

"Find them and do to them what they did to me."

Then he fired the gun, and his image vanished.

We were silent for a moment. I'd seen it, or something like it, more times than I cared to remember, but it was a new experience for Jebediah, and I could tell he was upset. I felt sorry for the kid; he was finally realizing just what it was that we were up against, and it disturbed him, probably more than anything had ever disturbed him before.

Finally Paulson spoke up. "I looked through the place before you got here," he said. "The man was a bibliophile. He had a first of Charles Dickens from almost seventeen hundred years ago. He had an inscribed copy of Jason Boorman from the 24th century A.D., and a first of Tanblixt's Canphorian poetry from the 9th century G.E. Those three books alone could have bought just about any farm on this planet. And they wouldn't take any of them." He turned to Jebediah. "They visited 143 farms. Twenty-eight owners turned them away; 115 are busy wishing they had—those that are still any condition to wish, anyway." He paused, and I could see the pain reflected on his face. "This world will never be the same again. Oh, they'll still grow crops, but people don't get over something like this. It was a nice place to live until now. I suppose I'll stick around for a few months, and then I'll be off to some other world the Star Gypsies haven't visited yet, and hope I die of old age before they discover it."

"I'm still trying to figure out why they wanted the holos of his wife," said Jebediah, frowning.

"Because *he* wanted them. They take whatever's most valuable to you, especially if it has no value to anyone else. They work for cash, but mostly they take their pay in pain and remorse." Paulson looked like he was about to spit, then remembered he was inside. "What kind of twisted minds take pleasure in that?"

"There must be a reason," insisted Jebediah, who was clearly shaken. "Why would they bring such misery to a man who had trusted them and kept his bargain and hadn't done them any harm?"

"There comes a point where you stop worrying about why evil beings do something, and you concentrate on stopping them," said Paulson. He turned to me. "That is, if you're as tough as Gabe here. Me, I couldn't face one more victim. That's why I quit."

"How long were you with the department?" asked Jebediah.

"Maybe a year, maybe a little more. Too damned long." He turned to me. "How about you, Gabe?"

"Too damned long," I said.

"You still remember your first experience with them?" he asked.

"It's not the kind of thing you ever forget," I said.

I could still see it plain as day, the tortured countenance of the orange-skinned fur-covered Bedorian. He was as unlike a human as you could get in every way but one—his grief. A storm was coming, a storm like Bedore VII hadn't seen in a century or more. His broodhouse needed reinforcement or it would blow away and leave all his offspring exposed to the elements before they were old enough to cope with them. The Star Gypsies showed up like magic and offered to work on his broodhouse and extracted their usual fee—local currency, plus one small artifact that was unique to Belore VII. He agreed, they did the work, they paid him—and then they took the artifact, a small piece of stone called a *rlymph*. It just looked like a stone to me, and, I'm sure, to them, but to the Bedorian it was a religious token that guaranteed that his brood, some 150 strong, would eventually find their way to the afterlife. In his mind—and who's to say he was wrong?—they had condemned his brood to wander eternally in limbo with no possibility of ever joining him or his mates in a Bedorian paradise. I spent the rest of the week visiting close to a hundred other Bedorians; every story was the same.

"Are you all right?" asked Jebediah, reaching out to touch my shoulder, and I realized I'd been motionless for a couple of minutes while the scene played through my mind again.

"Yeah, I'm fine," I said. "It's been twenty-seven years, but I can still feel it like it was this morning."

"And from that day to this, did you ever find anyone who was pleased to have dealt with the Star Gypsies?" said Paulson.

I shook my head. "No one." I turned to Jebediah. "As their reputation spread, a lot of people refused to hire them. Now they concentrate mainly on little out-of-the-way worlds like this one. And even when they don't try to hide who they are, there are always some people who think they can outsmart them, and some people who are so desperate they'll agree to anything. Then they find out exactly what it is they've really agreed to." I smiled ironically. "You might feel the same way. You agreed to join the department, and now you're finding out exactly what we're up against. If it was just one farmer here and one banker there and one alien elsewhere, it wouldn't be worth our time—but it's three dozen here and two hundred there and a thousand some other place."

"I'd heard rumors," he said. "But I didn't realize . . ." He let the words trail off.

"Everyone's heard rumors," said Paulson. "Most people don't believe them. That's why the Star Gypsies can function."

"They're sentient beings. No sentient being brings this kind of misery to other sentient beings without a reason," he said firmly.

"You never heard of a sadist?" asked Paulson.

"I never heard of a race of them," Jebediah shot back. He turned back to me. "Have they some grievance against the Republic or perhaps a local planetary government?"

"If they have, they've never voiced it."

"Did they object to being colonized?"

"You're barking up the wrong tree," said Paulson. "We don't even know where they come from."

"They must have a planet or a headquarters where they store all the things they've taken," said Jebediah.

"You know what I think?" said Paulson. "I think those things are as worthless to them as they are to everyone but the original owners. My guess is that they jettison them the moment they break out of orbit."

I'd heard all these theories before from dozens of men on my staff, so I began looking around. "I don't suppose they left any more clues than usual?"

"None," said Paulson. "Wouldn't matter anyway. We don't have a holo, a retinagram, a fingerprint, a DNA record, anything, on any of them."

"It would be a start," said Jebediah sternly, clearly annoyed at the officer's pessimism.

"I like your attitude, young man," said Paulson. "Don't let our failures deter you. You know you're going to hunt them down where everyone else has failed, and I salute you."

"Then why do you make it sound so sarcastic?" asked Jebediah.

"Because they've even robbed me," answered Paulson seriously. "I was just like you when I went to work for the department. It took them less than a year to rob me of something I once valued—my faith in my ability to put an end to the pain they bring. I hope they don't take the same thing away from you."

Not this week, I thought. *Maybe in a month or a year, but not this week. After all, he's only seen one victim.*

He saw more in the next few weeks.

There was the Ragobad, a race that lived in symbiosis with a little animal called a *lasphine*. The Ragobad had spent years building a complex system of burrows beneath the unhospitable exterior of Helena II. Due to earthquakes caused by sudden tectonic activity, the system had collapsed, and, right on schedule, the Star Gypsies showed up to help rebuild it. They did a hell of a job on it, too. All it cost the 823 Ragobadim who agreed was cash—and their *lasphine* symbiotes.

There was Homer Padoupolas, who lived alone on the mining world of Cassandra with his pet *braque*, a doglike creature from Alpha

Bednares V. He'd had it for close to twenty years and lavished all his affection on it. (You can see this one coming, can't you?) The Star Gypsies repaired his broken mining machines and helped him make his monthly quota. What they took for their efforts was 30 percent of his profits—and his *braque*.

There was Cold Steel, the outstanding cloned racehorse from the 27th century A.D. His owner had promised that 90 percent of the colt's winnings would be donated to his church if God would just cure his daughter of her terminal disease—and God, or something very like Him, stepped in and did just that. Cold Steel won race after race and became the most famous and popular horse in the galaxy, known far and wide as the Horse That Raced for God. Then one day he went lame, and no veterinarian could cure him . . . but the Star Gypsies knew what to do and made him sound again for a cash fee—and for the ugly little goat that lived in the stall with him and kept him company. Cold Steel never took another lame step, never won another race, and the owner's church soon found out that 90 percent of nothing is nothing.

On and on it went, the litany of misery and regret. We interviewed two men who had been sure they could outsmart the Star Gypsies, who haggled and narrowed down the definition of the keepsakes they would have to relinquish—and all they proved was that sometimes even you yourself don't know what your most valued possession is. It might be nothing more than an old coffee mug or a recording of a song or a lace handkerchief or a toy left over from your childhood, something as trivial as that—until it is taken from you and you realize that you'd give everything you have to get it back.

And you also know deep in your soul that once having been visited by the Star Gypsies, you will never see them again.

Things were quiet for the next month. That didn't mean the Star Gypsies weren't as active as usual, just that no one was willing to report them. Some of their victims were ashamed to tell us the value they put on whatever they'd lost. Some just gave up and didn't want to go on living. Most of them knew that they could report what happened and we'd go through all the motions, but we'd never retrieve what had been taken.

Jebediah's first experience with the Star Gypsies had motived him. He was still at his desk every night when I went home, and he was there every morning when I showed up for work. He watched every interview we had with every victim who'd been willing to talk to us. He crossed-checked every report on planets that were facing natural disasters, or economic crises, or anything else that might attract the Star Gypsies.

When I sat down at my desk at the beginning of his sixth week on the job, he walked over to me, and I could see he was disturbed.

"What's up?" I asked.

"They're driving me crazy," he said.

"They have that propensity," I agreed.

He looked at me with pained, puzzled eyes. "Why do they do what they do, Gabe? One sick mind I could understand, but why does an entire race go out of its way to ruin so many lives? What makes them that way?"

"You answer that and we're halfway to catching them," I replied.

"We're missing something," he said. "I can't believe what they do brings them pleasure."

"Why not?" I shot back. "The casebooks are full of psychopaths who got pleasure by inflicting pain."

He shook his head. "You're talking about individuals," he said. "No *race* can take pleasure from it."

"This race does."

"They don't," he said with total conviction.

I found myself wishing that I was as sure of anything in my life as he was of that. "Why not?" I said. "All the evidence says they do."

"Because it's against all logic for rational beings to take pleasure from bringing unhappiness to others."

"I don't know about that," I said. "We felt pretty good about winning the war against the Sett. The Canphorites were overjoyed when they conquered the Vostinians. Back when we were still Earthbound, I'm sure the Sioux felt happy about slaughtering General Custer."

"Those were military actions, taken to redress a real or imagined wrong," said Jebediah. "We haven't wronged the Star Gypsies. As far as I can tell, we didn't even know they existed a century ago."

"That doesn't mean we haven't harmed them or their planet without even knowing that we did it," I said. "We could have destroyed one of their military convoys by mistake, or crashed into their holiest shrine, or accidentally spread a virus against which they have no defense all over their home world."

"No," he said adamantly.

"Why not?"

"Because they're a sentient race, and this is not the reaction of a sentient race to a real or imagined abuse."

"So you say," I replied dubiously.

"All right, there's a better reason," he continued. "Even if we've unknowingly committed every act you mentioned, then their grievance is against the race of Man. But they've brought misery to over a dozen races, maybe more that we don't yet know about—and some of them aren't members of the Republic and have no social or economic ties to us."

I had to admit I hadn't considered that. Maybe there was something to the concept of fresh eyes after all.

"All right, I concede the point," I said. "But that doesn't put us any closer to understanding why they behave as they do. It just eliminates one possible explanation for it."

"If we can eliminate enough we'll narrow it down," said Jebediah. "And once we know why they're the way they are, we'll be able to stop them." He paused again. "We can't allow them to keep bringing such pain to their victims."

"I take it that means you've decided to stay in the department?"

He nodded an affirmative. "When I was a young man," he began, as if he was anything else, "I dreamed of battling the pirates who plague the spaceways, or rescuing beautiful young women from a variety of fates, each worse than death. They were glorious, romantic dreams . . ." The words trailed off and he looked at some fixed point in time and space that only he could see. "But you know something? People survive piracy, and they even survive fates worse than death—but nobody survives the loss of their most treasured memory. Of course I'm staying. This is where I belong." He paused, then continued after a moment. "This weekend I watched holos of more than two hundred victims describing their lives after their dealings with the Star Gypsies. I'll live with the memories of those interviews—and I'll never be rid of my memories until I can make sure no one else will be robbed of theirs."

"Well, it sounds like you've found your life's work."

"I hope not."

"I don't understand," I said, puzzled. "You just said—"

"If I'm here for a lifetime, that means we won't have solved the problem. I plan to stay with the department until I stop them."

"I felt that way once myself," I said.

"You still must," he noted. "You're still here."

"Where would I go and what would I do?" I replied. "I don't know that I'll ever catch one of them, and I'm pretty much convinced that I'll never find a way to stop them, but I can't just turn my back on the problem, not after seeing the damage they do. It's a war, but the collateral damage isn't shattered buildings and burned-out vehicles; it's shattered memories and burned-out dreams, and I think in the long run that kind of devastation is worse."

He stared at me for a long moment. "That's very interesting," he said. "I've been working with you for almost two months now. At first I thought you were just a cynical man marking time until he could retire on his pension."

"And now?"

"Now I think you're a cynical man who still wants to stop the Star Gypsies."

"Of course I do. But you have to insulate yourself emotionally, or you become Ben Paulson and eventually you run off to be the entire police force on an outpost world that's never had a crime."

"How do you drown out the misery?" he asked.

"We each have our own way. How does a doctor who deals with incurable diseases go home and lead a normal life away from his hospital? You make whatever adjustments you have to make. As far as I'm concerned, Ben Paulson, and half a hundred other Ben Paulsons, are victims the same as if they'd been visited by the Star Gypsies, because they never learned to protect their emotions." I looked at him. "How about you? Are you going to be able to protect yourself?"

"Yes," he said. "I'm going to catch them."

I couldn't remember for sure, but I'd almost have bet I'd said those very words twenty-seven years ago, before I grew up and lost something important along the way.

Our first break came three days later, and from the unlikeliest source.

Our computers were programmed to pick up and report any activity that might imply the presence of the Star Gypsies. Sooner or later they did—but it was always after the fact, after the deals had been made and the seemingly innocent payments had been extracted and the Star Gypsies had gone back to wherever it was they came from.

But this time it wasn't one of the computers at all. It was a subspace radio message from a small news organization on the colony world of Branson III.

I was sitting at my desk, going over reports from a dozen worlds at the edge of the cluster, when Jaimie Kwamo walked up to me, an odd expression on her face.

"Yeah, what is it?" I said.

"There's something I think you ought to hear," she said.

"Okay. What is it?"

"It's on Channel 173."

"Is it private?" I asked.

"Hardly."

"Then pipe it in so everyone can hear it," I told her.

She hit the controls, and suddenly the shaky, static-filled image of a middle-aged woman's face appeared to float a couple of feet above every desk in the office. Little flashes of light kept appearing and disappearing, but all it meant was that the signal was weak. It wasn't an especially memorable face; the skin was smooth, the eyes dark, the hair black and pulled back into the cone that was so popular on the more sophisticated worlds toward the Core.

"Hello," said the image, and the voice was also fuzzy and static filled. "I hope I'm contacting the right place. My name is Omira Maspoli, and I work for the *Branson Beacon*, a local newsdisk." The image began breaking up, and we waited until it stabilized. "Among my other duties here, I am in charge of the fraud investigation division. Prior to transferring to the Branson system, I worked on Matusadona II."

That brought quite a reaction in the office. Matusadona was almost legendary in our department.

"I was there when the tidal wave hit and the Star Gypsies came. The devestation from both was staggering. The planet recovered only from the tidal wave." She paused for effect, then spoke again. "That is why I have contacted you. This morning I received the following electronic query."

She leaned over and read from a small screen.

"Dear Omira Maspoli:

"My daughter is graduating from the University of Durastanti IV in 19 Standard days. I own one ship, and it is not functioning. I'm no mechanic, and I have no idea what's wrong with it. It cost all my savings to pay for my

daughter's tuition, and I simply cannot afford to buy a new ship or even repair the one I own. I can't even pay for passage on a spaceliner. I am a widow, and my daughter is all that I've got. I was afraid that I had no option but to remain at home and miss the most important day of her life, but yesterday a group of men suddenly showed up at my house. They told me they'd heard my ship had mechanical problems, and that they were itinerant mechanics, traveling from world to world looking for work. I explained that I have very little money to spend, and that the best estimate I'd gotten from the spaceship company was 32,000 credits. They offered to repair it for 3,000 Maria Theresa dollars, which as you know comes to less than 10,000 credits. It sounds almost too good to be true, but I'm really desperate. I told them I'd give them my answer later today. My question is: what legal recourse have I if they do a poor job and have moved on to the next world before I'm ready to leave for the Durastanti system?"

Omira Maspoli's image looked up from what she had been reading.

"If these are the Star Gypsies, I've seen what they can do, and I urge you to take prompt action. If not, I apologize for taking up your time."

The image vanished.

"Contact her immediately and find out how I can get in touch with the woman who wrote that message!" I said.

"I've got it already," said Jebediah. "She fed it into our computer at the time of transmission."

Suddenly the name and code appeared simultaneously on all our screens.

"Harriet Meeker," announced Jaimie. She uttered a terse string of commands to the computer. "Okay, Gabe—you're clear to send."

"This message is for Harriet Meeker," I said, looking into the transmission lens and pronouncing each word carefully since I figured that whatever was causing the static would be working both ways. "My name is Gabriel Mola, and your missive to Omira Maspoli was forwarded to my department. I am attaching my ID, which you can check with any government department on Branson.

"The men offering to repair your spaceship may be exactly what they appear to be, or they may be something very different and far more sinister. I need to ask you one question, and if the answer is Yes, make no bargains, sign no contracts, and contact me immediately. The question is simply this: have they asked for any form of payment, no matter how seemingly trivial, above and beyond the three thousand Maria Theresa dollars you mentioned to Omira Maspoli?"

"That's it?" asked Jaimie.

"That's it."

"Okay, it's sent. I'll resend it in a minute and route it through our station on Pinto. There should be less chance of it breaking up that way."

"Fine," I said. "Keep a channel open around the clock, and tell anyone we've got within fifty light-years of Branson III to monitor that channel, in case the static prevents her answer from getting through here." I got to my feet and turned to Jebediah. "You've got twenty minutes to round up your gear and meet me at the spaceport."

"You're going out there before you get your answer?" asked Jaimie.

"If we wait for an answer, what do you think we'll find when we get there?" I said.

"You're right, of course," she said with a grimace. "If she responds, what do I tell her?"

"Tell her to stall them, to say that she's got some money coming in. But she's a moral woman and she won't enter into an agreement with them until she knows she can keep her end of the bargain."

"And if they cut their price?"

"They won't," I said, walking to the door.

"What makes you so sure?" asked Jebediah as he joined me.

"They've never had to," I said. "Why do you suppose so many people who should know better deal with them? Because their offer is almost irresistable."

"Some people say no," he noted.

"Not many," I replied. "And like I say, the Star Gypsies don't bargain. Say no and they're on their way—and then you get to spend the rest of your life wishing you hadn't sent them away."

The irony of it wasn't lost on him. "So they deal in regrets even when you say no."

"That's right."

"Do you think your message will reach her in time?" asked Jebediah as we left the building and hopped the expresswalk.

"Probably."

"Will she listen?"

"Oh, she'll listen," I said. "But like she says, it's the biggest day in her daughter's life, and three thousand Maria Theresa dollars is such a reasonable price."

"So you don't think she'll send them packing?" he persisted.

"Would you?" I asked.

Branson III was a lovely little world with a temperate climate, a trio of freshwater oceans dotted with hundreds of islands, even a couple of impressive-looking snow-capped mountain ranges. There were no sentient native races, but evolution had taken a number of adventurous twists, and the planet had originally been opened up and operated as a safari world. Then the game had been shot out (it doesn't take as long as you think), protected parks were created for the multitudes of endangered species, and diamond pipes were discovered. The mining companies moved in, and they were followed by the support networks. The mines were played out in less than a century, but a number of towns still remained, going about their daily business, making Branson III one of the thousands of unexceptional worlds in the Republic that paid most of their taxes, obeyed most of their laws, and made as few political waves as possible. It seemed as nice a place to live as any other—until the Star Gypsies put it on their itinerary.

"How could the Star Gypsies know?" asked Jebediah as we stood in line at Passport Control. "This isn't a world with a widespread disaster, natural or otherwise, where your computer could pull up the information about a tidal wave or an earthquake or a typhoon. This is just one woman who can't afford to repair her ship."

"They always know," I said.

"They couldn't even have learned by intercepting Omira Maspoli's message," he continued. "She didn't send it until after they'd visited Harriet Meeker."

"If it *is* the Star Gypsies."

"Do you doubt it?"

"No," I said. "Not really."

"Neither do I."

I stepped up to the passport kiosk.

"Welcome to Branson III," intoned the robotic officer. "How long will you be on the planet?"

"Probably less than a day," I answered.

"I have scanned your passport, and it is free of all restrictions. I have approved you for entry and given you a three-day visa. If you wish to stay longer, please report to the Office of Immigration and Tourism, which can extend your visa for six more days at no charge. Our local currency is Far London pounds; we also accept Maria Theresa dollars, New Punjab rupees, and Republic credits. The gravity is 97.28 percent Earth Standard and the planetary day is 22.17 Standard hours. Have you any questions?"

"No."

"Enjoy your stay on Branson III," said the robot, and began asking the same questions of Jebediah, who was standing directly behind me.

When we had cleared Customs and were admitted to the lobby of the spaceport, a small, well-dressed man approached me.

"Hi, Gabe," he said.

"Hi, Wolf," I replied. "Jebediah, meet Wolfgang Spora, our man in this sector. Wolf, this is Jebediah Burke."

"Pleased to meet you, Jebediah," said Wolf.

"How many men have we got here?" I asked him.

"I have twenty-five posted around the spaceport," he replied. "We've got another dozen keeping the Meeker house under observation. By the time we got to the little port where she keeps her ship, the work had already been done on it, but I left five men there in case they come back for any tools or anything they might have left behind."

"Okay, that sounds pretty thorough. Meeker doesn't know she's being watched?"

He shook his head. "I don't want her peeking into the bushes or peering at the neighbor's roof if she starts getting nervous. If I can pick up signals like that, the Star Gypsies sure as hell can."

"How can we get to her house?" I asked.

"I'll take you," offered Wolf. "I've got a vehicle just beyond the exit."

"No," I said. "They might be watching the house, too. I want to take public transportation—and it'll just be Jebediah and me. She's only expecting two of us, and I don't want her to look surprised or curious when we show up, just in case."

He looked his disappointment, but he was too much of a pro to question my orders. "After you walk out of the spaceport," he said, "just summon a public transport courtesy vehicle. It'll be programmed with the address of every Branson III resident. There aren't all that many of them, well under half a million." He paused. "Do you want me to stay here or join my men out by the house?"

"I'd rather you stayed here," I said. "The less movement we have around her place, the better. And if they get by me, they still have to find a way off the planet. How are we doing on the private ports?"

"There are five of them around the planet. I've got men at each of them, and I have some police ships in orbit in case they get past us on the ground."

"You seem to have everything under control," I said. "I can't think of anything else, at least not at the moment. I'll contact you on the gamma frequency if I need to speak to you."

"Good luck," he said. "I'm trying not to get excited, but I have a feeling this time we've got 'em!"

"Let's hope," I said.

Jebediah and I walked to the exit, hopped a sleek-looking airbus, and ordered it to take us to Harriet Meeker's place. In a few minutes we were gliding through a charming little village that looked like it could almost have existed back on old Earth itself. It was filled with stone cottages and picket fences and colorful gardens. Of course, the stone was a façade over the titanium structures, the fences were capable of vaporizing any unwanted intruders, and the gardens were tended by robots, but you didn't think of that on first viewing. It just looked small and peaceful and old-fashioned.

After another minute we came to a stop in front of one of the cottages, and the vehicle informed us that we had reached the Meeker residence. We got off, walked up to the front gate, identified ourselves to the Spy-Eye hidden inside the bolt, waited until the gate swung open, and walked up to the front door. It scanned our retinas and bone structures, instantly tied in to the spaceport computer and matched its findings to our passports, then informed the owner of our presence and waited for her to order it to let us in.

A rather frail-looking woman, clearly at the far end of middle age, stood in the main room and invited us in.

"Good morning," I said. "I'm Gabe Mola and this is my assistant, Jebediah Burke. Did you receive the message I sent you yesterday from Goldenrod?"

"Yes, I did, Mr. Mola," she said. "I found it quite unsettling. What is going on?"

"Hopefully nothing," I said. "Did I contact you in time?"

"If you mean, had I entered into an agreement with these itinerant mechanics, no, you did not contact me in time. If you mean have they completed the work and asked for payment, the answer is: not yet."

I could see the excitement on Jebediah's face. Six weeks on the job and he might actually get to see a Star Gypsy, something I hadn't managed in twenty-seven years.

"What was the exact payment they requested?" I asked.

"As I told Omira Maspoli, they asked for three thousand Maria Theresa dollars, and I agreed to that amount."

"And what else?"

"How did you know even yesterday that there would be something else?" she asked.

"There always is."

"Are they criminals, then?" she asked. Suddenly a look of apprehension appeared on her face. "Does this mean they won't fix my ship and I won't be able to go to my daughter's graduation after all?"

"They'll fix your ship," I said. "They always deliver what they promise."

"*That's* a relief!" she exclaimed. "You had me scared for a moment there, Mr. Mola."

"You still haven't answered my question," I said. "What else did they ask for?"

"Oh, something small and trivial," she said. "Just some little keepsake."

"Did they identify it?"

"No," said Harriet Meeker. "They said they'd choose it later, when they finish their work on the ship and present their bill. But I don't understand why you've come all the way from Goldenrod. They even wrote into the contract that it can't have a market value of more than fifty credits."

"And they'll be coming here to the house for their payment?"

"That's what they said," she replied. "I'd be just as happy to pay them at the bank or the spaceport, but they'll want to choose their keepsake, and they can't do that if they don't come to the house."

"Do you mind if we wait here to meet them?" I asked.

"I knew it!" she said, and I thought she was about to burst into tears. "They've done something wrong and you're going to arrest them and I'll never get to Durastanti!"

"We're going to *prevent* them from doing something wrong," I replied, trying to sound reassuring.

"Who are they?" she demanded. "What have they done?"

"Have you ever heard of the Star Gypsies?" I asked.

"Just rumors and legends. Are you trying to say that they really exist?"

"They exist, all right," I replied. "You entered into a contract with them."

"Those nice men who are fixing my ship?" she said. "I don't believe it!"

"I'm sorry you feel that way," I said, "because that's who they are."

"Even if you're right, you yourself said they always do what they promise to do," she said stubbornly. "And they promised to repair my ship for three thousand Maria Theresa dollars."

"And a keepsake," said Jebediah.

"A trivial one."

He looked at me, as if to say: *How much do you want to tell her?*

It was a problem. I didn't want to keep any facts from her. After all, she was their target, and we were here to protect her. But she was so grateful that the Star Gypsies were going to make it possible for her to fly to Durastanti that I was afraid she might actually try to warn them if she thought we meant them any harm. I considered all my options and finally hit on a solution that I thought would satisfy everyone.

"I know you don't want us to wait for them here, and I think I know why," I said. "What if I promise that if they break their bargain or if your ship doesn't function for any reason, my department will see to it that you get to your daughter's graduation at no cost to yourself?"

"Do you mean it?" she asked suspiciously.

I repeated my pledge into my pocket computer, sealed it with my thumbprint, transmitted a copy of it to Omira Maspoli, another to headquarters on Goldenrod, and printed out a copy that I handed to Harriet Meeker.

She read it carefully, then looked up. "All right, Mr. Mola. You and Mr. Burke can stay. May I get you something to eat or drink?"

"Just some coffee or soft drinks," I said.

"I don't drink coffee myself," she said. "It will take me a few minutes to reprogram the robot chef."

"We're in no hurry," I assured her.

I looked out the window as she left the room. I couldn't see any sign of the Star Gypsies or of our own men.

"Her yard's a mess, and the house needs cleaning," said Jebediah softly when she reached the kitchen. "She doesn't have a robot, at least not a functioning one. She's going to cook and clean up after us herself."

"I know," I said. "But the alternative is going out to a restaurant—and I'm not going to be somewhere else when they arrive." I patted the pulse gun I carried under my armpit, a nervous habit I'd picked up over the years to assure myself that I really hadn't left it on the dresser or in the office.

"It's still there," said Jebediah, staring at me.

"What are you carrying?" I asked him.

"The usual—a burner and a screecher," he replied, referring to his laser and sonic pistols.

Harriet reentered the room a moment later, carrying two mugs of black coffee on a tray.

We each took a sip. It tasted like swampwater.

"This is very good," lied Jebediah. "Is it Antarean?"

"Bransonian—we grow it here ourselves," she said with a touch of pride. "And how do you like it, Mr. Mola?"

"Memorable," I said, hoping it wouldn't have me racing to the bathroom all night long.

"May I ask a question?" she said.

"Certainly."

"What have the Star Gypsies actually done? Who have they robbed?"

"Officially, no one."

She sighed deeply. "I'm so tired of you bureaucrats and your secrets."

It's not my secrets they're after, I thought. Aloud I said: "How many of them came here?"

"Three the first time they appeared. Then seven when they returned and I agreed to their terms."

"All Men?" asked Jebediah.

"No, there were two women."

"I meant the race of Man?"

"They appeared to be."

"Appeared?" I repeated.

"They just . . . well, there are all kinds of minor mutations now that we've spread throughout the galaxy and lived in different environments for generations."

"And how did these differ from you and me?" I asked.

"They didn't, not really," she said. "There are probably some tiny differences, but now that I think about it, there's nothing I can truly pinpoint."

"Did you notice anything unusual about their manner of speaking, perhaps? The timber of their voices, the way they pronounced words or strung them together?"

She thought for a moment, then shook her head. "No. I don't mean to mislead you, Mr. Mola. I've been under a lot of strain because of my situation, and perhaps I was imagining some minor differences that don't really exist."

"There are differences, all right," I said.

"What do you mean?" she asked.

"I mean that after all these years, we still don't know what they are."

"They're Men."

"No," said Jebediah. "If there's one thing we're pretty sure of, it's what they aren't."

"You must be mistaken," she insisted. "I know who I spoke to."

"There's no sense arguing," I said. "We'll see for ourselves when they arrive."

"They were *Men*," she muttered. Then: "I think I'll go into the kitchen and supervise the robot." She headed off to begin preparing our dinner.

"I feel sorry for her," said Jebediah, "having to put on an act like this."

"She doesn't have to," I said. "She *chooses* to. And you'd feel a lot sorrier for her if we showed up after the Star Gypsies got what they wanted."

"I know," he agreed. "Still, I—"

Suddenly he tensed.

"What is it?" I asked.

"I just saw someone outside."

"One of them or one of us?"

"We'll know soon enough," he said, and I noticed he had loosened his tunic to make it easier to reach his weapons.

I called Harriet in from the kitchen and told her to order the door to open.

Two men and a women entered. One of the men was tall, ash blond, slender, with piercing blue eyes. The other was burly and muscular, bald on the top, graying on the sides, with a prominent nose and a receding chin. The woman was in her early twenties, with short dark hair, narrow staring dark eyes, no jewelry or cosmetics that I could spot, maybe a few pounds overweight.

They didn't look at all surprised to see Jedediah and me standing there.

"The ship is ready," announced the taller man.

"We're friends of the family," I said, stepping forward. "I hope you don't mind if we inspect it before you're paid."

"You're no friend of anyone, Gabriel Mola," he replied. "But we stand behind our work. You are welcome to look at it."

"You know my name?"

"We know all about you," he said easily.

"Certainly more than you know about us," said the second man.

"Not for lack of trying," I said. "I've been waiting a long time to meet you."

"And now you have," said the woman. "I hope we haven't disappointed you."

"I'll let you know," I said. "After we've had a nice long talk back on Goldenrod."

"We're not going to Goldenrod," said the tall man.

"I wouldn't bet my last credit on that," I said, pulling out my pulsar and signaling Jebediah to produce his burner.

"Put those away," said the woman with no show of fear. "You know by now that we don't possess any weapons."

"Having it in my hand increases my comfort level," I said. "I want you to know that escape is out of the question. The house is surrounded, and I've got men at every public and private spaceport on the planet."

"We have no intention of leaving until we've been paid," said the tall man. He turned to Harriet Meeker. "Your ship has been repaired. Are you prepared to fulfill your obligation?"

"If it's been repaired, you'll be paid," I said. "You might use it as a retainer for a good lawyer. You're going to need one."

"I wasn't speaking to you, Gabriel Mola. We made a bargain, and we kept our end of it. Are you advising Harriet Meeker to renege on her commitment?"

"I told you: if the ship works, she'll deposit the money in an escrow fund that will be made available to you if and when we release you."

"That is only part of her obligation," said the tall man. "There is also the matter of a keepsake."

"I don't believe you've been listening to me at all," I said. "Let's get down to business. Will you surrender yourselves to our custody?"

"Of course not," said the tall man. "What laws have we broken?"

"We'll discuss it on Goldenrod," I said.

"I told you: we're not going to Goldenrod," he said. "At least, not as your prisoners. The day may come when we decide to pay it a visit, but that day is still far off."

I couldn't figure it out. I had all the aces. Jebediah and I had our weapons trained on them. They had to know I wasn't lying about the house being surrounded, surely they were aware that my men were all over the spaceports, and still they showed no sign of apprehension. It was like they simply didn't understand the helplessness of their situation.

"It is *you* who doesn't understand the situation," said the tall man, echoing my unspoken words.

"So you're telepaths," I said, only half-surprised. "Do you just receive, or do you send, too?"

"One or the other," said the woman with a smile.

"If you can read my mind, you know that you haven't got a chance of escaping, so don't make this any more difficult than it has to be."

The tall man turned to Harriet once more. "I ask you one last time, Harriet Meeker: will you honor your bargain with us?"

She looked at me questioningly. "What should I do, Mr. Mola?" she asked.

"I've already told you," I said to him. "If the ship works, you'll get your money."

"I think you know that we don't care about the money," said the tall man.

"And I think you know I don't give a damn what you care about," I said. I waved the pulsar at them. "Let's get going."

Jebediah stepped over and positioned himself in front of Harriet, in case things started getting out of hand.

"That is your final word on the subject?"

"That's right."

"You are a foolish man, Gabriel Mola," he said. "I expected better of you."

"We all have to learn to live with disappointment," I said sardonically.

"No," he said firmly. "Only some of us do."

And suddenly the tall man was no longer there, and I was looking at an exact duplicate of myself. I blinked furiously, but nothing changed. Then I was aware that there were two Jebediahs and two Harriet Meekers in the room.

I didn't know if they were shape-changers, or if they were simply exercising some kind of mind control, but it didn't matter. They were even more dangerous than I'd thought.

"Gabe?" said one of the Jebediahs uncertainly. "What do I do?"

"Help me, Gabe!" said the other in the identical voice. "There are two of you!"

"If you can't figure it out, shoot both of us!" I said. "Now that we know what they can do, we can't allow them to get away!"

"And aim straight!" said my double in my voice.

The Jebediah on my left tried to raise his burner. I could see his muscles tightening, I could see the sweat pouring down his face, but his hand didn't rise as much as a centimeter. I figured I was going to have to shoot both Jebediahs—and suddenly I found that I couldn't move either.

And now my mirror image stood in front of me and smiled again.

"Do you still think we won't walk right out of here?" he said. He took my pocket computer from my tunic, logged onto the gamma frequency, and spoke into it. "Hi, Wolf," he said, and even his inflections were my own. "False alarm. They really are just a bunch of itinerant mechanics. Call it off; we'll join you at the spaceport in an hour or so."

He broke the connection, and put the computer into his own pocket, while I wondered how he planned to dispose of our bodies.

"Nobody's killing anyone today, Gabriel Mola," he said in response to my thought. "You may be my prey, but you're not my enemy."

"The hell I'm not!" I grated.

"You know our history," he said. "Has one of us ever physically harmed one of you?"

"You have other ways."

He smiled again, almost regretfully I thought. "Now there you have me," he admitted.

He walked over to Harriet, who also was obviously unable to move. "And now, Harriet Meeker, it is time to complete our agreement. I know you meant us no harm, so I will not hold Gabriel Mola and Jebediah Burke's presence against you—but I will insist that you keep your end of the bargain. Gabriel Mola has promised us our money, and we will assume that he is a man of honor and will keep his word. We will contact him later with instructions as to its disposition." He paused. "There remains only the valueless keepsake."

He nodded to the other "Harriet," who began walking around the room, touching books, shelves, vases, paintings, a clock, a holo machine. Suddenly she seemed drawn to the bedroom, and she disappeared into it, emerging a moment later with a battered old hairbrush.

"No!" cried Harriet. "Not that! Take anything else you want!"

The false Harriet handed the brush to my double, who held it up and examined it. "Even new, I doubt that this would sell for as much as ten credits. Yes, this will complete your obligation to us, Harriet Meeker."

"Please!" she said, tears streaming down her face.

"And now I think it's time to take our leave of you," he continued, handing the brush to the female. He placed a hand on my shoulder and stared into my eyes. "You and I shall never see each other again, Gabriel Mola, but I am glad we have finally had this opportunity to meet." He turned to Jebediah. "You carry a heavy burden, Jebediah Burke. Protect it well."

At first I thought it was just an insult meant for me, that I was his burden. Then I saw the surprise on Jebediah's face and realized that he knew what they were talking about even if I didn't.

And then, as quickly as they had come, they were gone.

The three of us stood motionless for another half hour. I asked Harriet about the hairbrush, but every time I mentioned it she began crying, and finally I gave up.

Then we were able to move again, and I knew the Star Gypsies were off the planet.

We were debriefed for three full days when we got back to Goldenrod, but it didn't help much. Knowing that they could appear to be anyone didn't make spotting them any easier, and knowing they could read your thoughts didn't help you to protect those thoughts. The only change came when the government doubled the department's budget and added seventy-five Men and aliens to the staff.

Then came a rigorous series of physical and mental tests to make sure the Star Gypsies hadn't infiltrated the department. Somehow I knew we wouldn't turn up any of them, and in the end we didn't.

"Why would they come here anyway?" asked Jebediah. "We never act, we only react. They don't have any need to misdirect us."

"It's just a matter of touching all the bases," I said. "Probably nothing we do will make a difference, but we can't take the chance."

"I know," he said. "We should have shot one of them when we had the opportunity. At least we could have turned him over to our scientists and maybe learned how to spot them."

"The Republic frowns on cold-blooded murder," I said.

"The Republic's never been up against anyone or anything with these abilities," replied Jebediah.

"You're not thinking it through," I pointed out. "How are you going to kill a creature that can read your thoughts and knows what you're going to do as soon as you yourself know?"

"If I decide when he's twenty feet away, he's not going to be able to stop me."

"Unless walls can prevent him from reading thoughts, he'll know before he opens the door, in which case he either won't open it or he'll be prepared. Besides, any way you cut it, that's murder."

He sighed deeply. "I suppose you're right. I just hate to see what they do to their victims. The fact that they're willing victims doesn't matter; they don't know what they're going to have to give up."

"Anyway," I said, "the only way we're ever going to stop them is to figure out *why* they do what they do. Even if the department sanctioned a couple of shootings, what would we get from it? Two corpses, and maybe a way to spot them. It wouldn't stop them from visiting world after world and looking for work."

"As far as I can tell, they've never made a deal for straight cash," said Jebediah. "It's got to be the trinkets."

"Of course it is. But *why?* That's the question I've been asking myself ever since I left the navy and came to work here."

"You were in the navy before you put in twenty-seven years here? You don't look that old."

"I wasn't there long. Just under two years. Got my leg blown off in the Sett War. Ever since, I've been walking around on one the government gave me."

"I never noticed."

"No reason why you should have. It's not the handicap it once was. Hell, Marcus Quintoby was the best-paid Murderball player on the planet last year, and he's got two prosthetic arms."

We spoke a little longer, and then we got word that a team of Star Gypsies had struck again, if "struck" is the right word, out in the Corinda system. It was too late to do anything about it, but we dutifully went to the ship and set off for Corinda.

The Belage were a race of sentient marsupials, tripodal and covered from head to toe with bright orange down, that lived on Corinda IV. The world had been growing warmer and more arid for eons, and all of their water came from deep wells. The well supplying a local infirmary had collapsed. If it wasn't fixed within a solar day the patients were going to suffer; if it wasn't fixed in three days at the outside, most of them were going to die.

The Star Gypsies showed up, made their usual seemingly generous offer, and had the well open and the walls reinforced in just under a day. But they had signed their contract with the entire staff of the infirmary, and by the time we got there it was difficult to tell who was suffering more, the patients or the doctors.

We asked the usual questions, got the usual answers, made the usual fruitless search for clues as to where the Star Gypsies might be going next, and finally we left, glad to get away from the misery.

We'd just gotten clear of Corinda IV's stratosphere and were about to switch to light speeds when a subspace message came over the radio. Three human miners were stranded in the asteroid belt between the sixth and seventh planets of the Churchill system. Their ship had broken down and they'd sent out an S.O.S. There was a rescue ship on the way, but it would take a Standard day to get there, and we could reach them in six hours. We would help them if we could, of course— but more to the point, this seemed a perfect opening for the Star Gypsies. Maybe, with a little luck, we could be waiting for them.

Headquarters fed the coordinates into the navigational computer, we reached multiples of light speed, and then it was just a matter of waiting until we arrived. There was no sense entering a Deepsleep pod, not for a six-hour journey. We checked our weaponry, ate a light lunch, and waited for the trip to end.

About twenty minutes before we reached our destination we got another message. The miners had finally managed to get their ship running again, and it was limping toward port on the colony world of Greenwillow, which was two systems away.

"What do you think?" I asked Jebediah. "Do you want to try it anyway?"

"If they didn't hear the message, they won't know the ship isn't there. We've got the coordinates. If we can touch down on the asteroid before they show up, there's no reason why they shouldn't think we're the miners."

"Until they land," I said. "It's that damned telepathy." I considered our options, and realized that we really didn't have any. We were just about there, and if I didn't plan to confront them until they were unable to read my thoughts, I was never going to see them again. "Yeah, let's go for it."

We braked to light speeds in eighteen minutes and began weaving our way through the asteroid belt. I took over manual control and finally got Churchill Asteroid 1783-B—our destination—in my viewscreen when it happened. A tiny piece of solar debris—it couldn't have been the size of a tin can—ripped through the ship's hull and power pack. Had we been standing still it would have bounced off, but it had picked up speed in its orbit and we were still going about 75 percent of light speed, and it just tore right through nuclear pile and the power thrusters.

"Shit!" I muttered as the ship started spinning out of control.

"What happened?" asked Jebediah, clutching the arms of his chair.

"Some piece of space garbage," I said. "A rock, an iceball, something."

"How much trouble are we in?"

"If I can maneuver to where I can land on one of the asteroids, we'll be all right. If we keep spinning through the belt, sooner or later we're going to crash into something a lot bigger than what hit us."

It took me about two minutes to slowly bring the ship out of its spin. 1783-B was behind us, but I saw another asteroid about ninety thousand miles up ahead, and I figured if I could slow us down enough that was our best chance. The braking system was sluggish, and the ship wanted to spin again, but somehow I managed to get it under control.

"Brace yourself!" I said. "We're going to make it, but I can't promise a soft landing."

Soon the asteroid filled the entire viewscreen. I tried to set us down tail-first, but the controls weren't responding, and finally I settled for sliding in belly-first. It was damned lucky there were no baby mountains on that piece of rock, because we slid close to three miles before we finally came to a stop.

"Are you okay?" I asked.

"I can't vouch for my heart rate or blood pressure," said Jebediah, "but nothing's broken."

"Settle for it. Forty-five seconds ago I'd have given odds against our surviving it."

He smiled. "I'm glad you didn't tell me that earlier."

I checked the instrument panel. "We've still got problems," I said.
"Oh?"

"The radio's gone, and I have a feeling the ship's skin has been compromised. We're losing oxygen. We'd better climb into our spacesuits."

"What kind of oxygen supply do they carry?" he asked.

"About half a day."

"And how long before the ship's out of air?"

"At the rate we're losing it, maybe four hours."

I could tell what he was thinking. I could do the math myself. Four hours and half a day. Sixteen Standard hours. It was going to take the rescue ship twenty-four Standard hours start to finish, and even if it hadn't turned back—and there was no reason for it to still be on its way—it would arrive two hours after we'd run through all our air.

"We won't get into the suits until we have to," I said. "That'll buy us a little more time to see if we can get the radio working."

It was a fantasy. Even if we did get the radio functioning, there simply weren't any Republic worlds close enough to reach us in time. Oh, our signal might be picked up by a ship in transit—in fact, that was our only hope—but the odds weren't good, and they got longer every minute that the radio wasn't working.

After an hour I knew we'd never be able to fix it. Maybe a better mechanic could, but fixing broken subspcae radios just wasn't one of my specialties, and Jebediah knew even less about them than I did.

"Ah, well," I said, finally sitting down. "It hasn't been that bad a life, I suppose. I'm just sorry it has to end before I finish my work."

"Have you got any kids, Gabe?" asked Jebediah.

"A son," I said. "I haven't seen him in, oh, ten or eleven years. My wife left me—I guess I didn't exactly keep the job's frustrations to myself—and he went with her." I paused. "He was a nice enough kid. I've left him almost everything in my will."

"Almost?"

I pulled a small packet out of my breast pocket. "Everything but this. This I don't share with anyone."

"What is it?"

I opened it and held it up for him to see. "The Medal of Courage, from the Sett War."

"Was that when you lost your leg?" he asked.

"Yeah. I saved seven members of my squad and lost a leg. I think it was a good trade. So did the navy."

"I'm impressed," said Jebediah. "I've never seen one of these before."

"They don't give a lot of them out."

"You should be very proud."

"It was a long time ago," I said. "Doesn't seem to make much difference at this particular minute." I paused and considered my life. On the whole, it came out a plus. Not a real big one, but a plus. "Still, I don't have any regrets—except for never catching one of the Star Gypsies. How about you?"

"There's a lot of things I planned to do," he said. "Somebody else will have to do them, I guess."

"That's the future," I said. "Any regrets about the past?"

"Just one."

"And that is?"

"A regret."

Well, if he didn't want to talk about it, I wasn't going to make him. I figured we had maybe fifteen hours to get our thoughts in order and try to go out with a little dignity.

He kept fiddling with the instruments. Some were working, some weren't. The important one—the radio—was stone cold dead. I thought it was getting warmer. It could have been my imagination, or it could have been the oxygen seeping out. I decided not to get into the suit until I had to, or maybe not even get into it at all. When you've lived fifty-two years, what's another twelve hours—especially twelve hours of slow suffocation.

"I've never made a will," said Jebediah suddenly. "I just didn't figure I'd need one this soon. I suppose I ought to write one down so whoever finds us can deliver it to the authorities. Not that I own that much."

"It could be centuries before they find us," I said. "The whole system's uninhabited, and no one knows where we are." A thought occurred to me, and I chuckled.

"What so funny?"

"If you've got any money in the market or the bank, it could be worth millions by the time we're discovered. Too bad you won't have any descendants to collect it."

"It does make a will seem kind of silly, doesn't it?" he agreed.

"Leave it to your favorite church or political party," I said. "Someone will find a use for it."

"I suppose so." He turned to reach for the microphone to dictate his will to the computer. He sat perfectly still for a moment, staring at the small screen in front of his chair, then turned to me with a curious expression on his face.

"What's the matter?" I asked, wondering what else could go wrong.

"You said the Churchill System's uninhabited, right?"

"Right."

"And you never got off a radio message?"

"You know I didn't."

"Well, there's a ship approaching," he said.

"Are any of the weapon systems working, I wonder?" I said. "We could fire a near-miss to attract its attention."

"We won't have to. It's not flying by; it's slowing down."

I activated the main viewscreen. He was right. There was a small silver ship approaching us.

"I can't see its insignia," I said.

"What difference does it make?"

"If they've spotted us, they can probably tell we're disabled," I said, pulling out my pulse gun. "I hope they're here to help, but just in case they've come to rob us, let's be ready for them. Maybe we can disable them and take over their ship."

He pulled out his burner and screecher and laid them on the console next to him.

"Did you ever see a ship like this?" he asked as it came still closer.

"No," I admitted. "They must be aliens. There are no ships like that in the Republic."

"It's awfully small," he noted. "It looks like a one-man job."

"At any rate, he'll never fit both of us into it, even if he's a got Samaritan impulses," I said.

The ship was now hovering less than a mile above us, and it began lowering gracefully to the surface of the asteroid. For a moment it looked like it would land on top of us, but it missed us by inches.

Then we heard—well, felt—things being done to our hatch. It continued for a few minutes, and then I heard something I never expected to hear on an airless world: someone was knocking gently on the hatch door.

I ordered the hatch to open, but it was yet another piece of our equipment that wasn't functioning. I trained my pulse gun on it, then gestured for Jebediah to open it manually.

He did so, then stepped back as it swung inward.

A middle-aged woman with clear blue eyes, graying brown hair, and a muscular body entered. She was wearing some kind of all-purpose coverall, rather than a spacesuit, so I knew our ship was now connected to hers, or she'd never have been able to move between them.

She looked around briefly, then focused on me.

"I'm pleased to meet you, too," she said wryly, and I realized I was pointing the pulse gun at her. I lowered it, but kept it in my hand.

"Who are you?" I asked.

"Do you want the truth or a fairy tale?" she replied.

"You're one of *them*, aren't you?"

"And you're Gabriel Mola and he's Jebediah Burke," she said.

"How did you know we were here?"

"Is that really important?" she asked.

"I'd like to know before we die."

"You will. But I thought you might prefer to live."

"Did you have something to do with our ship's problems?" asked Jebediah.

"Of course not," she replied. "I know you don't believe me, but we really aren't vicious sadists."

"Do your fellow Gypsies know you're here?"

"They do now."

"And you're here to rescue us?"

"Well, that's what we have to discuss."

I uttered a harsh laugh. "How many millions of credits is this going to cost?"

"You're really not worth very much as a human being, Gabriel Mola," she said. "You hunt us for no reason, you persecute us even though we have never broken any of your laws, you warn people not to enter into honest and open negotiations with us. No, you are simply not a valuable member of your race. I think I will charge you one Republic credit to save your life."

"What's the catch?" I said.

"There's no catch. One credit, and a keepsake to remember you by." She smiled at me. "Payable upon demand after the job is completed."

"I saw your ship on my screen," I said. "You can't possibly fit us both on it with you."

"That was my offer to *you*," she said. Then she turned to Jebediah. "I will save you for free, Jebediah Burke. No money, no keepsake."

"Why?" he asked suspiciously. "You people never work for free."

"You have qualities."

"What qualities?"

"We will discuss them aboard my ship."

"There's something wrong here, something I'm missing," he said. "If you're going to save us one at a time, take Gabe first."

"I don't want him," she said firmly.

"I won't leave him here to die."

"If he'll agree to my terms, he will be rescued."

"And if not?"

"Then he will die alone and unmourned," she said. "His name will be forgotten, his body will never be found, and it will be as if he had never existed. Is that really the fate you wish for your friend?"

"Then save him first," repeated Jebediah adamantly.

"Don't be a fool, Jebediah," I said. "Go with her while you've got a chance."

"I'm not deserting you," he replied.

She turned back to me. "Do not argue with him. He will come of his own free will when the time arrives. Do you and I have a deal, Gabriel Mola?"

"One credit?"

"And a keepsake."

"What the hell," I said. "If I die here, none of my keepsakes will do me any good. Yeah, you've got a deal." I turned to Jebediah. "If I don't make it back, I want you to give every single thing in my apartment away, or burn it or atomize it, before you let her get her hands on any piece of it."

"I'm not going anywhere until you do," he insisted.

She walked over and extended her hand. "I prefer a written contract, but under the current conditions, I will settle for a handshake. Have we got a deal, Gabriel Mola?"

I shook her hand. It felt just like a real woman's. "We have a deal. Now, how are you going to pull this off?"

"I will take Jebediah Burke with me. This will give you almost two more hours of oxygen. Someone will be here to take you away before it has run out." She paused. "Try not to be too hostile to them, Gabriel Mola. After all, they will be saving your life."

"This doesn't mean I'll stop hunting you down," I said.

"I think perhaps a credit was too high a value to place upon you," she said. Then she shrugged. "Still, a bargain's a bargain."

She walked back to the hatch and turned to us again—and suddenly we weren't looking at a middle-aged woman any more. Somehow she had become a lithe, slender girl, probably still in her teens, with dark sad eyes, long wavy honey-colored hair. She looked young and innocent and untouched by life.

"Come, Jebediah Burke," she said in a voice that perfectly matched her body. "It is time for us to leave."

"Oh, God!" murmured Jebediah. "How could you know? I put her out of my mind!"

"You have lied to yourself," said the Star Gypsy. "She is the most prominent image in your mind."

"Don't do this to me!" said Jebediah. "I lost you once. I've made my peace with the universe. Don't make me do it again!"

"You've lost me, and now you've found me," she said.

"Who is she?" I asked.

A tortured expression spread across his face. "Her name is Serafina. We were going to be married." He forced out the words. "And I killed her."

"It wasn't your fault," she said. "The police cited the other vehicle."

"I was so busy looking at you instead of the road I never saw it coming at us," he said. "*That* makes it my fault."

She reached a hand out toward him. "I forgive you."

He tried to look away from her, but he couldn't.

"Come with me, Jebediah," she purred. "Time is running out."

He stood as if hypnotized. "You're not Serafina," he managed to say.

"I will be Serafina for you for as long as you wish," she said, backing out through the hatch. "Come, Jebediah."

"Gabe, I . . ." The words caught in his throat.

"Go on," I said. "You can't do us any good by staying here."

He seemed to resist for another second. Then, with a sound that was halfway between a sigh and a sob, he followed her into her ship. A moment later the hatch closed, and I watched them take off on the viewscreen.

For the next two hours I wondered if she would keep her bargain. The interior of the ship grew uncomfortably warm, and breathing became an effort. I was about to climb into my spacesuit when a ship, larger than the last one, dropped down gently right next to mine. There were five Star Gypsies on it. They attached our ships, opened the hatch, and very politely told me to enter their vessel.

We took off a moment later. They offered me food and drink, which I refused, and pleasant conversation, which I found ridiculous under the circumstances. It took us a couple of hours at light speeds to reach Greenwillow, where they touched down at a small private spaceport and let me off.

"Where's Jebediah Burke?" I asked, looking around at the empty landing field.

"He'll return to you when he's ready to," said the one who seemed to be their leader.

"How do I know you haven't killed him?"

He seemed amused. "You know more about us that anyone else. Have we ever killed anyone?"

"No," I admitted. "But why do you do the things you do?"

"Why do you eat?" he responded. "Why do you breathe?"

"What the hell kind of answer is that?" I demanded. "Are you trying to tell me that you're compelled to bring heartbreak and misery wherever you go?"

"We are not the enemy, Gabriel Mola."

"Then who is?"

A look of infinite sadness crossed his handsome countenance. Then the hatch closed, and a moment later the ship took off.

I got in touch with the department's closest office, which was on Hesporite III, reported what had happened, and waited while they sent a ship for me.

When I got back to Goldenrod, I half-expected Jebediah to be waiting for me, but he hadn't shown up. I put out a Priority Search order for him and transmitted it not only throughout my department but to every police department in the entire Quinellus Cluster. Nobody had seen him, nobody knew anyone who had seen him, and after a year I finally had to face the fact that the Star Gypsies had committed their first murder. I hoped he had enjoyed his last few minutes or hours of life with his pseudo-Serafina.

The Star Gypsies seemed to get bolder. Oh, except for Jebediah their crimes were no different, but they seemed to anticipate every trap we laid for them. Prior to this they had confined themselves to small outpost and colony worlds, but now they began operating on the more populous worlds as well. The situation was always the same: there was work that had to be done, they appeared almost by magic, they did the job for an incredibly low price—and an incredibly high one.

I thought I had a couple of them trapped on Daedalus IV, but they simply waited until my reinforcements showed up, took the shapes of the first two men to arrive, and walked out in the confusion. I took a shot at one of them in a dingy Tradertown on the Inner Frontier world of Covenant, but he ducked into a deserted building and I never saw him again, though I examined every inch of it.

I directed half a hundred searches for their home world, but it was no use. No one knew what they really looked like when they weren't busy looking like someone else, so there was no way to tell whether we'd found it or not.

The job was really getting me down, so much so that I was thinking of taking early retirement. I just couldn't take much more of the misery I saw and the frustration I felt. If I'd thought drinking or drugging every night would have helped I'd have done it, but I knew the problem would still be there the next morning.

Then one evening, toward the end of summer, I stopped by my usual restaurant for dinner, and decided to walk home rather than ride one of the express slidewalks. It was dark when I finally got there, and I was surprised to see a light in my window. I could have sworn I'd turned the lights out when I left in the morning.

I approached the door carefully, pulse gun in hand. I uttered the combination, waited for the door to dilate, then stepped through—and found myself facing Jebediah Burke.

"I can't believe my eyes!" I said, putting my gun away. "I gave you up for dead almost three years ago!"

"How are you, Gabe?" he said easily.

"Shocked," I replied, making no effort to hide my delight at seeing him. "What are you doing here?"

He looked around the angular living room. "I've been admiring the paintings on your wall," he said. "And your library. It's been a long time since I've seen a real book."

"How the hell did you get in here? That's a state-of-the-art lock on the front door."

"I learned a lot of tricks from the Star Gypsies."

"How did you get away from them?" I asked.

"That's what we have to talk about," said Jebediah.

"You've learned something about them!" I said excitedly.

"I've learned everything about them."

I walked over to my favorite easy chair, ordered it to hover a few inches above the floor, and sat down. "Tell me about it."

"That's what I'm here to do."

"Start with your escape," I said.

"I didn't escape," said Jebediah.

"I don't understand."

"I know. But you will." He summoned a hard-backed chair, waited a few seconds for it to arrive from the corner, and sat down a few feet away from me. "Let me begin by saying that they weren't lying to you. They've never broken a law."

"No," I said. "They just break hearts and destroy dreams."

He nodded. "Yes, often they do. It can't be helped."

"Of course it can be helped," I shot back. "They don't have to rob their victims."

"They didn't rob anyone, Gabe. They never forced anyone to make a bargain, and they never took anything that hadn't been promised to them."

"Come off it!" I said. "You sound like one of them."

"That's not surprising," he said.

I reached for my pulse gun again. "Are you telling me you've joined them?" I demanded.

"Put it away, Gabe," he said with no show of fear. "Do you want answers or do you want blood?"

"I haven't decided."

"I'm all through talking until you choose one or the other."

He folded his arms across his chest and waited patiently. He knew that after thirty-one years of chasing the Star Gypsies, I wanted the answers. Finally I muttered a curse and put my gun back in its holster.

"That's better," said Jebediah.

"Talk," I said. "And it better be good."

"The first thing you have to understand about them, Gabe, is that they're aliens, with all that the word implies."

"I know."

"You *don't* know," he said emphatically. "You think you do, but they appear as humans, they speak flawless Terran, they do the same work that Men do, they accept payment in Republic currency, and you think of them as human. Cruel and unfeeling, to be sure, but human just the same."

"That's what they are," I said.

"That's what I thought, too. But I was wrong, just as you are."

"Go on. I'm listening."

"I know you are. I just hope you're *hearing*."

"Spare me your word games and get on with it," I said.

"All right. The Star Gypsies have been blessed with a number of abilities. You've seen many of them, and I'm sure you're aware of others. But they are also cursed with a defect, one that probably outweighs all the virtues." He paused. "They have no emotions. They can't *feel*."

"What are you talking about?"

"Just what I said. They are incapable of generating emotions. But they are not incapable of appropriating the emotions of others. They realized both this lack and this ability when they first came into contact with an alien race. They saw how empty their lives were, and they went about solving the problem."

"And the only emotion they seek is misery?" I said. "I'm not buying it."

"No, Gabe. They don't seek misery. They don't take all those keepsakes to make the owners miserable. They take them because through means that are all but incomprehensible even to me, they can assimilate the love, the happiness, the tenderness, the fond memories that are associated with them. That's what they're after: a sense of love and joy, even a borrowed one. They know the pain they bring. That's why they work so cheap; they're trying to make up for it. And they know most people will get over the loss sooner or later. But without these objects, they themselves would go through life eating, sleeping, working, but never feeling a thing."

He fell silent for a moment while I considered what he had said.

"If that's true, I sympathize with them," I said at last. "But I don't sympathize enough to let them bring emotional pain to members of every other race in the cluster."

"Is it really so terrible, given the alternative?"

"You've spoken to their victims," I said. "What do you think?"

"I think it's an unfair universe," said Jebediah, "and that in the long run the best you can do is choose the lesser of two evils."

"They've brainwashed you," I said.

"I went with them of my own free will," he said. "I can leave whenever I want—but I don't want to."

"You think you joined them willingly, but you were chosen, kid," I said. "That Star Gypsy appeared as your Serafina because they could read your mind. They not only found her there, but they saw that you were young and impressionable, and that you could tell them how I think, how the department functions."

"No!" he insisted. "I've joined them because I want to help them."

"I thought you wanted to help their victims."

"Everyone has to make choices," said Jebediah. "They're not always easy. I've made mine."

"Have you thought about what's going to happen to you when they no longer have any use for you?" I continued. "You've turned your back on your own kind. You're not one of us any more. You've joined the people that cause us pain and misery. We'll never take you back."

"I don't want to come back," he said. "All my life I've wanted a purpose. Now I've got one. They were getting clumsy. You found them on Branson III, and again on Daedalus IV and Covenant. They needed someone to direct them."

"So you didn't just join them," I said accusingly. "You're *leading* them."

"Somebody has to, or sooner or later the department is going to start killing them. You're a reasonable man, Gabe, and I truly don't think you'd stoop to murder, especially now that you know why they take what they do—but others would, and once it started there'd be no stopping it."

"So what do you and I do now?" I asked.

"Now we complete a final piece of business, and then we go our separate ways."

"All right," I said. "But after tonight I'll be coming after you."

"You'll never find me."

"That won't stop me from trying," I promised him. "Now what's this business you're talking about?"

"Four years ago a Star Gypsy saved your life. The agreement was that payment would be made sometime after the job was completed. I'm here to collect it."

I took a coin from my pocket and tossed it to him.

"This is a five-credit piece," he said.

"It's the smallest I've got. Tell them they can keep the change."

"No," he said, pulling four one-credit coins out of a pocket and handing them to me. "A deal is a deal. We never accept more than a contract calls for."

"All right," I said. "Now we're done. Get out."

"We're not quite done," he said. "You still owe us a keepsake."

I waved an arm around the apartment. "Choose one and leave."

"It's not on a shelf or in a drawer, Gabe," he said. "It's in your pocket."

"What are you talking about?"

"Your Medal of Courage. That's the keepsake we want."

"You go to hell!" I yelled.

"You made a deal, Gabe. Nobody forced you to."

"Take anything else and I'll give you a week's head start before I go hunting for you."

"We don't want anything else. You're an honorable man, Gabe. We expect you to keep your word."

"I didn't make that deal with you," I said. "I made it with a Star Gypsy who looked like a girl you once knew. When she shows up and demands payment, I'll turn it over to her."

For a moment I thought he was going to try to take the medal from me, but then he shrugged and walked to the door.

"Tell her I'll be waiting," I said.

He walked out of the apartment, and that was the last I saw of Jebediah Burke, who gave up his own hopes and dreams to help the Star Gypsies steal theirs.

He was a basically decent young man, probably better than most, filled with idealism. He wanted to make the galaxy a better place, and he found a race that managed to engage his services and his loyalty. But you don't help one man or one race by harming another, especially when you take those very private things they hold most dear.

I said we'd never take him back, but I didn't mean it. I hope someday he'll realize that and come back. Of course we'll forgive him his transgressions, because that's the way we're made. The Star Gypsies have one major advantage over us in this undeclared war: we're both capable of harming innocent parties, but only we regret it, and only we try to avoid it. It's strange, but I've never thought of compassion as a problem before.

I don't know if we can win with that kind of handicap, but I know it's why we've got to try.

About the Author

MIKE RESNICK has won an impressive five Hugos and been nominated for twenty-three more. He has sold fifty-one novels and almost two hundred short stories. He has edited forty-three anthologies. His work spans from satirical faire, such as his Lucifer Jones adventures, to weighty examinations of morality and culture, as evidenced by his brilliant tales of Kirinyaga. The series, which, with sixty-four major and minor awards and nominations to date, is the most honored series of stories in the history of science fiction.